Praise for The Night Stalkers series

Wait Until Dark

"High-energy military suspense at its best… this book has it all."

—*RT Book Reviews*, 4 Stars

"Buchman mixes adrenalin-spiking battles and brusque military jargon with a sensitive approach… readers will feel real tension."

—*Publishers Weekly*

"Exquisitely written, sensory-loaded, and soul-satisfying."

—*Long and Short Reviews*

I Own the Dawn

"Fascinating… a classic tale of socioeconomic opposites who fall wildly into love—and passion."

—*NPR.org* (An NPR Best Romance of 2012)

"Buchman writes with eloquence and a feel for emotion that drew me right into the story. The characters are realistic and fun, as well as darned good with guns."

—*Long and Short Reviews*

"A compelling military romance that vividly captures the complexities of life on the front line."

—*Fresh Fiction*

The Night Is Mine

TAKE OVER at Midnight

THE NIGHT STALKERS

M.L. BUCHMAN

sourcebooks
casablanca

Published by Sourcebooks Casablanca, an imprint of Sourcebooks, Inc.
P. O. Box 4410, Naperville, Illinois 60567-4410
(630) 961-3900
Fax: (630) 961-2168
www.sourcebooks.com

Printed and bound in the United States of America
VP 10 9 8 7 6 5 4 3 2 1

*To Colonel Jim Baker and those like him
who've been kind enough to share their stories with me
of the moment they stepped forward.
And my deepest thanks for taking that step.*

Drag *n*.
The aerodynamic force that opposes
a helicopter's forward flight.

Drag *v*.
To pull down,
as in opposition to a positive force.

Chapter 1

"Chief Warrant LaRue?"

Lola couldn't see who addressed her despite the bright airfield lights driving back the nighttime darkness. The helicopter that had come to fetch her kicked up a whirlwind of fine brown dust.

The dust coated everything, everywhere in Afghanistan, and Bagram Air Base felt like the worst of it. It had taken less than ten minutes from arrival in-country for it to penetrate every pore of her being. Clearly you didn't need to brush your teeth here, you just chewed the air and they'd be sanded clean in no time.

Now she stood, bathed by the whirlwind, duffel in one hand and her free arm wrapped across her face to block the worst of the chopper's rotor-driven brownout with her uniform's sleeve.

"Yo!" she called out in what appeared to be the right direction.

The turbines didn't cycle down, the blades didn't even slow to idle, they stayed at flight speed, and the dust continued to roil upward in a never-ending supply from the ground.

No previously imagined neat little meet-and-greet on the ground.

No "Welcome aboard! We're so glad you're here!" entry to the innermost circle of U.S. military heli-aviation.

They had come to fetch her and return to base as if

she were as exciting as a new artillery piece rather than only the fourth woman in history to qualify for the 160th SOAR and only the second female pilot.

A hand appeared from the dust and wrapped about her upper arm, firmly but not hard, and guided her into the maelstrom. Clearly she should've pulled on her flight helmet rather than clipping it to the pack strapped on her back. And tied back her hair, which now beat her about the face and neck until her skin tingled with the stings of the wind-whipped ends.

A pause and a shout in her ear stopped her before she could bang her knees on the Black Hawk helicopter's cargo deck. Considerate.

She was barely aboard before she heard the blades biting the air more deeply. Could feel the weight change as she was pressed heavily into the hard metal deck by the chopper's accelerating lift.

The hand guided her to the rear cargo net where she clipped her duffel and pack. As she dragged on her helmet, the hand snagged the D-ring on the front of her survival vest and snapped a monkey line to it. She was now attached to the helicopter by the three-meter-long strap, just in time before the chopper's nose plunged downward and they roared forward. Only a quick grab of the cargo net kept her from sweeping forward and sliding right into the console between the pilots' seats.

One tug by the unseen hand confirmed the line's solid attachment to her chest. Decently, the hand didn't use the opportunity to grab her breast. Even the heavy SARVSO vest and flight suit didn't stop most guys in such a situation. She'd had to sprain more than a few thumbs during her military career, one she'd even had to break before the jerk backed off. Sent him squeaking all the way to his commander, who'd thankfully booted him down two grades and shipped him stateside. It was the goddamn 2010s, but jerks still thrived. Or thought they did.

Despite no welcoming committee, she'd take the lack of a grab as a good sign on her first mission assignment with the Army's 160th Special Operations Aviation Regiment, the Night Stalkers.

In the backwash of the airfield's lights, with the dust now cleared from the cabin by the draft of the open cargo doors, she could see the man who'd guided her aboard. As much as anyone could see anyone in full flight gear.

Not a big guy, but clearly a strong one by how his grip had felt and the way his uniform's sleeves were tight against the skin rather than flapping in the wind like most soldiers' would. Definitely a weight lifter. She could appreciate that.

A lot of military time was spent waiting. Waiting for the next round of training, waiting for the "go" on a mission that could come in two minutes or two months. Different soldiers burned off the time differently. Some gals just stopped, lying on their bunk and reading or watching movies or something. That was fine for ten minutes at a time, but not as a lifestyle.

There was a whole generation of techno-geeks that were always tinkering with their toys, whether a smartphone or a four-million-dollar Predator drone. Lola often wondered what the geeks had done in olden times before tech was such a big deal. What did they play with back in 'Nam, their FM radios?

Most troopers stayed active. U.S. Army grunts had left a string of jury-rigged basketball hoops at thousands of temporary bases around the world. She was tall enough and fast enough to do well in these games, but she wasn't much of a team-sport gal. She did better in solo endeavors. Some soldiers ran. A lot of them, like the guy who'd helped her aboard, clearly liked moving iron up and down. Weights were her second choice. Her first choice was swimming long distances.

The guy's helmet appeared black in the dim cabin with an incongruously crossed knife and fork painted on the side, oriented like crossed bones on a pirate flag beneath a large smiley face.

The only other thing she could see clearly as they left the last of the airfield's lights was a smile. Not a leer, but a genuine smile before he slapped his visor down. Another point in his favor.

She smiled back.

He plugged a comm line into the jack on her helmet. She could immediately tell that this ship flew with open communication channels. Some pilots kept the intercom system off so that the crew had to key in to speak, but she could hear the quiet chatter of the pilot and copilot. A radio squawk from the field tower wishing them "safe flight."

"Sergeant Tim Maloney, ma'am. Welcome aboard *Viper*. Major Beale drew escort on a forward flight tonight, so she sent us to fetch you."

"Uh, thanks."

"My pleasure, ma'am." Made it sound as if it was completely his doing and really was a pleasure. Clearly a southerner. Not deep-fried South, definitely not

Louisiana, no real accent, but a soft, pleasant weave to the words. Unhurried speech. And an inborn politeness that was too often lost these days. She could feel the familiarity of Tim's speech pattern relaxing her.

He saluted—she could make out the motion as a silhouette against the soft glow of the cockpit readouts behind him—then his bulk was gone and back into the left-side chief's seat.

She hadn't seen the bird falling out of the night sky until it was too late and the dust had blinded her. It was definitely a Black Hawk, but she hadn't heard it until it was right on top of her.

They'd made her wait outside the normal circle of field lights, beyond the edge of the pavement. And still the bird had surprised her.

Looking around, it took her only moments to assess why the unusual treatment.

The cargo net behind her kept extra cans of munitions from sliding around. Outside the bird, she could make out the weapons pylons sticking out to either side where some serious missiles and cannon were hanging.

They'd picked her up in a DAP Hawk. A Direct Action Penetrator Black Hawk was the nastiest piece of hardware ever thrown into the night sky by any military, and only the Night Stalkers regiment of U.S. Special Forces flew them. There were only a dozen or so of these on the planet. Even inside SOAR, it wasn't exactly clear how many.

If a girl was gonna hitch a ride, this was about the sweetest muscle car she could land in. She'd always had a dumb-as-a-brick weak spot for guys with muscle cars, but never stuck around long because they always had to drive. Half the reason she'd gone pilot was that she got to drive.

But the rotors sounded odd. Wrong. She'd flown over a thousand hours in Black Hawks, over a hundred in a DAP during training. To have the sound be so different was as if she'd gone to sleep and woken up on a different planet.

She leaned out the cargo door, but there was nothing to see in the night.

"She's a quiet one, ma'am." Tim must have noticed her actions.

A quiet one.

Stealth.

Lola had forgotten. She'd flown a quieted DAP Hawk on an actual mission once, well, at the end of one. She'd been so wound up and terrified of screwing up that she hadn't noticed the differences at first. The stealth one that had hard-landed in bin Laden's compound back in 2011 was the only one the public knew about. Here was another.

They'd fetched her in a stealth DAP Black Hawk. This wasn't a muscle car. This was a friggin' big-block GTO with a turbocharger and nitro. Made a girl feel really special. It made up for any lack of a "welcome aboard" moment. And made up for some of the dust that still coated her like an oil slick.

No wonder they'd had her stand in dirt beyond the field lights and kept the rotors going. This bird was not a sight meant for casual eyes. She had to take a pull on a water bottle from her thigh pocket, rinse a bit, and spit out the door and into the roaring wind to clear the last of the grit from her mouth.

Clear of the airfield, her eyes were adjusting to the night. Lola could make out the stars above. And the complete lack of lights below. Primitive agricultural. As soon as you were away from the cities, fires and oil lamps were the only nighttime lights Afghanistan had going for it. It wasn't just dark down there, it was a blank slate visible only by night-vision gear.

Inside the Hawk, she could make out just enough in the darkness to identify the miniguns in front of both of the crew chiefs who lived their lives facing sideways and craning their necks out the gunner's windows. If they were using the standard setup, the guy who'd helped her aboard would be a dead-on gunner who could also fix a helicopter blindfolded, and whoever hunched over the right-hand gun would be the chief mechanic who could also shoot better than most people in the Army.

Copilot forward to the left and pilot forward to the right. That was her seat. But it wasn't. She bit her lip, really hoping she'd made the right choice. She'd given up the pilot's seat in a combat search and rescue bird to fly copilot in SOAR.

Two years of training before they'd let her aboard for a mission, and that was after she'd already been flying for seven years. She'd thought that was ridiculous when she heard about it. Two years later she wondered if that had been enough time. Even from combat search and rescue, CSAR, the jump to SOAR was like going straight from a tricycle to NASCAR. It had been a hard two years.

"Y'all welcome aboard, Chief Warrant 2 Lola LaRue."

She could see the pilot turn his helmet slightly toward the gap between his and the copilot's seat. The

voice wasn't the guy who'd helped her, Tim Maloney.
Normally lousy with names, his had stuck easily. That
meant it was the pilot speaking.

This guy was clearly trouble. He said her name in the
drawn-out slurring way so many had before. Not even
the accent was real–faked Texas. Badly faked.

So, if it was gonna play that way, it was time to "pull
on her soldier."

"Yes, sir. Appreciate the lift."

"Lola LaRue." He said it again like he was rolling it
around on his tongue.

Shit! was the only thought she could come up with.
She'd really hoped SOAR was above this. More than
hoped, believed. *Stupid, girl. Really damn stupid.*

"Somebody named y'all that?"

Upbeat and chipper, LaRue. "My daddy. I think he
wanted me to grow up to be a stripper." She'd discovered
that taking it head-on was the only thing that worked.

"Looks like y'all've done gone and disappointed
him and probably many other men besides. 'Specially
if you're even half as purdy as your file photo says you
is." He actually drawled "purdy" into some weird kind
of over-Texas-saturated slur.

"Disappointed the hell out of him. And I look way
better than my stupid Army photo." It was true and to
hell with him.

A deep chuckle.

She swallowed hard and dug down into her Creole
badass, street-girl soul for the serious load of rude she'd
be needing to launch. A deep breath to tighten her gut.
*Okay, here it comes. Stupid joke about maybe a private
performance, or maybe just a little one for his crew, or—*

"Well done, Chief Warrant. Welcome to SOAR." His words now sharp and crisp, untraceable except as Army.

Lola had to bite down hard on the sharp retort she had loaded in the chamber and ready to fire. Best she managed was an, "Uh, thank you, sir." A test of her patience or just messing with her head for the hell of it?

Tim cut back in using an airline voice. "Your pilot tonight is Major Mark Henderson, lovingly called 'Viper' by his crew and the few unfortunates who survived—"

"Very, very few," the pilot offered in his normal voice.

"Facing," Tim continued without missing a beat, "the wrong end of this bird."

Major Mark Henderson. Holy crap! This wasn't a muscle car, this was a notorious weapon of death wielded by the most decorated officer of SOAR. His reputation was sterling. He must have just been teasing her, though he wasn't known for a sense of humor.

"Your copilot," Tim continued as if first steward on a 787 full of tourists, getting that bored flight attendant tone so perfect that she had trouble not laughing, "is the famous and dashingly handsome Captain Richardson. For your entertainment in the cabin you are joined by Mr. recently married Big Bad John, really is his name. Scout's honor. And you thought Lola LaRue was bad. I'm called, by those who know me, Crazy Tim Maloney. John and I are the best crew chiefs in the sky."

"My wife might have a thing or two to say about that. And those who don't know you call you odiferous." Big, deep voice wrapped around a low laugh. Must belong to the massive dude seated before the starboard-side minigun. How did someone that big even fit into a Black Hawk gunner's seat?

"Ignore him, Ms. LaRue. John's awesome. It's that his wife is just plain scary. You'll be meeting her later. Tonight the *Viper*, that would be this finest helicopter in the U.S. Army, not to be confused with 'Viper' your pilot, will be flying you over such scenic sights as the village of Mehtar Lam—"

"Which you won't see because," Big John explained, "though they have electricity, it's been offline for three days."

"The pleasant little hornet's nest of Loy Kalay will be given a wide berth…"

"As they tried to fry our behinds last time we flew over there," the Major filled in. She could hear the easy closeness of the crew. A team that flew together and fought together.

"We anticipate a quiet flight over Asadabad," Tim continued, "because we're going nowhere near it."

Lola waited for a comment from the copilot, but he apparently flew quieter than the rest of the crew. He had yet to speak.

"Estimated time to arrival is thirty-five minutes, so food and beverage service will be preempted for this flight. Our in-flight movie is an oldie but a goodie about an invisible six-foot-tall heli-pilot who—"

"*Viper*, this is *Wrench*." A radio call came over the headset in her helmet as clearly as if someone had been sitting right next to her, except some of the high end was missing. Encrypted transmission.

"Air Mission Commander Archibald Stevenson III, how's married life, you old cuss?" Major Henderson's voice, now filled with bonhomie, didn't quite hide the professionalism.

"You tell me, Major. Your wife is in it again."

Were all of these guys married? Slim pickin's for a girl fresh from training.

"Crap!" The humor was gone. "Heading?"

Already the twin GE turboshaft engines were winding up closer to the yellow line.

"310 will get you on the right track…"

The chopper twisted to the left and roared to life as five thousand horsepower poured into the main rotors before the AMC had even finished speaking.

"…you're twenty minutes out."

"Not for long," she heard the Major growl over the intercom.

"The nearest fast mover is thirty minutes out."

That meant all of the jets were on the ground tonight.

Lola heard the rotors deepen another couple notes of pitch as he twisted them for more speed, and the turbines spun up to a pitch that she knew was well into the yellow zone. Just barely below redline.

"LaRue, you wearing armor?" Any sign of banter gone from his voice. Pure steel remained.

"Full vest, sir, but not loaded into the flight suit." Kevlar plates front, back, and under the arms. Itched and rubbed when you were traveling but she'd pulled them on before landing in the "zone." Armor was just something you did in Iraq and Afghanistan, something you did all the time. She tugged up the back collar so that no one slipped a nasty surprise between the vest and the back of her helmet. But her arm and leg armor was stacked in the bottom of the duffel clipped to the net behind her.

"Best we've got. Tim, get her up and running on the M60. Set it on your side. You're responsible for her."

Lola considered responding that she was responsible just fine for herself and had been since she'd run away from home at fourteen. But the Major's current tone of voice made it clear why he was nicknamed "Viper." At the moment he sounded bloody dangerous. She wasn't going to mess with that.

The shadow that had helped her aboard was beside her in an instant, working on the cargo net. She grabbed Tim's arm to help keep him steady so that he could work with both hands. She'd been right. Really serious weight-lifter's muscle. Warm too, a heat against her hand that had chilled unnoticed with the night and the altitude. He was probably married like all the others, which would explain the politeness. Some woman had trained him well.

Too bad. She liked strong. Appreciated a muscle man in her muscle car. She liked funny too. Mixed in with polite, that could be fun, as long as he wasn't too polite.

The rest of the story came in by the time they had the big machine gun set up on a swivel in the middle of the cargo-bay door. They also rigged a strap so that she had some chance of remaining in place behind the M60 during sharp maneuvering.

Major Emily Beale, flying protective escort on a "meat" mission, a pick-up-a-load-of-troops-here-and-dump-them-off-over-there mission, had watched her load of "meat" be dumped right into a grinder. Despite the best intelligence, they'd landed two full squads of U.S. Rangers just below a Taliban camp in the front range of the Hindu Kush mountains. The ground-pounders were taking heavy fire from a seriously armed enemy. Emily Beale was trying to break it up, but one of the transports had been hammered out of the sky and the whole operation was going to hell.

"Popping one," Lola called out and kicked a single round out of the M60. A satisfying jolt against her palms as the hammer pounded home and drove a single round into the side of a passing mountain. The belt of ammunition jerked forward one position so fast she probably wouldn't have seen it in broad daylight, never mind at night.

Been a long time since she'd sat in back, at least a year, and that had been a training flight. She'd always been hot for the pilot's seat, ready to really rock and roll, not just shoot at things picked out by the pilot.

Tim had also patched in a data feed for her helmet. She swung her head around to get used to the tactical display across the inside of her visor. The camera system projected an all-around view outside the helicopter in a thousand shades of gray. It sensed the direction she was looking and projected the image from outside cameras in precisely that position, both horizontally and vertically. On top of that were dozens of symbols that she'd need for fire control.

A whole sector was missing. The blankness irritated her until she realized it was the piloting information that she didn't need until she was in her proper seat.

Dead of night, and she could see the rolling hills that had surrounded the airbase quickly shift into towering mountain terrain. She'd certainly seen it enough during SAR flights, but search and rescue was about cleanup, not about bringing the hammer.

Tonight, they were the DAP Hawk hammer.

—⁓—

Lola cursed under her breath when they were close enough to see the battle. Constant streams of tracer green death hammered down from a helicopter that danced and twirled like a ballerina gone mad. The bright streak of a rocket-propelled grenade slithered upward, but the chopper wasn't there and the RPG went wide. The dancing chopper had to be the other DAP Hawk.

She cursed again.

Lola had thought she was a top pilot now, knew she was. But no way could she do what that other DAP pilot was doing. Hell, she could barely keep track of it. That had to be Major Beale. While her husband Viper Henderson was the most decorated SOAR aviator, she had the reputation for being the best.

A nearby hiss, just one notch below a roar, brought Lola's attention back to their situation. Four rockets shot forward from the *Viper*'s own FFAR pod with a sharp sizzle. Her makeshift gun mount was not limited like the miniguns. The minis had stops so that you couldn't shoot your own armament where it stuck out on the chopper's side pylons or chop up your own rotors spinning above you like a room's ceiling. She had to remember to be careful. A glance showed the rockets raining down around the origin point of the RPG.

The explosion bloomed and sent a small fireball flowing skyward.

"Whoo-eee!" Crazy Tim yelled out. "Who brought the weenies? Time for a roast."

A couple of dazzling bursts as the baddies' armament

blew up. She saw three, four, five figures running or crawling away from the center of the explosion.

"Kick 'em in the buns!"

She and Tim opened up at the same time. His tracer-laden green buzz-saw of destruction and her own steady hammer pounded into bad guys, cleaning up the work begun by the rockets.

Big Bad John's minigun pounded out the other side of the chopper at more targets. The minis didn't have the ta-ta-tat sound of her machine gun. They howled like the largest and meanest vacuum cleaner ever built. Their electric motors wailing and the fifty-plus supersonic rounds a second roaring like a freight train. It was an eerie sound of the unleashing of death.

Causing the demise of at least one RPG nest, they too were now a target of interest to the baddies. Her tactical display started showing gunfire coming their direction. The array of microphones around the fuselage gathered and computed the most likely point of fire. She pounded short bursts down into the dark at target after target identified merely by crosshairs and a small circle on the inside of her visor.

At one point she blinked and her vision shifted to the outside world beyond the display. A nightmare landscape of soaring peaks, impossibly narrow valleys, and the flashes of attack and counterattack filled her vision. A vertical terrain shrouded in moonlit glow, black shadows, and a hundred sparks of fire from the muzzle flash of hand weapons.

Another blink returned her focus to the inside of her visor, and she saw a mortar track across the tactical display as it launched skyward. Even as the shell descended,

Tim wiped out the mortar crew. The explosive landed against the downed transport bird. Figures dove out the other side of the bird and into the night. Figures with the small infrared reflectors on their sleeves indicating they were friendlies. Even as the bird caught fire, the pilot and copilot scrambled clear, one more dragged than moving under his own power.

"Major," she started to call out. Every instinct of her CSAR background was driving her toward that spot, no matter how ugly the battle.

"I see it. Can't!" was all he replied, his voice tight as he rolled them through a heavy-gee maneuver. He flung them down into the canyon where the latest attack had come from.

She shut up and followed the flow of battle as well as she could with only a back-ender's tactical display. As copilot she was used to receiving far more information in overlapping graphics and visual enhancements. She was also used to having a broader view of the overall scope of the battle with a front-seater's view.

As a gunner, she had to simply trust that the pilot was making the best use of his assets by the targets that he made available to her side of the craft. Of course, as a pilot, you had to trust that your back-enders could follow through on what you gave them. The Major was giving their side of the Black Hawk a lot of opportunity. At first she'd thought it was because of having two guns mounted on their side of the craft.

But the more she watched, the more she understood that Tim was a master with his M134, wielding the minigun with brilliant acumen and immense effectiveness. He compensated for the Major's twists and turns as if he knew what was coming before the Major did. His lead for the helicopter's airspeed was flawless. She felt as if she were better and more competent simply for gunning alongside him.

Despite the two DAP Hawks and the one transport bird still aloft, it still took half an hour or maybe an hour more to scour the area clean. Time blurred with firing, reloading. Dodging out and back. Waiting for someone hiding to foolishly make a break for it.

Wrench, the married Air Mission Commander Archibald somebody, guided the air and ground troops on threats and opportunities that could only be seen from far above. Whoever he was, he too was damn good at his job. A master of tactics, he appeared to anticipate the enemy's moves as easily as Tim anticipated the helicopter's.

Lola let herself settle into the adrenal-hyperawareness where a thousand hours of training had taught her to blend tactical displays, helicopter motion, the AMC's guidance, and her own judgment into a single lethal flow.

At long last, the transport Hawk ducked in and took out the injured, but the ground-pounders stayed. Moving fast, the squads faded into the landscape and were moving on before the local militia could recover and reinforce.

The Major sent a final rocket salvo into the burning transport chopper, ensuring its complete destruction. Nothing left for any bad guys to salvage.

"Thanks, honey." A smooth voice, so calm that Lola, for a moment, thought it might be a recording of a woman's voice.

"My pleasure, babe," the Major replied.

"We should do this more often."

More often? Lola was limp as a rag from the pounding of battle and the shaking of the gun. Always knowing that the next round could find her and not even having the time to worry about it. The adrenaline letdown was already making her hazy.

She dug an energy bar out of a thigh pocket as the Major leaned the chopper on its side and turned for what must be home. The move was so abrupt that the bar floated above Lola's palm for a moment. Before she could grab it, the sharp turn and dive sent it tumbling out the open cargo door and falling toward the dark landscape below.

She watched the bright foil catch the light of breaking dawn she hadn't noticed sneaking over the horizon.

Checking one pocket and then the other unearthed nothing useful. She hadn't restocked after pilfering from her emergency rations during the forty-three hours in transit from Fort Campbell, Kentucky. Without food, she knew the adrenaline rush would descend into a nasty little headache. Great. Just what she wanted on her first day at a new post.

She set the safety on the M60 and locked it into resting position with more violence than necessary. The gun had performed fine. Her sudden peevishness wasn't its fault. Lola had been in transit too long, then flown into battle as a gunner, not a pilot. Back-enders didn't trust officers, ever. And here she was on Day One treading on their sacred turf. They'd probably turn out to be territorial, hazing, never-forgive-you-for-intruding-on-their-space types who—

A bright paper packet was floating just beyond her

visor. For a surreal moment she thought the energy bar she'd dropped had come back to her, somehow falling up as the Major beelined for base.

Then common sense intervened. Tim Maloney had noticed her actions and offered one of his own bars. Paper wrapped, not foil. Right, foil might have too big a radar signature.

She took it. Too wiped to do more than nod her thanks. Rather than a nasty back-ender, yet more proof of decent guy.

Chapter 2

"AIR BASE" WAS FAR TOO GRAND A TERM TO DESCRIBE the SOAR base in Bati, Pakistan. Lola assessed her new base of operations as they slipped down through the morning light, swinging wide over the village that stretched a mile along the narrow river.

On a rise to the east, on the boundary where land shifted from houses and irrigated fields to arid soil and an endless flat plain of dust, huddled an old, concrete soccer stadium. Dull gray with flaking whitewash. Not quite the sort of home a girl always dreamed of.

A ring of guards, Army Rangers, perched along the top row of the seating, all facing outward very attentively. Clearly not a friendly place to have a base. That U.S. Army helicopters were squatting in Pakistan at all meant that some strange negotiations had happened at a level way above her pay grade. The U.S. and Pakistan governments were barely on speaking terms, yet here they were.

The field itself was an inventory catalog of the birds that SOAR flew. Two of the big, twin-rotor Chinooks lurked down at one end. An array of tents beyond made up what must be the main camp huddle.

Midfield was taken up by a half-dozen Little Birds. The MH-6s were the wasps of the unit. Small, fast, and nasty. Pilot and copilot, plus either a decent array of weapons or four passengers who sat on benches outside of the helicopter because there was no room inside.

Down at the other end of the field was another small cluster of tents and a half-dozen Black Hawks. Six transport birds each able to move a dozen troops and all of their field gear. Also, room for their two birds, and the blank spot just big enough for the bird they'd left burning on the ground.

Between the edge of the field and the concrete bleachers ran a wide running track. Most of it was covered with helicopters and at either end by tents, but a path had been left open. Even now she could see a couple of grunts out for a run around the track. Clear message, nothing to do here but fly and run. Probably enough of the former that the latter didn't have time to get too dull.

This time she waited for the blades to spin down and the worst of the dust to settle before jumping down.

She landed true, but she crumpled to the ground. When she tried to stand, pain from her leg flashed bright stars behind her winced-closed eyelids.

Someone was beside her in a moment.

Any attempts to declare she was fine were ignored, first by the others who jumped down from her own Black Hawk and then from the other bird which had landed next to them.

She shut her mouth when she spotted the red stain and hole in her pant leg. She flexed her foot.

The pain spiked and twisted, but the foot moved and the pain stayed on the surface.

"Just a graze," she managed through gritted teeth. She had enough training from her CSAR work to be an aid rather than a hindrance in a medical situation. "Some antiseptic, a bit of glue, and a bandage, and this should be fine," she announced for anyone who could be bothered to listen, which totaled absolutely no one.

She went to stand just as someone leaned down to pick her up. She felt a thump through her helmet followed by a loud curse as she dropped back to sit in the dust.

Shoving up her visor and looking over her shoulder, a vista of bright red greeted her. In the growing daylight she could now see the weight-lifter guy clearly. Tim. His hair crew cut, his skin a natural sun-kissed shade made deeper by the sun, and his nose flowing bright red where she'd smashed it with the back of her helmet.

A huge man loomed up beside him, the starboard-side gunner, and stuffed a rag in Tim's face, none too gently.

Tim yelped. "Damn it! Go easy, John. I think she broke it."

Ouch! She really hoped not. Especially after he'd been nice to her.

The big man flashed a grin almost as large as he was. "'Bout time you spilled some blood for the Black Adders."

"Black Adders?" Lola stripped her own helmet as some corpsman squatted before her. In moments, he'd cut back the pant leg and revealed exactly what she expected. A thin groove and blood already clotting. She'd need new pants and have to really wash out the sock. Not much more. Certainly less blood than Tim. He sat in the dirt, his head leaned back against the Black Hawk's cargo deck as he held the bloody cloth to his nostrils.

By now, both crews were gathered around her. Here was her "Welcome to SOAR" moment, sprawled in the dirt with a bunch of guys staring down at her. Only they weren't all guys. *Do not*, she ordered herself, *do not squirm*.

She distracted herself by inspecting the crews that were in turn inspecting their latest addition, like they were a neighborhood welcoming committee really unhappy about who just bought the house next door.

Lola could identify Tim and Big John. And when the knock-'em-dead blond slipped up beside the equally handsome, blue-eyed Major with the distinctly amused grin, she knew she'd spotted Major Emily Beale and Viper Henderson. Damn, their kids were gonna be something amazing to look at.

The two other women had taken one look at her and turned back to shut down their bird. So, these were the first three women of SOAR. Not exactly the warmest of welcomes. Well, they were going to have to deal. She made four.

The two copilots were already working on their post-engagement reports, flight suits peeled down with the arms tied around their waists, white T-shirts clinging to their frames, damp with the heat. If the weather was this hot in mid-March, what was summer like? Both guys were nice enough to look at, but the excitement of a little blood was insufficient to distract them from their jobs.

"Black Adders." Big John flashed her another one of his big, easy smiles. "Those lucky enough to fly with Viper Henderson and his wife. That's what you are now, a Black Adder."

"We'll see." One of the women paused long enough in cleaning her weapon to glare down at Lola. "Gotta have more than a lousy scrape to be a Black Adder."

Stung by the automatic dismissal, Lola pushed to her feet. Resisting the urge to steady herself on the shoulder of the corpsman who even now was taping on the final bandage, she stepped over to the Sergeant. She looked down at the woman, a full head shorter than Lola. She had long, Asian black hair with a single, dyed-blond streak, narrow eyes, and a brick-shithouse body. Real breasts, something Lola had always wanted and never grown.

Lola moved up until she was toe to toe with the woman.

"Sergeant, I got way more *couilles* than you ever dreamed of. And that's Black Adder Sir to y'all. We be clear here?" She could feel the Creole flowing out of her. She bit down on her tongue before she could go too far. She knew that once her own temper was really rolling, it would be hard to reel it back in before it burned her.

She could see the woman's temper rising fast and hard. *Well done. Screwing up the team before she'd even stepped aboard.* She'd just turned a bit of derision into a battlefield. Well, to hell with her.

Before she could let loose another round, the other crew chief stepped up. Hazel eyes, a cascade of soft brunette hair around a quiet face.

"Give her a break, Kee. She's flown with me before. She's alright. And you know how long a haul it is from the States."

Lola recognized the voice. She'd never seen the woman in daylight without a helmet, but she knew her. Sergeant Connie Davis. Yeah, they'd flown together, once, on a mission that she'd been told she was never allowed to mention to anyone, ever. She'd been on a SOAR training mission in Germany when an emergency call had gone out for a CSAR crew. That combat search and rescue mission was also the last time she'd flown as pilot-in-command.

"Hello, Sergeant Davis." The quiet mechanic had rarely spoken as they flew together, but they'd gotten it done.

"Chief Warrant LaRue." Connie Davis returned to her weapon as if nothing had happened.

Sergeant Kee last-name-unknown glared at her as she stripped down the top of the flight suit and tied the arms around her waist with such a hard tug that Lola winced in empathetic pain. Then she turned, making it clear Lola wasn't worth even dirt. Well, maybe that much. If she were lucky.

Lola's first instinct was to tackle the little bitch and solve it here and now, but she knew better than to follow her first instinct. Had learned that the hard way. Especially with someone of lower rank. Officers weren't supposed to pound the crap out of enlisted, no matter how much they deserved it.

Still, the whole holier-than-thou attitude pushed her buttons real damn hard.

She turned back to the others. Tim still leaned his head back against the cargo deck as the corpsman inspected his nose. His big friend hovering protectively despite his dismissive words.

"Not broken," the corpsman announced. "You're almost done bleeding."

"Yeah," Big John rumbled, "stop whining. You such a wimp, boy." You could hear the affection in the way he said it. These guys clearly had some serious history. They'd been through it together.

The Majors were still watching her. She felt herself straightening as she faced them, could feel the pull of the bandage across the graze along her calf.

Major Henderson was still smiling at the little display. It wasn't overt, but he wasn't the pure steel of legend either. He struck Lola as a man who found humor in any situation, despite his reputation. Well, perhaps any situation other than someone shooting at his wife.

Major Emily Beale was wholly unreadable.

Lola snapped a salute, as clean and sharp as she could with her bloody pant leg cut open and Afghanistan dust penetrating every pore of her exhausted being.

"Chief Warrant 2 Lola LaRue reporting for duty, ma'am."

The Major simply stared back at her with those crystalline blue eyes.

Lola retained the salute for several long seconds before remembering. Then she lowered her arm hesitantly, remembering too late that you didn't salute in the field. A salute could tell a distant sniper which one to aim for.

When her hand at last returned to her side, the Major nodded slowly.

"Welcome to the Black Adders." She then slid on mirrored Ray-Bans exactly like her husband's. Suddenly there were four of Lola staring back at her.

Beale and Henderson turned and were gone, taking only moments to disappear into the shimmer of heat already rising from the packed earth of the abandoned soccer field.

Lola let out a sharp breath and turned for her gear. Only Tim remained, his head still tilted back, the red cloth still covering much of his face.

She could see Big Bad John Wallace walking away with Sergeant Connie Davis. Holding hands.

"What the hell?"

Tim opened his eyes that he'd kept closed against the bright desert sun because there was no way to put on his sunglasses with how his nose felt. About the size of his mama's favorite soup pot.

He noticed where the new girl was focused. John and Connie. Who'd have ever guessed? Connie'd sure pissed off John enough in the beginning. Half a year back Tim would've bet good money there'd be death before marriage, and now you couldn't turn around without them being all lovey-dovey. *Sad state of affairs, my man. Sad state. Bachelors hitting the mat right and left. Down for the count and, even worse, looking all happy about it.*

"Married two months. Only way to keep 'em apart is when the Majors assigned them to different choppers."

He watched her back as Chief Warrant LaRue shed her vest and peeled down her flight suit against the rising morning heat. A thin, white tank top outlined strong shoulders and that sharp taper to a soldier's slender waist. But a woman's hips. Not some anorexic nymph, just a shapely woman in fine shape. Damn fine shape. And that cascade of thick, dark chestnut hair curling down past those strong shoulders. Nonregulation hair wasn't all that common in SOAR, but it was allowed and LaRue's mane was a serious statement in that direction.

Serious eye candy from behind. She'd made SOAR, which meant she was an awesome flier, though Major Beale would make her better. Be fun to watch those lessons. But he wasn't gonna complain for a second about sharing a camp with a woman so easy on the eyes.

Then she turned to look down at him where he still leaned back against the side of the chopper. Skin naturally the color of the most perfect summerlong tan and a face that stopped him cold.

He could see her incredible figure, hard to miss from where he sat at her feet looking up at her, all sleek and lean and perfect. But her face. He didn't want to look away from that face for a moment.

He knew her, but didn't. She had a face that a man, having seen it even once, could never forget. But where? When?

Poland.

He'd never been closer than thirty meters across a wind-torn cruiser's deck, but it had to be her. It wasn't just her beauty or her amazing wave of flowing hair. It was how she stood. Something radiated from her that he couldn't turn away from.

She studied him with narrowed eyes, then eased off and smiled down at him.

"You're sweet."

"What?" But he didn't need to ask. She'd been eye candy from behind, but from the front she was incredible. And she'd caught him staring stone cold. Tim could always be cool around a woman. Mirrored shades on, T-shirt with the sleeves and collar torn off, muscles on show—the women flocked and he didn't complain. And he treated them all nice enough that he never heard them complain one little bit either. He was always smooth, even, steady.

He reached in his mind… and came up with nothing. No smooth line. No easy shrug. No Mr. Casual. All he could do was watch as her eyes shifted from curious to friendly. She tugged a pair of sunglasses out of a thigh pocket and slipped them on. Then a crazy smile pulled up at one corner of her mouth, dimpling the cheek on her left side. A burst of laughter came forth like from an insane elf.

"Come on." She offered a hand. "Get up out of the dirt and show me where to get food and a shower, in that order."

He took the offered hand, and though his nose throbbed as he made it to his feet, it didn't start bleeding again. Regrettably, he still wore his flight gloves, but he could feel the strength. Long, lean strength in fine-fingered hands.

He turned to help her with her gear, but she pulled on fifty-plus pounds of pack and slung her duffel over one shoulder with the ease of a soldier's long practice. Slender and strong. Stunning and funny.

Tim was so screwed.

Big John was gonna laugh his ass off.

Chapter 3

THE MESS TENT WAS, WELL, A MESS.

Lola dumped her gear by the tent flap and followed Tim toward the chow line along the back wall. She could see the territorial boundaries laid out like an airstrip.

Far right taxiway belonged to the U.S. Army Rangers. Crew cut and muscled up. A lot of them had their green berets on. One guy had a T-shirt that proclaimed, "Rangers—often mistaken for the wrath of God." They were a rowdy lot with a lot of back slapping and stories flying between them. Good guys when you needed a hammer blow.

Down the left taxiway guys huddled around a couple of quiet tables. Three things made them stand out. Their motions were small, precise, tightly controlled. Some had long hair, others a beard or mustache. And they were speaking in whispers that wouldn't carry to the next table, even if the rest of the tent were silent.

D-boys. No mistaking them anywhere, except in public where they were frickin' invisible. You'd pass them on the street and never notice them. She hadn't known Delta Force was encamped here. That meant there was some seriously nasty shit going down here.

Lola was good with that.

Deltas weren't muscled like Rangers, though they trained longer and harder. Tricycle and NASCAR again. Rangers might rock 'n' roll, but D-boys were the best warriors on the planet. Even the SEALs gave them respect.

Like the SEALs, Delta operators also let their hair grow to civilian lengths, making it easier for them blend in. They looked like, well, any guy. They'd be hard to pick out of a crowd, hard to remember them even if you did.

SOAR made a career of moving Rangers into battles, D-boys and SEALs into clandestine tactical situations, and getting all of them back out. It's what she'd signed up for. And after two extra years of training required after making SOAR, she was ready. Beyond ready.

Down the middle of the chow-tent runway, SOAR. No more chance of mistaking the Night Stalkers than the Delta operators. Many had arm tattoos of a sword-wielding Pegasus, a flying horse of death. Quieter than Rangers, of course everybody was. Their stories were more focused but still physical, planed hands swooping to demonstrate a flight path, a jabbed finger to indicate rocket fire. Some crew cut, most not.

She liked that about SOAR and had let her hair start growing the day she'd signed up. She liked the implied companionship with the D-boys. The most lethal fliers carrying the most lethal fighters.

"Hey, c'mon." Tim snapped his fingers in front of her face to get her attention.

Lola had come to a stop to observe this first assignment card she'd drawn. There'd be a thousand missions and a hundred camps and bases, but this was her first as a SOAR copilot and it looked as if boredom was not going to be an issue.

She followed Tim down the chow line. He loaded up

on dinner. It was the end of her day after all, but Lola
had always been a fan of breakfast for dinner. She also
didn't feel right eating a burger and fries at six in the
morning. Despite the base's remoteness from any other
signs of Western civilization, the cooks here obviously
tried, since they were serving both meals. She went for
a short stack, bacon, juice, and fruit.

Tim led her over to a table where she recognized
most of the two crews. Clearly this was where the DAP
Hawks chowed down together. She counted seats and
came up one short. Nowhere for her to land without taking someone else's.

Tim must have read her mind, he nodded to the
corner. Not far from the D-boys, the two Majors sat at
a table with one of the D-boys. She watched from the
corner of her eye just long enough to observe everyone
giving that table an extra-wide berth. Even the Delta
operators swung wide.

"Who?" she mouthed at Tim. The extra guy looked
rugged and tough. Then he smiled at something one of
the Majors said. The rugged remained, and the tough,
but it looked right on him.

"Colonel Michael Gibson. Medal of Honor and all that."

Lola glanced over at him one more time. They had
a D-boy colonel stationed in a tiny camp like this?
Clearly they were not in any normal place. *Duh, Lola.
You're at an unreported camp in the middle of the
Pakistani desert, fifty miles, about fifteen minutes, from
the Afghanistan border.*

Without the Majors they'd have a chair to spare at the
SOAR table. Not sure where to land, she ended up at one
end of the table across from Tim, shoulder to shoulder

with Big John. Connie Davis, the mechanic she'd flown with in Poland, sat on John's other side. Might as well be a mile away with that wall of man-flesh between them.

A tall and lean man slid in next to Tim and began setting his table. Taking napkin and silverware off his tray. Even setting knife and spoon to his right, fork on napkin to his left, with plate and water glass in place. No insignia, already showered, and wearing civvies. Uptight priss by the look of it.

A hardback book thumped down on the table beyond him. A small, dark girl in white native garb jumped onto his back and wrapped her slender arms around his neck.

He ignored her. Continuing to set his place as if he sat alone in the whole tent.

The girl covered his eyes. "Guess who?"

The guy stopped, tilting his head one way and then the other, not trying to shake the small hands loose, rather considering. Then he proclaimed solemnly, "President Peter Matthews. What are you doing in Bati, Mr. President?"

Lola recognized the voice. Took her a moment to place it. Air Mission Commander. *Wrench*. The voice that had called them about Major Beale's flight being in trouble. The married AMC. Well, he'd gone native and his kid had completely favored her mother, there was no sign of the AMC in the elfin face grinning over his shoulder.

"Need see my best peoples." She lowered her voice as far as a young girl's could go.

"People."

The girl repeated it dutifully but still in her pretend-adult tone.

A woman arrived bearing two trays. Must be the AMC's…

Lola looked at Sergeant Kee as she ground to a halt toting two trays of food. Glaring at Lola as if she shouldn't be there. Kee stayed still long enough that the little girl took one of the trays from her hands and set it beside her book. *The Secret Garden*.

The Sergeant finally set her tray down with a sharp snap.

Lola was glad Kee sat at the other end of the table, down with Connie Davis and Henderson's silent copilot, Richardson.

"Where's Terry?" Kee asked loudly.

"Packing his gear," the mountain man next to Lola rumbled out. "Now that we got our new copilot, he's stateside for R-and-R, then some training."

So Lola had counted the number of seats and crew-members right, but she hadn't known about the kid.

The kid. She'd arrived with the Sergeant but latched on to the AMC. They were a family. What in the hell was the kid doing on a forward air base?

Lola bit down on her tongue rather than make what-ever was between her and the Sergeant even worse.

Besides, a forward, secret air base in one of the nas-tiest little wars in history was probably safer than the house Lola had grown up in.

Chapter 4

CHIEF WARRANT 2 LOLA LARUE LEANED FORWARD TO get a better view through the DAP Hawk's forward windscreen. It was pointless, all that existed out there was darkness. Anyway, the image was across the inside of her visor, not out the windscreen, but she couldn't help the body reaction.

She'd lost sight of one of the Little Bird choppers they were supposed to be guarding. The two-seater attack helicopters barely weighed a tenth as much as her Black Hawk and were so quick in tight spaces that it was hard to keep track of them. You spent one lousy moment trying to find where some raghead bad guy was pinging your windshield with rifle fire, and the Little Bird slipped into hiding.

Major Emily Beale, who sat to her right in the pilot's seat of their Direct Action Penetrator Black Hawk, pointed casually down to the left just in time for Lola to spot the Little Bird swinging into sight from behind a pillar of rock. How did the woman know what Lola was missing even before she did?

She gripped the cyclic and collective controls even tighter, crushing them in her frustration. Her first flight in-country and she was already letting the Major down. The cyclic wiggled in her hand. Then wiggled again hard enough to rock their helicopter a bit side to side. Right. Pilots fly with a loose wrist.

"Ease up, LaRue!" The order transmitted as clearly through the controls as if it had been shouted in her ear.

Lola did. Flexing her fingers a moment and feeling Emily Beale's sure and reliable control take over.

The Major had risen in just a few short years to be one of the most highly successful officers in the U.S. Army's 160th. Lola had almost killed herself trying to get on Beale's crew, and now she was busy screwing up by not measuring up.

Lola could feel Sergeant Kee Stevenson sitting directly behind her, glaring at the back of her seat as if she could punch holes through the Kevlar armor built into Lola's chair.

She shook her head to clear the thoughts and glared down at the battle scene spread out below and around them.

The Hindu Kush mountains of northeastern Afghanistan punched upward like a madman's drawing of a nightmare. Impossible crags of barren rock with an upside-down forest ecology. Down below was arid desert. Here, high on the ridges, holly and oak trees of impossible size loomed out of the near-vertical cliffs, just dying to snag an unwary helicopter's rotor and send them crashing into the valley far below.

That would be bad enough without the added distraction of the bloodthirsty Afghanis, spending every penny that should have been spent on food for their families on ammunition, just so they could pour it into helicopters that were trying to protect them from the Taliban they hated even more and from… she didn't even know what. She was just getting more pissed off the more times gunfire pinged against their hull.

The two crew chiefs behind her were using the opportunity to unleash their miniguns against anyone foolish enough to show up on their threat detectors. Fire at a DAP Hawk and your likely position of fire was fed directly into the crew's visors as targeting information. It was about the deadliest choice you could make on the entire planet, shooting at a DAP.

Not her worry. Her concern was the Little Birds, and damn, she'd now lost the other one.

There, roaring out of a cleft with a stream of fire chasing its butt. Without even thinking, Lola sighted up the cleft, the target sight on her visor lining up with the location that the Little Bird was zipping away from. A moment's pause to make sure that the tactical display didn't place any other friendlies on the ground there. Not a one. The few remaining Afghani soldiers were huddled deep inside the remains of their firebase.

Lola fired off a salvo of three Hydra rockets.

They roared a dozen feet over the Little Bird, briefly illuminating its bulbous windscreen and tiny cabin with their trails of hot fire. The rockets slammed into the cliff with a very satisfying explosion.

A nice little rockslide started above the impact site and erased anyone marginally lucky enough to have survived the initial explosion.

"Splash one!" she called out. Not quite right, they hadn't just dropped an enemy jet into the ocean, but rather a half-dozen Taliban into their Maker's keeping forevermore, but it sounded good. Felt good too. A half dozen down probably meant an equal number of U.S. troops would be going home in one piece.

She glanced over at Beale. No word. No nod of

acknowledgment. Not even a glance toward where she'd just axed some of the baddies. The woman had a reputation for being made of cold steel, and Lola hadn't seen anything different. Didn't even know why she expected anything else.

A quick scan of engine and airframe reports said that if anything had been hit, it wasn't critical enough to show up… yet. Constant vigilance was something beaten into her by a dozen instructors and a hundred missions. And the woman beside her demanded no less than perfection. Not by her words, but by her actions.

Lola again thought back to that emergency CSAR mission into the heart of Poland. Six months ago, three quarters of the way through her training, she was the closest asset when they'd called for a rescue flight.

She'd been sent to fetch Major Beale who had just flown twelve hours, the last part with a serious concussion and bleeding from where she'd been shot up. The Major had been worried first about her crew, then her bird, then their precious cargo. Never about herself.

Lola had helped shove the barely conscious woman onto a stretcher, had to strap her down so that she didn't get up to check on her crew herself rather than take anyone else's word for their well-being. That was the kind of woman Lola wanted to fly with. The kind of woman she wished she could be. The kind of woman she knew she wasn't. Anyone she fooled otherwise simply didn't know the real Lola LaRue.

But no one really did know her. Not with Mama Raci dead and gone. She'd be best off if she could just keep flying below everyone's radar.

The Major backed off the DAP Hawk, not enough to

be out of the action but enough to give the Little Birds room to maneuver and to provide Lola with an overview of the mayhem that was tonight's firefight.

The local militia had decided to shoot up a forward base and tear the Afghani army a new one just for existing. The U.S. Army had been trying for a dozen months to turn the battle against the Taliban over to the Afghani regulars, but they couldn't stay organized long enough to stay alive. So now, instead of the troops doing primary protection and wide-perimeter patrols that were standard around a U.S.-run base, the Taliban were able to slip in until they were right on top of the Afghanis, dug in wholly undetected before they opened fire.

That left it up to the U.S. SOAR 160th, the Night Stalkers, to come in on emergency call and do the heavy cleanup that should never have been needed, if the Afghani regular army had done it right to begin with.

At long last Major Beale jerked up and back on the cyclic, flipping them from close hover support through about the smoothest roll maneuver Lola had ever seen, and twisted them back toward base. The collective and cyclic controls in her hands were hard-linked to the Major's, the pedals beneath her feet as well. Lola had felt every tiny adjustment of the maneuver, and she still had no idea how the woman did it.

The four Little Birds—she counted them twice to make sure they were all accounted for, then counted them once more to be sure—danced and zipped just ahead of them. The Major kept their speed down so that they didn't overrun their flock. Little Birds were more agile but not as fast as a Black Hawk.

Lola was drenched with sweat inside her flight suit.

She was used to the deceptively hard work of sitting in a copilot's seat and wrenching around ten tons of helicopter. And she'd been in enough firefights to not flinch at a spray of rounds smacking into the forward windscreen right at eye level.

What she wasn't prepared for was the exhaustion from the hyper-focus required by close-in battle flying. A couple years of flying forward patrol support with the Screaming Eagles of the 101st Airborne hadn't prepared her for tonight's flight. The Eagles hung back and depended on the superior reach of their rockets, 30 mm cannon, and whatever other nasty armament they were carrying for that flight. They also flew far more often in the daylight than the dark. At night they sent the 160th.

When she'd flown in a search and rescue bird, she'd sat yet another step behind that. Most of the time. There was a reason for the *C* in combat search and rescue. It meant going hot into heavy situations to pull out the wounded. It was the *C* that had hooked her out of CSAR.

Flying forward combat rather than SAR meant she'd be saving guys before they were already injured. She could fight the battles and prevent the troops being injured in the first place. But she'd never flown consistently this close in during combat.

Major Beale had rarely been more than a dozen rotor widths—the fifty-six feet from one tip to the other of their main rotor blades—away from the action. It was easier to think in "rotors," especially when trees or power lines were always reaching out to snag you.

Anyone who thought that airborne battles weren't up close and personal had clearly never flown with Major Beale.

"Quiet night." One of the crew chiefs. Sergeant Kee, of course, spoke calmly over the intercom.

The woman had to be bragging for Lola's sake to make her feel even more incompetent.

"Didn't even use up two cans," the Sergeant continued. Two cans of ammo through their miniguns. That was an immense amount of lead they'd fired in just, Lola checked the clock, forty-five minutes. She checked the clock again. It had seemed like six hours. Their fuel still showed enough to get home without a midair refueling. The battle had been so intense that she'd lost all track of time.

"Clean and green," the head mechanic, Connie Davis, announced. She could have been a prerecorded machine voice for all the emotion she portrayed.

Lola wanted to shove up her visor to wipe away the salty sweat that was trickling into her eyes and stinging. Would have, but she didn't want to embarrass herself even more than she already had in front of the Major.

She tried to resist glancing over at the woman. Barely a foot separated their shoulders. A foot and about a thousand miles. Not a single comment. Not a gesture. No feedback at all on how she'd done.

"Take us home, Chief Warrant." Major Beale's voice was quiet over the intercom. Real quiet, in a way that didn't bode well.

"Aye, sir." Damn! "Ma'am." She couldn't even get that right. In the old Army, the way it had been when she'd signed up just six years ago, all superior officers were "sir" regardless of gender. Now it was shifting and you never knew. The older women still expected a "sir," but the younger ones wanted a "ma'am."

Hard to believe that Major Beale was only a year older than Lola. Made Lola feel like a total slacker. Like that comedian had said, "When Mozart was my age, he'd been dead for three years."

She followed the Little Birds and checked her heading for the Bati soccer stadium. Just concentrate on getting them back in one piece. She could fly that well at least.

Chapter 5

"LET'S GO!" TIM MALONEY stood from the chow table but didn't head off.

"Go where?" Lola had just finished breakfast, for which she'd had dinner, as the sun set, and they were about to have a whole night off. No missions tonight, which was good. For a whole week, all Lola had done was prove that she'd been a total idiot in signing up for SOAR in the first place.

Now, with nothing to do for a whole night, she dreaded what she knew was going to happen. She'd overthink every action for the last week, each flight, each maneuver. She'd dwell on them until she'd spiraled into a place of depression and self-disgust at her own incompetence. She'd land in a place that reminded her far too much of living with her father. A helpless downward spiral of crashing self-esteem that she'd always been powerless to stop once she got caught in the downdraft.

"Go where?" she repeated when Tim didn't bother to explain.

He just gave her enough of a light punch on the arm to get her moving. She shrugged. What the hell, why not? Maybe he'd keep her from dwelling on how badly she'd screwed up her career. Two years of training and now she was flunking out. Not in testing, not in training; it was the real world where she wasn't good enough.

Well, that didn't come as such a surprise. After all, it was right on track with the rest of her life.

Tim rousted the rest of the table, snagging the Majors and the D-boy colonel along the way. A couple of the Little Bird crews tagged along and enough Rangers that soon twenty or so of them were trooping out into the dark of Bati air base. Probably a trip into town. It was dangerous to go with less than a squad, but they were nearer a platoon now, and that was too big and would just tick off the locals.

Tim had scooted ahead. Just outside the chow tent he was handing out old second-generation NVGs. The monocular night-vision goggles were monstrous by today's standards. Where in the world had he dug up these dinosaurs? They were heavy and covered the face from tip of nose to top of forehead to block interfering light. A single lens stuck out like a stubby misplaced unicorn's horn right over the bridge of the nose.

Soon everybody had one and Tim was gesturing to put them on.

Lola decided to play along. He was the only reason she'd felt welcome at Bati. Every day he found something to amuse her or help her out. He'd showed her where a pretty decent weight set had been gathered in the back of a supply tent, complete with a couple of benches and enough iron to keep a half-dozen grunts happy. When he'd discovered she played backgammon, he'd turned a couple of games into a daily morning ritual between breakfast and sack time. They were fairly well matched, which kept it interesting.

She pulled on the NVGs, adjusting the straps so that they settled not too uncomfortably. With the goggles on, she could see that Bati field was brightly awash under a half-dozen infrared lights. Shadows of helicopters were sharp-edged and overlapping against the bright green wash. A small flag stood in front of her with a number *1* on it.

Tim held out a golf club. No, it was a golf putter and a ball with a strip of infrared reflecting paint and the letter *S* on one side, a *1* on the other.

"I knew color wouldn't show up," Tim said loudly enough for everyone to hear. "So your balls are marked for your group."

A number of vulgar jokes were tossed back from the crowd as Tim distributed putters and golf balls. A couple of the ruder remarks were aimed her way. Typical. Army grunts always tried to see if they could offend or embarrass the women entering their ranks. Lola knew from watching others in the past that once you showed the least weakness, they'd drive it home until you wanted to curl up and die. But she'd spent a lot of her teen years working the kitchens at Mama Raci's, nothing was offensive after that. And years of search and rescue had long since cured her of any squeamishness.

"Just 'cause I got no balls, mon," she shot back at one of them, "don' mean I ain't gone kick you in yours." That got the expected laugh and they eased off.

A *D*-marked ball for the colonel and the two other D-boys. A dozen *R*'s for the rangers. *S* for the rest of SOAR. He fished into his bucket and came up with *A* balls for a couple of Army folks who were there in support roles—three armorers and a couple kitchen guys. Tim even had little scorecards and stubby pencils. Where the hell had he gotten all this?

Only when everyone was outfitted and people were knocking around their golf balls on the rough dirt of the hard-packed running track did Tim continue.

"Twenty bucks!" he called loud enough to stop conversation. "Twenty bucks each into the kitty. Three prizes: a half, a third, and a sixth. Cough it up!" Some grumbled, though most pitched in with good humor. With Tim cajoling them, no one walked away and he soon had five hundred bucks stuffed into his pocket.

Tim set them off down the course in pairs. Eighteen holes around Bati stadium. Obstacles were rough ground; some oddly placed boards; a ramp that led four tiers up into the bleachers, thirty feet along the narrow seat ledge, and back down; and the undercarriages of helicopters and service gear. He must have worked on this through the whole day when the rest of the crews had been sleeping.

She and Tim ended up together as one of the last teams. Just before they teed off, Colonel Gibson came up. Even with the NVG covering most of his face, there was no mistaking the man. The smooth movement, the lower jaw marked clearly by a broad scar that looked piratical rather than disfiguring.

Without saying a word, he took the ball out of Tim's palm and dropped his own in its place. He glided back down toward the tee-off for the second hole.

Tim laughed quietly. "Didn't think I'd get that by him."

"What?" Lola watched Tim as he fished out another ball with an *S* on it.

He glanced around, but they were alone at the moment. He took the two balls, the *S*- and the *D*-marked ones and rolled them together on the ground. The one with the *S* bounced and gyrated over the rough ground, but went generally straight. The one with the *D* wobbled, then stabilized into a long, curving track. They came to rest a dozen feet away and several feet apart.

He gathered them up and dropped the one with the *D* back into the bucket with a few other leftovers.

"Saw them in one of those party game catalogs. Couldn't resist."

Lola looked at him aghast and then glanced down the course to make sure that no hoard of angry putt-putt golfers was fast approaching. "You gave rigged balls to everyone?"

"Everyone except SOAR." He held up his *S* for her to see. "Gotta keep our reputation in place."

"And if the Rangers figure it out, they're gonna beat the shit out of you." Even as she said it, she thought over the start. Tim had only paired SOAR with other SOAR. Everyone else was paired with some-one with a rigged ball. They'd attribute all of their problems to the rough course. She shook her head in grudging admiration.

"You really are Crazy Tim."

Tim shrugged negligently. "Seemed worth the risk. Besides, they're just Rangers. How would they ever know?"

And they didn't. Lola patted the eighty-five dollars in her pocket for coming in third. Henderson won, not a big surprise, and Colonel Gibson placed second with his *S*-marked ball. She'd finished only a stroke ahead of Tim and Major Beale. Kee was three strokes back and was laughing about it right until Lola finished and tallied up a winner. Well, screw her. Lola had had fun.

More than just the game, though. She'd really had fun because of the time with Tim. For a couple of hours she'd forgotten herself. Laughed a bit. Laughed a lot.

Tim told stories of his prior escapades. He'd done everything from the dumbest stunts to the most elaborate. Offering around pepper chewing gum for Marines the moment before his chopper had dumped them in central nowhere for a weeklong, deep-country survival training class.

He'd once gotten really pissed at a lousy commander in his early days of flight. He'd snuck out and unmounted the pilot's seat, turned it around, and bolted it back down facing backward. "Not that he'd have noticed the difference, he was that bad. Problem was, he was too sick to fly the next day. That was the first time I met the Viper. He was the substitute pilot."

At Lola's inquiry, he'd finished the story. "All Henderson said was, 'Either give me a mirror so I can see where I'm going or turn that damn thing around.' John and I had it back in place before he finished pre-flight. Flown with him ever since."

They'd laughed together. They'd lagged behind everyone else. He'd told her stories of growing up in his family's restaurant kitchen.

Tim didn't push when she declined to fill in the spaces he left for her to offer her own stories.

Lola compared his upbringing to Mama Raci's kitchen. Close family and good food versus a nasty, old, black Cajun brothel-owner stingy with the girls—"Mon don' want 'em plump"—and not much nicer to the customers. "Enough cheap booze and I don' have to feed no mon much to get der money."

But when Lola had finally had the good sense to run away from home, Mama Raci had taken her in. Fed her the same as the working girls, and Lola had paid for it by washing dishes and sweeping the cracked-out linoleum. She'd even had a small room off the kitchen all her own. Way better than living with her criminal father and his creepy buddies always hanging around and eyeing a growing girl. And way, way, way better than joining the bloodthirsty street gangs. That was no way out of anything. It was a trap in the shape of a bottomless pit.

Lola wandered toward her bunk after the game. Eighty-five dollars would have been a fortune back then. Still nothing to sneeze at.

Tim left her feeling strange. He'd been easy around her. Made her easy around him. Left her relaxed and forgetful of her differences from all of those around her. Almost made her feel as if she belonged.

Chapter 6

"IT WAS WEIRD." LOLA ROLLED THE DICE AND MOVED her backgammon marker three and two. Safe.

"What was?" Tim Maloney sat across the table from her, shaking his dice cup in the nearly empty chow tent. Sitting with Tim Maloney had rapidly become her treat to herself. Ever since the crazy golf game a half-dozen flights ago, he'd dropped the goggle-eyed expression he'd been aiming at her when he didn't think she was watching. In its wake there remained an amazingly handsome, easygoing guy she enjoyed spending time with.

Breakfast had been cleared, and most of the base's personnel had drifted away to do whatever they did. The fliers to kill some time before sleeping through the day. The 160th SOAR was called the Night Stalkers for a reason. They flew at night, slept in the day. The maintenance guys were normal shifters. They worked on the birds—refueling, rearming, and repairing through the day, then sleeping while the crews flew.

A couple of the Little Bird guys were lingering over coffee. Some Rangers were going back to the line for seconds or maybe thirds, despite the rising heat of the day making the air too oppressive to allow minor considerations like hunger. Rangers were tough; she'd made it through Airborne and Ranger school herself, and she knew how tough they were. But only an idiot kept eating in this heat.

At the far end of the tent, a group of D-boys sat in their own little world. Even the Rangers were careful to leave them a wide berth. Most of the time. Except every now and then one would go suddenly "Ranger stupid." Something would go sideways in a Ranger's brain and he'd choose death by Delta. It was like the idiots who shot at the White House with a .22 trying to arrange suicide by cop. Neither action typically led to actual dying, but in most cases that would have been less painful.

Weirdly enough, Sergeant Kee Stevenson was over sitting with the D-boys. And that little native kid who always followed in her shadow. D-boys tolerated nobody outside their own circle, but they let the Sergeant, the kid, and her *Secret Garden* book sit with them.

Lola had tried talking about Mary and Dickon with the kid. Not much luck with Mother Superior looking over her like Lola would somehow break the child just by speaking with her.

Tim rolled a four-six. Great. He was about three moves from totally barricading her in.

She returned her attention to the game and what was really bugging her.

"I'm a good pilot. Damn good. But flying with Beale…" She shrugged. She had no better words for it.

Tim had the decency to not laugh at either her statement or the useless one-four he rolled. She could either play safe and make no real progress or play messy and hope he didn't roll on top of her.

She played messy, leaving three pieces open. As long as he didn't roll…

Double-twos. Crap! He knocked all three of her open pieces back to the bar.

"I always outflew everyone." Even her SOAR trainers had given her nothing but praise. Okay, that wasn't
right. They'd insulted her less than anyone else in her
class, which was as high as their praise ever rose. But
the slick grace and perfect control Major Emily Beale
had demonstrated again tonight was at a whole other
level. Like Lola was an outsider looking in at something
she barely understood.

She really, really needed double fours to stay in the
game. She rattled her dice cup hopefully. Tim's silence
was companionable, inviting her to talk. Men were
never easy to be around. They always wanted something, sex usually, or at least dominance of power.
Around Tim she felt strangely mellow. He was easy to
talk to. No agenda.

"I had this friend Rikki back when I flew with the
Eagles. Best shooter you ever saw. World-class sniper.
Then she told me about this Special Forces chick who
fired twice Rikki's normal score. She tried to explain
what she saw but couldn't, didn't even know what the
woman had done that she wasn't doing. I never understood what she was saying until now."

"She say who? Your roll."

Lola rolled. Four-six. She moved one piece off the
bar and back into the game, but the other two were still
blocked by Tim's pieces. Military snipers were a small
world, but she couldn't remember the name.

"Smith. Maybe. All I know is some little Asian chick
with a weird rifle."

"An HK MSG-90A1?"

Tim doubled-down on her lone piece and bounced
her back to the bar.

"Yeah." You didn't forget a weapon like that. "How did you—"

He pointed over at the D-boys' table.

You'd expect a D-boy to be able to shoot like… But there was only one woman at the table. Sergeant Kee Stevenson.

"Smith was her maiden name."

Great. Another damned overachiever. And Big John and Tim had agreed that Connie Davis was a scary-good chief mechanic, even by their own caliber of excellence. She'd signed aboard a flight of goddamned super-women. Which meant she'd never measure up.

She rolled again.

Nothing.

She was in over her head and getting absolutely nowhere.

Chapter 7

"WALK WITH ME."

Walk with the Major? Lola wanted to just go stand in the shower and try not to cry as she washed this latest flight off her skin and out of her brain. Seven missions in six days. Tonight they'd gotten back to base barely in time for an emergency extraction call. The second flight had been beyond ugly, pulling broken bodies off shattered hillsides under a fusillade of flying lead.

With luck maybe she'd be washed right down the shower drain along with the prior evening's misplaced hopes. She hadn't killed any friendlies, but she'd come damn close. And she'd wiped out some bad guys, but not enough. Two soldiers had died even as they boarded the choppers that were there to save them.

But the Major's "Walk with me" hadn't sounded like a request.

Lola set her helmet on the copilot's seat, wondering if she'd get to fly again. She hesitated, but the Major didn't protest her leaving it there. She'd take that as a good sign.

It was still dark as they left the chopper and moved toward the running track that circled the Bati soccer field. She could feel the others watching her. *Well, Sergeant Kee Stevenson, tonight you may get your wish.* But Lola had worked too hard for this, even if she wasn't any longer sure she wanted it. No, she wanted it but didn't deserve it. If they were planning to be rid of her, they'd have to do it themselves.

"Hey, Major. Do you—" Crazy Tim came trotting up.

"Get lost, Mr. Maloney." The Major's voice was calm, perfectly polite, and stopped Tim cold in his tracks.

Nice of him to try and run interference. Too late for that. Lola sent him a look of thanks, wishing she could just curl up against his shoulder and let the shame run out of her. That was weird. Guys were a place you went for sex and entertainment, not for safety.

He shrugged helplessly as she turned away. Whatever the medicine, Lola was, as usual, on her own and would have to take it.

She and the Major walked out onto the track, barely visible beneath the stars. The disappearance of the very dimmest stars indicated dawn lay not far off. Continuing around the track, Lola started to worry at the problem. Half a lap and still not a word. Should she speak first? Bite her tongue? Run away screaming?

By a full lap neither of them had spoken. She glanced toward the helicopter as they came by it and wondered if Tim was still there. If her gear was still there. Or had the Major already assigned someone to pack up all of Lola's equipment in preparation for shipping her out?

"Do you want to be here?" The Major's question was so soft that Lola barely heard it. Almost asked the Major to repeat it, but finally registered the words before she had to ask.

Lola looked up at the stars and all she felt was exhaustion. Rooted right down into her boots. She didn't often think about what she wanted. She just kept moving forward. As long as it was new, she was game. Military, flying, helicopters, Special Forces, CSAR, SOAR... It was always the next thing.

She shrugged, knowing the Major couldn't see her response. Still far too dark.

"You're a damn fine pilot. Maybe as good as I was when I hit SOAR. But we have a problem."

A problem? Other than she couldn't walk or talk or even think? Wait. Something. The Major had said she was a good pilot? *No way*.

Major Beale circled back to where Lola had come to a stop without realizing. The sandy soil and uncertain surface threatened to pitch Lola to her knees. When they stood face to face with just a hint of dawn revealing the light oval of Major Beale's face, though not her expressionless blue eyes, the Major stopped and crossed her arms.

"I'm your commander. That's means more than you might think. I need to build a team. One I can trust. Trust without thought. Without consideration. That takes time. Before you and I invest that time, do you want to be here at that level? A hundred percent in with no questions. No doubts. You can't be any more a little bit SOAR than you can be a little bit pregnant."

Lola had faced a lot of tough questions in her life. She'd faced questions that had changed her past and her future. After Mama Raci, the SOAR review boards had been a cakewalk. After Mama Raci, anything was a cakewalk... except perhaps Major Emily Beale.

She'd struggled so hard to be here. Years of Army, years of SOAR training, and the Major had the gall to ask if she wanted to be here? Lola considered getting angry and lashing out with some vitriolic derision. But when she reached for it, it wasn't there. Whatever her self-defense mechanism, the Major had triggered something else. The question had raised doubts and fears instead. Something she always tried her best to avoid, but there they were.

Was she good enough? Lola didn't know. Strong enough? Sufficiently dedicated?

"How did you decide?" She didn't know where she'd found the question or the nerve to ask it. By not giving herself time to think.

"I didn't." Major Beale turned to look up toward the reddening of the eastern sky over the tiers of concrete bleachers that encircled them. Now they stood side by side facing the same canvas of empty sky. The silence stretched around them as infinite as the desert beyond the walls and the sky above. A held breath. In the far distance she could hear the muezzin of Bati calling the faithful to morning prayer.

"For me it wasn't a decision. It was simply the only thing that made sense. Flying, SOAR... Mark too. I didn't think about them. I actually fought hard against the last and best, but thankfully Mark is even more stubborn than I am."

Reaching up, the Major unclipped her dog tags and slipped a wedding ring off the chain. She re-latched the clasp and pulled the ring on. Jewelry wasn't good in flight or a combat situation. Exposed, it could catch light or snag on fabric. It could hurt and cut if you were firing a weapon and the stock jammed against the ring. If your hand needed surgery, they might have to shear the ring... Many soldiers Lola knew didn't wear rings at all. That the Major did wear one revealed a softer side evident in no other way.

Lola turned to watch the last stars fading in the morning sky. Shoulder to shoulder with the finest pilot she'd ever seen. With a woman that everyone respected. She wanted that, more badly than she'd thought.

But what she'd really wanted was to feel what she'd witnessed the first time she'd met Emily Beale. The Major had hovered closer to death than life but had cared more about the safety of her crew than anything else. More than for her craft or herself.

Now that Lola replayed the memories of that brief meeting, she realized that the Majors had already been married by that time. But the first thing Emily Beale had asked about was her crew.

Lola wanted to care that deeply. She wanted to care that much about something, about anything. Wanted to care so badly it hurt like an ache around her empty Tin Man heart.

She blinked her eyes, gone dry with staring at the sky, and turned to the Major.

But the woman was gone, had left her alone with her question.

The Major's answer was clear. Either figure it out, or clear out your gear and get on the next flight to somewhere else.

Well, Chief Warrant 2 Lola May LaRue knew her answer. Absolutely clear. Five by five. Truly, deeply, even madly.

Yes.

The feeling roared into her with a clarity and power she could barely contain.

For perhaps the first time in her life, she knew exactly where she wanted to be.

Flying right next to Major Emily Beale.

Chapter 8

TIM HAD LOUNGED IN THE SHADOWS AROUND Lola's bird.

The grapes had come by, the fueling crew in their safety-identifying purple vests. Once they'd cleared, the reds from ordnance had rolled in with cans of 7.62 mm cartridges, Hydra rockets, and rounds for the 30 mm cannon. They'd even checked over the personal weapons hanging in their door clips, though it was clear that the FN SCARs hadn't been used. He'd hovered in the shadows as they checked the barrels of the miniguns, but no maintenance was needed. Kee and Connie had left theirs as clean as he and John always left their own.

Once they all left, he set into pacing. He knew something wasn't right. He just didn't know how to fix it. When his sister came home from her first high-school breakup, he'd made her laugh through her tears and fed her chocolate ice cream. When his brother had burned himself so badly with hot oil that his whole arm blistered, Tim had been the level-headed one to call the ambulance and keep his mother too distracted to weep, much.

He could think of a thousand times he and John had…

For the life of him he didn't know what was up with Lola LaRue. But he wished he did. Wished he knew how to fix it.

He glared at her black helmet with the silver fleur-de-lis where it rested on her seat. It wasn't giving him any answers either. French? So, was she French? Her accent, soft, enticing like a summer breeze, had eluded him. Whenever he thought he'd pinned it down, it shifted. As if she didn't come from anywhere. Had no anchor.

Tim had an anchor as deep as the ocean. The fact that it had led him to the itinerant Army lifestyle was only one of the many odd turns of his past. But the odd turn that kept bugging him at the moment was how the Major was treating Chief Warrant LaRue.

Beale had never taken a copilot, or any other crew member, straight into battle before. She'd always given them a week or so in the backfield to settle in. The operational tempo was high, but it wasn't that fierce. *Viper* could easily have flown the last two weeks' forward missions, but instead Major Beale had taken *Vengeance* and her new copilot straight in.

He finally spotted Major Beale heading back toward the tents through the soft dawn. Probably gone to change and get some chow. Still no sign of Lola.

Five minutes later, he leaned back against closed cargo-bay door and started to wonder just how stupid he was for waiting. Who knew what they'd talked about? Maybe Lola went back to the tents down the other side of the bird. The sun cracked enough over the horizon to light the top row of stadium seating, flooding the field with soft reflected light. Maybe just five more—

Something slammed into him, full on. Not even giving him time to blink or react.

One instant, standing there…

The next moment, his breath knocked out of him and Lola leaned hard against him. She clamped his face in her hands as she gave him a smacking kiss.

She started to pull back, but Tim's reactions finally kicked in and he wrapped his arms around her and pulled her back in.

For a moment, she held back, a breath separating them. Her eyes aglow with a joy he'd not seen before. She'd shifted from merely gorgeous to radiant.

Lola laid back into the kiss, driving her body against his, kissing him so hard his lips were stinging.

He slid one arm around her slender waist and dug the other into the lush cascade of softly curling hair he'd been dying to toy with since the first time he'd seen her. It had been another time, another mission; an unknown woman standing on the wind-blown ship's deck in the wintery Baltic Sea. Even at a distance, she'd captivated him. Though she was a little taller, their bodies shaped and molded closer together more perfectly with each passing moment.

An energy coursed through her that drove his body's attention into overdrive. Every nerve ending vibrated where they touched.

And her kiss! Rocket fire and the scorching heat of his family's chicken fricassee. Lola LaRue tasted like fire and heaven.

She started sliding back and forth against him. First a slow gyration side to side, building rapidly until she shifted out of his arms. Their last point of contact, her teeth dragging across his lower lip.

Grabbing one of his hands, she gave it a sharp tug and pulled him from where he had been plastered against the chopper. In a moment she stood cheek to cheek with him, one hand on his right arm, their clasped hands pointing toward the *Viper*. He slid his arm back around her waist, blown away by the perfect way she fit there, and pulled their bodies together with a sharp tug.

She threw her head back with a laugh that reminded him of starlight, and with a kick and step, they were sliding ahead in an impromptu tango. Five steps, slow-slow-fast-fast-slow, he spun her into a twirl and pulled her back.

Their bodies slammed together, and again the starlight-sparkling laugh.

This time the kiss was quick and fast, with just the slightest linger.

When she moved away this time, he was powerless to stop her. As she danced downfield between the choppers, her hips sliding side to side in a way designed to make a grown man go blind, he heard her voice whispering back to him.

"I was right. You are sweet."

All he could do was watch her go.

He looked down at his feet. So light a moment ago, they weren't going anywhere now.

Yep! No doubt about it. He'd been absolutely right when he'd assessed their first meeting.

He was totally screwed.

Chapter 9

MAJOR EMILY BEALE SAT WITH MARK AND COLONEL Michael Gibson of Delta Force, her usual breakfast partners. But she wasn't really paying attention. The two of them were, as so often happened, trading fish stories. One a Montana boy and the other Colorado born and bred. High mountain streams, lakes that were a three-day horse ride in, pan-fried versus grilled on a green maple twig directly over the fire.

Mark had taught her to fish, and for a city girl, she'd discovered camping suited her very nicely. But she'd rather lie on the bank nearby and read a good book while Mark strode hip-deep into freezing water.

She let them talk, let her body eat, paying some attention to her steak and eggs, but mostly she watched her crew halfway across the tent. Taking her chance to assess their attitudes unobserved.

Archie and Big John were busy entertaining Dilya. And the little girl, who had bloomed over the last year, teased them right back. Clearly smart, she was consuming culture and schooling like water. Kee sat beside her chatting with Connie.

Kee lacked the playful streak that was such a surprise in Archie, but she and Dilya had something special. Some understanding and feeling that went deeper than anything Emily had ever imagined. Made her yearn for a child of her own.

Without turning, she reached out a hand. Without pausing in his story about a remote California lake of golden trout originally stocked by Chuck Yeager and an illegal Air Force mission he'd arranged, Mark slipped his hand into hers and held it tightly.

Not yet. But someday. Today she had other concerns.

Her first cue was Kee's sudden stiffening.

Emily didn't have to see her face to feel the scowl.

Silhouetted by the brightening daylight, Chief Warrant LaRue stood in the entry of the tent. Emily didn't need the woman's careful nod in her direction to know the answer.

The woman who had flown with such a desperate need to please was gone. LaRue no longer stood stoop-shouldered as she'd been out on the track just a few minutes ago.

The woman about to enter the chow tent now was a tall and confident woman. Emily would bet safe money that if she could see LaRue's face, it would be flushed. She wanted to take them back aloft right now to see how it translated into her flying.

Whatever LaRue had decided, it had also put a dance in her step as she moved toward the chow line. A number of the Rangers tracked her across the tent, she was hard not to watch.

As Emily returned her attention to her food, another shadow darkened the entry.

No mistaking the powerfully shouldered silhouette. Tim Maloney also stopped when just a step inside. It was a common event, waiting for your eyes to adapt from the bright sun to the dim tent.

But the morning wasn't that bright yet.

He scanned the room, nodded slowly to Big John, but still didn't move. Took a step toward the chow line, but stopped again. Then he turned slowly, not just his head, but his whole body turning as he tracked...

Emily looked over her shoulder and saw Lola LaRue crossing from the chow line back to the crew's table with a laden tray.

When Emily looked back at the entry, Tim was gone.

She bit her lower lip. Hoped she wouldn't have to warn Mark. Tim was on his crew now.

And she hoped for Tim's sake that a cold shower would be enough.

Five get you ten, it wouldn't be.

Chapter 10

Tonight's mission started differently.

Lola could feel the old Lola, the one who had been starstruck around Major Emily Beale, start to slide over her during the briefing. That shield of awe that there was so much that could be attained, even if it would never be attained by Lola.

Then she shook it off. Did her best to toss old Lola out of the briefing tent. She'd done near enough a thousand flights, she had skills. Had cracked over five thousand hours not counting simulator time, a huge mark in a chopper pilot's life. Tonight she'd bring them. Bring them hard. And maybe Major Beale would start learning to trust her new copilot. *Hell of a high bar to live up to, girl.*

Screw that, gel. Y'all be bedder dan dat. Mama Raci's thick-accented voice sounded clear and grouchy from out of her past. Maybe it was time she listened to the old woman.

The briefing tent held fewer flight crews than usual. Must be a light night. Viper Henderson was up at the front with Captain Archibald Stevenson, Sergeant Kee's significant other.

Lola wanted to ask Tim what was going on. But he hadn't shown at breakfast after last night's flight. No backgammon. No pleasant chat after everyone else drifted off. Probably just hit his rack and passed out.

Now it was evening before a night's work and he still looked fairly ragged, as if he hadn't woken up yet. He'd barely acknowledged her cheery "good morning" over dinner. He'd sat down past Connie, invisible beyond the wall of Big John. Others looked at him in surprise. Readjusting for his failure to occupy his usual spot. And he ate quietly, not chatting with Connie or Kee, who sat across from him, even though he'd apparently sought them out.

In Lola's opinion, it at least had the advantage of distracting Kee from her usual pissed-off-at-the-world-but-especially-Chief-Warrant-LaRue attitude. Instead, she'd spent her energy worrying about Tim while still appearing tough as hell.

The briefing tent tonight held the two DAP Hawk crews and two five-man teams for the monstrous Chinook choppers. The Delta colonel also sat there. Back row. Quiet. Looking impossibly powerful.

A shadow slipped in and perched on a chair beside Kee. A small shadow in a white *hajib*, the native over-smock that covered the girl from shoulder to knees. White pants and incongruous red, blue, and yellow sneakers below that. Without even turning, Kee wrapped an arm around the girl who snuggled in. A gentle side Lola never would have guessed existed.

No one else reacted. No one acknowledged the girl, but neither did they dismiss her. Somehow this kid was just a fixture on the military base.

"Tonight"—Captain Archie Stevenson pulled up a map on the projector—"we're on the move. Tonight we're going here." The Air Mission Commander ran his pointer south over the trackless desert southwest of Lashkar Gah.

That would be fine, if it weren't in the incredibly lethal Helmand Province. Everyone—French, NATO, British, and U.S.—had lost choppers there. Though there was nothing except dunes and sandstorms that far south.

"Continuing to here. Camped by first light."

Another place with absolutely nothing.

"We'll be staging a single mission from a temporary base in Western Afghanistan. That information is, by the way, classified 'secret.'"

Nothing there except—Lola took a deep breath—the Iranian border.

"Flight in one hour. Minimum duration two days each way, two to seven days in-country. Dilya, you'll have to stay here with Base Clerk Reynolds. We'll be gone about a week." Briefed in the same tone as any soldier.

Kee squeezed the girl tighter, but Dilya nodded her head matter-of-factly. Showed she was a trooper and used to the routine.

"Dismissed."

Chapter 11

AN HOUR LATER, LOLA WAS FINISHING THE PREFLIGHT check on the *Vengeance*. Kee and Connie were stowing gear, and the Major was already in her seat making sure the mission route was keyed into the onboard nav displays.

Nearby she could see Tim and Big John prepping their bird. Captain Richardson mirroring her own flight checks. Major Henderson was down the way a bit talking to the Chinook pilot. She could see them loading gear into the back of the monstrous helicopter. Instead of the forty-odd troops the bird could carry, there were a half-dozen guys and a lot of gear.

No. She'd been wrong.

There weren't a half-dozen guys. The group was working together in absolute silence and perfect synchronicity. Definitely not just guys, they were Delta Force. The Colonel hadn't been sitting in the back of the room for his health. The Chinook was taking them somewhere very nasty. Somewhere nasty enough to shift some serious assets across two thousand kilometers of hostile territory.

Two Chinooks, two DAP Hawks, six D-boys. Nothing else. This was about the nastiest crew the U.S. military forces could field. If this group couldn't get it done, no one on the planet stood a chance.

She turned to see Tim watching the Chinook as well.

A long, assessing gaze. He saw it too, so it wasn't just her imagination.

He turned to her, and across the full rotor width that separated their birds, she read his thoughts clearly. They were headed into some shit.

Lola thought of that impulsive kiss and the heat that still rippled through her body from it. He hadn't done any of the expected grab or fondle. He'd just held her like she was the most precious thing on the planet in that moment. And then he'd proved that all that strength didn't keep him from busting out some smooth moves.

She shot him a saucy smile.

―――⋙⋘―――

Tim did his best to smile back.

Honestly, he did.

Apparently it worked because Lola spun lightly on her heel and went back to her preflight inspection.

That's Chief Warrant 2 LaRue to you, flyboy. Sergeants just didn't get it on with gorgeous female officers. Though somehow Sergeant Kee Smith and then-Lieutenant, now Captain Archie Stevenson had hooked up. He'd never be comfortable asking an officer how they did it. Maybe he could ask Kee.

Who was he kidding?

First, Kee hated LaRue for some reason. Second, he knew he was just dreaming anyway. The Major had given her some news on their walk that had been something to be ecstatic about, and so Lola had smacked him a good one in celebration. Joy had just radiated out of the woman like a shining sun. That was it. Nothing more.

Big John slapped him hard on the shoulder. Then held

on and shook him back and forth like a leaf. At least his marriage made sense, two sergeants. Two people who loved their machines as if they were their own children.

"You set, John?" Tim asked just to have something to say.

"Yep! *Viper*'s ready for flight. You?"

"Stowed and locked down."

John shook him again, a bit more gently.

"You got it bad, don't you, buddy boy?"

Tim shook his head in denial, then realized he was still watching LaRue as she climbed into the copilot's seat and pulled those long legs of hers inside the craft.

"Don't know what you're talking about." He slapped aside John's hand and went to check his weapons for a third time, just to have something to do.

Almost out of earshot, but not quite, he heard John's soft, "Uh-huh."

Chapter 12

LOLA WAS WIPED OUT AS SHE CAME DOWN UPON THE agreed coordinates. The dark still lay upon the desert. They'd chosen a lonely spot, flat and free of any sand dunes. She'd thumped the chopper down harder than she'd expected. Lola could taste why in the night air, salt. Rather than soft sand, they were on a hard salt pan. That and she'd been sloppy with fatigue.

As the turbines wound down, she could feel the last tiny bits of energy draining out of her until they both ground to a halt in unison and she couldn't move. She'd been so full of energy just eight hours, three midair re-fuelings, and two thousand kilometers ago.

She'd gotten them down, not clean, but she got them down. She tried flexing her fingers from where they'd been curled around the controls, and pain rocketed up her arms. They joined the complaint and finally her shoulders admitted they'd be happier if she just let go and wept.

She'd been first down and the other birds landed around her. *Viper* close to starboard. To her port side, one of the Chinooks settled so smooth and soft that it pissed her off even more. Too much grace in such an ungainly monster.

Another ten seconds and the other big twin-rotor Chinook settled down to the other side of Henderson's Hawk. Looming above her bird and twice as long, not counting the long blades that looked like an ungainly afterthought. Four birds in a row.

In moments two Delta operators were perched atop the Chinooks, one looking south and west, the other north and east.

She finished the shutdown, pulled off her helmet, and just lay back in her seat, as much as the thing allowed. Too damn tired to move. To breathe.

For the whole flight, Major Beale hadn't said one damn word. With the fact that Kee wasn't speaking to her and Connie apparently never spoke, they'd flown dead silent for more than eight hours.

Well, she'd shown she could fly. She'd stayed dead on profile. She'd nailed the midair refuels on her first try, all three times.

Her muscles ached. Not from holding on so tight, just from not having a moment's break.

She felt the slight motion in the bird as Kee, then Connie, stepped off.

Lola kept her eyes closed, waiting for the Major to step down. To get away before Lola said something really, really inappropriate. It was just plain cruel to leave a pilot at the controls for eight solid hours. It took—

"Next time…" Beale's voice was quiet beside her.

Lola rolled her head against the seat back and opened one scratchy, aching eye to look at the Major in the dim light of the instrument panel.

"Next time, ask for help when you're tired. There are two of us here for a reason. You don't have to do it all yourself."

Lola closed her one open eye and rolled her head back to center. Just too plain tired.

Of course. It wasn't Major Beale testing Lola with a brutally long and painful flight. Instead another goddamn lesson. A chopper flew by teamwork. Lola knew that. Should know that. Wouldn't forget it again, that was for damn sure.

Mama Raci had taught her to trust *no mon but she self*. Hard to break that despite a half-dozen years in the service. Time to blast that old tape out of her brain with some serious explosives.

Merde! She had been a total *teet peeshwank*. Mama Raci had called Lola a "small runt" for all of her teenage life, long after she towered over the old woman. She'd called Lola that right up until the day she joined the Air National Guard. The change had been jarring. The loss of the demeaning nickname a far greater marker of the achievement than the swearing-in ceremony.

Lola climbed down to help rig the camouflage nets over the choppers. She had to bite her tongue near to bleeding to stop the groans from her aching muscles.

Chapter 13

WHEN THE SUN CAME UP, IT WAS AS IF SOMEONE WAS attacking Lola with a sky-sized hammer. In minutes the chill air of the desert was replaced by air that burnt her lungs to breathe. A parching wind arose and drove the fine dust and sand in billowing waves across their site.

Everyone started shedding vests and flight suits. All facing away from the wind.

Lola didn't care that she had nothing but a T-shirt and panties on under the flight suit. She stripped first and then dug out loose white slacks and a long-sleeved shirt. Guys were down to their boxers or tighty-whities just as fast. Sunglasses and a bandanna over her face so that she could breathe completed the outfit. She tried dampening it, but the air dried the bandanna faster than she could wet it.

The dawn light had revealed that they were parked in the middle of a salt plain that had probably been a lake in a former life. Low, dry hills stretched into the distance. Not a blot of green anywhere to the horizon.

Tactically good. First, no could slip up on them here. Second, it was the largest district in Afghanistan and the least populated, with 8,000 people in 22,000 square kilometers. Easy to see why, there was nothing here but sand and salt. The nearest track of any kind was over ten klicks away. The nearest thing that could be called a road was more like fifty.

Now, in the full light of day, the sunlight was blinding, even through sunglasses. "Bright enough to burn a black man." Yeah, well, not quite how her father had said it, but he could make Deep South white trash look good by comparison. Never made sense that he'd married a mixed-breed Creole. She'd been parts French, African slave, Choctaw, and who knew what else. Dead before Lola was five. Knowing her father, the woman had to have been dead inside long before that to survive him as long as she did.

Lola shook it off and headed for some shade. Most of the crew were squatting in the shadow of one of the Chinooks. A filigree net of sand-and-earth tones fluttered above, hopefully hiding them from casual inspection.

Don't mind us. We're just a lump of nothing interesting squatting in the middle of a blazing salt pan. A blazing salt pan about ten miles from the Iranian border.

Lola swung by the chopper's rear ramp. Dinner had been set out. A box of mixed MREs and a case of water bottles. Meals-Ready-to-Eat were not all that different from one another, no matter what they said. She grabbed whatever came to hand.

A glance forward into the big cargo bay showed that the D-boys had packed in some serious gear. Six guys, packs bigger than should be humanly possible. And a range of armament. They couldn't be taking all of this with them. They must be ready to make selections at the last minute as needed. That was their problem. Her problem, as the DAP Hawk weapons platform, was to make sure the Chinooks got them there and that they got them back out.

She dropped down near Tim and Big John. "I can feel the salt sucking all the moisture right out of my skin."

Big John nodded slow and easy. "Long way from a hot shower."

"Ugh!" Tim ripped the top off his MRE and started pulling out the bits and pieces. "Don't even say the word 'hot.' Just hearing it is killing me."

"Heat doesn't bother me none." Born and raised in New Orleans made heat easy. "Dry. Not used to the dry." She sliced open her own MRE with her field knife. She'd grabbed Mediterranean Chicken, could have been worse. She pulled out the packets, considered the flame-less heater and decided she'd rather eat the meal cold. It left the sauces a little glutinous even in this heat, but that was better than hot.

They all sat in a row, backs to the wind to guard against the dust, as they opened packets, spread cheese on crackers, munched on corn bread. Hers didn't have any hot sauce. Stupid. The little bottle of Tabasco should be in every one of the twenty-four different meals.

She dumped the carbo-electro powder packet into her water bottle and gave it a shake. Definitely going to be needing that.

"Where you from, Chief Warrant?" Big John worked his way through Meatballs with Marinara and Garlic Mashed Potatoes, then started on a second meal of Sloppy Joe with Peanut Butter (Chunky) and Jelly Sandwich.

"You're gonna get fat eating all that," Tim mumbled around a mouthful of Nuggets (Turkey).

John, for all his size, didn't have an ounce of fat anywhere. He ignored Tim as if he'd never spoken.

"Can't quite place your accent, Chief."

"Call me Lola." She'd done her best to not have an accent at all. "You're from Oklahoma."

"John," he acknowledged in return. "Muskogee bred and buttered."

Big John was easy to talk to, but not comfortable like Tim. They'd only had their after-breakfast backgammon game a few times, but she already wished she'd thought to bring a board. A little backgammon, a little quiet time to just shoot the breeze after a long damn flight. A single haul that put her at her rated daily limit of eight flight hours. Of course, when the shit was going down, it was less of a rule and more of a really strong suggestion. Only shit going down today was her own stupidity. Not again.

"Didn't answer the question there, long lady."

And she didn't intend to.

"But you wear it on your helmet. Why's that?"

She glanced toward the *Vengeance* where she'd left it on her seat.

"Hunh. Guess I do. Never thought about it that way."

"Where?" Tim shuffled a bit forward so that he could see her around John.

"She's a Cajun lady, our copilot is."

"No, Sergeant… sorry, John. Creole, yes. Cajun, no."

"Which means what?" Tim had shuffled further forward and turned sideways to the rising wind to partly face her. A blast of dust and sand washed over his meal. He'd have to get another and start over. She thought about pointing it out to him, but some wicked part of her thought better of it. Let him find out the hard way.

"Cajun is all fashion and style. Also, it implies Acadian heritage. As far as I can find out, my mama was a lot of things, but none of them Acadian."

"In other words," John observed, "something nobody cares about who isn't one of you."

Lola considered, had always insisted she wasn't Cajun because… She had no idea and shrugged in response. Time to let that one go except if she was ever dumb enough to be back in New Orleans.

"What about your dad?"

"Dead."

"Oh, sorry. Didn't know." Tim looked chagrined. Like it really pained him.

"He was run over by a beer truck while lying drunk in a tavern parking lot. No loss to the world, trust me."

They sat in silence while she finished her Fruit (Dried) which she liked way better than the Fruit (Wet Pack).

"Who named these things anyway?" She pointed at Tim's Cookies (Patriotic). A safe and common enough topic of speculation among those who lived on them from time to time.

"Still must have been pretty awful when he died."

"Hey, that's way more than he deserved." Which was completely true. "New topic. C'mon."

"How old were you when—"

"Same old topic, Tim. Something new."

"Okay. Where did you learn to play backgammon?"

"Mama Raci. She took me in when I needed someplace to be. Ran a kitchen in a house in Storyville." Didn't know why she said any of that. Could only hope that they didn't get what that implied.

The blank looks said she'd dodged that bullet.

"Nice old lady. Nice to me, anyway." When it had really mattered. Actually a nasty old bitch to the girls who worked there earning their keep by the hour. To this day, she still didn't know why Mama Raci had given her a place to work and sleep. Available only so long as she never missed a day of school or a single homework assignment. Tough old biddy, and Lola did her best not to grimace over the pain of her loss.

Tim was clearly itching to know more about a past she'd left as far behind her as possible.

Lola was busy trying to find an excuse to brush off a man who made her a little crazy in a good way and more than a little hot in ways the temperature couldn't explain.

"How did you learn backgammon?"

That brought a roar of laughter from Big John. Tim simply smiled as if he were trying to be some sweet and innocent child instead of a gorgeous chunk of U.S. Army warrior.

"This here pipsqueak…" John clapped him on the shoulder hard enough to hurt.

Tim shrugged it off.

"Got his nickname playing backgammon."

"Circle up," Mark Henderson shouted out.

"Story for a later time," Big John offered in a smaller voice, though not much smaller.

"A much later time." Though Tim didn't look as chagrined as his tone indicated. Perhaps even a little proud.

Everyone shuffled to their feet, and Lola made sure Big John stayed between her and Tim. When Connie joined John, she didn't complain about the extra distance.

She was liking Tim far too much.

Chapter 14

SOME PEOPLE WERE STILL EATING AS THEY CIRCLED UP on the Major. Tim remembered the last of his meal in his hands and took a big bite of one of his crackers. Chewed it a couple of times thinking about Lola. She was smooth, slick, like the way she flew. Sliding out from under questions.

He had to give her a break, she was new. But he'd thought they'd built some connection. And... he coughed.

Then inhaled.

And got a lungful of dirt just as the Major started speaking. He tried to suppress the reaction but couldn't. He hacked up a tiny cloud of dust and spewed out half-chewed chunks of cheese-coated crackers now turned brown with desert dirt.

John's thump on his back drove him to his knees. The Major ground to a halt and turned to watch. Everyone did, but Tim couldn't stop.

Lola handed him her water. "Small sips."

He hacked up another chunk of cracker and desert sand.

His instinct was to knock back the water, but he did what she said and the small sips worked. Softened the cracker, eased the dust-dry coating on his tongue and throat.

He hacked again and got the last of the cracker out, right between Lola's knees where she knelt before him. *Attractive. Real attractive, Tim Maloney. Sure know how to impress a girl.*

But she didn't look grossed out. If he didn't know better, he'd say she was on the verge of laughing. As if she'd covered his meal in dirt herself, which was impossible.

"You two done?" Clearly Major Henderson was done, so Tim had better be.

"Yes, sir. Sorry, sir." His throat was sore and ticklish, but he managed to swallow hard and stop the next cough.

The Major was being downright serious. Well, they hadn't come here for the fun of it. Tim spit one last time to clear his mouth, looked like the spit dried before it hit the salt pan.

"Okay. Who knows what lies about six hundred klicks northwest of here?"

Everyone turned to face northwest. A dozen kilometers of salt pan and then the Iranian border. The only place on the whole planet that was more godforsaken than this was—

"Desert One." Lola got there a beat before he did. And the Major was just nodding.

Tim looked at those around him, and they all looked a little sick.

You couldn't be SOAR and not know every detail of Operation Eagle Claw. It was the birth of SOAR, or at least the event that had led to its birth. It was also one of the most public disasters in the history of the U.S. military. It had reshaped foreign policy and toppled a U.S. president.

The failed rescue attempt of the Iranian hostages in 1980.

Tim tried to make his voice light. "Bad juju there, Major. Let's stay way clear."

The Major stared at him levelly, the gaze steady through those mirrored shades he never removed. Scuttlebutt had it that he didn't even remove them when making love to his wife.

"By tomorrow sunrise," Major Mark Henderson said in a flat monotone of absolute authority, "we'll be parked two thousand meters west of Desert One."

Chapter 15

THEY WERE AT THE DROP-OFF.

No one had slept through the heat of the day, a doze was all Lola had managed. She knew none of the others on her crew were any better off. She and Major Beale had traded off the flying every hour so they'd be as fresh as possible.

A half-dozen kilometers northwest of Ravar, Iran, at one in the morning. *Viper* and *Vengeance*, the two DAP Hawks, stayed high. Well, forty feet off the ground, about where they'd been flying since crossing the border.

One of the Chinooks hovered nearby, her main purpose backup and the massive bladder of fuel sitting on her cargo deck. The days of a flock of C-130 tanker planes flying into the center of Iran undetected were long gone. The nation, which in 1980 had been without radar except at a few airports, was now one of the nine nations able to launch a satellite into space. The Chinook carried enough Jet A for four refuelings of the little fleet, and her guns were manned and not to be underestimated. Wrench, Captain Archie Stevenson, sat on that Chinook as the Air Mission Commander.

The other Chinook swung down, skimming an empty road in a low-speed pass. Her rear ramp lowered and the six D-boys spilled off it without the bird ever touching down.

Bicycles. Lola zoomed in the view projected inside her helmet, but they were gone so fast into the night she couldn't tell more. They'd been mounted on electric bicycles. High-speed electric bikes. Small and lightweight, easy to hide and probably silent, they were moving at least twenty miles per hour and still accelerating as they moved out of sight.

Before they were gone, the choppers headed out to Desert One. There to wait until called for, at the very earliest, two days from now. Or rather two nights.

––––

And now they were here.

Lola glanced back at the shallow valley among the dunes. The choppers hidden by their camouflage, guards in place.

Eight of them, most of the two DAP crews and Archie, stood atop the low bluff at the edge of camp. Captain Richardson had hung back at the camp with the Chinook crews and the Deltas.

Fifteen minutes walking across the low dunes, the desert so silent it made your ears ring and echo. The soft slide of sand underfoot the only indication that members of the U.S. military walked the Iranian night.

They climbed a final bluff barely outlined by the starlit night, and Desert One lay before them.

Lola looked right and left. She'd never met better nor flown with better. But how many would be standing six months from now, or a year? How many would a CSAR pilot come for? For how many would it be too late?

She was getting pretty morose, but the locale lent itself to that.

The moonlight revealed each true to their form. Connie leaning back against Big John for comfort. Kee holding hands with Archie but still standing a little apart, the woman always strong and independent and still riding Lola's ass. It ticked her off, but she was coming to respect the contradictory woman despite that, the kick-butt soldier combined with the loving stepmother of an orphaned native kid.

Emily and Mark stood close, an arm loose around each other's hips. Tim had planted himself close to Lola's right, both hands jammed into pockets, looking down toward the empty plain below.

In 1980, the new Iran under their new Ayatollah took fifty-three Americans hostage. Operation Eagle Claw was an elaborate and poorly coordinated rescue effort of immense bravery that flew eight Sea Stallion helicopters and six C-130 tanker and cargo planes below radar and into history. A mash-up team of Navy, Air Force, Rangers, and Deltas made the effort.

A sandstorm tore their equipment apart. A busload of natives showed up at the remote landing strip by pure chance just as the aircraft landed at midnight. And then, on takeoff, a chopper lost in its own brownout of dust rammed a refueling plane. The inferno cost eight lives, seven helicopters, and one of the refueling planes. It also created an international political disaster of epic proportions that had cost President Carter any chance of reelection.

SOAR had been founded months later by a couple of fliers determined to never let such a travesty happen again. And it hadn't. The 160th, one of the smallest and most specialized regiments in the U.S. Army, had become feared the world over by those few adversaries unlucky enough to know about them and still be living.

"Dad said it was like waking up in hell." Henderson's voice was rough, though not loud.

Lola glanced over at him, as did the others, including his wife.

There was the answer. With all of the desert in Iran to hide out in, why here. They'd want to be far away from the Deltas so they didn't attract undue attention there. The planners must have also wanted somewhere well known, and Desert One was among the most carefully mapped sections of Iran in SOAR history.

And Henderson's father had been here.

"Dad was Special Forces for the Navy. Not a SEAL yet, that came later. He came as a shooter. After too many helicopters broke down in the sandstorm and they declared a no-go on the mission, he said they climbed aboard the C-130, dumped their gear, and just lay down on the fuel bladder. Settling in to sleep the whole way home."

Lola could see the layout. Each fuel plane with a couple of choppers pulled close for fueling. A bus of hostages parked nearby under guard. Deep, deep darkness of a moonless night.

"He woke up in the center of an inferno. Someone grabbed his collar and practically threw him from the fire. He said that the pillar of fire that lit the night would call anyone within a hundred miles to come see.

"They abandoned the plane. They abandoned the six choppers without waiting to destroy them. The Iranians got four of them running that we know of. They abandoned the bodies of eight of their comrades. They fled for their lives in utter defeat, fled from themselves without Iran having to raise a single finger."

Henderson turned to face them. As if somehow he could see them each clearly despite the darkness.

Lola could feel when his gaze was upon her. A probing assessment of whether or not she deserved to be a part of such a legacy. Of whether she had the tenacity and drive to repay the past with committed action in the future.

This was hallowed ground, the birthplace of SOAR.

"Michael Grimm." Lola spoke to fight the dark, making her voice clear and strong. "Bob Johnson."

"Randy Cochran." Tim picked up the note. He took her hand in the dark and squeezed it tightly. The surge of it shot through her. Knowing she was a part of something bigger, more important. Along with that surge came a heat upon her cheeks that she was glad the night hid.

Others continued, listing the founders of SOAR. A catalog of those who'd looked at defeat not as failure, but rather as the need for a stronger, more capable future.

Glad for the privacy because something else was opening up inside her. Not just her pride in flying alongside these people. No just knowing that she maybe, just maybe, was good enough to belong here. There was something inside her every time her orbit swung her too close to Tim Maloney. Something she didn't know, nor want to know.

Whatever she felt when he was around, down in that deep core somewhere unidentifiably near her heart, was scaring the shit out of her.

But she didn't release Tim's hand as the litany of

names continued. Didn't want to. Wouldn't simply because there lurked something that rooted her to the desert with fear.

She was SOAR and would face her fears.

They were SOAR. The 160th. The Night Stalkers.

They'd flown through three of the most dangerous countries on the planet in the last thirty-six hours, and in the next few days they'd be flying back out. And if they didn't make it and the mission was needed, someone else would try again until they succeeded. That was their legacy.

"NSDQ." Lola closed the circle of names with their motto.

Night Stalkers Don't Quit.

Others answered in the dark, "NSDQ."

Lola knew she would never quit again. Not quit on herself. Not on others.

But she couldn't quite bring herself to look over at the man who still held her hand.

Chapter 16

TIM CALLED LOLA OVER AFTER THEIR SECOND NIGHT AT Desert One. Dawn was just breaking with its achingly beautiful light, and its threat of blistering heat and brutally dry air within the hour.

One of the main problems with this part of any operation was staying sane. Boredom was killing her. There were only so many times you could check the dust seals on the aircraft. The entertainment of re-anchoring a camo net torn loose by the omnipresent wind waned after you'd done it enough times that you could do it in your sleep.

But she just couldn't settle, couldn't sit down with any of the trashy novels they'd stowed away. Because while she was busy bitching about being bored in the middle of nowhere in the Iranian Lut Desert, six D-boys were still after something. Something nasty a hundred miles to the south.

"Please God, Tim. Give me some damn thing to do."

He grinned like a fool. She didn't need to see his mouth hidden behind his scarf. Everyone had some fabric wrapped over their mouth and nose to fend off the dust. Nor did she need to see his eyes safe behind the shades they each wore against the desert glare.

It was simpler than that. Like he brightened somehow whenever she came around him. It wasn't an effect she was used to having on anyone. Unless they were just trying to get between her legs. With Tim it might include that, but even if it did, it also included far more than that.

They hadn't touched since holding hands out at Desert One. Even if she'd wanted to, there was no damn privacy squatting night and day under the same camo net with four flight crews. Sitting watch duty high atop the back of the Chinooks was the only break any of them had from each other.

But he'd been there for her.

Some piece of her heart had ripped open that night, and it was a piece she wasn't so comfortable with. She had a past. One she'd spent her entire adult life pretending didn't exist. But even before she'd been born, men had stood here. American helicopter pilots fighting for what they believed in. Fighting for their lives. And some of them losing that battle.

Lola just couldn't quite wrap her mind around what was going on inside her. She'd always faked it. Didn't know what she believed in for herself. Had been able to leave the thinking up to the Army. They were good at that. They liked giving you things to do. Keep you busy. That worked for her.

Except now.

Now she was bored out of her skull and thinking too damn much.

"Save me, Tim. I'm begging you." Even if he was the one her thoughts kept circling back to.

He just kept grinning behind his mask.

"Well, if you're gonna beg." He took an odd sideways step and looked down at the ground behind him.

Nuts and washers. Aligned in a familiar pattern.

Then her focus shifted and she saw it.

Lola threw herself at Tim and hugged him tight. Gave him a good quick, hard kiss right through both their scarves.

Carved into the salt, right down to the last painfully long triangle, was a backgammon board.

—⁓—

"How?" Lola sat cross-legged on a small air mattress and stared down at the board. Tim had even etched a pretty scrollwork pattern into the salt surrounding the board. She rubbed a finger on the alternating dark brown and white points.

"I got the chocolate candy packs from a bunch of people's MREs. Rubbed it into the salt. Made a nice brown."

"Cool!" Good use of materials. No self-respecting Special Forces personnel would eat the candy in an MRE, especially not on an op. Guaranteed bad luck. Debates would occur whenever the MRE designers didn't include candy in a particular menu, but shoved in an alternate treat. Does it rate as candy? Everyone agreed that a brownie could be eaten safely without hexing the mission. But what about pudding? Sometimes pudding came with a Candy III pack, so then it was safe, but what about as a stand-alone like Menu 23? The Chicken Pesto Pasta MRE was rarely packed on active missions because of that unresolved question.

Instead of dice, Tim had six quarters.

They talked about backgammon boards and stupid MRE menu designers through the first half of the game. Easy, safe topics.

Tim tossed the six quarters up in the air, let them fall on the salt.

Three came up heads.

"That's a three." He gathered them and tossed again. Two more heads.

"And a two. And I am…" He drew it out dramatically. "So screwed."

He was. It was about the worst roll he could have at the moment.

Lola crowed as she gathered up the quarters and tossed them. "A four!" She gathered them up and gave them a good shake in cupped hands. "Oh baby. Bring mama another one, just another measly little four." She tossed the quarters high enough that the ever-present wind scattered them a bit.

"Yes!" She leaned over and fisted Tim's shoulder hard enough to rock a lesser man over backwards. Tim just shrugged. She not only hammered two of his pieces, she also closed her home board. He wasn't getting out of the trap any time soon.

"So, you refuse to talk about your past."

Lola tried not to cringe. Hoped it didn't show. Light and airy, that was the trick.

"Don't have one." She regathered the quarters. Tim wouldn't get to move until she was forced to unblock her home board, and that was going to be a while as she had a pair of serious strays to bring home.

"Everyone's got one."

"Nope," she assured him as lightly as she could, and she concentrated on her one-two toss. "I was born in 2005."

Tim looked at her with a tilt of his head. "Not to be rude to the lady officer, but you look like you've long since passed through puberty. Very nicely I might add."

Then Lola swore she could see him blush between the scarf and his shades.

Damn, he was cute. A guy hadn't blushed around her... well, ever that she could think of.

"I was flying a supply and maintenance bird for the 225th Engineers out of Camp Beau, Louisiana. Just an old Bell Kiowa hand-me-down from the 6th Cavalry. Poor chopper was so old it might have dated right back to the Civil War."

She tossed a four-six and a three-two before Tim spoke again.

"You were there." His voice almost softer than the wind sighing around the helicopters baking and pinging in the mid-morning heat.

She nodded. No need to ask about "there." During 2005 in Louisiana there would only ever be one "there." Katrina.

"So were we."

She looked up and was confronted by her twinned reflection in his mirrored shades. She looked a mess, worse than he did. They both wore shades and kerchief, were windblown and dirty. On Tim it looked rough and rugged, only making him even more handsome. Her hair looked as if it had been teased to twice any previous volume and cluttered about her head in a Medusan snarl. Guys got off so easy.

Tim had been there. Flown there. That demanded an honesty she typically did her best to avoid. "I flew the shoreline and the shrimp boats. And oil rigs. I flew to an awful lot of oil rigs, or the remains of them."

"I'd just made it into SOAR." Tim traced one of the chocolate-brown triangles of the board with the tip of his finger. She felt a shiver echo up her spine as he did so, as if it had been her body rather than the salt that he stroked so gently. "I was down at Fort Rucker for training when Hurricane Katrina slammed through. I flew out with Viper Henderson's wingman, riding up and down the hoist for days pulling folks off of rooftops."

Lola could only nod. Flying support from first light to last, with little thought of sleep or maximum allowed flight-hour rules. First, pulling people out. Later dropping food and especially water after it was no longer safe to send down a crew chief.

Never daring to come down close, to land. That would risk the bird being stormed by all of the desperate and the suffering. If a dozen people leaped aboard a machine designed to carry six, it could crash in a moment. Always lift them up with the long-line even if you could get close enough to hover. She'd had to let go of more than one long-line because four or five people would latch on to the wire and refuse to get off no matter what she said about the impossibility of her lifting so many.

"It was how I got hooked on CSAR." Lola finally found her voice, somehow speaking past the death of a city. "Guess my commander recommended me upward because the U.S. Army sent round a recruiter a couple of weeks later." She shook the quarters in her cupped palms a few times.

"No." Lola listened to the memories among the tinkling of the coins. "That's not quite right."

She tossed the coins against her palm a little more, gazing over Tim's shoulder. Then her eyes focused on the two Majors. Deep in conference over a flight chart pinned to the ground by the weight of their FN SCAR rifles.

"No. The recruiter had said a Captain Henderson had watched me flying rescue and thought the Army needed folks who could fly like me. The recruiter didn't even blink about a woman flying a chopper for the Army. Though enough others did."

Viper Henderson indeed. Did he even remember that he'd changed her life? That he'd reached down into the lowly National Guard and elevated a Creole train wreck of a woman to become a SOAR pilot? Did he even know the flight he'd admired had been done by a woman? If so, would he have cared? She'd guess not.

"I was born that day. This"—she pointed down— "this is where I belong." She could feel the heavy weight of it. But also the truth of it. As if she'd slammed down the gauntlet for any who might dare challenge her. Her decision back at Bati that she wanted to fly with Major Beale had turned into a rock-deep core that anchored her in place for the first time in her life.

She'd flown Army. And almost five years from the day she'd joined, the minimum time requirement, a SOAR recruiter had showed up on base. Actually off base. In a local bar. She'd never thought before how unlikely that circumstance.

She glanced over at Henderson again. They'd followed her career. Followed her record. Made sure she ended up in SOAR's ranks.

"You belong here?" Tim asked half incredulous.

"Yeah! Here!" She fisted her hands until the quarters were cutting in her palms.

"Really?"

She cocked her fist half back, ready to rearrange his jaw. And she'd been attracted to him for what reason?

She wasn't ready for the fury of betrayal that slammed into her as she realized Tim was just another misogynistic asshole.

"You belong on a backgammon board?"

—⁓—

Tim watched Lola look down startled and realize she'd pointed at the board when declaring where she belonged.

He thought about the stiff punch she'd delivered to his shoulder and the one she'd been readying for his jaw.

Back in his early days, he'd been on the receiving end of enough hard punches to know hers would have hurt. There'd been a time, back when he'd earned his Crazy Tim nickname, that he'd thought a big, messy bar fight was actually a good way to unwind after a tough mission and well worth the resultant time in lockup.

"Funny," Tim said, finally pointing his finger exactly mirroring her gesture. "I belong on a backgammon board too. Crazy fates, hunh. You and me both belonging right here. Cool. Now we have to fall for each other. Absolutely fated."

She pulled back her hand and continued to glare at him.

He grinned back at her.

"Well." Tim turned so that his legs were stretched out to one side, leaned back on his elbows, and looked up at her. Even in shades and scarf the woman was bleeding magnificent. He wished to God he dared reach across the narrow gap and fool with her stunning hair, but she just might break his jaw. He figured it might be worth the risk, maybe he'd try it later.

"Back when I was a young punk of a two-striper, I was just known as Corporal Maloney."

"Not odiferous?"

Tim laughed that she remembered Big John's tease, though he wished she hadn't. He decided to ignore the comment. Maybe if he could distract her with the story, he could make her forget the game he was absolutely going to lose.

Again Tim eyed Lola's clenched fist.

Her fighting form was excellent.

Who was he kidding, her form was downright incredible! He resisted the urge to look down at that sleek, T-shirt-hugged torso of hers. He did his damnedest to suppress the memory of how awesome she'd looked yesterday standing on the salt pan in just that T-shirt and some of the skimpiest panties it had ever been his pleasure to observe. Plain white panties on Lola LaRue were far sexier than any thong he'd ever helped remove.

"Not odiferous, just stupid. Picked a fight with an entire Marine squad one night. John says I declared I could whip the whole squad buck naked and using only one hand. Can't say as I exactly remember that part." He remembered it perfectly, but there was a level of stupid that the average guy didn't want to admit to.

Lola stretched out her legs in the other direction and lay on her side facing him across the board, her head propped up on one arm. The light pants and shirt flowed over her with sinuous perfection.

Focus on the story, boy, unless you want to embarrass yourself.

"I made a pretty good showing of it until the MPs showed up and tossed all of our butts in the brig. Same cell. Even Big John who'd stayed out of it. Man, was he pissed." Actually, he'd sat back on the sidelines laughing his ass off.

A shift in the breeze flapped the camouflage netting over the helicopters. They both looked around, but the anchors appeared to have finally been driven into the salt pan hard enough.

"Anyway, there I am in the cell with these idiot Marines. And the Gunny came over. Big damn guy named Bear Garry with one black eye swelling shut. Rather than beating the crap out of me"—though John had been cheering the Gunnery Sergeant on—"he dubbed me the craziest damn flyboy he'd ever met. Big John, the helpful jerk, tagged me with 'Crazy Tim' and it stuck. Then old Bear taught me to play backgammon for the week we all spent cooling our heels for brawling. So I really do belong on a backgammon board in some ways."

Lola gave an appreciative laugh.

He'd left behind his brawling that day, or at least most of it. He still didn't know what he'd been trying to prove or disprove. Big John had called it "taking up his man space for such a short shrimp." But Tim was only short compared with man-mountains like his best friend and Gunny Garry.

Lola quieted. Went dead quiet as if thinking about something really major.

The silence left him again admiring the sinuous woman stretched out before him. Damn, but her legs looked like they just went on forever.

He knew the heat of raw lust was rocketing once more to his cheeks, but he couldn't stop. God, he wanted this woman. Not like others. He enjoyed women and they enjoyed him, making for a neat mutual passage at arms.

But Chief Warrant Lola LaRue, this woman sitting so at ease just within reach, this one he wanted unlike any other before. Wanted, hell. Needed! Had he even slept since she'd hit base? Certainly not since the moment she'd kissed him.

He'd even enjoyed the hot fire that flamed forth in her nearly black eyes. The heat that burned torch-hot inside her. Her eyes had flared with joy the two times they'd kissed. And with fury as she declared where she belonged.

He couldn't help but wonder at what fire passion might place in those mesmerizing eyes. And could he be the man to place it there?

"Yes!" she declared.

Tim startled with the abrupt affirmative answer to his question. Then knew he hadn't spoken aloud. So what in hell was she "yessing" about?

"I bloody well, as sure as all-fired hell, do belong on this here backgammon board."

"Then drop your damned quarters and get back in the game."

She did, with a laugh. That starlight laugh. That's what really killed him.

Chapter 17

"YOU AIN'T SHIT."

Lola spun to face the snarl.

The D-boys had called for pickup after three days and nights. For the last twenty minutes the flight crews had been scrambling about in the dark erasing any sign of their time perched in the desert plateau above Desert One. Anchor spikes pulled, camo nets folded, area swept for trash.

Lola had been squatting to gather the fifteen nuts and washers and six quarters from Tim's impromptu backgammon board. She'd wished she could chip the board out of the salt and take it with her, but maybe it was better this way. Now she'd always know it was here, could picture it here in the high Iranian desert.

Sergeant Kee Stevenson stood close behind her.

"I've got you in my goddamn sights, LaRue! Don't think I don't see what you're doing."

Lola unfolded from her low squat to full height and stared down at the diminutive woman. Lola considered slamming Kee to the hardpan for sheer bad attitude or failure to respect rank. But that wouldn't solve whatever was eating at her.

"Personally, S—" She bit off the Sergeant's rank before she could put that between them and managed to substitute the woman's name. "Stevenson, I don't know what the hell you have against me." And she didn't give a good goddamn either.

But she did.

A couple of red work-lights had been set to shine across the camp. They weren't bright, but just strong enough so the crews could see what they were doing without totally destroying their night vision. The work-lights turned the white salt into a plain of blood, the perfect place to square off. It was past eleven o'clock at night, and they were to be airborne in ten more minutes. More than long enough to hash this out.

Taking the approach she'd like to, busting the woman a good one in the face, wouldn't do a damn thing to help build a team. Was this another Major Beale test? Had she put Kee up to this? No, the Sergeant's dislike of Lola was genuine and deep.

Stevenson's straight finger jabbed Lola's breastbone hard enough to really hurt.

Lola grabbed Kee's hand, barely fast enough. The woman was quick, but Lola was faster. She bent the wrist backward against a nerve point she found with her index finger. The woman showed no sign of the pain, which must be excruciating. Lola held it a moment longer to prove her point before tossing the hand free as if it were no threat, though the center of her chest still throbbed where she could feel a bruise forming.

"You think I don't see what you're doing." Kee was actually snarling. "Well, you're wrong. I grew up on the street. I know your type. You leave Tim alone. He's too good a man for the likes of you."

Leave Tim alone? They were friends. What more was she talking about?

"You're just like a girl I knew, black-widow chick named Shasta. Called men with a wave of her hips and then crushed any hope and life out of them. So I'll only warn you once — stay the hell clear of Maloney, or a stray round just might find you some day when you least expect it."

Lola felt that blow harder than any physical jab. This was one of the Army's top snipers, she could be a mile away when she pulled the trigger to end Lola's life with no one the wiser.

That she could have the woman court-martialed for the threat didn't make it any less real.

But that wasn't the reaction Lola could feel boiling up inside her. A rage built from deep down. Deeper than the place that had driven her to the Army, from as deep as the misery of her childhood.

Lola snagged a chunk of Kee's hair, a dyed blond streak now devil-red beneath the worklights, and wrapped it in her fist, putting enough of a twist on it that she could keep the Sergeant still as she leaned in until their noses were inches apart.

And her anger poured forth not as a shout, but rather as little more than a tight whisper.

"What's eating at you, Sergeant?" This time she used the title with all of the derision she could lay into it. "Isn't what's between Tim and me that's eating you, which if you had a goddamn brain you'd see was just friendship. I like him. And that's all."

Kee's glare despite the pain in her scalp told Lola that the Sergeant didn't believe a word of it. But there was more.

"No." Lola twisted harder, bringing tears to the Sergeant's narrowed eyes as she leveraged the hank of hair harder.

"What's eating at you is that Major Beale thinks I can do the goddamn job. How long did it take you to prove yourself to her? How long did it take Connie? Bet I've got both your asses beat because I'm just that damned good. And that must just grind your soul."

A flicker in the woman's eyes told her she'd struck home. Lola hadn't even known what she'd been going to say before she started, but now she got it. The Major was treating Lola far better than she had started with Kee Stevenson or Connie Davis. If this was better, the Major must have put them through hell.

Her anger drained away. She shoved Kee away, not using her hair as a lever to do so. The woman staggered aside but didn't come back at her.

Lola, who'd finally decided not to be the outsider, had become just that because for the first time in her life she'd really and truly cared about something. She'd committed to SOAR and to Major Emily Beale.

And it didn't feel any damn better than before when she hadn't committed to anything.

Chapter 18

LOLA KEPT AN EYE OUT ON THE NIGHTTIME DESERT streaking by close below. Low and fast, they flew into the night, racing back to Ravar. They were fully fueled by the Chinooks and, unlike the unfortunates of Operation Eagle Claw, had not overflown a single vehicle or through any sandstorms. Now something was bound to go wrong. Had to.

The desert had been clean when they left. No sign of their stay in the heart of Iran other than Tim's damn backgammon board.

Crap!

She'd been so pissed at Kee that she'd forgotten and left the playing pieces on the salt pan. For half a moment she considered turning back to get them, knowing such a thing was impossible, foolish, and dangerous combined. Someday, would a desert nomad pick up those six American quarters and wonder how they'd come to be there scattered among little bits of hardware? She hoped so. It would make up a little for their loss.

God. Damn. Kee. Stevenson.

There was nothing between her and Tim. That she knew for sure.

And if she didn't get her head back in the game, Major Beale would make her life even more hellish than it already was.

Consciously she unfolded each finger from the cyclic

control. Shook out each muscle. Calmed her thoughts and focused once more on the empty desert. One secret of being a top pilot: staying loose and flexible, always able to react, always ready to act.

She thought about the woman seated just two feet behind her through a layer of Kevlar armor that wrapped around Lola's seat.

The second secret of a great pilot was never losing sight of your enemies.

Ever.

Kee Stevenson, you I've got on my radar!

Lola was slipping along at twenty knots, going backwards.

She'd picked up a visual on the D-boys barely two kilometers out from the rendezvous. As DAP Hawk pilots, she and Major Beale had the job of providing protective cover. *Viper* flew at the far side of the two Chinooks, making sure the road ahead stayed clear.

So she and the Major let the D-boys go by and were now flying backwards behind them and their electric bicycles that were moving at almost thirty miles per hour.

Lola swallowed hard. Only five of them. Two days ago they'd dropped off six men. There was no possibility of carrying a body on their rigs, so someone was still back there in the desert, and it was only safe to assume the worst.

Letting the rotor wash wipe all tracks from the dirt road, she kept an eye down the road.

And there, far down the narrow bit of path across the trackless waste, almost lost in the dark, rose a plume of dust. A plume that was coming on fast.

A quick selection on the camera system that fed the image to her helmet visor, and she glanced directly behind. It showed the hovering Chinook, tail ramp down on the road, but nothing else touching the earth. The first of the five bikes shot aboard. There would be no mark that they'd been there, the road dusted clear by the DAP Hawk's rotor downwash.

And up ahead, the lone, distant plume shot ahead faster.

"Major." There was no way Beale could miss it in the hyper-awareness they all had at a moment like this.

"Roger, keep on it."

That meant the Major was paying more attention to what was happening below and behind them with the recovery of the five surviving operators, and leaving Lola to focus on the oncoming problem.

She started to turn the chopper to port to expose the starboard-side gunner to the target. Connie's minigun could be more tactical and selective than the forward weapons under Lola's control.

"No. Kee."

Lola dutifully began to slew the chopper the other way to turn Kee Stevenson face-on to the oncoming threats no matter how she felt about the woman. What was important now was the mission, and she'd trust Major Beale's knowledge of her own crew.

As they faced momentarily head-on down the road, Lola noticed a second dust plume through the darkness of the night. She loved these new cameras on the DAP Hawks. Far better than the old, green night-vision.

The first plume resolved itself into a single vehicle, the second into a string of three or four. And they were gaining ground on the first vehicle, an aging Iranian van.

"Any bets on D-boy six?"

They hovered for three long seconds while the Major considered if the lead vehicle, which they could now see had a sole occupant, might be the missing Delta Force operator.

Beale keyed her mike. "Letting one through the gate. Betting it's Michael."

Michael who? But Lola was too busy to take the time to ask. Oh, right. The colonel with the scar on his jaw.

"Roger that," Viper answered. He flew on patrol ahead of the big Chinook but would now be swinging in to check out the vehicle they let roar by beneath them.

Lola finished the swing to turn Kee toward the oncoming string of vehicles.

"Keep it quiet," the Major ordered.

Lola felt a small mechanical sound transmitted through the back of her seat. She'd noticed the rifle case mounted there but hadn't thought much about it. Kee must be opening it now.

A sniper. Kee might be a bloody bitch, but Tim had said she was also one of the highest ranked sharpshooters in the Army, male or otherwise. Somehow Lola hadn't connected that skill to the case behind her.

Lola counted to five to give Kee time to get ready, then slid into a stable hover, high enough to not roil the dust and low enough to hopefully stay off any radar.

That gave her an idea.

With their lights out, the helicopters would still be invisible to approaching vehicles. And with their truck engines roaring, the quieted helicopters would be inaudible as well.

"Hold," Lola called over the intercom.

Leaving a vehicle with a bullet through someone's forehead wasn't exactly the subtlest action when invading a foreign country you never wanted to admit to entering.

Lola slid sideways until she was over the dusty desert rather than the paved road. She shoved the collective down with her left hand, cranking the throttle wide open as she did so, until she was ten feet above the road. She jerked the control back up and the rotor blades groaned. They stopped the chopper's descent barely a foot above the dirt surface.

Dust bloomed upward around them. An impenetrable wall rose thirty feet or more into the air.

Now, between the oncoming vehicle and the D-boys rolling aboard the Chinook was a shield of invisibility hundreds of feet across. Even a brave driver wasn't likely to go into a desert dust storm. Or to make it through if he tried. He'd be driving totally blind and could follow the road only by a guess. And best of all, in the dark of the night, he'd have no way to tell that it wasn't a natural dust storm.

She held the hover another ten seconds, expanding the cloud by pumping up more dust, before pulling back enough to rise through the center of her own maelstrom. She had to watch the instruments closely. For the moment, she was as blind as her adversaries.

Sideslipping the chopper, she was soon in the clear. A line of vehicles approached the cloud from one side, the flight of choppers and D-boys hidden on the other side by dust and darkness. Then she spun to give Sergeant Kee the best possible view of the truck they'd let through.

A glance toward the Chinooks revealed the lone

driver flashing a thumbs-up, then roaring up the ramp of the hovering Chinook.

The monstrous bird lumbered aloft even before it started closing the ramp.

Lola twisted back to watch the dust cloud and continued to backpedal into the night. *Vengeance* was the trailing bird as the whole flight turned perpendicular to the road and aimed for the border.

By the time they reached the first rise, still no one had come through the dust cloud.

Just as they cleared the top to slip down the backside, one vehicle showed in the slowly dispersing cloud.

Well off the road, mired, and rolled onto its side in the sand.

Lola slid over the top of the rise and down the far side.

They were gone.

They'd never been there.

They were the U.S. Army's Night Stalkers.

Lola had one clear thought as she turned to follow the others back to friendlier places.

Flying with SOAR was a seriously cool thing for a girl to do.

Chapter 19

BY THE TIME THEY REACHED BATI, TIM WAS HAMMERED-down tired. They hadn't stopped at their outbound camp in southwestern Afghanistan as planned. The D-boys made it clear that wasn't an option. No explanations, but no landings allowed. So they flew through the night and the morning into early afternoon.

Once out of Iran, the first of three KC-135 Stratotankers fell in with them. Three midair refuelings and fourteen hours of flight at the end of four mostly sleepless days.

After landing at Bati, Tim stumbled out of the *Viper*, felt the earth solid beneath him, and just stood. The ground buzzed through his boots because his foot nerves hadn't yet figured out they were no longer on a vibrating helicopter.

Major Henderson climbed out beside him and stumbled to a halt with a low curse.

Tim rolled his own shoulders and cursed right along with the Major. He could hear his joints popping as he flexed and twisted to loosen his back and neck.

The women in the next chopper over didn't look all that much happier. Connie climbed down and, for the first time in his memory, didn't start checking the helicopter first. She simply sat down on the dirt and hung her head, clearly too tired to even pull off her helmet. Kee stepped down to the earth, but then just lay over backward until she stretched prostrate on the cargo bay deck of the *Vengeance*.

John gave Tim no wallop as he staggered by. He simply sagged to the ground beside his wife and began peeling off her helmet for her. When he finished, he dropped it in his lap, clearly too tired to realize he still wore his own.

Tim managed to get his feet working. As he walked by, he tapped John on his helmet so that the man didn't fall asleep while still wearing the thing.

Lola still hadn't opened her door. He stepped into the shadow cast by the weapons pylons, a cool relief. Seen through sunlight-adapted eyes, the helicopter's interior was almost black. He blinked for a moment to help his eyes adjust, but it didn't help. They'd arrived well into midday and the light was blinding despite his shades.

A sudden image of Lola passed out in her seat, half choked on her seat belt, had him yanking open the door.

She had her helmet off, had clearly scrubbed her fingers through her hair so it bloomed about her face in a lush brown halo mostly hiding her face. She was finishing the shutdown checklist. Captain Richardson was probably doing the same thing for *Viper*.

She finished, cleared the checklist from the main screen on the dashboard, and shut down the main power.

Tim stepped aside, back into the blinding sun, and held the door as she clambered down. Even in the bulk of a fire-retardant flight suit, with a layer of Kevlar armor slid into the special lining, her legs just went on forever.

He stood, holding open the door and weaving. Not sure what to do next, his mind so muddled he couldn't think. The midday heat hammered against his brain until salty sweat dripped down and stung his eyes before evaporating into the impossibly dry air.

She slipped off the FN SCAR carbine that they each wore while flying in case they were downed unexpectedly and snapped the rifle into the door clips.

He still held the door, or rather the door was the only thing that holding him upright.

In moments she shed her survival vest, tossing it back on her seat, then opened the front of her flight suit down to her panties.

"Salope chien lacou."

It sounded light and musical and mysterious. He expected it was also foul. And he couldn't agree more… whatever it meant. If he'd been less numb, or they didn't have an audience of physically wrecked aviators, he'd just reach out and drag her against him. Officer or not, screw it. Some things would be worth getting in serious trouble for.

She reached up and stretched.

He could hear her joints popping.

Then she twisted and turned with more energy than was decent after such a flight.

He realized he was staring at what her motions were doing to that fine, T-shirt-clad torso of hers as it was revealed and hidden by the open flaps of her flight suit.

Blinking hard, he looked away. And had to wonder how long he'd stood watching her. It couldn't have been more than a few seconds. Couldn't be. But the others had drifted away. He could see John and Connie moving slowly far down the field, hard to tell who was helping support whom as they headed for the showers. The others were just plain gone.

Lola appeared to realize the same thing at the same time. Her dark gaze turned on him.

Think Tim. Do something. Anything. All he did was hang on the door.

Chief Warrant Lola LaRue shook back her hair like a mane, exposing that magazine-ad face of hers and a slight, teasing smile, with just a hint of the dimple showing on one cheek.

His body had some clear ideas, and he was too damned tired to argue.

Somewhere between one heartbeat and the next he'd driven her back against the narrow panel between the pilot's door and the chief gunner's window. They were shadowed by the open door and the 30 mm cannon hanging from the weapons pylon. He drove his hands in the front of her flight suit and dragged her against him.

His mouth hard against hers unleashed a fire that had been burning hot and deep since the first moment he'd seen her. It blew forth. She tasted of hot spice and fire, of heat and that impossible richness of a perfect, soul-scorching jambalaya.

—✵—

Lola had huffed out her breath when Tim had slammed her against the side of the chopper. His hands on her were rough—no, strong. He drew her so tightly against his body, they could have been one person.

His mouth was on hers before she could draw breath.

His need dragged hers forth. All she could think was how badly she'd needed something, wanted something. Anything that wasn't a goddamn battering copilot's seat. Every muscle in her body ached... except where

Tim held her. Even as he crushed against her, his hands worked on the tight knots in her shoulders, her hips, her buttocks.

All she could manage in response was to groan against his driving tongue. A low groan like an ancient vault door creaking open.

He stopped abruptly. Froze.

She opened her eyes, not remembering she'd closed them.

His eyes were wide. But they weren't looking side to side, not like a schoolboy afraid he'd been caught. But they were afraid.

He pulled back enough to unlock their lips, but she let him get no further than that with the arms she'd wrapped and locked around his neck somewhere along the way.

"I shouldn't... We shouldn't... Sir, I'm..."

She'd been right. He was so damn sweet.

Then she wondered. Wondered if he'd have stopped if she were any other woman. It was an odd thought, but she'd bet that with any prior woman he had just let his lust run them both happily into the ground. She couldn't think why he felt the need for control around her, other than their disparate ranks and the potential of career-ending disciplinary action, but Tim's control of that much need showed core-deep strength.

That only revved her up all the more. She wanted to unleash his power, see what he could do to her when he really let go.

Lola usually drew the demanding ones who knew the game as well as she did. None of them would have hesitated in this moment, no matter what their rank. Tim Maloney was actually being decent on top of gorgeous and owning a body built precisely to a woman's order. His hands betrayed his need, digging into her of their own will even as he struggled to hold back the tidal wave of lust between them.

"Soldier?" She growled it soft.

"Yes, sir?" He actually answered with a straight face, though his hands were still tangled in her underclothes.

"If you call me 'sir' one more time before you finish what you started..." She slid a hand down inside his flight suit and wrapped him in her fingers. "I'm gonna bust you one in the balls."

"Yes, s—" He stopped himself. It took him a moment, but not a long one. He wasn't stupid. Like a good aviator, he also didn't waste time acknowledging anything. When the tower cleared you for takeoff, they didn't want a lot of chatter, they wanted you out of their airspace. Tim got right back to the task at hand.

She could feel his smile against hers as he reached down and drove her upward. Drove her on until she was flying and her head was lost in the clouds of the perfect, clear blue sky.

Chapter 20

TIM FELT HE COULD STAY HERE ALL DAY, RIGHT HERE. Holding warm woman up against the side of the Black Hawk. Breathing in that spicy, unique scent that was Lola LaRue. As a matter of fact, he wasn't sure he had any choice about actually spending the day.

Partly it was their position. Her head resting on his shoulder, an arm thrown around his neck, one of her legs wrapped around his hips still holding him tight against her.

Partly, if he moved, he was afraid they'd both slide to the ground in a puddle of damn-pleased-with-themselves.

He'd never seen a lady who could just let go like that. Women always held on to some self-awareness or with some agenda, or he didn't know what. Or they offered nothing back, expecting the man to give all so that the woman could simply lose herself in her body's reactions.

Lola had totally abandoned herself to the surges rocketing through her. But neither had she gone anywhere blank, past action, past anything but receiving. She'd given as good as he had. Her hand still held him, clenched around him, gentle now where she'd been frantic moments before. She had driven him right off the deep end with her.

They stood there long enough for the sun to shift a bit, to move them from the barely forgiving shade to the unbearable sun. Slowly, gently, they slid apart, straightened clothing, brushed pointlessly at hair messed by four days in the field before they'd found other ways to disarrange it.

"Thanks." She gave him a toe-curling kiss and dragged at his lower lip with her teeth. "I really, really, really needed that."

"Me, too." *Stupid. Lame.* He could see some of the light go out of her. She wasn't that kind of woman. He didn't know what kind she was, other than his kind. She'd gone and charmed him right out of his goddamn brain. And his body.

"If that's the road to a court-martial, sign me up." And it was true. With how she made him feel, he didn't give a damn.

That got her radiant smile back, but that wasn't right.

Right for her, but it was more for him. That's what had stopped him cold for a moment. Why he'd suddenly gone all awkward and rank formal on her. He really didn't care what happened, not as long as he could be with Lola LaRue.

He'd never felt that way before, and the shock had snapped his head back like a hard slap.

He'd spent a career running away from his own past. And he was damned good at it, though it helped that he loved his job. He'd spent a lifetime not ever really connecting with a woman or really caring beyond a happy tumble.

But he'd throw it all away in a heartbeat for this Lola LaRue.

They turned for the showers and then some chow and shut-eye. He didn't feel nearly as sleepy as before, still couldn't wrap his mind around whatever he really wanted to say to her. Something he'd bet she wouldn't want to hear. He—

"What are they doing?"

Lola was looking toward one of the Chinooks that had flown with them. A cordon of D-boys had formed around the chopper that had taken aboard the racing Iranian truck. They had rifles in their hands rather than slung across their backs.

In the middle of a secret U.S. airbase, they were facing outward, protecting the aircraft from other members of the U.S. Army Special Forces.

He and Lola shared a look. Another mission that they'd probably never know the end result of.

Perhaps one they really didn't want to.

Chapter 21

DANIEL DRAKE DARLINGTON III HATED THESE MO-ments. He listened to the phone ring. Sometimes it was the worst part of his job. It rang again in his ear. He could feel the pain he was causing the man at the other end of the line, though he'd never admit it.

On the fourth ring, it was picked up and dropped. But Daniel was used to that and had held the phone away from his ear in anticipation of the moment.

"Wha-ish-hit?"

Daniel didn't bother suppressing his smile. The whole world thought that Peter Matthews was always erudite and calm. At the moment he sounded like any other man woken from too little sleep.

"Good morning, Mister President."

There was a distinct pause.

"How long I been ashleep?"

Daniel glanced at his watch. "Almost two hours, sir."

Another long pause.

"Shit."

"Yes, sir, Mr. President."

The pause was shorter this time.

"Who this time?"

"The Iranians, sir."

"I'll be down in ten minutes." That had put the snap back in his voice.

About the only thing worse Daniel could have said

would be the North Koreans. Most rogue nations were Third World, some practically pre-technology. It was hard for them to hurt people other than themselves. On the other hand, Iran, North Korea, and sometimes Pakistan all shared Most Dangerous Rogue Nation status.

It had certainly rousted Daniel's brain quickly enough when they'd had woken him after only twenty-five minutes of sleep.

He hung up the phone and looked up at the man across the Situation Room table from him.

"He'll be down in five."

General Brett Rogers, the Chairman of the Joint Chiefs of Staff, a grizzled warrior and former commander of USSOCOM, Special Operation Command, nodded. They'd both served with this President for two years now.

Delta Force Commander Colonel James Andhauer didn't react, of course. He simply waited in stillness.

Peter Matthews was the youngest President in history, and his energy was legendary, even among those who worked with him. Of course he'd be down sooner than he said.

Daniel was five years his junior and, despite eighteen months as Matthews's Chief of Staff, still had trouble keeping up with the man.

The President cruised into the Situation Room wearing sweatpants, a T-shirt, and sneakers at 2:00 a.m. sharp, four minutes after Daniel's wake-up call.

"What have we got?" The President dragged his fingers through hair long enough to brush his collar. It made him appear even younger than he was, and Daniel had watched many negotiations in which that youthfulness, backed up by a presidentially sharp mind, had totally disarmed those around him.

Daniel knew even as he watched that, with a single sweep of the Situation Room boards, the President had gathered more information than most men could with careful study.

Only the General, Daniel, and the commander of Delta Force. No political officers like the Secretary of State or even the head of the Iranian desk.

That would tell the President the perceived delicacy of this matter and how limited the present scope of knowledge.

The display screens and status board were blank, which told him they weren't even trusting this information to a graphics orderly, despite the Marine Corps staff's notoriously impeccable security. Just three men waited for him in one of the most secure rooms on the planet.

"Good morning, gentlemen. Why do I think I won't be going back to bed anytime soon?"

"Operation Cat was initiated due to satellite imagery."

Daniel clicked a remote and, once the Sit Room's screen flickered on, selected a document from the secure desktop. It opened to reveal an image of a power station against a broad background of brown.

General Rogers took the lead.

"It's a small electrical generating plant. There is a very small line to the nearby city of Ravar in Eastern Iran. This line couldn't carry a quarter of the plant's capacity."

Daniel clicked to the next image. A map of Southwest Asia and a small red circle where the plant stood.

The President whistled. "I remember approving this, but I didn't realize we were going so far in. That had to be Emily's team."

Who else. The President's childhood friend had flown numerous black ops for this administration, including the one that saved the President's life.

"Yes, sir. Majors Henderson and Beale led a four-bird flight, and Colonel Michael Gibson headed the ground operation and the six-man Delta infiltration squad. Everyone got out clean."

"I can't believe Michael's still in the field."

A colonel was the commander-rating for Special Operation Force Delta. Men with the bird on their collars didn't lead small operational squads in the wild deserts of Southwest Asia.

James Andhauer offered one of his rare remarks. "If you can figure out how to get the man off the front line, you're wiser than I am, Mr. President."

That didn't even warrant a nod of agreement from around the table. Promoting the man to general wouldn't get him out of the field. He was the most dedicated and successful Delta operator in the history of the unit. And he was still alive and in one piece after an impossibly long list of clandestine missions, which merely proved that he was indeed the right man in the right place.

The next image showed a mid-range satellite image. The power plant, the few electric lines leading to the nearby city, but no explanation for the size of the plant.

An arrow-straight road, looking like a rail line, led from the power plant to a small cluster of buildings a kilometer into the desert.

"My wife dug this out of archival imagery as part

of the mission-planning phase." Daniel had managed to slip out without waking her. Almost a year now married to a top CIA analyst and loving every second of it, except of course when he had to crawl out of her bed in the middle of the night.

The image Alice had found, clearly dated two years before, showed a deep trench, heavy construction equipment lining either side, and massive cables being laid down the trench between the power plant and the outbuilding.

"So, what did they find?"

Daniel went to the last image, the reason he'd woken the President in the middle of the night.

"This is the image we shot with a high drone on an overflight two hours ago."

Peter Matthews jerked upright in his chair and stared at the image.

"Did we do that?"

"No, sir. We didn't. We asked the forward team, and all we received was a dumbfounded response. They didn't do it. Didn't see it."

"Is it on the media wires?"

"No. Nor any announcements of American imperialism on Al Jazeera either. We're not even sure they knew we were in there."

They all stared at the massive crater that had replaced the small desert building.

"As far as we can tell from sources, they blew this up themselves. See the circle of vehicles along the rim? We've positively IDed at least three of these in the chase group that followed our team into the desert." Daniel put up the next slide, "Here's an image from twenty minutes later."

Smoke billowed from each of the returned vehicles, and bodies sprawled around the vehicles in a way only dead bodies could lie.

They sat in silence for a long minute while the President of the United States contemplated images seen by fewer than a dozen people in the world.

"Colonel, bring them here. Now. Your full team and whatever they found."

The commander of Delta Force reached for the phone.

"And, Colonel?"

"Sir?"

"Have them bring the DAP Hawks and their crews with them."

Chapter 22

OVERTIRED, TIM RETREATED TO THE WEIGHT ROOM TO jam some iron. The back corner of the base's supply tent had been cleared by stacking gear dangerously high to either side, but what wasn't dangerous in the Army? A pair of benches and some stacks of free weights were jammed in the small space. A couple of the heavier dumbbells pinned the tent canvas to the dusty ground.

Though the midday heat was scorching beyond the tent, the cool iron felt good, felt familiar in Tim's hands. He liked the ritual of it. Choosing the start weight. Sliding on the right number of disks. Counting out the reps. Building through days, weeks, now years. Ten pounds here, five reps there. Constructing a routine layer by layer until you could do it in your sleep. Until your body tingled in anticipation, and afterward thrummed and burned from the actual workout.

He knew he was tired, even if his personal sleep-switch didn't, and he didn't have a spotter, so he loaded the bar light and lay down to knock out some tonnage. A hundred pounds made twenty reps to the ton. He'd normally push enough weight for fifteen or even ten reps to the ton, but he judged his reactions and response time and ran light today.

John wandered in during the middle of Tim's second ton, or was it the third? Didn't matter. Today he was after wearing himself out, not some program plan.

"Pussy," was all John said after glancing at the weights on Tim's bar. He settled onto the other bench.

Tim could see that John's bar wasn't all that much heavier than his own, but John didn't bother changing it, though he could out-press Tim two-to-one. John had proved it once by clamping his massive hands around Tim's arm and thigh and pressing him for a half-dozen reps to honor a bar bet that Tim had made with some rowdy Air Force jocks.

Tim waited until John had settled and dug into moving some iron up and down.

"Same back to you, bro."

After his fourth ton, or maybe his third, Tim slotted the bar back on the hooks. Knew no sleep awaited him yet, but remained too addle-brained to think of what to do next. Leg lifts maybe. He scrounged up some sets of ankle weights, sat back on the bench, and began kicking twenty pounds up into the air.

"What's got you so strung?" Big John's voice didn't even waver as he shifted his barbell up and down.

"Who says I'm strung?" Not that Tim had ever been able to hide squat from Big John. They'd been flying together since before SOAR. Had sailed through SOAR evals together. Okay, made it through by the skin of their teeth only after having their asses handed to them. Five years they'd flown together. Five years and they knew what each other was thinking.

Right until John met Connie. Tim hadn't seen that one coming at all, and it still bugged him that he hadn't. He kept telling himself he was cool with it, because that was never going to happen to him. Now look where the hell he was. And with an officer, to make matters even worse.

John continued to pound the weights up and down, not really paying attention to such a light load.

"Not getting any for too long. It ain't good for you, buddy boy."

"And you saying you just got some?"

"Sure did," John shot back. "With the purtiest lady ever married a fool like me. Left her sleeping sweet. She's even cuter when she's asleep."

Not getting any wasn't Tim's problem. He switched to the other foot. He'd gotten plenty, far more than he'd expected. The problem was he'd also gotten far more than he'd bargained for.

He'd gotten Lola LaRue on the brain. She traveled down his bloodstream, pumping him up for even thinking of her. Her scent, which he could still savor in memory despite a hot and later a cold shower, was burned more clearly on his memory than his mama's *sofrito*. The taste of Lola's skin had cleared his palate of a desire for any other flavor. And her skin. The impossibly smooth sheath to those magnificent muscles.

She fit against him. His hands had always seemed overlarge and clumsy, until he'd wrapped them around her. There they fit perfectly. He was gettin' plenty — too much.

He hadn't even noticed that John had dropped his weights on the hook and sat up beside him.

Tim continued to stare straight ahead, trying desperately to erase the image of her easy smile that slipped crookedly across a face that would have been too perfect with a standard smile.

"You're kiddin' me, man." Big John leaned in to look at him even closer. "Kidding. Right?"

Tim didn't answer. Couldn't. It wasn't supposed to be that obvious.

"Oh shit." John picked up a couple of thirties to do some reverse curls, more to keep his hands busy than anything else.

"What?" Tim still didn't look over.

"Like Archie, man. It's all over you. You remember?"

Couldn't forget. Lieutenant Archie Stevenson had been all cool and collected Bostonian upper crust. He'd flown with Beale since the beginning, since before the beginning, all the way back to West Point. But it had all evaporated the day he met Sergeant Kee Smith from the streets of LA, the wrong side of those streets.

"No way." Tim had not done that with Chief Warrant LaRue. Whatever her past, she was so out of his league. He hadn't pulled an Archie and fallen in love at first sight. But he had. If not love, the most damn serious case of lust John had ever run into.

"You couldn't stand Connie when you met her." Tim needed to push back some, build a safety zone.

"Nope." John sounded cheerful as could be. "She made this dumb Okie completely nuts. So beautiful and so friggin' smart. But once I got past that…" His shrug was eloquent.

Tim didn't need to bother pointing out that neither of them was stupid. They'd both made SOAR and that took some serious moxie. But John was right. His wife operated in a whole other world, like eighteen levels above mere mortals.

"But she fell for a big slab of meat like you."

"She did." John tossed down the thirties, which landed on the packed sand with a heavy thump, and picked up some fifties. His first flyaway almost tagged Tim in the chest.

Tim slid back on the bench until his shoulders rested against the barbell, well out of John's way. He hadn't gotten all stupid about a woman. He'd only traded some of the finest heavy-petting sex of his life with a superior officer against the side of a military attack helicopter in the middle of a secret U.S. Army air base during broad daylight.

"Well, I don't have that for Chief Warrant LaRue."

John just laughed and kept flapping the dumbbells up and down through the air like the goddamn giant goose that he was.

Lola remained where she'd come to a stop in the tent, her right shoulder against a stack of supply crates, just around the corner out of sight from Tim and John.

Nobody ever "had it" for Lola LaRue, and that's exactly where she wanted to be. She knew her body drove some men kinda nuts and that was just fine. If she was in the mood, she welcomed them, other times not so much. When they got too persistent, well, she wasn't a soldier for the fun of it. Okay, not only for the fun of it.

She closed her eyes and thumped the side of her head against the crates, lightly, so they wouldn't hear her.

She knew she wasn't that kind of woman.

Emily Beale had found her everlasting joy with a man as terrifyingly skilled as herself, Viper Henderson. Apparently the woman without a call sign had one, but nobody dared use it for fear of the lightning-fast repercussions. When she was known to be out of earshot and gunshot, and perhaps general geographic region, the name "Viper-Bitch Beale" was bandied about in whispers. Bandied about with the absolute highest respect. The toughest woman any of them had ever met, without a single moment of macho bravado. No one ever even tried "Vipress" in her presence, just Major.

Big John and Connie made some sense, both wizard mechanics, even if he was twice her size.

Archie and Kee and the little Uzbekistani girl made no sense at all. Weird-ass family: Boston rich, Los Angeles bitch (not in a good way), and war orphan. Lola had tried to make nice with Kee over food in the chow tent, which had gone absolutely nowhere. Her husband too distracted by the little orphan's antics to pay even the slightest attention. Kid was pretty damn cute, hard not to notice that, even while her mom was trying to roast Lola over some imaginary fire. Wouldn't put it past her to set up a good old Creole barbecue if Lola were the long pig on the spit.

And now here she stood, her aching head leaning against a stack of cases of, Lola looked, potato chips, with trail mix on the other side. The fourth woman of SOAR and here she stood lost among the snack foods. Well, she'd come to fly, not to make happy noises with the first flyboy she ran into.

She turned back out into the sun, feeling even more restless than when she'd arrived.

⌘

"Mad dogs and Englishman."

The new flying lady jumped as if Dilya had poked

her with a sharp stick when she stepped out of the tent
and into the sun.

"It what my dad says when people are walking around
in the sun when they supposed be sleeping."

"Where is your father?"

She pointed toward their tent. "He with The Kee. I
think they want to try make more baby."

"Too much information, kid."

Dilya wondered how a girl could have too much information. She loved to learn. She shrugged to show she
didn't understand, but the lady did not explain.

"I go for walk around spindly thicket." Dilya squinted
against the sun to see the woman's face, but it was clear
she didn't understand.

"Spindly thicket, like Pooh ther Bear, him that kind of
bear. With Piglet?" She stopped and tried to think of more
words, more English words. The Kee had said that spindly thicket was like tall pointy bushes all in a clump. So,
when The Kee and the Professor Archie looked at each
other that way they did, Dilya went for a walk among the
helicopters, all tall and pointy, and felt better too because
she was like Pooh. She often wished she had a Piglet.

"Want you to walk like Pooh and Piglet?" She waved
her hand to show them weaving between helicopters.
"Then maybe you find own tracks too."

The woman shrugged. So different from The Kee.
The Kee did everything as if it was so important. When
she hugged Dilya, it was always so hard it would have
hurt if it didn't feel so good. She remembered how The
Kee and the Professor had fought each other so hard
when they first met that she was afraid one would break.
But they didn't.

The new lady, La Roo, wasn't very much like Roo, the baby kangaroo in *Winnie-the-Pooh*. She was more like Mary Lennox before she found her secret garden. Never happy where she was. Always so mad at the world. The La Roo made Dilya tired just to watch her.

"Sure, kid. Lead on."

Dilya had her favorites. The Big Bird with two spindly heads and the big dent by the rear ramp had a mechanic who saved chocolates for her. Every time, he said that it couldn't hurt for a kid to eat them. But he never explained.

There was one of the Little Birds that the pilot had said she could sit in anytime and pretend, as long as she did not touch anything. Sometimes she pretended to take Piglet to see places that Piglets never got to see. Sometimes she flew them to the Hundred Acre Wood to visit with Owl and Christopher Robin. But mostly she flew with The Kee to build castles in the warm sand.

But her favorite, Dilya took La Roo to her favorite. Not straight there, still pausing to visit friends and familiars along the way.

The La Roo didn't speak, but followed her. Stopping when she stopped, touching what Dilya touched. Like the rough skin tape that covered three holes in a perfect straight line on one helicopter, or the smooth, cool blade on the back of another. So smooth it felt like water.

She reached The Kee's helicopter and tugged on the cargo door.

Dilya liked that the La Roo didn't help but let Dilya do it herself. She could move the heavy door, but The Kee always just grabbed and heaved it aside as if it weighed nothing and the Professor always did it for her like it was something special.

Dilya hopped up and sat on the edge with her legs dangling over the side, still a long way before they would grow down to touch the ground.

The La Roo just stood there as if she did not know what to do.

Dilya patted the open deck beside her, and finally the La Roo settled beside her.

This was Dilya's best imagining place. Here she felt safe. Here she had found a father and mother to replace the ones she lost. Here she could sit and look out and see the world not rushing by. She could just sit in the cool shade of the *Vengeance*.

"What is *Vengeance*?" It struck her that maybe it was more than a name. Like she now knew that her grandmother wasn't really "Calledbetty," because part of that she now knew was more than a name. But it sounded wrong when she tried to make it two parts and it had made Calledbetty sad when Dilya tried using two words so she'd stopped. Did "Betty" mean something too?

"Vengeance is to get even with someone. To pay them back. To make them hurt for hurting you." The La Roo's voice sounded nasty when she said it. As if she was angry and wanted to hurt someone. Dilya watched for a moment, but it wasn't Dilya she wanted to hurt, so Dilya went back to thinking about the name.

"Like if Pooh pulled out Owl's tail feathers to make him sad like Eeyore sad when Owl took his tail? Doesn't that just make everybodies sad?"

The La Roo was silent for a long time. Shifted back and forth as if sitting hurt her, even though her legs were so long they could touch the ground.

"Yeah, kid, you got it about right."

Chapter 23

T IM SAT HUNCHED OVER HIS BREAKFAST. H E FELT LIKE a Neanderthal protecting his prey from wild scavengers. Not that anyone was messing with him, but that his brain and his body were now both impossibly tired and his thoughts were little better.

Except for the last two hours in the scorching afternoon heat, he pretty much hadn't slept a whole night's worth in the last five. On a mission, there were tricks to keep yourself sharp. Your team worked with you, and you all helped charge each other up.

But they weren't on a mission. Kee, John, and Connie looked too damn self-satisfied to be tolerable. Clearly well slept and enjoying the benefits of cohabiting with their married partner. Not a reminder he needed so much.

Archie was off somewhere, which was good. It saved Tim from hating him too, always so neat and tidy and pleasant as if they were in week two of being deployed on a Hawaiian beach and not month eighteen in an abandoned soccer stadium in northwest Pakistan.

So here he crouched over his tray of eggs and bacon and toast and a side of steak as the sun went down, almost daring someone to mess with him.

Then he spotted Lola and Dilya entering the tent, the low sun striking them from behind and casting them in silhouette. They could have been sisters. Dilya, sprouting up like a weed, was going to end up long and slender like Lola rather than seriously short and seriously built like her adoptive mother.

As they moved into the tent, he could see that they even walked alike. A slow, sliding gait designed to make no noise as they moved. Not the kind that is trained in, like the D-boys, but something that was learned young. They both came from worlds where silence was a survival trait.

Their faces, as they moved out of the back-lit tent entrance and toward the chow line, also tied them together. Both quiet and thoughtful, each possessed of a good chin and clear, dark eyes that looked as if they could see right through you.

"I don't like that," Kee growled beside him.

"Don't like what?"

John twisted to look over his shoulder and see where Kee and Tim's attention was focused.

"That woman with Dilya!"

Tim turned to face Kee. She was serious. Had that determined fighter face that she wore when flying or practicing her sharpshooting.

"Why not?"

Kee leaned forward and lowered her voice. She never did that. If anyone in the entire camp was willing to tell you exactly and precisely what they were thinking of you, it was Sergeant Kee Stevenson.

Tim and John leaned in.

"She's a goddamn phony. Everything about her is wrong."

"But she's an awesome pilot. Even the Major says so." Tim had overheard Beale talking to the Viper when they didn't realize Tim was still cleaning his minigun not two feet behind their seats.

"I don't care. Whatever she's telling you, Tim Maloney, that has your head all turned around, it's a lie."

Tim felt his blood flowing and his head clear. He'd flown into battle with Kee plenty, knew she was someone he could trust his back and his life with. But this time Kee was flat wrong.

"But she hasn't told me anything!" It made him crazy to know so little about someone and want to be with her so much.

"Well, that's a lie too."

"What's a lie, too?" Lola put her tray down across from Tim, with Dilya landing at the same instant between her and John.

Kee simply snarled at her, grabbed her own tray, and walked away.

There was a painfully awkward silence that stretched on and on. Tim was trying to think of how to change the subject, but he was too tired to come up with anything.

Finally Dilya spoke, a soft aside to Lola that Tim had to strain to hear.

"Sometime The Kee more like the helichopter than the Pooh. But she always get better."

Whatever the cryptic statement meant, it earned a nod and a smile from Lola, and the tension slipped away from the table.

Tim had to figure out what was going on—and figure it out soon.

Chapter 24

LOLA WAS REACHING FOR THE SALT AND TRYING really hard not to look at Tim when Viper Henderson appeared at the end of their table.

He spoke softly, clearly for their ears only. "Twenty minutes. Full gear. We're gone. Dilya, you're okay with us for stage one." Then he was gone as if he'd never been there.

Lola could feel her heart beat two, three, four times before anyone reacted. Then they stood up, not all at once, but rather as if just going about normal business, dumping half-full and full trays at the cleanup station. A quick pass up the chow line, this time for fruit, energy bars, and maybe a sandwich that could be demolished while they headed for their tents. Dilya moved with similar grace and speed. A little trooper who knew the drill.

Lola followed close behind Tim; they were the last ones to clear the tent. No one had paid them any mind.

Just at the exit from the tent, Tim hurried his pace and bumped square into a Ranger while pretending to look the other way. They'd been clear, then Tim had purposely drawn attention to his hurried departure. Lola hung back trying to figure out why.

"Hey." The Ranger made sure Tim was steady on his feet. "There a mission to fly?" It had been a quiet couple days for the Rangers and they were getting itchy for some action.

Tim leaned in and whispered something that Lola couldn't quite catch.

She sidled in and caught the end of Tim's spiel. "We'll call from fifteen minutes out. Promise not to tell anybody before."

"I swear on yo mama!" The Ranger held up what might have been a Cub Scout salute. Then he hurried into the chow tent, clearly excited to spread whatever news he'd just been sworn to secrecy about.

Lola moved up beside Tim as they headed for the tents to pack their gear.

"Alright, what was that?"

"That, oh nothing." Tim waved a hand as if it didn't matter. "Told him we just got a secret call to fly down to Peshawar. Carrier was sending in twenty gallons of ice cream and we had to be there whenever it arrived or we'd miss out."

Ice cream.

"That was so cruel." Lola knew that Bati air base had never in its history had ice cream. Troops mooned over it on the blistering hot days, talked about favorite flavors, got into fights over waffle versus sugar cones just to have an excuse for a brawl to break the boredom when times were really slow.

She looked back over her shoulder. They'd wait for hours. Twenty gallons would be enough for everyone on base to have two or three bowls. They'd wait all night rather than sleeping as they normally would.

"The fifteen minutes warning." Tim sounded terribly pleased. "That was really the cherry on top."

"I don't get it."

Tim just smiled as if he really had just eaten the cherry.

"Oh." Lola got it. They'd have tables and bowls and spoons all set out and lined up within minutes of the helicopters taking off. And then a couple dozen Rangers, and about fifty base and SOAR personnel would wait. And wait.

When the ice cream never showed up, everyone would pound on the poor, dumb Ranger who'd bought Tim's line. With one sentence he'd stirred up several days' worth of entertainment.

Almost a pity that they'd miss it.

———～～～———

In ten minutes flat, they were all at the DAP Hawks in full flight gear and stowing their duffels. Tim felt far better than he had in days. Nothing as fun as deep-sixing a Ranger; they were almost too easy for target practice, but still fun.

He and John kicked into high gear on the preflight.

Dilya was coming, so that meant weapons shouldn't be needed, but Tim checked them anyway, while John preflighted the engines, fuel, and exterior of the craft. Captain Richardson, the copilot, was already on the avionics. Tim made sure that fresh belts were laid into the miniguns and the Vulcan 20 mm cannon. He grabbed the nose of each Hellfire missile and gave it a good shake to check the seating of the clamps. He checked that the reds, the armorers easily identified by their red vests, had indeed refilled both 19-tube FFAR rocket pods.

At twenty minutes from the warning, Major Henderson climbed aboard and thirty seconds later they were airborne. Tim glanced to the side in time to see the *Vengeance* rising up in their wake. The knife-edge desert sunset slashed the day from night, darkening the arena even as they cleared the stadium's rim.

Right behind them, the big Chinook, which had the captured truck aboard, lifted clear. Only after they were airborne did the ring of Delta Force who had been guarding the chopper disperse.

Tim wondered what the hell the Delta Force operators had dug up out in the Iranian desert. An itch between his shoulders told him that his first guess was wrong. He was going to find out.

With the sole instruction of "Full force protection, follow *Viper*," Lola found her mind free to wander. It was dark night now, but *Viper* was a clear beacon on the projection against the inside of her visor. Four rotor diameters ahead and one to the side, allowing for concentration of force while also providing clear forward vision and an open field of fire.

Their heading made no sense, but that wasn't a first.

And there was no question what they were to be protecting—the laden Chinook floated along right behind them.

They had a child aboard a fully armed, secret military helicopter, which was a new one for her, but she could shrug that off if others could. And Sergeant Kee could be a bloody pain in the ass, but she guarded over the kid with her whole heart. No chance she'd put the kid in harm's way.

Lola was starting to see the woman's strong core through all of the rough edges. Could see that Kee had clearly grown up like a wild weed running loose on the streets. Word around camp said East LA, which was a hard road to be sure. But it was as if she and Kee came from rival gangs and no quarter could be granted, ever.

Well, that wasn't how Lola had pictured SOAR. She'd pictured camaraderie. She'd pictured a tight team that flew together, partied together, kicked ass together, and unquestionably had each other's backs. Lola would lay safe ten-to-one money that Kee wouldn't even miss Lola if she fell over dead this instant.

The feeling was mutual. If Kee was shot, there was no chance that afterward Lola'd be wishing it had been her instead of Kee.

Then she glanced to her right and eyed the Major. Not that you could see anything beyond the helmet not much smaller than an astronaut's, the full flight suit, survival vest, and FN SCAR carbine folded across her chest, but she sat there like an absolute rock. An icon to her crew.

Lola wanted that. Suddenly wanted it so bad it was like a knot in her chest. So sharp that if she didn't know better, she'd think she was having a heart attack. But it wasn't.

Nor was it envy.

It was hope. A hopeless hope. She knew the combination well, and the diagnosis was easy—she was totally screwed. She could dream of being like Beale all she wanted. She could strive all she wanted.

And in the end she'd choke on it.

Then Major Beale took her hand off the collective control, not a problem as Lola was pilot-in-control at the moment and Beale was just feathering along out of habit.

But what she did was rub that hand gently across her

belly despite all of the heavy gear. A gesture Lola had
seen many times in Mama Raci's Storyville kitchen.
When some working girl would come in, scared to death
and knowing she was—

Beale jerked her head around at Lola's gasp and then
punched mute on the intercom. Not just for her station,
but for the whole chopper. She never did that. Major
Beale always kept all of the comm channels open so that
her crew was always informed.

Lola agreed wholeheartedly. She didn't like her first
trainer who had insisted on isolating the back-enders
from strategic chatter with other birds or the Air Mission
Controller. Kee and Connie had their butts on the line
just like Lola and the Major, so they deserved to know
what was going on at all times.

It took Beale three tries but she finally managed to set
the intercom so that only she and Lola were in the circuit.

"Not one word!" With that tone, Emily's voice could
have commanded a battalion to fly into the valley of
death. "I'm late is all. I'm just late. Not a word to the
crew. Not to Mark. Not to anyone. Do you understand
me? Not one word."

"Yes, sir!" Lola snapped it out instinctively even as
Henderson began curving his helicopter down toward
a landing in the middle of nowhere. She checked the
charts again, truly nowhere southwest Pakistan.

"May I ask one question, Major?"

Beale paused before suddenly puffing out a breath
and in a much quieter voice saying, "Go ahead. Ask it."

"If you're not 'just late,' are you to be congratulated
that there will be another generation of Viper in the
world? Or not?"

Again the silence and the long puff of breath as Lola landed in desert-nowhere-in-particular, close behind Major Henderson.

If the rotors hadn't already been winding down and the cabin growing quieter with the last of the descent, Lola would not have heard the expectant mother's response despite the intercom feeding her voice directly to Lola's helmet.

"Damned if I know, Chief Warrant. Damned if I know."

Lola reached across and squeezed the hand of the Major, who clutched at it convulsively. Lola's left hand on the collective, the Major's right hand controlling the cyclic, they descended the last few dozen feet together.

"It'll be okay, Major."

"How do you know?"

Lola laughed and tightened her grip to match the Major's.

"Damned if I do, Major. But it's what Mama Raci always told the girls who came into her kitchen to tell her they'd just ruined their livelihood."

"Was it okay?" The Major's voice was a bit thin and breathless. Grasping for hope.

All Lola could do was shrug and tell the truth as the wheels touched the ground. "Not often, but sometimes. Sometimes it was definitely alright."

Beale waved Lola off from the shutdown, so she jumped down to see what they were doing out here in the untracked desert. She peeled her helmet just in time to get a face full of dust from the big Chinook that landed right behind them.

Once their rotors began winding down, she heard

Major Henderson's call from where he stood by the other Hawk, "Wrap 'em up tight." Well, that answered that. They weren't going to be staying anywhere local, nor returning soon to Bati. They were headed beyond the range of a simple chopper flight.

In moments Connie and Kee had closed the cargo bay doors, exposing the footholds built into the side of the chopper behind the door. They scrambled up onto the top of the fuselage. Lola grabbed a monkey-line strap from where it hung inside her door.

The two women up top shoved the rotors around until the fixed blade lined up with the tail, then they set to work unpinning the remaining blades one by one from the rotor's head.

Lola went to the end of the blade they were working on and heaved the strap up and over its tip.

"Walk 'er in," Connie called out softly, and Lola grabbed the two strap ends and began towing the released blade around on its pivot, dragging it toward the tail. When she got it nearly to the tail, she slid the strap free and the blade swung home under its own momentum, nestled against the blade already lying in place.

Lola still wasn't used to the five-blade rig. The blades were quieter and the rig let them fly faster than the standard four-blade Hawk. She was starting to learn that because the blades were shorter, she could slew a turn about ten percent harder. The DAP Hawk with the five blades and the bigger engines really did make her feel all-powerful when she flew.

So why did she feel so powerless in the face of this crew?

Major Beale arrived at her shoulder, and they watched

the two crew chiefs finish buttoning down the blade and start unpinning the next one.

Without turning to Lola, the Major whispered, "Not a soul."

Lola only had to think a moment to realize the comment wasn't about the mission, but rather about the possible change to the Major's future. Lola raised her right hand in a three-fingered salute. "Scout's honor."

"You were a Girl Scout?"

"No." Lola grinned at some of the memories. "But I tripped more than my fair share of Boy Scouts. Does that count?"

Beale laughed aloud. "God, it feels good to laugh. We were careful. We were always so damned careful."

"Nothing's a hundred percent. How long have you known?"

"Yesterday. Maybe."

Lola could hear the tentative in the Major's voice. "Not a lot of pee sticks in a forward operations theater. The military still isn't used to women."

"I know. Ticks me off."

Lola could think of a thousand things that ticked her off about how the military didn't understand women, but that was something you signed up for. You had to outfly, outfight, and outsmart the men, especially in the lower services. By the time you got to SOAR, the worst of the jerks had been winnowed out, a surprising number actually.

It was just surreal that the ones she was having problems with were the women. Lola towed the third blade around for the crew chiefs before returning to the Major's side.

"You do recall that I used to fly CSAR?" she asked the Major.

"I do. Remember you saving my butt. Literally."

And Lola had. "Wasn't sure you remembered that. You were pretty far out of it by the time I came along."

"Not that far."

Again Lola's respect for the woman went up another notch. Concussion and pain and way too much blood loss, and the Major had not only completed the mission but remembered the medical crew who had come for her. No, more likely she remembered the pilot who had finished flying her helicopter home when she was no longer capable.

"Well, I've restocked our med kit knowing we'd have four women on board. I'll get you a couple EPT sticks the next moment no one is around."

"You stocked a military bird, a DAP Hawk, with early pregnancy tests?" Lola could feel the woman's smile in the dark. "Thanks, Lola. I'm really glad you're aboard."

Lola laughed but couldn't hide the bitter edge to it. "That makes you and nobody else."

"What do you mean?"

"Connie won't speak to me."

"She doesn't speak to anyone except Big John. Mr. Garrulous and Ms. Silent. No one understands that relationship except them, and I guess they're the only two that matter. But don't take that one personally."

"Sergeant Stevenson wishes I were dead."

Lola could see Emily's nod in the dark. "She does. That one you're going to have to work out."

"Why me?" Lola felt cornered. Trapped. They walked

side by side as she hauled the next rotor blade into place and returned to wait for the last one.

"Part of being a pilot. You are responsible for making your crew into a team."

"But it's your team."

Lola could hear the distant roar of the big jet engines that must be on a C-5 Galaxy transport, the only military plane big enough to carry the Chinook and both of their Hawks.

Beale didn't bother responding, she just stood there.

Someone must have scattered some infrared markers to lay out an impromptu runway in the desert.

If Beale really was pregnant, Lola would bet she'd want to keep the kid. Most of the girls in Mama Raci's wanted to keep the kid, even when they didn't dare or couldn't afford to.

The C-5 roared down onto the desert a couple thousand meters away, quickly looming larger and larger in the night. The reversers doubling the volume and tripling the dust cloud that the transport kicked up as it came in. An experienced desert pilot would be throttling back right about now to make sure he didn't get lost in his own personal dust storm. Right on cue, the engine roar faded and the jet rolled more slowly toward them.

If Beale kept the kid, she'd be out of the pilot's seat almost immediately. Then it really could become Lola's flight.

That thought was even scarier than Tim being all gone on her.

Chapter 25

THE NEXT THIRTY MINUTES OF HAVOC PASSED AS THEY always did—in meticulously ordered and well-orchestrated military mayhem fast enough to keep Lola very warm despite the cooling night air, but slow enough to allow no mistakes.

The monstrous C-5 jet transport, as large as a 747 but lower to the ground, rolled to a stop with its nose less than a rotor from the Chinook. With a characteristic groan, four stories worth of nose cone detached from the fuselage and began swinging up into the air on giant hinges until the nose cone towered high above the cockpit. The raised nose exposed the cavernous cargo bay interior, lit softly in red light to preserve everyone's night vision.

The moment the loading ramp hit the dust, two small tractors descended the ramp. Too small for a person to sit on, but strong enough to move a C-5 fully loaded if they were run in tandem. Two loadmasters followed each tractor, one with a wireless remote control strapped to his wrist. They steered the tractors toward the waiting Black Hawks.

Almost before the two crews could tie down the last blade and scramble out of the way, the C-5 loadmasters had latched the two Black Hawks' front wheels onto the tractors and begun towing them backward onto the looming airplane. Just under a football field long and with a cargo bay that could swallow of couple of Abrams main battle tanks, the C-5 quickly gulped down the DAP Hawks.

By the time they were up the ramp, inside, and tied down, one of the tractor crews came back out to the Chinook. With the help of the D-boys, the SOAR crew had the two three-bladed rotors folded with seconds to spare. Not tens of seconds, but they beat the tractor crew.

All four loadmasters worked to make sure the Chinook made it up the ramp clean and was pegged down so that it couldn't shift in flight. They went over their checklists again, double-checking that the choppers were placed properly on the position markers running down the inside of the plane's cargo bay. Off by just a couple feet and the center of gravity could be far enough off to cripple the jet in flight. Or cause a crash on attempted takeoff.

The ramp was already lifting as the crew stumbled aboard.

As soon as the nose cone thudded into place, the engines roared from idle back to takeoff speeds. In the trackless desert, it didn't matter. No taxiing back to the head of some runway, no other air traffic or buildings in their way. They just continued pointing into the wind and opened up the throttles wide.

Lola checked her watch. Total time on the ground for the C-5, twelve minutes, forty-seven seconds. For the Black Hawks and Chinook, just a few ticks over half an hour. They rotated and became fully airborne faster than Lola and the rest of the SOAR crews could find jump seats down either side of the aircraft and buckle in.

A plane capable of carrying 125 tons shot upward with a load of barely forty-five.

There wasn't any point in asking where they were going. When Major Henderson wanted them to know, he'd tell them.

Once they reached cruising altitude, Lola unbuckled and wandered as nonchalantly as possible toward the rear of the aircraft where *Vengeance* had been tied down.

The Chinook had been resealed. A lone D-boy had apparently decided to toss down his pack and sit on it where he just happened to have a perfect view of both the chopper's rear ramp, where it had picked up the stolen truck, and the pilot's door, both closed. At least the pack was probably more comfortable than the folding jump seats that lined the walls.

Lola rather hoped that his eyes tracked her for her looks instead of the package he was guarding.

What in the world had they uncovered out there? Seemed like a good old snatch-and-grab operation. Gather a bunch of intel and turn it over to the CIA or whoever cared about such things. But a twenty-four-hour watch and a surprise trip on twenty minutes' notice…

Stateside. That's where they were headed. Pentagon probably. They had to be going somewhere seriously secure. New bomb design maybe? Perhaps final proof that the Iranians really had become the planet's newest nuclear power. Maybe their first bomb, stolen right from under their noses.

Well, her current mission had nothing to do with whatever lay inside the Chinook. She was half past the *Viper* when she heard the double footfall close behind her. The sound of someone dropping from the Black

Hawk's cargo deck down to the steel plating of the C-5's deck.

She turned and, sure enough, Tim Maloney stood there looking all handsome and swaggery. It was easy to imagine just letting him wrap her up in his arms and burn away all of her fears about the crew and her own abilities with one of his searing kisses. Well, more than one.

But then again, he was also becoming one of her fears. Time to deal with that. If what she suspected was coming down the pipe at her with Major Beale's news, she didn't need any distractions, no matter how cute.

"Hey there, Sergeant." Lola did her best to keep her voice light.

"Hey, yourself." He took one of those easy, swagger-style steps toward her, but stopped when she took a step back.

She could see the puzzled look flicker across his face. Crap! She was setting up to hurt him, and for the first time, she cared enough about a man to not want to do that. How do you let a guy down easy? No one had ever taught her that and she'd never bothered to learn. If they bore you or get all possessive, you boot 'em out and move on. She didn't want to do that to him.

"Tim, I—"

It was as far as she got before Big John clambered out of *Viper* much more lightly than his smaller friend. He eyed Lola for a moment, then smacked a hand down on Tim's shoulder with enough force to have driven a lesser man two feet into the steel decking.

"Hey, Timmy. Poker game setting up. C'mon."

For a moment she thought John might try tucking

Tim under his arm. That would be impossible for any man smaller than John, but he just settled for a headlock. He looked back over his shoulder at her as he dragged Tim away toward the front of the plane.

"Connie's playing and I need someone to be putting dough in my wife's pocket besides me. She doesn't share her winnings." His voice was light and funny, his look back to her was anything but. The message was clear—if she hurt Tim, the rest of the crew was going to turn on her, and turn on her hard.

Merde! She didn't sign up for this shit! Nothing was making any sense. And now she was all tied up in whatever they'd found in the bloody desert before she could even settle in properly. A dozen flights, a couple of really fine kisses, and now her world was comin' apart at the seams. She hadn't even gotten any real sex out of the deal.

Maybe she'd taken a wrong turn out of CSAR, should never have joined SOAR. Or picking up Beale in the middle of Poland in the dead of night. Never should have accepted that mission.

Beale. Right. Lola had a small mission and wasn't even getting that done. A quick check showed she was finally alone. She clambered aboard the *Vengeance*, sat on the cargo deck, and rummaged around behind the cargo net until she found the extra med kit in a small, bright red duffel that she'd stowed behind the .50 cal ammo. Bottom right corner farthest from where the zipper opened. She pulled out two sticks, thought better of it, and scooped a third into her grip before pulling them out.

"Pooh the Bear keeps honey jars in his pantry."

Lola spun around. She snagged the three white-plastic-wrapped packages on the safety netting and they scattered across the cargo deck. Dilya, the little kid, was sitting in the shadows on Kee's gunner seat. Her book sat in her lap. A small book light cast a soft glow onto the open pages, which was how Lola had missed her in the dimly lit end of the jet's cargo bay.

"Mary Lennox found her key under the ground. She keeps it in her pocket. What does La Roo keep in her helicopter?"

"Uh." Lola collected the pregnancy test packets and slipped them into a thigh pocket. "Medicine."

"Is La Roo sick? Piglet had the worst case of hiccups once. Could you make him better?"

"No. He did? Maybe."

Dilya nodded her head with the sage wisdom of an elder crone.

"Mary Lennox has met a very sick boy. Maybe she can make him better."

Lola almost said, "She did." But that would give the ending away. "Uh, when you finish the book, you can let me know. I like to make people better."

"With medicine?"

"With medicine."

The girl was quiet for long enough that Lola had time to restow the med kit, fasten the cargo net, and consider leaving. But something made her wait. Lean back against the net and the steel ammo boxes and just wait for the little girl to think her thoughts.

"Making people better is more good than making people dead?"

It was. But it wasn't the choice she'd made. She'd

gone from Search and Rescue to a DAP Hawk, from saving lives to taking them. Which had saved more people? Picking broken bodies off battlefields one by one, or killing the bad guys before they killed others?

"Sometimes," she answered the girl's silence. "Not always."

Again, the crone's nod of wisdom.

"Dilya only help make people dead. Not good. Dilya not do that no more."

"Anymore," some knee-jerk part of Lola's brain offered up. At her age, Dilya had helped make people dead?

"Anymore," Dilya responded. This little girl who had apparently dispensed death also worked at correcting her English. She returned to her book. "I let La Roo know if Mary Lennox makes little boy better or dead."

Clearly dismissed, Lola left the helicopter and moved toward the front of the plane. Walking away from the little girl for whom death was as natural as life.

Lola liked flying the Hawk. Liked reaching out and saving people before they were hurt, even if it meant hurting others. She'd chosen to believe that those she fought to save were worth saving and those who wished them dead—those who flew planes into the Twin Towers— were wrong and best off removed as fast as possible.

But it left her queasy and a little unnerved as she walked up the length of the roaring cargo bay. The massive jet engines, barely a dozen feet away through a very thin fuselage, washed the bay in noise so thick you could cut it up with a knife. This was a military cargo jet, not some dressed-up passenger liner. No pretty beige walls, carpeting, or little plastic windows. The only way to tell night from day was to glance up at the flight deck three flights of steel stairs above the cargo deck and look for light through the pilot's windshield. No security doors around the pilots. Again military, no need.

No light shone down from above. Clearly night, wherever they were. No one had said where they were headed, so no one had asked. They'd taken off right after sunset. If they were indeed flying to the States, they'd be in darkness the whole way, chasing the night halfway around the planet.

The only lights this far back in the bay were the small, red jump lights. Up forward, everyone was hanging around the front of the Chinook. She could hear their voices and laughter, a muffled overlay to the engine's noise. The D-boy who'd been pretending to relax while watching the locked-up Chinook had set up on the other side of the bay.

From the shadow of *Viper*, a shadow separated itself from behind a 20 mm chain gun hanging from a weapon's mounting hard point.

Lola slipped the three packets into Major Beale's hand and said very softly, "Pee on the end, wait three minutes. Even if all three come back positive, it could be false. Still see the doc."

"I'm so looking forward to a career-changing talk with a doctor." Beale's voice almost cracked. The Major held Lola's hand for a long moment of thanks and bestowed a brief hug before moving off.

Lola didn't know which was more unnerving, a child who talked of causing death or a grown woman whose hands shook with the possibility of life.

Chapter 26

TIM HAD WAITED FOR HIS OPPORTUNITY. HE'D LOST A quick twenty bucks at the poker game, not much left to chance when Connie and Major Henderson were facing off. Then he'd found a sandwich and stood back a step as Big John managed to take two hands in a row.

Tim faded down the side of the Chinook and nodded to the watching D-boy. After eight years in, Tim had learned to just accept what came next, at least on the Army side of life. He'd find out what they'd uncovered in the Iranian desert soon enough. Probably too soon once the truth was told.

Dilya drifted by, a book clutched in her hands, probably headed forward for food. A full year since they'd rescued her from starving in the heart of the Hindu Kush, and she still ate like a vacuum cleaner. She'd eat six meals a day if she could, often did, and all she did was grow a little taller. The gaunt was gone, showing that she'd be a great beauty some day, but still just a slip of a kid.

Always a bit too serious except around Archie, always a little reserved except around Kee. Tim messed up her hair as she went by. She brushed it aside enough to show her world-deep eyes and her smile before continuing forward.

As Tim crossed into the shadow between the Chinook and Henderson's *Viper*, he spotted Lola and

Beale having a little tête-à-tête. Tim pulled back into the shadow to give them their moment and finish his sandwich. He couldn't hear them over the engine noise, but he could see that whatever the conversation was, it had drawn them close.

Even in jeans, a T-shirt, and a light vest, Major Beale still radiated strength and power. The woman was pure, unbending military. Tim knew from long experience that she was unflappable, never blinked first, and the best damn pilot he'd ever met. Other than with her husband, Major Beale never showed anything beyond pure military. The perfect, textbook, kick-ass-and-don't-take-names blond.

Lola, by contrast, slouched casually against the side of the Black Hawk while they talked. While Beale's off-the-shelf jeans fit nicely enough, Lola's followed every skintight curve. She wore a dark blouse of thin material that both revealed and hid her shape. Unbuttoned enough to suggest no bra without actually revealing the truth of the promise. Her natural stance heavily flavored with casual, she could look like she was leaning comfortably against the air if nothing stood nearby for her to lean on.

Everything that was so perfectly controlled in the Major was loose and easy on Lola. Her dark hair fell in long, messy waves. Burying his face in that soft mass had been a true joy, one he was looking forward to repeating at the first opportunity. Where the Major's hands were quiet, Lola's waved about and shaped the air as she spoke. And all of the Major's serious attitude turned to smiles and head nods in Lola.

Yet for all of the contrasts, there was a similarity deep inside. Something that made both of them fly like no man he'd ever seen. When they flew, it was some kind of magic. He'd spent more time than he should have watching them fly nearby on missions. He could tell instantly who had the controls.

Major Beale was a surgeon, always in exactly the right place at exactly the right moment.

Lola LaRue was a dancer, a quick bob-and-weave placing her where the casual observer would least expect, suddenly hammering away at the exact heart of the problem but from a wholly unexpected direction.

Kee's distrust of Chief Warrant Lola LaRue had set him back on his heels. Kee was wicked savvy about people. And with Lola her dislike was deep and wide, though she still refused to explain why. Her attitude had made him doubt what he was feeling.

But here was Major Beale, clearly trusting Lola deeply. The Major had always taken weeks and sometimes months to burn in a new crew member, doing easy runs in patrol zones, then light action before trusting them with full-action missions. Even then, they had to earn her full stamp of approval through some extraordinary action, like Kee stopping a war or Connie stopping a holocaust.

Major Beale was the litmus test of SOAR. Within a week, he'd seen her discard plenty of fliers that any other commander would have been thrilled to keep.

With Lola, Beale had taken her to the front lines on the first mission. Now, after just a couple weeks, when Beale might normally let a newbie know they had a chance of being almost acceptable if they just tried harder, she was being all friendly with her new copilot. Actually gave her a long, tight hug before returning forward.

He felt almost as dazed as Lola appeared to be. The Major never did that. Ever.

Lola remained there in the shadows, blinking rapidly after the Major. Turning one way and then the other but not going anywhere, as if she couldn't get her feet moving. Finally just leaning back against the chopper and hanging her head as if exhausted.

Tim came to her, as if drawn by a stout cargo-lifting line, unable to simply watch her wrestle with whatever was in her heart. She didn't startle when she spotted him. She raised her gaze until he stopped a mere breath away.

He waited there. Waited for her. He'd never wanted a woman so much, to hold, to help, to care for. Normally, he'd make some joke, slide an arm around the likely woman's waist, and pull her in. He'd earned a few slaps, but only a few. His timing and judgment had long since been honed with practice.

With Lola, he stood and waited.

Even in the dim lighting, he could see the tears in her eyes. Not weeping, he'd never seen her cry, but far from her normal laugh-at-it-all self.

She didn't wrap her arms around his neck and bury her face on his shoulder. As if she were made of stronger stuff, she just leaned there and looked at him, eye to eye. She swallowed, a lovely motion on her long neck, and blinked a few more times. Then without a change of expression, she slid a hand into his. The shock of contact coursed up his arm and straight down his body.

Not releasing her hold, she turned and headed for the very rear of the jet. As they passed the *Vengeance*, she stopped for a moment and indicated he should stay where he stood. She ducked inside for a moment, then once again led him to the rear of the cargo bay.

The massive rear clamshell doors sloped upward from the cargo deck at a forty-five-degree angle like a rising hillside twenty feet wide and more than that tall. The rear rotor and tail section of the *Vengeance* cast a shadow of near impenetrable darkness. When Lola stepped into it, she simply disappeared.

Tim stepped into the darkness with her. When he did, she did exactly as he first imagined—turned and slid up against him. Wrapped her arms about him and buried her face against his shoulder, holding on as tight as she could.

He slipped his hands around that perfect waist and held her tight. Traced up the length of those magnificent shoulder muscles that only soldier-training could develop. Civilians simply didn't train at the level of a soldier, not the workout queens, not the aerobics instructors, none of them compared. Especially not to the standards of a Special Forces soldier.

Her hair. He buried his face in her hair and breathed her in. Inhaled the intoxicant of her skin, breathed in until he became light-headed.

His hunger for her at the end of the last mission was no less now, but instead of ravenous, it took a gentle, savoring turn. He nuzzled her neck, tasted her earlobe with a light tug of his teeth, kissing her on the eyelids after they had fluttered shut.

His hands that had previously been so greedy for butt and breast now lost themselves in her hair, cradling her head as he kissed her, digging fingers into over-tight shoulder muscles until she groaned against his lips.

Her fingers slid up into his hair and massaged until all he could do was stand there with his forehead against hers and revel in the sensation. With an easy motion, she pulled him down enough to kiss his forehead, then guided him lower.

She encouraged him to feast on collarbone, one of her finest features on a startlingly beautiful woman. His fingers leading the way, he unbuttoned her blouse, the promise of no bra come true, but opened it no wider than the trail down to her belly. He knelt before her and nuzzled the impossible soft flesh there, and all she did was encourage, hold on, and press him closer, her hands still in his hair.

His hands traveled where his tongue did not, discovering what a perfect, generous handful her breasts made against his palm. How the lower curve of her glutes stood proudly above powerful thighs, a well-defined and awesome behind.

Her strength lay in long layers of smooth muscle. He never moved his head from where his cheek rested against her belly, cradled in her long-fingered hands, not as he studied the curve of her calf, not as he explored every curve back up the length of her body. He wished he could memorize her, every shape, every inch, every taste.

He leaned back to look up at her in the dark. He couldn't see her face, shrouded in a deeper darkness by her hair cascading down either side, but he knew she looked at him just as intently.

There was no need for the question. Nor the answer.

Tim pulled her down atop him as he leaned back against the cargo bay doors.

———

Lola sank to her knees over Tim. Let herself sink until they lay pressed so close together that what little clothing separated them didn't matter. Wasn't there. Just her heart pounding against his.

She slid down enough to lay her ear on his chest and listen to the quick double-beat of his heart. His hands gathered and combed her hair with a gentleness belied by their size and strength. She'd watched him hammering the side of a powerful fist on a reluctant piece of Black Hawk, trying to repair a panel. Another time, when an armorer's lift broke, Tim had easily helped him lift fresh munitions onto the chopper's hardpoint mounts.

And he brushed her hair through his fingers as if he were little more than a breath of spring breeze.

She lay there, her body buzzing but oddly content to remain silently tended while she listened to the double-tap of his heart. But the buzz in her body kept growing, and Tim's clearly had similar feelings. There was no mistaking the point of contact where his hips lined up with her belly.

She sat up and began undoing his pants, testing shape and texture as she went. The hard, six-pack abs. The soft hair tickling the backs of her fingers, the impossibly smooth skin where hip met upper thigh.

When she cupped him, he made the first sound that had passed between them, the low moan of a beast in pain, exquisite pain.

She toyed with him, slowly, gently, feeling him get harder and harder until she could take his pulse there against her palm.

Without releasing him, she leaned forward to kiss him. He slid his hands up inside her open blouse until he supported her weight easily with her breasts against his palms. As if she were as light as a feather. As if she were floating.

"I don't..." he managed to groan out before she covered his mouth with hers.

His kisses were so strong, so powerful that she momentarily forgot her hand still wrapped around him or his palms pressing against her breasts. Tim's lips could drive a woman mad. Soft, teasing, lush. Backed by strong teeth that nipped and pulled and a stronger tongue that drove as greedily against hers as hers did on his.

She knew what he meant, of course. She sat back up and freed one hand. Slipping it into a pocket, she held forth the foil packet she'd snagged from the chopper's med kit.

His soft noises as she rolled it over him were all she needed to make her sure.

She'd wanted to be held. Needed to be held. Tim had done that. Made her have needs beyond mere release.

Lola had hoped that, with some sex, she could stop all that was going on in her head. Tim had offered an opportunity to do that.

But he'd given her more. From that impossibly deep strength wrapped around his heart, he'd offered her far more than she'd ever anticipated.

He was making love.

She stripped out of her pants, until only her open blouse covered her.

He was making love with her.

She settled down over him where he lay against the cargo bay doors.

This one time she would let it happen.

They moved together in such perfect harmony that neither of them could have spoken had their lives depended on it.

She would let herself be made love to.

He drove upward into her until she floated, feeling nothing but where they connected at hip, hand, and lips. Filled so thoroughly in body and soul.

She would let herself love back.

For the moment.

For this one time.

When she came, and he followed her over the peak, she floated free of herself and simply reveled in the cleansing waves that rippled up and down her body.

Floated 35,000 feet above the world.

Had the clamshell doors supporting them swung open and tumbled them out to float in space, she could not have felt lighter than this moment as she lay against Tim. His hands cradling her like a lover as the last shivers slid up their bodies in perfect harmony.

Chapter 27

THEY MOVED TO THE FRONT OF THE PLANE SEPARATELY. She sent Tim ahead well in the lead.

Standing alone in the dark and the roar at the rear of the plane, Lola tried to convince herself it had just been sex. Much needed sex.

She'd have been able to convince herself if she couldn't hear the memory of Mama Raci's cackle. A fifteen-year-old Lola had asked her about love.

"It is de woman's power to take de mind from de mon. She can make de mon stone blind until he see no one but she. It is de mon's power to take de woman's heart until she can no find it nowheres else but in him's arms."

Lola cursed the crazy old woman who had become her only family. Cursed her for her coarse ways, her harsh love, and for dying when Lola still needed her so badly.

Game face, Lola. Game face. She braced her insides, took a couple deep breaths, and ran her fingers through her hair one more time. She did her best to effect a lazy stroll as she moved forward to join the others at the head of the plane.

The first thing Lola noticed when she arrived was where Tim stood at the edge of the poker game. It also struck her that he was the handsomest man in a circle of very handsome men.

The second thing that struck her was the way Major Emily Beale sat close beside her husband, hands wrapped around his upper arm, her head resting on his shoulder.

Major Mark Henderson might be concentrating on his poker game with his legendary card-sharp prowess, but it was clear what answer his wife had found about the change that would be entering their future in just under nine months. Her head curled against his shoulder, her arms around his neck, her eyes closed.

The rest of the crew were clearly trying to hide their shock, but they couldn't stop looking over at the two Majors, so far out of character. Mark's ease with his wife's action was a view into how they were together in private. But it was obviously the first time anyone had seen even a hint of it in public. PDA, public display of affection. Not just their normal holding hands, this was serious PDA.

Well, this was going to be damned interesting and Lola wanted a front-row seat.

Henderson called Connie's play and his three ladies beat her two pair high.

"Room for another soldier?" She grabbed a soda from the cooler and stood at an empty crate positioned like a seat.

Henderson looked up and considered her over his wife's head. Major Beale popped open her eyes and aimed a worried look at Lola. As soon as it became clear that Lola had a poker face about more than card games, Beale offered a quick, shy smile. At Lola's nod, she slowly relaxed back into her favored position against her husband.

Henderson's eyes, hidden as usual by mirrored Ray-Bans that must turn the darkened cargo bay into an eerie black cavern, clearly inspected her.

"If you've got the chops. And the cash."

"I won't need the cash, but I've got it. And I've got Creole chops. You ain't messing with that, *mon cher*, no matter what you be thinking." She laid it on thick. Mama Raci's old voice coming almost as easily as her own.

An ancient, black, uneducated brothel cook. Probably never read a book, but well-educated in the ways of the world. An education she'd worked hard to pass on to Lola. A crone to the girls who worked there, but the closest thing Lola had to a mother. She'd first come into that kitchen while hiding from her father's groping friends at seven years old and later when she'd finally left home for good at twelve.

Henderson looked around the circle. Big John and Connie sat on opposite sides of the small table. Archie Stevenson, all long and thin, sat between the Major and Connie. Colonel Gibson of the D-boys sat between her and Big John. This placed them all shoulder to shoulder, have to be very careful to not reveal your cards.

Tim and a couple of the D-boys milled around behind the card players. Dilya and Kee sat on a pair of jump seats along the side wall, reading the ever-present book together. Lola found herself hoping that the boy was doing well in the care of Mary Lennox. Hoped that his recovery might offer even more brightness to the dark child. And maybe a tiny bit to rub off on her adopted mother.

The Major cleared his throat and kissed his wife absently on the top of her head. "All in favor of letting the wild Creole play, y'all better ante up." He flashed one of his killer grins at her. "Your deal, LaRue."

Lola took the deck and riffled it a few times quickly. The sharp snap and slap of the cards was one of many tricks she'd learned in the Storyville brothel. If you appeared really competent with the cards themselves, it unnerved your opponent more than they might like or comprehend. She'd spent hours and hours learning to manipulate the cards.

Not that she couldn't deal a mean deck.

She started spinning out the cards, keeping her voice loud enough to be heard over all the background noise of jet roar.

"Seven-card straight, that's the game." Twice around. Just before tossing down the first faceup card, she added, "Suicide king, wild."

"Oh, give me a break. That isn't poker." A couple of them protested, others settled in to the play.

"You give the girl the deal," Lola crooned in her old woman voice, "you no say anything about no special rule." She called the cards as she dropped the first round. "Nine, seven, a pretty lady for the Major," as she dropped the Queen of Diamonds in front of him. "A deuce, a ten-spot, and a—"

When she dropped the last faceup card of the first round on her own pile, the King of Hearts lay there stabbing a sword into his head.

"Oo." Lola let out her crone's laugh, the one that had always creeped her out when Mama Raci let it loose upon the world. The woman had always found the strangest things funny.

Tim sidled closer to watch the game, but she couldn't

be thinking about him right now, she had a card game to play. Yet he remained there, on the edge of her awareness. God, he'd made her feel good.

Lola didn't even bother to look at her hole cards. She watched the other players as they did inspect theirs.

The D-boy colonel clearly didn't play poker much, but D-boys were tricky, so she'd keep an eye on him. He could be playing the fake inside the fake. He had one of those rugged faces, not one you'd ever find in a magazine, but one that you'd learn to trust and appreciate with time. A face of strength, but how well he could play poker, that was a different question. The small smile that Colonel Gibson aimed her way told her that he was well aware of her scrutiny. Definitely expect the fake-within-the-fake is what that smile told her. Unless he was faking.

Big John, just like you'd expect, looked like a stone wall of grim determination. The Major was expressionless and oddly careful not to show his cards to his wife, despite her not being in the game.

Archie's lips definitely tightened, and she'd bet not in a good way. Connie, the silent mechanic, now there was clearly her main opponent. Lola couldn't read a single thing about the girl. This was going to be fun.

Everyone bet cautiously, except Archie who folded.

"An eight, possible straight." Lola started dealing down the next round. "A four, a bad inside straight. A deuce, the Captain, he should have stayed in the game, he should. But the deuce, she does the woman no good at all. And a Jack of Hearts for little Lola. Lola she bets two bucks."

This cleared Connie from the table, which was

information in itself. Her cards weren't that bad, she was clearly messing with the other players' heads and it would come around as payback three or four hands from now. Master poker player.

On the third round they all held, but the last card up killed off the Colonel.

Last card down and it could still be anyone's hand. Big John studied his final card carefully. Lola flipped up the corner of the last card. Maybe. Just maybe. Depended on the first two cards, but she still didn't look at those. Didn't want to get her hopes up. Didn't matter if she won or lost the first few hands, it was what she learned about the others, especially whether or not she could scare them.

Big John could be spooked and folded.

"You are a wise man no to mess with the Creole Queen."

The Major wasn't looking at his cards, he was watching her. That smile that made him so handsome tugging at the corner of his mouth. She'd also wager that few outside of his and his wife's crew even knew the man could smile.

He hadn't inspected his last card. He was going into it almost as blind as she was.

"Five to stay, mister. You play or you gonna run away?"

He tossed the fiver into the pot.

She considered raising him blind, but left it alone. Letting him call.

She pulled up a second jack. With the wild king, it could be three of a kind. From the first two cards she'd not seen, she dug out a pair of threes for a very nice full house. Jacks over threes.

"Can you beat dat, meester?"

Her smile, she knew, was as big as his.

His first two hole cards left him with three queens and three pieces of crap. But if the last hole card matched anything, she was toast.

"I'm counting on you, my queen," he informed Major Beale before turning the last, unseen card.

Another queen rolled into view. Four of a kind.

It was worth it to hear his roar of laughter and the tight, hard hug he gave the woman at his side. Her smile bloomed huge.

Definitely worth the loss, at least until Henderson raked in Lola's money along with everyone else's.

Okay, mostly worth the loss.

Chapter 28

THE DOWN PITCH OF THE FOUR JET ENGINES WOKE Lola for the C-5's descent. Some water and a slightly stale turkey sandwich from an Air Force cooler helped wake her up. The hundred bucks in poker winnings in her pocket as she changed into her flight suit left her feeling positively cheerful despite not enough sleep lying on the hard deck.

By the time they hit the tarmac, they'd been in flight for fourteen hours and several midair refuelings. Sleep on a couple blankets over the steel decking left her stiff, and she did some stretches along with the others to work out the kinks.

Frankly she'd have preferred to curl up somewhere cozy with Tim, but there were some things you didn't do with a sergeant, like getting caught in a relationship. Especially when you were a chief warrant.

A relationship? Was that what they had?

Crap!

That thought blasted the last of the sleep and most of the poker-winnings joy from her mind. She glanced over at Tim, strapped in a couple of jump seats down, while the plane turned from runway to taxiway. He looked better in a flight suit than most guys in a tuxedo. And when he was happy, it just slayed her. Like now. He was laughing about something with Big John, all cheerful and at ease with himself. He and Big John were like peas in a pod. No question who would be best man at Tim's wedding.

Double crap!

She really had to get the man out of her head. Out of her blood. She wished she could go and get one of Mama Raci's useless potions and accompanying good advice. But Lola hadn't been back to New Orleans in years, not since after Katrina when she'd discovered that the hurricane had taken the only person she cared about from the face of the planet.

Mama Raci had survived the Great Depression, race riots, civil rights, police crackdowns on the bordellos, and who knew how many waves of gang wars that swept across New Orleans every decade or so—from Prohibition to the Bloods and Crips to the new "clique" gangs ruled by individual OGs. No original gangster was stupid enough to mess with Mama Raci. She had hidden powers that no one understood, not even Lola.

She'd survived a lifetime in the worst neighborhood in the nation's deadliest city. She'd ridden out Katrina and all of the bloody desecrations that followed, only to die in the aftermath due to bad water and no medical care.

Lola hadn't been there to evacuate her. Her service range hadn't been around Storyville. Her National Guard unit had been working the coast and a couple of badly damaged offshore rigs.

She tried to imagine what Mama Raci would say to her grown-up adoptive girl, if she were still around. What she would say about Lola finally being totally charmed by a man?

Lola glanced sideways at Tim again. Careful not to indicate that she was aware of how he was watching her.

Charmed? Crap a third time. Who was she kidding? Other than herself? Mama R. had always said Lola was the world expert at that. She'd done her best to purge it from her system and yet here it was again.

She closed her eyes for a moment as the plane made its final slow, smooth turns to wherever they were parking. "Straight up, girl!" She could hear the old woman's voice. "If you can no be truth with self, you can no be truth with no mon."

Straight up. Sex with Tim was brain-crunchingly awesome. But that wasn't where he was getting past her armor. It was all that gentle aimed at her from such a powerful man. She could lose herself in the world of safety that seemed to surround him wherever he went. He battered at her defenses with a world she knew nothing about. A world she'd always assumed to be a fairy tale.

The plane finally rocked to a halt and the engines began to wind down after more than a half day of service.

There was no man Lola would ever be spending her life with. Not no how.

But the man looking right at her with those dark, gentle eyes, him she could spend some serious chunk of time with. *Could do that easy, mon, vera easy.*

<hr />

Fourteen hours of nothing turned into a full-on military sprint the moment the two ends of the C-5's cargo bay opened up. A wave of cool, fresh air washed through the cargo hold.

Tim didn't choke on a cloud of dust or gag on smells that were an overripe mixture of cooked lamb and raw sewage spread upon local farmer's fields. He stepped out onto the rear ramp and breathed deeply to fill his lungs with good old USA-brand air. They were parked inside a massive hangar, one big enough to swallow a C-5, which was saying something.

Then he froze. One of the C-5's loadmasters actually had to shove him aside to clear the ramp. There was another plane parked beside theirs in the hangar. The overhead lights were soft on the blue-and-white paint job of the most famous 747 of them all, Air Force One. They were at Andrews, inside the hangar for the President's personal transport.

No one was allowed in here without massive security clearance.

That's when he noticed the phalanx of guards. Every twenty feet between Air Force One and their C-5. Each soldier held an M-16 at ready arms. From that position they could target and fire in less than a second. Way less. So, the Army had been allowed inside the hangar, but that didn't mean the Air Force was one bit happy about it.

He leaned over toward John. "Opportunity, my friend."

"Oh, no."

Tim sidestepped before John could grab him and muzzle him.

"Howdy, boys!" he called over in his best country yokel voice. "How're y'all doin' tonight?"

Not even a peep of a response.

"When are they gonna let you Chair Force nuggets fly a bird that doesn't have an autopilot to hold your hand every inch of the way?" He slapped the nose of the *Vengeance* as they trundled her down the rear ramp.

"The same time you learn to fly something better than an army lawn dart," a master sergeant called back from the line. "Goddamn Crash Hawk jock." "Lawn dart" for how abruptly some of the early Black Hawks fell from the sky after their tails fell off.

By the time Tim turned back, they had the *Vengeance* clear and the *Viper* was coming down the rear ramp. Through the vast cavern of the C-5 open at both ends, he could see that they had the Chinook going out the front.

Connie and Kee were unfolding the first blade of *Vengeance*. Well, no way two girls were gonna outdo him and John just because they were unloaded first. Clearly John was of the same mind. He slapped a wrench into Tim's palm, and they were both climbing up the sides of their bird while the loadmasters were still rolling it out.

Tim gave a final shout as he reached the top of his bird, "Got no time for a lousy slick sleeve." Which was about six ranks and twenty years low for the Air Force master sergeant.

That earned him a single bark of laughter. A quick glance revealed that the rest of the Air Force squad hadn't eased off from their alert position by a single millimeter.

He bent to work with a good heart. Always worth the extra moment to demean another arm of the service. And how often did a guy get a chance to tease the crew of Air Force One? Now he had to make up for the wasted time.

It was a close thing, but he and John pinned the fifth and last blade into place just before the girls. Maybe only by a minute, maybe half a minute, but they were first. Henderson and Richardson were right on the pre-flight, but Lola and Beale were on the hustle too.

"Just not gonna happen!" He didn't need to guess what John was talking about. Tim jumped from the top of the bird, landing with a roll and coming right up on his feet. They pulled engine covers and pitot sleeves while the Captain and Major checked fuel and began powering up instruments.

Weapons locked and loaded, all the covers folded and stowed. Tim and John high-fived with a sharp slap that would have echoed in a smaller space just as the first sound of their turbines began winding up.

Tim glanced out at *Vengeance*.

"Shit!"

John swung over to look out the cargo bay door with him.

"How did they do that? We were awesome!"

Vengeance's rotors were already spinning nicely, while *Viper*'s were just finishing their achingly slow first rotations.

"They cheated," Viper said over the intercom. "Must have."

Tim nodded in agreement. Unless Lola was as good as Beale. If that was true, then the two of them could have done it. Now there was a thought. Someone that good in the sack who was that good in the air. There was an image that made his body burn just sitting here.

When he caught her cheery wave of victory through the windscreen, he considered turning aside as if he hadn't seen it. Too petty. He cast a casual, two-fingered salute. Dilya leaned out the cargo bay door to wave happily so he waved to her as well, then turned away.

To his next surprise.

The C-5 was already gone. In all the hurry, he hadn't

even noticed the hangar doors open to the April night or the quiet sound of the electric tractor dragging the big jet clear.

He glanced over at the Chinook, just now starting up its twin rotors. The D-boys clambered aboard, their rifles slung over their shoulders. A single one trailed behind, scanning the hangar with his sniper rifle at ready arms. For the tenth time, Tim wondered what the hell they had dug up out in the desert.

He didn't like it one bit. In unison, he and John slid into their seats and buckled in, and Tim made sure everything was ready on his minigun. Friendly soil or not, if a D-boy didn't trust it, he wasn't about to either.

The hangar doors opened, allowing the three choppers to roll forward into the night. A glance back showed that the guards still hadn't moved from in front of Air Force One as the hangar doors slid closed behind them. They'd probably spray the floor with disinfectant where the Army helicopter might have touched their precious patch of concrete.

They headed northwest, the National Mall a blaze of light off to the north. In a half-dozen miles, they slipped down low over the Potomac and continued northwest.

No one about. No police choppers. Not many vehicles either, not at four in the morning.

Just three Special Forces military helicopters flying over home soil, ready for battle. Was that even legal? The military was forbidden from carrying out force operations over U.S. soil, courtesy of a half-dozen laws going back a hundred years and presidential orders on top of that. This wasn't force, at least not yet.

But that wasn't his concern. No one was talking

about it on the radio either. The pilots were silent. Communicating by some weird tele-psychic thing SOAR pilots sometimes did, where everyone just knew what to do and where to go.

So he kept his mouth shut and watched the sky and the roads for possible inbounds. Tim wondered if he'd be able to fire at a perceived threat and risk accidentally taking out some guy with his girl looking for a place to neck.

At a large office complex they slowed, staying below a hundred feet.

The Chinook began to settle to the ground as the two DAP hawks hovered above. Langley, Virginia. CIA headquarters. Tim had never been here, no reason. He kept his attention on a sweep of the sky and tried to find enough spit to swallow against a dry throat.

The Chinook swung so that her stern rotor was passing within a dozen feet of the building. Even as the bird touched down, the rear ramp hit the ground and a pair of D-boys were driving the vehicle backwards off the ramp. They didn't even slow or turn, just backed right off the chopper and straight into a garage door that had slid open to receive them moments before it would have been struck. The others stayed on the big bird.

Henderson must have been as fascinated as Tim was. The *Viper* had to suddenly jerk aside to get clear of the ascending Chinook.

The Major let out a long, slow whistle. "Why do I think we haven't seen the last of that?"

"Giving me the willies there, Major." And he was. Tim had fought plenty of battles but not often been creeped out by what he'd seen.

"Well, I'm glad to be rid of that package," Big John rumbled.

"No question. Where to now, sir?"

"Anacostia." The Major headed them south, his voice a little easier. "A bit of down time."

The Chinook turned southwest and climbed into the night. Just before it completely disappeared off the edge of their night-vision gear, its crew turned on their nav lights. Probably making the three-hour transit down to SOAR headquarters in Fort Campbell, Kentucky.

The two DAP Hawks swung in unison back down the Potomac and slipped quietly into Anacostia Naval Support Facility where the U.S. Marines stored the Marine One helicopters for the President. Again, within minutes of landing, they were tucked out of sight inside a closed hangar.

Chapter 29

"Greetings, Nephew."

Mark Henderson climbed down from the *Viper* and saluted the commander of Anacostia smartly. "General Arnson, sir!" He couldn't help smiling down at the General, still ramrod straight as you'd expect from a forty-year man. Mark could remember when his uncle had seemed tree tall and larger than life.

Then the old man grabbed Mark and slapped him on the back a couple of times in a quick half hug. He kept a friendly hand on Mark's shoulder as Emily came up, followed by the rest of her crew.

They traded salutes.

"Looking good, Emily."

"You too, sir."

"That's Eddie to you."

"Yes, sir, Eddie." She saluted him again saucily.

While still a colonel, the General had happily busted Mark's butt over and over until he met the old man's flight standards. Rarely doling out a smile of any variety. Then Emily came into Mark's life and completely won the old man over. Pre-Emily, Mark would never have dreamed of calling him Uncle, except maybe at the most casual family gathering. And here she was required to call him Eddie.

A year married and he'd still like to know how she'd done that. Her only answer was an uncertain shrug, then one of those smiles she aimed at Mark whenever she wanted to wipe all possibility of brain function out of his body.

"Looking damn good," his uncle continued, still watching Emily.

"Should I be getting jealous?" Mark was actually surprised to feel a slight twinge of just that. His wife was damn beautiful, and he still couldn't believe that she'd said "yes" when he asked. Actually, she never really had, but she'd stood with him at the altar and said, "I do," when it counted. Good enough for him. Right this moment she looked beyond beautiful. Middle of the night, halfway around the world from their last bunk, and still the woman glowed.

"When do I get my cigar?" The General glanced over at him.

"Your what?" Mark couldn't make any sense of it when his wife went sheet white.

"Watched my Ellen through five kids, and with my youngster, Tessie, already through two, you get to know what a woman looks like at certain times."

"Why would I give you a ciga..." Mark could feel the words slowing down and clogging his throat as he watched Emily's face.

Several of the crew startled and stared at the two of them.

"Whups!" His uncle clamped the hand harder on Mark's shoulder for a moment before withdrawing it. "Excuse me. I think your birds are messing up my nice, clean hangar floor." He pointed to the rest of the crew. "All of you can come help me clean that up. Nephew, this mess you'll have to clean up on your own."

The General walked away and the others trailed after him. With the loss of the support of his uncle's steadying hand, Mark could feel himself swaying in the breeze despite the breathless air and his dry throat.

"Are you… Are we…"

His Emma tipped her head sideways and smiled tentatively, which he'd always thought was her cutest stall tactic of all of them, but it wouldn't distract him this time.

Then she shrugged. "Maybe."

"*May*—be?" The first syllable a shout, the second a whisper.

"Self test says yes. Lola says I need to see a medico to be sure."

Mark shook his head to clear it. Something wasn't making sense. Something—

"When?" How long had she known and not told him?

"Last night."

Last night.

During the flight.

Just last night. He could deal with that. When she'd curled up against him as if the three flight crews weren't even there. And now, he was… She was… This he couldn't deal with.

A hundred images flowed through his mind and he had no idea what to do with them. A storm of confusion inundated him about what she'd do if she couldn't fly. Of how he could ground her without breaking her heart. Of how he could possibly love her more than he already did.

Thankfully, his body was smarter than he was and knew exactly what to do. He reached out and folded her against him.

In moments his personal beacon of strength had buried her face against his shoulder. He heard the first, ever so gentle sob, and held her tighter.

Her words were muffled and it took a moment to make sense of them. "I'm so scared."

Something fundamental shifted in that moment. He could feel the change wash over him.

Major Emily Beale wasn't scared of anything. Ever.

In that instant he was being asked to protect her; in that moment he became the strongest man alive. He kissed her atop her beautiful hair and whispered in her ear.

"We'll figure it out, honey. As long as we're together, we can figure out anything."

Her nod against his chest reassured him. The hand she raised from his chest to stroke his cheek, without looking up, told him how much she trusted him.

Now he just had to figure out himself how to live up to that trust.

Chapter 30

"Okay, y'all. You're free to go." Major Henderson kept his wife clutched close by his side.

Lola didn't need to see anything more to know that Emily Beale had picked a good man. He looked as if he were about to explode with pride and protectiveness and a dozen other conflicting emotions.

Since they'd just broken the news to all of both crews, whether intentionally or not, and they'd all seen the wonder and joy cross his features, it didn't matter exactly what he showed to them anymore. Not one of them would ever question that he was the most competent commander any of them would ever have, or that he loved his wife with his whole heart.

"Stay in the D.C. area and keep your pagers on." Henderson was clearly trying to pretend his entire world hadn't just changed. He wasn't fooling anyone, except maybe himself.

Lola didn't try to hide her smile.

"Stone sober. If you drink wine with dinner, it better be a half glass, watered down." He looked down at his wife. "And you don't get any at all."

His voice a caress as gentle as a breeze, a voice Lola had never heard except in the movies. It completely stole her breath away to hear it in real life.

Henderson's voice shifted back into commander mode as he finally found enough rudder to get control of it. "Be ready to scramble on a couple hours' notice. We could be on hold a day, we could be a week. We could be shipped back to the front."

Not much of a bet on that last one, and Lola could see that no one else thought it likely either. Come war or peace, they were wrapped up in this particular mission until it reached the end.

"Couple of vans out front can take us into town once we shed our gear. What's today's date?"

"April 1st," Connie offered in that inflectionless voice of hers.

Henderson nodded once solidly.

"April Fools' Day," Lola couldn't resist pointing out. Tim grinned at her. Clearly about to say it himself. Fellow in crime.

Henderson started to nod again, then twitched. He spun to face his wife as she burst out laughing.

"You wouldn't—" His tone threatened dire consequences.

"No! No!" She covered her mouth to block her mirth at the random chance of it.

After a few more chuckles at Henderson's discomfiture, everyone started drifting off to grab their civvie gear. Trading flight suits for street clothes, combat boots for some nice leather with decent heels, sidearms for wallets with cash, and digging out their cell phones. About the only things to survive the transition from soldier to civilian were dog tags and sunglasses.

"We are one damn fine-looking crew," Crazy Tim remarked as they spilled out of the hangar into the light of the rising dawn.

"Even if you have to be the one to say so."

Tim nodded at Lola's riposte. But it was true. The level of fitness made them all fine specimens. And they were a handsome lot. Lola didn't mind being included in the group for one moment.

"Who's up for breakfast at my place?" Tim called out. Lola had been thinking of hitting a hotel with a deep bath and immersing herself for a couple hours, but John and Connie chimed in with wholehearted agreement. She still might have dodged it, but Kee and Archie opted in with Dilya in tow. Left her no way to chicken out.

"Sure, why not. You keep a place in D.C.?" Maybe he had a deep tub, deep enough for two after the others left.

"I'm from here. My parents' place actually. Family breakfast is usually in about half an hour."

A couple of the others tried to hide smiles.

Big John was about to speak up, but Tim forced a cough and John shut his mouth.

Okay, whatever the game was, she was clearly being set up and she'd just have to roll with it. Fun or hideous? She'd wager on "it's an experience" by the looks people were giving each other.

Richardson hooked up with a couple of the guys from the base and declared they were going over to Annapolis, something about the opening day of striped bass fishing.

The Majors opted out in favor of going to her mother and father's place in Georgetown.

"Director of the FBI? Her dad is the director?"

Tim just nodded cheerfully in response to her shocked whisper as if it was no big deal. She double-checked with John just to make sure Tim wasn't messing with her.

Lola knew the Major was something special, you couldn't miss that. She kept glancing over at Beale to see if she'd somehow changed. But she still looked like a SOAR major on leave, who was expecting a baby and was pretty damn confused about it.

So, the seven of them piled into a van and headed into the city. Lola had never been here and kept pressing her nose to the glass like any tourist. For the most part, it looked like a city. But when she started to turn away, a small voice spoke, barely loud enough for her to hear above everyone else's cheerful chatter.

"I like the castle of the Smithsons." Dilya. The girl pointed out the right side window clearly figuring out that Lola was a newcomer by how she'd been acting. How much did the kid see about the people around her? How much had she learned while surviving her childhood?

Suddenly it wasn't just any other city. The Smithsonian Castle rose in magnificent piles of red brick. Beyond that…

"The Capitol. Where people sit around and make no laws."

Maybe she meant "new laws" or maybe she had it right.

Dilya tapped her shoulder and pointed left. They were cutting across the middle of the National Mall. The Washington Monument soared like a needle into the sky. Giant buildings down the opposite side turned out to be museums. And off in the distance, at a height above everything else, perched the Lincoln Memorial. She definitely had to get there.

Then they were back into office buildings.

"There." Dilya pointed proudly at a block-long mirrored building. "Mr. Frank works there."

"Oh," was all Lola could think to say as she spotted the sign at the front. The orphan girl from Uzbekistan apparently had made a friend in the United States Secret Service. "Is he a nice man?"

"Yes, I hope he never must stop bullet with his chest."

The only ones who really did that were on the Presidential Protection Detail. She looked at the little girl again and at Kee, clearly a street kid herself. They had a friend on the PPD. Didn't seem likely, but Lola had had enough surprises to not second-guess anyone in this car ever again. Maybe Kee had been an astronaut. Or Connie had commanded a submarine.

Tim directed the van's driver to the back door of a place about a block west of the Secret Service office building. Seemed an odd place to live.

Two things assaulted Lola as she entered the door last of all and dropped her duffel bag with the others.

First, the face-slap power of a top-notch commercial kitchen. She could pick out rich stews, sharp curries, and the deep warmth of soups that must have been simmering since the founding of the nation to smell that way. For all of Mama Raci's stinginess, her soups had that same richness that permeated the air like hope and comfort.

But instead of a narrow, poorly lit space that had been cramped into the back corner of the building as an afterthought, this kitchen sprawled and gleamed. Long steel counters, rows upon rows of burners, several already bearing large pots despite the early hour. Giant walk-in coolers beyond. Off to the right was a large wooden prep table, half set for a meal and sporting a dozen chairs, all underlaid by a burnished parquet floor.

It was a world-class surgical suite compared with a CSAR flight where a corpsman huddled in the center of a Black Hawk's bay covered in the blood of those he was too late to save.

Gods, what a place. It made her want to pull on an apron and dive in.

The second thing that assaulted Lola's morning was the joyous screams of men and women who threw themselves at Tim. He disappeared into a swarm of bodies who were clearly family. Some in aprons, some still in street clothes. Tim's nose on an older man, his warm eyes on a well-rounded woman. Others who must be siblings or cousins gathered round. Everyone demanded a hug, and many didn't let go once they got their turn or just piled in on top of someone else's hugging two, three, four people at a time.

Big John and Connie were greeted warmly. Dilya was propped up on a counter with a glass of orange juice so big that she needed both hands to hold it. Kee and Archie were clearly known as well.

Lola was hugged a half-dozen times before she was actually introduced to anyone. Drive-by huggings, which was a huge step up from her old neighborhood.

Hugs were Lola's favorite thing. Ignored by her father, harassed by his buddies, and growing up in back of a brothel, human contact wasn't high on the list of what was happening. Lola actually barked out a laugh, picturing herself hugging Mama Raci with even half the abandon Tim's family threw in the direction of this stranger in their perfect kitchen.

It always confused men she dated that she'd rather hug than crawl into bed. This was just a perfect combination, and she wallowed in the by-blow joy of Tim's unannounced homecoming.

As the tide of hugs once again pooled around Tim, Big John loomed up beside her.

"You're awful important to him, sir."

"I don't want to be." Though she knew she was.

"That's a problem."

She slumped against the steel counter behind her. "I wish I knew what to do about it."

At that Big John smiled. It warmed his face and lit his eyes. She could see how a woman could fall for a man with that smile.

"Well, pretty lady, I couldn't wish a better man on any woman. And if he thinks you're worth it, isn't that all that counts?"

She shrugged.

"My Connie, she thought I was worth it no matter how wrong I was sure she was. Surprised this big, dumb Okie no end. To be sure I ain't complaining though." He gazed off to where his wife was working on a stove that looked half taken apart. "She'll have that fixed and running before breakfast unless I miss my guess. I'll just go see if I can help her a bit. 'Scuse me, sir."

Connie did nothing to acknowledge her husband when he arrived, but maybe she didn't need to.

After a glance at the progress, John picked up a screwdriver from the floor and began disassembling a panel. Connie held it steady as he pulled the last screw,

and then they bent down in unison to study what they
had uncovered.

Chapter 31

TIM UNSNARLED HIMSELF FROM HIS FAMILY AND crossed to where Lola still leaned against the counter, its stout support barely sufficient to overcome the weakness in her knees.

Tim worked his way back into the crowd with her hand firmly clasped in his. Cousins, two older sisters, little brother… All went by in a blur, but not a one of them missed that her hand was firmly clamped in his.

Oh shit!

She was being dragged forward to be introduced to the family. Which was great. Except she was being presented as the chosen woman of the prodigal son. No! a voice screamed in her head. No! No! No!

Everyone went quiet when she landed in front of an older man. She could feel every occupant in the room completely focused on her. Time to put on her game face. She had to have one around somewhere.

"This is my da, Jackson Maloney."

Jackson was a narrower version of Tim. Still strong despite graying hair and enough early wrinkles to be in his fifties, but not with Tim's sheer physical strength. Though it was easy to see where his son had come by his magnetism. Though Tim's eyes were dark and his father's blue, they both shone with the man inside.

Jackson shook her hand heartily and she felt warm for the welcome though she couldn't pick out most of the words above the buzzing in her ears. A bit of an Irish lilt, but that's all she could discern.

The chosen one. She so didn't see that one coming.

Lola hoped she said something nice back to Jackson.

"And this is my ma, Cara."

Lola's free hand was enveloped between a splendidly full-figured woman's two hands. Lola saw the gentle eyes that the mother had passed on to her son, along with the sun-warmed skin. And she saw the fierce hope that maybe she was the one for her boy. Her accent was Puerto Rican, her words just as meaningless as her husband's, but her hug communicated all the warmth of that island to Lola's chilled skin.

Run! Away! Every instinct in her body and soul told her to drop to the floor in a sprinter's crouch and dash across the kitchen for the closed door. Forget about the duffel bag she'd dropped with the others, just go. Dive through a window if necessary, open or not.

But Tim and his mother, each in possession of one of her hands, anchored her in place against all her better instincts.

She smiled. At least she tried. She was so numb that it was hard to tell if she succeeded. If anyone knew, it wasn't her.

Within moments the silence, which had held while she met Tim's parents, returned to its previous roar, far louder in some ways than the steady inundation of the C-5's four massive General Electric CF6 jet engines. Her head spinning as fast as the turbofans in full flight, she sought some focus but gathered little more than scattered images.

A wall of awards hung in an arc over swinging doors that must lead to the dining area.

A side of beef sprawled on one table.

A headless fish nearly the size of the cow flopped on another, swimming in a giant tray of ice. Swordfish. She recognized it from having seen the movie *The Perfect Storm*.

While still a teen, she'd snuck in the back door of the movie theater to get dreamy over George Clooney. Little had she'd known that the movie would change her life.

Not beautiful George, but rather Sergeant Millard Jones whose chilling death had been portrayed when his pararescue helicopter crashed at sea. That was the moment to which Lola could trace her desire to fly search and rescue. It took her a while, but the idea started that day, three rows from the back in a stuffy New Orleans theater with a broken air conditioner.

Somehow, her life had moved from that movie to this moment. And her feet felt less certain, less stable with each passing day.

In a daze, she found herself escorted to the prep table set for breakfast and seated between Tim and his father. Tim still held her hand captive, thankfully under the table, so at least a bit out of sight. He was chatting away about produce supplies with his brother or cousin or someone.

The old man. He was looking at her. What was his name? John? James? Jeff? Jackson? Jackson Maloney.

"You fly with my Timmy?"

"No. Yes. Sort of." *Smooth, Lola, real smooth.* She took a breath, held for a count of three, and puffed it out. Trick she used to re-center herself if a battle slapped her silly.

Okay, now she was present.

"Same company, a different helicopter. But we fly on a lot of the same missions."

He picked up a large mug of coffee that some cousin had just filled.

"I barely understand why he does it. Why do you?"

"That's not an easy question." Then she looked into those bright blue eyes and couldn't look away. "Tim's reasons would be different from mine. He flies for you, I'd guess. To protect his family."

"And you don't?"

"I," Lola considered, "I fly for myself."

Jackson nodded as if being polite and still not understanding.

He searched for a distraction, and thankfully one arrived as large platters of food were delivered to the table, the steam wafting upward in tongue-watering layers. First the spicy edge of a dark, dark chili, then corn tortillas, so fresh she almost wanted to sneeze for how they tickled her nose. Eggs topped the tortillas with just a sprinkle of what might be pulled pork.

It looked Mexican, but the spicing smelled different, richer, more varied. And fresh fruit was worked into the dishes rather than an addition on the side. The warmed maple syrup must be destined for the steaming bowls of oatmeal. And large mugs of coffee all around.

"I apologize." Tim's mother leaned forward to look around Jackson. "Tim did not warn us he was coming or we would have made something special."

Lola assured her that this would be just fine. After a day of cold sandwiches and warm soda, and MREs for most of the last week before that, anything would taste great. But this was incredible by any breakfast standards.

She calmed down a little as the meal progressed. For one thing, Tim released her hand so that he could use both of his to focus on his food. That made her a little less self-conscious. No one had wanted to always be holding her hand since Joey in eighth grade. Last boy she'd let get away with that, now that she thought of it. Still, Tim's knee rested lightly against hers, oddly comforting.

Constant contact. That's what was different about this table. They almost couldn't talk without touching each other. And they all were talking continuously, all at once. Tim and his sister each had a hand on the shoulders of the cousin seated between them. Lola tuned in enough to hear about some girl he shouldn't let get away.

Everybody who passed by Dilya stroked her hair or gave her a special treat. Once it was discovered how much she liked cherries, by her sneaking the ones that had adorned Kee, Archie, and Big John's oatmeal, a whole bowl of them appeared by the girl's side. Even the silent Connie had her attention engaged by a boy barely eighteen who was clearly infatuated.

Jackson and Cara whispered together as they ate, while holding hands. He ate left-handed and she right, so they could hold hands and still eat. About the tenth time Lola bumped elbows with Tim, she realized they could be doing the same if they switched sides.

An advantage to being a southpaw. One of the few plusses she'd found in her life for that particular trait. If it was an advantage.

She nudged her knee against his to get his attention.

"You never told me your family were cooks."

"Something like six generations."

It finally clicked. "That's why your helmet..." She recalled the crossed knife and fork emblem on his flight helmet.

He nodded. "I enlisted as a chef. The plan was to do my two years and then come cook in the kitchen. Army put my butt in the air and I never came back down. I love cooking, but flying with the Majors, Henderson and Beale, and with Big John, it's the best experience a man could ever have."

Lola believed him as she took a bite of the best corn tortilla with sausage and egg that she'd ever had in her life. There was no questioning his sincerity. Or his choice, really. Even after only a couple weeks of missions, there was no questioning how exceptional the Majors were. She hoped they were okay. Such a short time and she already felt a pang of what it would be like to fly without Emily Beale beside her.

———〜〜〜———

"I'm stuffed." The food was so incredible that Lola hadn't been able to stop eating. She struggled from her wallow and onto her feet to help collect dishes, despite the family's insistence that she was a guest. It wasn't burdensome, they just stacked everything and took stacks down to the dishwashing station where the teen with the crush on Connie had already manned what was clearly his station. Any attempt to offer help there was an obvious insult to his manly ability to crank out clean tableware, which he did with immense efficiency.

"He'll make a good crew chief some day."

Tim nodded. "Jimmy's a sharp boy. We're all hoping

he goes to college rather than Army. He's smarter than all the rest of us put together, but I'm afraid I've been a bad influence on his generation. And Connie isn't helping things. He's totally in love with her ever since she helped him rebuild his motorcycle engine last year. My little sister is in boot camp right now."

Lola could hear the pride in his voice. It wasn't that they were an Army family that struck her. Nor was it the pride in the service. It was that there was a feeling of pride of family. Tim cared enough about his sister to have strong feelings about her. To care. She'd never had that in her life.

If Mama Raci had ever felt pride about Lola, it was only expressed by a decrease in the old woman's general nastiness. Her father's only emotions had been, well, nonexistent on the subject of his daughter. Her moving in with Mama Raci was no secret, couldn't have those in New Orleans, but not once had he bothered to come by and check on her or...

She shook herself before she could walk down those dark paths of memory.

And noticed that even in the last moments, the environment of the kitchen had changed. The rest of the SOAR fliers had left with warm hugs and large bags of leftovers. Those of the family without aprons were pulling them on. Long trays of unprepared vegetables were being pulled from the coolers. The sharp "wick, wick, wick" of knives being run over sharpening steels. They were preparing for lunch service, just another day in the restaurant.

She could see Tim wanting to drift in to help.

"I'll just grab my stuff and find the hotel."

That stopped him cold. "No. Don't. They won't let me help anyway." He grinned. "Watch."

He grabbed a perfectly white apron from a pile stashed under the near end of the counter. He headed to the side of beef, pulling a knife from a large wooden block. And stopped.

Dead square in front of him stood his mama. Hands on her hips. Fire in those gentle eyes as she glared up at her son.

"You no come home to cook."

"Mama, I bragged about your cooking, our cooking. I gotta."

"You are no' a good boy to leave your lady friend to stand there alone."

Lola could think of a hundred things she'd rather do after an all-night flight, but dutifully pulled out an apron to put it on. She'd become a fair cook under Mama Raci's watchful eye.

Tim's broad smile and wink were almost worth the price she'd have to pay out in work.

"I'm glad to help."

The glare now turned on her, strong enough to stop Lola in her tracks though the woman stood the better part of a foot shorter than she did.

"He put you up to this. I know my son and his jokes, better than his father. Better than his sister. You, young lady, you come back for dinner and we make you something nice. And you"— she spun back to face her son—"you take your girlfriend somewhere nicer than this old kitchen."

The rest of the family, who'd paused for the drama, plunged back to work. The swordfish was unearthed from its deep tray of ice, and three of them started in to break it down.

It was actually the nicest big kitchen Lola had ever been in, and "old" wasn't even close to right. "Old" was Mama Raci's bordello with the cracking brick and ceiling paint flaking into the thin soup, the creaky stools and the rusting old wood stove that was only lit during the hottest weeks of the summer when canning was going on.

Then Cara's words caught up with her and Lola choked. A spasm deep in her throat and she had to cough so hard to clear it that it actually hurt. She'd heard the space Cara hadn't put in "girlfriend." Lola hadn't been labeled "girl friend" who was one of Tim's flight mates. Lola had just been labeled "the girlfriend" of the eldest son.

She hacked and swallowed against the bristly pain in her throat as someone ran for a glass of water and someone else thumped her sharply between the shoulders.

"The girlfriend" who'd just been brought home to meet "the family." It was so weird that it surprised her each time the thought came back.

Lola straightened abruptly, took the glass of water, and sipped at it a few times to steady herself before setting it down.

Tim was out of his God. Damn. Mind.

Chapter 32

TIM PULLED OFF HIS APRON, TOSSED IT TO HIS MOM LIKE a bouquet of flowers, and wrapped himself up in one of her deep, warm hugs.

His dad and a couple of the others grinned at him. They'd clearly known the strategy he'd just played on his mom. He hugged her again.

"Love you, Mama. More than your soup."

"More than my stew?" He smiled. He hadn't heard the ritual in too long, six months since he'd last been home.

"Well, not that much," he completed it.

"Good!" She patted his cheek as if he were twelve. "Then I have not lost my touch. Now you two go play. I have lunch to get ready."

Tim turned to Lola. "Wanna go for a run? Best way to see the city."

She had the oddest look on her face. He'd only seen her run once. After *Viper* had flown a twelve-hour mission, he'd hauled himself up on one of the concrete risers that surrounded the soccer field at Bati, too tired to move. Too tired to breathe without considering it a burden.

He'd napped briefly in the sun, then woken to a dream image—Lola running the track that followed the inside perimeter of the soccer stadium. There was almost always someone running there because there was almost nothing else to do at Bati base between missions.

You sure didn't go into town unless you took an armed squad with you.

So, he'd sat there, feeling too hazed to do more than watch, as she ran lap after lap.

Lola had run like a goddess. Or maybe a nymph. Her hair blowing back, her step light and fast. He could have watched her for hours. He did, for at least a dozen laps. It had taken him a while to realize that she hadn't come around again. He waited a while longer, then finally gave up and went to crash-land in his bunk.

This time he wanted to see her up close. And D.C. was an awesome city to travel on foot.

She shook her head. Nodded. And finally shrugged.

"You're a nutcase, Maloney."

He shot her his best smile. "The few. The proud." And he snapped a regulation salute.

"Okay, you're not as nuts as a Marine, but you're really, really close." He didn't need to turn around to know that they were still the spectacle of the moment. The lunchtime prep was less than half of the normal volume and almost no one was talking. They wouldn't want to miss a word.

"C'mon." He snagged her elbow and led her toward where they'd dropped their gear, which was now cluttering up the middle of the butchering area.

As soon as they were out of the way, Jamie and Sally moved in to start breaking down the beef into steaks, tenderloins, roasts, and the parts to be fresh ground.

"You try to sleep after a long flight, you'll end up twitchy and all out of sync. You gotta stay awake until nightfall if you wanta flip into the right time zone."

She shrugged again. "Okay, I guess." She knew that

trick. It was just a question of how to stay awake for at least another dozen hours.

He aimed her at a bathroom. Again couldn't help noticing the nice way she filled out those narrow jeans she wore. He definitely wanted to see as much of what lay beneath as possible. He'd had his hands down her flight suit against a helicopter and up her body in the darkness of the C-5's cargo bay. But he'd actually seen very little of Lola LaRue's skin except a brief moment in a wind-blown desert.

"Gonna be a scorcher in another hour or so. Don't bother with layering up." Seemed like an efficient way to phrase his lust as she disappeared into the bathroom.

Tim considered following her in. Reliving an early fantasy when he'd gotten Suzanne Sanchez back there during his fifteenth birthday party… and been caught by his dad with his pants half down and her skirt half up.

He glanced up to see his dad watching him. Watching with that smile of his.

Dad tipped his head toward the door for a moment, indicating that Tim should follow Lola in.

Nope. Not with Dad watching. Not even if he'd had condoms with him and no longer needed the lecture he'd suffered through at fifteen about a man's responsibilities.

He turned for the other bathroom.

He couldn't hear the old man's laughter in the noisy kitchen.

But he could feel it.

⌁⌁⌁

What Lola was wearing, or rather wasn't wearing, was exactly to Tim's liking. He watched her come across the kitchen toward him. Running shoes with short socks. Brilliant red shorts and a sports bra to match. Wraparound shades and her hair out loose.

There was so much glorious skin that it was blinding. He couldn't help but stare.

Apparently neither could anyone else. Tim could feel the kitchen growing quieter and quieter behind him as he looked her up and down.

He'd been right—the woman had the longest damn legs in the world. And they were amazing legs. The thighs rippled smoothly as she flexed and stretched, oblivious to all watchers.

Tim turned around and glared at his family. They all grew very busy with their prep work, the volume rapidly skyrocketing to several times the normal mayhem of a working kitchen.

Jimmy still gawked, but at that age, Tim remembered, it was impossible not to.

Tim also decided they'd better get to running unless he wanted to embarrass himself completely.

"Your shorts aren't hiding much," Lola whispered from close enough beside him that he could feel her breath on his ear.

He swallowed hard. He should have followed her into the bathroom.

"Let's go!" She led him out the door, indicating he should lead the way. Tim tried to set up a steady trot though it was hard with his knees turned to Jell-O.

Chapter 33

LOLA WATCHED TIM'S TIGHT BUTT AS THEY HEADED down the sidewalk. Turnabout was fair play. She'd seen his body's reaction to her and found it actually pleased her more than she'd care to admit. He wanted her. He wanted her so bad.

She should have stuffed a credit card in the pocket of her shorts. Then they could just get a room and… Okay, she wanted him pretty bad herself too.

She glanced at her own reflection in the front of a mirror-glass building. Almost didn't recognize the woman who could want a particular man so much.

Free of Tim's family, and the constant stream of attention and friendly but persistent curiosity, she started to ease back into herself and settle into the run. She had no idea how they were going to do this. Cities were not made for running. Even Bati field was better than this, though the endless circling eventually got pretty old.

Wide open spaces, country roads, field and pasture, that's where you could run.

Running in a city was about getting out of a trap. About getting away from someone.

The scenery in this city wasn't so different from any other if you were out for a run. Tall buildings. Bankers and lawyers and women in ridiculous dresses that were a cross between office worker and fashion model, which gave off more of a high-end hooker motif than anything else. They all hustled about as if what they were doing was so damned important.

And Tim and his nice butt just ran through them so smooth and easy, as if they weren't even there. He barely stirred the slightest wake in the crowd with his passage. Lola felt clumsy because men stopped and gaped at her, often completely in her path, and she had to keep circling around. One actually walked head-on into another, neither of them watching where they were going. At least she was looking good on the outside, however she felt on the inside.

She and Tim jogged in place waiting for a light, then crossed the street. A half block later, she forgot about everything else.

Looming large before her was the White House. Just there, across the street, through a black iron fence and a bit of lawn sporting a small fountain amid a bed of red roses. Impossibly white. Impossibly daunting. It seemed to rise up out of the ground as if it grew by magic. The seat of the most powerful ruler in the world, her Commander-in-Chief, stood just across the street.

Lola ground to a halt trying to take it in. Every mission she'd ever flown had started here, in some form or other. Every military operation of the U.S. forces and most of the ones done by the UN and NATO forces had originated right here.

Tim circled back and jog-trotted in place beside her.

"Didn't realize you'd never been to D.C. Kind of a showstopper, isn't it?"

All she could do was nod.

"Okay, I'm going to change our route a bit. There are some things you have to see."

When Tim started off again, she followed along in his wake. They turned and crossed streets, and still the White House dominated the area. Sometimes lost in trees, sometimes in clear view. It was as if the building was the main rotor hub and the rest of the world was spinning around it. Roads radiated away from the hub like the main blades of a chopper, but you could feel them reaching far beyond the mere limits of the city. Lola just couldn't get over the feeling that they extended south to New Orleans and east all of the way to her little airfield in Pakistan.

Then they broke out onto the National Mall. The Capitol building shone to the left, the Washington Monument soared straight ahead, and in moments they were running along the Reflecting Pool, straight toward the Lincoln Memorial.

As if he were teasing her, Tim led them right past the memorial. At her protest, he called back, "We'll loop around to it," and led her onto a bridge over a river.

"Got a silver dollar?"

"No. Why?"

"Right about here is where George Washington chucked his silver dollar over the Potomac. Thought you might want to give it a try." Clearly he was trying to lay it down as a challenge. She found herself half surprised that he didn't produce a coin for her to try with.

Lola looked from one bank to the other, glanced up at the "Welcome to Virginia" sign as they ran along under it, and decided against picking up his tease. Maybe with a golf ball in space, like that cosmonaut. The ball had remained in orbit for about two days, which would make it about a million-mile shot. That would clear the Potomac and then a bit. But trying to throw a silver dollar across a mile-wide chunk of river? Not so much.

At the Virginia shore, Tim turned south. This time he slowed until they were running side by side.

"Kind of makes you think, doesn't it?"

Then she saw the building and again ground to a halt, feeling like a tourist idiot, but she couldn't help herself.

The nearby roadway roared with morning commuter traffic. She could see it, but it seemed to flow in perfect silence. The waterfront park they were standing in was teeming with early joggers, cyclists, moms with baby carriages; they appeared frozen in place.

Tim took her hand, and that was the only thing holding her steady.

"That's the Pentagon," she managed a whisper.

"Largest office building in the world. Did you know that you can walk from any office to any other office in seven minutes flat? That's the coolest part."

The thing was so massive, an aircraft carrier parked in a sea of fishing boats, impossibly huge in both size and power. But an aircraft carrier at full speed could outrun most enemies. Not here. This building hadn't managed to outrun the terrorist-controlled airliner.

"Which wall did they hit?"

"The one we're facing."

Lola studied it carefully. "I was cutting classes in high school when the planes hit. You know, kicking around with a couple other girls who were trouble waiting to happen but had nowhere to go. Some were listening to their Walkmans. One girl had a small ghetto box. She'd tuned it to a Cajun station, and we all stood there pretending we were too cool to want to dance to the fast beat of Buckwheat Zydeco's latest."

The building wall looked no different. She'd seen the diagrams, knew the shape of the hole in the wall, but the same company who had built it in 1941 had dug stone from the same quarry and refinished it to match. She couldn't see the lines where old joined new.

"I remember the radio bulletins."

Tim squeezed her hand in quiet sympathy.

"It's like I became so much smarter that day. Until then I'd been making a conscious life choice to not play the game. I mean, what was the point of playing if you knew you were going to lose?"

Lola tried to stop her voice, but it all spilled out anyway.

"The fact that Mama Raci would've beat the shit out of me was the only reason I hadn't gone to whoring. Not yet. That day, between feeling all rebellious and the total emptiness of my wallet, it looked pretty good to an attractive, seventeen-year-old Lola LaRue. Since sex was the only power I'd ever have, I figured that maybe it was time for me to start using it."

That one day older had made all the difference in her life.

"They killed all of those people too late for me to make anything of myself in high school, but I was the only one of those girls to finish and graduate. LSU let me in for reasons I still can't fathom. ROTC got me some money and a ride into the Air National Guard. The rest came from a swim team scholarship and tips from being a bar waitress every weekend and weeknights when I didn't have a practice or a meet."

Tim stood close in simple support. She just told the

man she'd almost become a whore and still he stood by her.

Funny. Her whole journey since then had all led back to here, to this starting point. To standing in front of the Pentagon on a beautiful summer day. Her life had changed because people had died here. Right here. For some reason, the attack on the headquarters of the Department of Defense in the nation's capital had hit her harder than the Twin Towers. Harder than the jet that had augered into the Pennsylvania farmland.

"I once spoke to a Colonel Jim Baker," Lola recalled.

She could feel Tim's silence as he turned to look at her, though she couldn't take her eyes from the massive building.

"I met him at some conference a couple of years ago, right before I applied to SOAR. He'd gone out for a run that day, kinda like we are now, up the National Mall and back." She glanced across the river and squinted toward the Capitol building made hazy by distance and the rising heat of the day.

"He described it as being a day just like this. He'd circled the Capitol and was just jogging off the bridge when the jet came in." Lola looked back and forth at the land and the highway. "He must have been right about here. It came so low, he said, that you wanted to duck. A roar of full power and they drove it into the Pentagon."

She and Tim both looked up into the sky, scanning, checking the vast expanse of blue for a predator, the worst predator, a human who is sicko enough to think that their god justifies murder. But the sky remained achingly clear.

"His office was almost dead center and all his staff

died instantly. His assistant—who had almost come on the run with him but changed his mind at the last minute—gone. His entire group ceased to exist."

Tim didn't reach for her. Didn't try to console. The ones who'd been through it knew better. You couldn't. You just had to stand up on your own and face the Devil.

When he spoke, his voice was barely louder than the wind and the morning traffic. "I signed up that day. I've always told my family I signed up as a cook. My family always had. Five generations in five wars we've been Army cooks. The story I tell them is that Army thinking put me in helicopters. That the story I tell everyone."

He pointed across the river.

"I stood right over there."

Tim's face must be a reflection of her own, grim, angry, betrayed.

"And I watched it burn. I watched the tape of the towers going down. So I signed up for Army, real Army. Never mentioned to them that I could cook. I learned to shoot better than anyone I met before Kee Stevenson. I learned to fix helicopters. I learned to reach out and do my damnedest to make sure this never happens again."

He turned his gaze to face her, and she saw something more than just grim determination. What she saw on Tim's face was an absolute commitment to the cause of protecting his family. A man of immense honor watching the world of his family across a vast field of inner conviction. She felt hollow to be standing beside him, knowing her own inner drive had only recently found first gear.

Lola wished she could be like him. Wished she didn't feel every action she took might be the wrong one for the wrong reasons. Wished for the certainty that she was serving someone, something, besides her own petty whims. Maybe she was finally getting a taste of it. Major Beale and Tim Maloney, they were teaching her more and more about herself and what drove her.

"If this is what you brought me here to see, thank you."

His smile was slow in building. But when it came, there was no doubting the joy behind it.

"Nope. Not what I wanted to show you at all. C'mon." He settled back into a medium run and Lola fell in close behind.

"Damn fine butt, Mr. Maloney!"

Even from behind, she could see the blush going up his neck until it hit his ears.

Chapter 34

Tim faded back until he was beside Lola as they crossed the bridge back into D.C. He guided her down the right pathways but wanted to make sure she had an open view when they arrived.

He liked the feeling of running beside her. She did it so naturally. He always felt like a bulldozer struggling against a headwind when running. He did it by brute force. He'd grunted out twenty-milers with a fifty-pound pack with the best of them. Nothing was going to stop him.

But Lola LaRue floated. She was a natural-born runner and a complete joy to watch. Even without the skimpy attire. Though the idea of resting his head on that sleek, tight belly on a lazy summer afternoon was definitely high on his to-do list.

He kept her face slightly turned toward the river until in a single burst they were right on top of the Tidal Basin.

It was perfect.

She gasped aloud. But didn't stop.

No chest-blow impact of man-made objects. Instead the breeze that swept up from the Chesapeake, alive with the scent of the sea and possibilities, shook down a gentle pink shower of fluttering petals.

Lola spread her arms and laughed aloud as she ran. Ran as if she could catch the beauty of three thousand blooming cherry trees. As if every one welcomed her personally with fluttering pink petals in a blue sky.

She changed for him in that moment. He'd been enraptured since he'd first seen her in Poland. He'd been totally lost ever since she'd bloodied his nose with her helmet. Some combination of wild beauty and wilder vibrancy had captivated all of his attention.

Now Lola laughed again. From the heart. A sound of pure joy. She didn't shine—she radiated.

As if he ran beside a goddess of old, the joy flowed over him, into him, until he too was laughing, unable to hold it inside.

Like children three years old, they jumped and chased after the petals falling like pink and white rain. Tim scooped up a handful of cherry petals from atop the grass and tossed them at Lola. A hundred, a thousand caught in her hair. One stuck to her nose, another to her cheek.

He hooked a hand around her waist and they turned into each other with all the force of their stride and all the joy, and he feasted upon her mouth knowing he could never have enough of this woman. Not today, not tomorrow, not in a lifetime, not in a dozen.

He'd fallen in love with a woman who tasted of heaven and smelled of cherry blossoms.

Chapter 35

THEIR RUN FORGOTTEN, LOLA HAD BEEN COMFORTABLE to wander through the falling blossoms hand in hand with Tim. She'd rarely been to a place like this, never such a wonder of natural beauty.

New Orleans had its moments, but the Deep South was about lazy heat and the people. For all her time in the service, the dice had rolled against her. She'd never served in such a place. Air National Guard had kept her close to home. The Army had shipped her off to Iraq the first moment it could. SOAR had trained at Fort Rucker, Alabama, and in the Nevada desert. Then they'd fired her off to Pakistan.

"Why do the crazies always live in the desert? Why can't they live somewhere like this? Or maybe the Bahamas?"

"Flew security there once. Nothing much happened. Some nice beaches. A lot of women wearing even less than you are. But I'd rather be here."

He turned to look at her and squeezed her hand lightly, just as if they'd been walking hand in hand for years.

"Feels right here. Feels like home."

The wind curled around and chilled her skin for a moment.

"Not a feeling I know." Actually she knew what home felt like, and it wasn't something she'd ever wish on anybody. The only thing worse than home was family. Tim's was different, though. Overwhelming.

Overbearing. Overprotective. She bet his family was talking about her right now and how she'd never be good enough for their boy. But despite all that, at least they didn't leave you with your skin creeping no matter how long you scrubbed in a shower.

Well, screw 'em. All she wanted from Tim was a good time and some good feelings.

Wasn't it?

It had to be. Whatever hesitation preceded that thought was to be ignored as stupid and foolish. Lola LaRue lived her life loose and easy. Sure, she'd committed to her crew. Flew hard. Had their backs and they had hers. That was enough for any soldier. It was enough for any girl. All she needed.

She let Tim lead her wherever he wanted to go. He led her from the glorious avenue of falling petals and somewhere back toward the city through long parks and manicured trees. For now she did have all she needed. All she wanted.

They wandered down tree-covered paths, moseying like any other couple on a warm spring morning.

Tim was easy. They chatted about nothing and he made it easy. He talked about growing up in the city and visiting family in Puerto Rico during the winter and Boston during the summer. He told funny stories about his brother and sisters. Discovering that he'd probably served Emily Beale and her family at their restaurant when he was a teenager, but neither of them remembering.

Connections. To Tim everything was connections. His best friend had fallen in love with Connie Davis, and now she and Big John were his two best friends. His

loyalty to his crew, to those who flew on the two DAP
Hawks wasn't something felt, like hers; it was integral
to his being. To him they were family. Perhaps closer
than. When someone else on the crew got shot, everyone
wished it had been them instead. She'd feel that way
even about bloody Kee Stevenson. The difference was,
Tim would leap in front of the bullet if he could.

Tim remembered the name of every teacher from kin-
dergarten to SOAR. She'd be challenged to remember
half, never mind name them.

"Really," Lola insisted when Tim pushed. "I was the
weird kid in the back of class."

"What did you do there, polish your nails?" Tim got
her to laugh the way he said it.

"No, that was Betsy and Jeannie. I read."

"What?"

"Anything about anywhere that wasn't where I was.
I read mostly... You'll laugh."

"Of course I will. C'mon, give. This sounds good."

Lola ignored him.

He leaned forward and kind of looked up at her like
a sad puppy dog.

She turned away and studied a blooming bush of
vibrant yellow.

He stepped around her and held her other hand, repeating the puppy dog look from the other side.

When he whimpered she lost it.

"Science fiction," she managed between her laughs.

That stopped him. "Last thing I was expecting to
hear. I figured gothic romances or war history."

"Nope. Arthur C., Heinlein, Card, anything I could
lay my hands on. Our local library only had a couple

shelves, so I read them from Douglas Adams to Roger Zelazny. I started stealing them from bookstores by the time I hit high school."

"Ever get caught?"

"Once." She left it as a tease. She'd never thought talking about books could be flirty. She usually kept her passion quiet and to herself. Those worlds were as far as she could get from the one she lived in. She'd lived for Diaspar and Dorsai. Regulus Base and the Benden Weyr. Kept the books hidden. They were just for her. Tim was the first one she'd ever told.

"And…" he picked up on the tease. So fun to be with.

"I got caught putting a book back."

Tim snorted. "Putting one back?"

"Well, I had nowhere to keep them."

"What about your room?"

That killed any sense of fun. "I had nowhere to keep them." She knew her voice had gone cold. Couldn't help herself. Ran her free hand down the length of his muscled forearm in apology.

All it did was raise goose bumps on her own flesh.

She could feel him turn to look at her a few times. She just kept her attention straight ahead. Focused on the line of marble steps ahead. Steps that led to some-where hidden by the low brow of the trees they'd been wandering under.

Tim remained quiet as they continued forward.

"Holy crap!" Lola couldn't stop the exclamation.

Tim started. Clearly he had been thinking deep thoughts or he'd have expected her reaction. The Lincoln Memorial rose abruptly out of the trees. The massive columns towered stories and stories above them.

Even on a weekday morning, the place was swarmed with tourists. Buses were emptying load after load, yet the place was so massive that Lola didn't feel in the least crowded. They climbed the stairs.

Right near the top, with old Abe looking down on them benevolently, Tim stopped and turned her to face the city.

All she could do was sink to the warm marble steps. Washington D.C. laid out before her like a road map. The great green of the center of the city, as if saying, "We're so powerful, we can afford to leave the whole center of the place empty for a park and pretty buildings. Our power is hidden. Our hammer is out of sight. Be careful not to forget that."

"We're part of that hammer." Her voice came out as little more than a hoarse whisper.

She could feel Tim's nod from how he sat so close beside her that their shoulders rubbed.

"We rule the night." Tim made it sound like a prayer.

"The Night Stalkers." Something to be proud of. Something to belong to.

Perhaps it was a prayer.

Chapter 36

"THEY'RE IN OUR SPOT."

"They are. Should we have them shot?"

Lola looked up in surprise to see Major Beale and Major Henderson standing just a few steps below them, profiled with the Capitol Building peeping up between their shoulders.

Despite their civvies, jeans, and T-shirts, there was no mistaking their military bearing. They looked good together, as if they'd always stood side by side. The broad-shouldered man and the stunning blond. As if they belonged side by side.

"Well," Beale answered her husband as if Lola and Tim weren't sitting right there listening, "officer and enlisted. Holding hands. Not good. Not good at all. Firing squad might be too kind."

Lola tried to shake her hand loose but be subtle about it. Tim didn't move. They were too close, and her elbow was caught inside of his.

"Right." Henderson aimed his mirrored Ray-Bans at them like twinned miniguns. "We, at least, were the same rank. We had some respect for the military code."

Beale elbowed her husband.

"Okay, we were eventually the same rank."

So, they'd been different ranks when courting. At least they'd both been officers.

Lola knew the Majors could hang both of them out

to dry. Fraternization was forbidden. It sometimes fell under the "Don't ask, don't tell" rules like the one the gays had served under until 2012, and sometimes it didn't. Depended on the commander. Commanders.

Everyone ignored Lola's efforts to disentangle herself from Tim's grasp, until she finally stopped for feeling too damn foolish.

"I don't know, dear," Beale continued as if Lola and Tim were just specimens under a magnifying glass. "I'm off duty. How about if we convene the court-martial some other day?"

"I could get us ice cream instead." Henderson nodded toward the rolling cart at the base of the steps.

"How did they do it, sir? Kee and Archie?" Lola had blurted it out without intending. Without even knowing where the question came from. Sure, she'd wondered as they were an officer and enlisted couple, but she and Kee weren't exactly on close speaking terms so as to hunker down and have a friendly girl chat on the subject.

Lola also couldn't figure out why she was so interested. Having now started it, this was not a conversation she wanted to be in. For one thing, it implied that it was part of a conversation she and Tim would be having. For another, she didn't want to care about Kee but was finding that she did. For all of the woman's in-your-face nastiness, she was an amazing soldier, a devoted wife, and an amazing mother.

Major Henderson continued speaking to his wife rather than to them. "The youngsters these days, no respect. That should be Sergeant Kee Stevenson and Captain Archie to them. How did they pull that off anyway? I missed it until they invited me to be the best man opposite my wife."

Beale patted her husband's shoulder with the hand he wasn't holding. "You're sweet and they were discreet. Mostly. Though there was one morning at Bati… I'll just say that Captain Stevenson has very cute knees." The woman's smile was huge and wicked. Lola would give some fair chunk of her next paycheck to hear the story behind that smile.

Her husband harrumphed at that.

Beale stared down at them for another long moment, considering. Long enough for Lola to start squirming again before she spoke.

"Orange Creamsicle." Major Beale spoke as if passing final judgment and life sentence.

"Fudgsicle!" Tim piped up.

"Didn't ask you." Henderson aimed a finger at him. "Wasn't I about to court-martial you?"

Lola couldn't help smiling. "I'd—"

"Ice cream sandwich," Henderson finished for her. "You're definitely an ice cream sandwich kind of girl."

She nodded. She was. And even if she wasn't, she'd have said yes so that he could be right.

"C'mon, Maloney. You can help carry."

Tim rose to follow the Major down the steps. "As long as you're buying."

"Damn! Should have court-martialed you while I had the chance."

Major Beale sat beside Lola and they admired the two men descending the broad marble stairs.

"Damn, but they look good, don't they?"

Lola could only nod in response. They certainly did.

Though she hoped her face didn't look quite like the Major's. There was a palpable look of true love across her features.

Time for a subject change. She faced Major Beale. "Have you seen a doctor yet, Emily?" It felt strange to say the Major's first name. But asking a commanding officer about her baby was a little too strange. It was easier to ask a woman.

By the way she slid her hand over her belly, Lola had the answer to her question.

"What are you going to do?"

"Knowing, really knowing," Emily whispered to her, "changes the world."

—∿∿—

They had lunch at a hot-dog vendor's cart after going up the Washington Monument and peeping out the small, grimy windows toward the four points of the compass. They happily paid tourist prices for that and a snow cone covered in Blue Dye No. 1. Lola shared her snow cone with Tim, both of their tongues turning bright blue, which they made a point of sticking out at each other like a couple of kids.

They all strolled through D.C. together. Sometimes walking as couples, but more often two men together and two women. Lola felt that was a little clichéd, but she was discovering that in addition to respecting the Major, she also was coming to like Emily Beale quite a bit.

They talked about nothing much, at least nothing much that stood out as important. They spoke of their first flights: Lola's during a ROTC recruiting event which had inspired her to be a front-seater, Emily's on one of her father's business flights. They spoke of first battles, that moment that proves the chosen path: Hurricane Katrina and the Opium Triangle respectively. At first boyfriends, Emily went coy and Lola didn't want to talk about it anyway.

They circled back a dozen times to the regimen suggested by Emily's doctor. A civilian doctor, because a military one would have grounded her immediately, had been horrified at what she did for a living and told her she had a maximum of four weeks to get off the chopper if she wanted to keep the child due to the g-forces alone, never mind the possibility of being shot.

Knowing that, Mark and Emily had decided that whatever happened as a result of their trip into the desert and this morning's escort flight, this would be her last mission until after the birth.

Lola didn't ask what would happen then. Neither of them was ready to face that question: Emily to stop flying, Lola to fly without her.

"Do you have any dinner plans?" Tim broke in on a discussion of jungle-flying tactics. "Ma's lookin' to feed some people."

"Sounds great." Emily considered for a moment. "Though I was thinking of dropping in on Peter."

Tim busted out a big grin and a wink that Lola didn't understand but that made Viper Henderson smile most evilly. "Invite him along. More the merrier."

Emily stepped aside and pulled out her cell phone.

"Your ma doesn't mind feeding us in her kitchen? We won't be in the way?"

Tim pointed down the street.

Lola knew they'd come full circle through D.C., but she didn't quite know where they'd started. Before, they'd arrived at an anonymous back kitchen door in an alley. Now she saw a building with a broad glass frontage and elegant wood-carved sign naming one of the hottest restaurants in D.C. Its reputation reached far and wide. Pauley's Island had made Caribbean food one of the newest foodie trends.

It took her heart about three more beats before she made the connection. A side of beef, a whole swordfish, the freshest ingredients.

"That's your family's restaurant?"

"Ma's the head chef, Dad's the marketing and business guy." His smile shone huge.

Viper Henderson was also clearly enjoying her complete discomfiture.

She jabbed Henderson in ribs, not even horrified that she'd just poked a superior officer hard enough to hurt.

"Hey, he's the one who hoodwinked you." He grinned down at her and didn't even bother to rub where she'd hit him.

"I'll make him pay later," she managed to growl out.

"Too bad, I'd be glad to hold him for you."

"No need." Lola made a fist with a slightly raised knuckle and pounded her fist into the nerve nexus where Tim's deltoids met biceps. It was like punching a brick wall, but still it elicited a very satisfying "Yowtch!" as he clutched at his upper arm.

Emily came back over, clearly trying not to laugh at what she'd just witnessed.

"Peter?" Lola mouthed at Tim.

"Sure." He turned to Lola. "Old friend of Emily's.

They grew up together. That's the only way we refer to him out in public."

Lola narrowed her eyes at the last cryptic remark. Tim just grinned at her. She considered punching his arm again, but he dodged away behind Major Henderson who raised his hands palm out to show he wanted no part of this.

Emily interrupted before Lola could offer chase, one hand over the cell's pickup.

"Room for Daniel? Alice is out of town."

Tim shrugged a "Sure."

Emily finished the call, "See you at seven?"

"I'll tell Ma."

Lola glanced up at the clock tower that loomed above a building labeled "The Old Post Office."

As the Majors left, she observed to Tim, "Any suggestions on what we should do with the next four hours? Other than a hot bath."

"Oh." Tim's smile bloomed, again proving he was quick on the uptake. "Oh yeah!"

Chapter 37

TIM SWUNG THROUGH THE KITCHEN OF PAULEY'S Island and waved at Becca and Bobbi. Everyone else was too busy serving late lunches to stop for even that. He grabbed his and Lola's gear. He reached for the key to the apartment, but it wasn't there. Crap!

It had always hung next to the back door, unless someone else was using it. This couldn't be happening. Who could possibly be using the upstairs apartment in the middle of a Monday afternoon? Occasionally his parents slept there if the restaurant closed late. Grandpop had lived there the last few years of his life. If one of the kids partied too hard downtown, better to crash upstairs than on the road.

After the third time he tried unsuccessfully to slow someone down long enough to ask about the key, his ma came in through the back door dangling it from her finger. "I made it all nice and clean for you. Some nice roses from this morning's arrangements."

Tim hugged her, making sure to secure the key first. "You're the best, Mama. The very best."

"I am. You remember that always, *sí*? I like the girl who you leave outside waiting. She's very nice."

Tim could only nod. Lola was very nice. And that Ma liked her was about the best thing that could happen. She had a great sense about people. More than one girlfriend had not passed the kitchen test. And he'd learned the hard way that no matter what he and his hormones were convinced of, if Ma simply shook her head, the truth would turn out that the girl wasn't worth the trouble. He was often accused during breakups of being a "mama's boy." He wasn't. She just kept being right.

And she liked Lola. Made his heart hurt a bit, got caught in his throat somehow.

His mother turned him toward the door and slapped his butt to send him on his way, exactly as she'd been doing since he was able to walk on his own.

Half out the door, he remembered. "Ma, can we have a table for six of us?"

"Sure"—she waved him out—"next week."

Their game continued. He'd always done this to her. Before the Army, his lousy sense of procrastination had made most planning short notice. After the Army had cured him of that, the very nature of his visits had caused the same situation. He couldn't help smiling.

"No, tonight. Seven o'clock."

Fists on hips, jaw grim, she faced him. "You idiot. We are booked solid for three weeks. No stupid table for no stupid son who doesn't even call to say he's coming home. You want a table? You eat right here."

She thumped a palm on the big family table, presently covered under tubs of iced fish now broken down into fillets and cutlets.

He considered for a moment. Some battles were better not to fight. Besides, he'd rather eat here than out front. He just hoped the others felt that way. He shrugged.

"Perfect, Ma. You're the best. Though some flowers would be nice."

"Flowers?" She glared at him, but it didn't quite work.

He waited half in and half out of the kitchen door. Finally she turned away, but not in time to hide her smile.

"Seven," she called out loudly enough to be heard over the busy kitchen. "You and your friends be on time."

Tim slipped out to the woman he'd kept waiting far longer than intended.

Chapter 38

His mother had done more than put out a few flowers in the apartment above the kitchen. She'd placed little vases in a half-dozen places. Folded back the sheets on the bed. Slid the gauze curtains into place so that there was light as well as privacy. In the bathroom, fresh towels and a new bar of soap—and more roses.

"I think my ma likes you." He turned to Lola, who hadn't moved from the center of the little living room.

"It's not much. We don't use it very often." It had a living room big enough for a couch, chair, television, and a bookcase of cookbooks and trashy novels. Two bedrooms, neither big enough for more than a queen-size bed and a dresser. No real kitchen, but with the restaurant downstairs, just a couple burners and a mini-fridge were plenty. He pulled the fridge door open to see fresh juice and a bottle of bubbly. He looked down at the floor that separated them from his ma's kitchen and sent a thank-you.

He slipped up behind Lola and did what he'd been dying to do all day. He slid his hands around her waist and across her belly, slowly pulling her back against him until she filled his arms.

He could feel her loosening up. Whatever was bothering her, she started to let go. She laid her head back against his shoulder, and he slid a hand up to rest between her breasts, over her heart.

"I—" Her voice sounded strained.

"Shh." He made it soft in her ear. "It's just me. Just us."

"Oh." She laughed a little, a ripple where her back lay against his chest. "Like that isn't scaring the shit out of me."

Tim puzzled over that, letting his hand that wasn't over her heart rub back and forth across her belly, like soothing a child with an upset stomach.

"I'm scaring you?"

"No. Yes. We—" Again she stopped. Then she reached up and back, sliding a hand behind his head. She turned her head enough and pulled him into a kiss. A long, slow lingerer of a kiss.

With her other hand, she took his hand from her heart and set it over her breast. Even through the sports bra he could feel her growing arousal.

As she continued to kiss him, not releasing her hold on him, he slowly explored the front of her body. Her hands sometimes just rode along on his arms, other times guiding him with the slightest pressure, first over her shorts, then under. Her long fingers riding smooth over the backs of his own.

She arched back against him, pressing his hands harder against her, breast and loins. She broke the kiss to simply lay her head back against his shoulder as Tim explored, massaged, reached.

He nuzzled her neck as his fingers entered her. She drove her hips back against him and used her own hand to increase the pressure he applied.

For a moment he opened his eyes and caught sight of her. The full-length hall mirror faced them, showed her front on.

He could see her writhe as he moved against her.

"You are so damned beautiful. I can't even think around you." He knew his voice was rough, as if the words were all he could throw forth.

Apparently past speech, she drove against his hands and he wrapped her tight in his arms as her body convulsed.

He'd never seen a woman come. Not like this. Beneath or atop him, yes. But never fully exposed like this. His hands moved as if they belonged to someone else, his arms and face the only part of him that showed in the reflection.

The rest was Lola, her head thrown back against him. One leg raised, the ankle hooked behind his knee to open herself further to his explorations.

Even as he watched, she reached her arms up behind his neck, clasped them together and held on as her body bucked.

A low, primal sound started where his hand disappeared inside her waistband and echoed upward. Not finding release, he could feel it roll up her body where it lay against his, past diaphragm and chest until at last it poured from her throat. The sound of a woman in pure rapture.

A sound Lola didn't recognize ripped through her, shattering something deep inside. The sound of Lola LaRue coming alive. Her body bucking to a familiar and soothing rhythm, her heart doing something else entirely.

Slowly returning to herself, she managed to open one eye. One that was quickly followed by the other.

A mirror.

A mirror reflecting her well-ravaged self, limp with pleasure, held in place by a man's strong arms.

He'd rested his head on her shoulder and was swaying her gently back and forth. Tim was a damned genius at making her feel totally incredible. She hadn't felt this good since, well, just since. He'd known exactly what to do for her. Exactly.

She tried to identify the other feeling. The change. What was different, but it eluded her hazy consideration. She had tried using sex to bury the fear of how much she liked Tim, of how easily she could see herself living in a small, cozy yet elegant apartment like this one with him. A world of a perfect mixture of fine glass and cozy furniture, a hideaway nest that welcomed and protected. Lola had kissed him until she could forget. It had worked and it hadn't. She'd forgotten the fear, but with Tim the sex was never just sex. It was something more. Something different.

As she became more and more aware of her body, she finally became aware of his body and how its need still pressed against her. That she knew how to solve.

The other feeling was unfamiliar, of being so exposed in the beveled-glass oval mirror yet so at ease. That was less certain.

Lola shoved her shorts the rest of the way off her hips, retrieving the foil packet she'd stuffed there before letting them slip to her ankles.

At ease in a man's arms, that was new. Enjoying herself, sure. But at ease?

When he made to move his hands, she clamped them back on her. She liked how she looked in Tim's embrace, one arm wrapped around to hold her opposite breast, one still between her legs, still reaching inside her. Holding her.

Sex was about fun. Or release. Or usually power.

She leaned forward against his grasp to open a little airspace between them, her languid body reawakening already against the slow-dance massage of his hands. She pulled his running shorts down, though they caught before she could finally get him free. With her hands slipped between their bodies, she managed to sheath him.

Sex with Tim was about something else.

He didn't look down, he just watched her in the mirror. Watched her watch him.

Tim was about safety.

When he was ready, she moved his hand from her breast to her hips, then slowly bent forward. Bent until she could reach out to the side and hold on to the rose-patterned couch accented by the dozen bouquets scattered about the room in contrasting vases.

She'd never felt safety as a part of sex.

Still their reflections retained eye contact. She wanted to close her eyes as he slipped into her from behind, filled her like no one ever had, as he still cupped her in front. But she didn't.

With Tim, she felt absolutely safe.

She kept her eyes open, her head tilted just enough to see his reflection as he took her with those strong arms and powerful legs. He drove into her, his eyes slipping helplessly closed, yet Lola remained transfixed by the image they made.

Safe was not a feeling she knew anywhere.

She kept her eyes open as they both peaked and flew.

Safe was a feeling she wouldn't mind having more of. A lot more of.

She watched a woman in the mirror who she didn't recognize. One whose body was flying upward, yet at the same moment was falling, tumbling out of the sky, right toward this man.

Right toward Tim Maloney.

Chapter 39

THEY MADE IT DOWN TO DINNER BY SEVEN, PERHAPS with a little less time to spare than Tim would have preferred, but they made it.

He'd lost some time, and his brain had lost any access to his blood supply, when Lola stepped out of the bathroom. With her hair brushed back into a flowing mane, that lopsided smile solidly in place, and a clingy, mostly backless red dress custom-made for Lola's sleek shape that spoke of elegance and roared of sex, she took his breath away.

He'd told her to dress nice even though they'd be back in the kitchen. He knew the others would as well.

They were the first downstairs, but the Secret Service detail was well ahead of them. They'd discreetly staked out the kitchen.

When Tim and Lola entered, his mama came over clutching a big soup ladle that she'd been about to use. She gave the much taller woman a big hug. Lola looked startled but quickly leaned down and returned the gesture. A bemused smile on her face.

"You look beautiful, my dear girl. Far better than my lump-head of a son deserves." She now wielded the soup ladle close enough to his nose that he backed away into one of the Secret Service agents who had the indecency to prop him up and then nudge him forward, back into the fray.

"'Oh, some friends they coming for dinner, Mama.' You, boy, if the lady you're so trying to impress were not here, you would get such a smack. I should have known better. All these years, I think I should know your games."

Tim ducked inside the arc of the swinging ladle and scooped her into his arms. "You *should* know me that well. I love you too, Mama," he whispered into her ear and was rewarded with a tight and hard hug.

When he let her go, she looked flushed with pleasure, though doing her best to hide it with a frown.

"Go, sit. Stay out of my way or I hit you but good." She wielded her ladle again and then nearly danced her way back to the soup tureen.

Tim turned for the table and wished he'd found a way to tell her just how much he loved her. She'd not set the table as if just for his friends. She'd made it beautiful, but not like the front of house. Rather than each place setting being laid with the perfection of a three-star restaurant, it was perfectly casual. Perfectly.

The centerpiece included flowers and some vegetables scattered as if the table was still being used for food prep and sorting. The tableware was the family's stoneware, not the fine-colored glass that was served out front. Napkins were varicolored accents tossed beside the plate as if hurriedly dropped, but he'd been trained by his parents and knew how much work it took to create that casual appeal.

Lola was eyeing the several agents in black suits intently.

When Tim came up beside her, she reached out and hooked her fingers under the edge of his pectoral muscle near his underarm. It took a moment to figure out what was happening, but he was too late to react by the time he did.

Lola dug her fingertips into the brachial plexus nerve cluster and clenched her hand into a fist, vising it against the edge of his pecs with a shockingly strong grip. Pain rocketed across his chest, so sharp he didn't dare move, actually stopped breathing because even the slightest motion hurt like hell.

Lola leaned in until their noses were less than an inch apart, and for the first time Tim didn't feel the least bit romantic about their proximity. By the look on her face, what he could see of it through his pain-squinted eyes, his death might be imminent and he was powerless to stop her.

"Who the hell is coming to dinner?" A feral growl from the queen of the pride, the alpha lioness about to rip out his jugular with her clenched teeth.

He'd have answered if he could, truly. He was feeling a bit light-headed, suffering from the anoxia of holding his breath too long, as if they'd flown above 15,000 feet without oxygen masks.

He heard the kitchen door swing open behind him and Major Beale call out, "You'll never guess who we found lurking in your alley, Mrs. Maloney. You really need a better level of security."

Lola turned enough to glance over Tim's shoulder.

He didn't dare turn and his vision was tunneling slightly. He'd have to breathe soon or pass out, but he wasn't looking forward to the agony the motion would cause.

Her expression eased briefly, but then her fist clenched impossibly harder.

He squeaked. He heard the sound escape his own throat. He could do nothing about it.

She looked at him, bewildered for a moment, and then released her hold as if shocked that she'd done such a thing.

Blood roared back into the nerve cluster Lola had grabbed, the pain spiked, and his knees folded until he sat abruptly on the hard floor.

—⁓—

Emily looked at Lola, then cast a quick, surprised glance at Tim on the parquet floor. Lola could do nothing about it, she was too busy gawking at the man hugging Tim's mother.

Her body snapped to attention. Even as her mind registered how stupid she must look doing so in a red cocktail dress.

President Peter Matthews wandered over and clapped a hand on Tim's shoulder where he still sat on the floor.

"What are you doing down there, Tim?"

·"Breathing, sir." He clutched his chest with one hand. Maybe she had been a bit rough.

Lola was trying to hold strict attention, but she could feel her eyes turning to watch the President's progress. He was a good-looking man on television and in the magazines. But in real life, while he looked about the same, his magnetism radiated outward. He had a narrow face with a good strong chin. Hair that famously flowed free to his collar. Then he aimed his thousand-watt smile at her.

"By how you're standing, you must be one of Emily's crew."

"Sir! Yes, sir!" was all she managed.

Emily came up and hooked a hand through Lola's goosefleshed arm. "At ease, Chief Warrant."

At the command, Lola's body automatically stepped her left foot out to shoulder-wide, keeping her right foot in place, hands clasped tightly behind her back, her spine no less stiff. At least Major Beale was also wearing a nice dress, a knee-length of darkest blue, so Lola didn't feel too exposed by wearing a skimpy cocktail dress.

"Peter, this is Lola LaRue. A damned fine copilot and a nice lady besides"—Emily shook her by the arm as if trying to shake the cyclic loose from her iron grasp—"once she learns to relax a bit. Clearly I don't need to make introductions in the other direction."

With Emily's assistance, Lola managed to drag a hand forward and have it warmly shaken.

A wicked twinkle entered the President's brown eyes as he glanced down at Tim still on the floor. "Didn't warn you I was invited?"

"No, sir, Mr. President."

"Bet he won't be making that mistake again."

She couldn't stop returning the smile. "I'd bet not, sir."

A beautiful man talking on a cell phone came up behind the President. The White House Chief of Staff Daniel Drake Darlington III was almost as popular with the newsies and even more photogenic than his boss. Mr. Darlington was the sort of man to adorn the poster-covered walls of teenage girls.

Lola had read about him. He looked like a studly California surfer but was actually an intellectual Kentucky farmer. He'd rocketed upward to become the most powerful non-elected person in government.

Yet even the most vitriolic D.C. gossip mills seemed to agree that he was doing a magnificent job.

Introductions complete, she managed to unlock her knees, and they all drifted to the table. Tim recovered his feet with some assistance from Mark and ended up to her right. She turned to discover the President landing to her left and her heart rate at least doubled, leaving her light-headed and a bit giddy.

Appetizers, soup, and salad all passed before Lola's nerves quieted enough for her to taste anything. Her mouth told her that she'd missed richness, sweet flavors, and had apparently eaten some food too hot even for a Creole to eat unnoticed as her lips still burned though she had no memory from what.

All she'd been able to do was listen and keep her right knee hard against Tim's left under the table. He anchored her in place, helped her find her center with his presence alone. He reached for her hand under the table a few times, but she jammed her heel down on his toes. There was no way that she'd be holding hands in front of the Commander-in-Chief.

The conversation rolled around her, teasing and sharp ripostes shimmering back and forth between Emily and the President. Daniel tossing in a few of his own lobs that Emily or Mark or Tim caught and shot back without hesitation.

During the swordfish course, Lola finally unwound enough to get Tim's attention by brushing his abused pec in apology, under the guise of dusting away some crumbs.

"'Emily's friend, Peter. That's the only way we refer to him in public'?" His phrase from earlier in the day finally made sense.

Tim shrugged. "It is. Makes it easier to talk about him. Less security risk."

It made sense. It didn't make her happy, but it made sense.

"Enough with the goddamn surprises. In the future, just tell me."

Tim's shrug was easy. "Sure." He pressed his hand briefly against his chest, right where she'd just brushed, to show she was forgiven for abusing him.

Then he smiled wickedly. "It only works for so long anyway. I had the unit going nuts trying to figure out who the practical joker was until I was shot in the arm. Just a meat shot, but I was a month in R and R for recovery. They were all waiting for me in a line when I came back. Had to kind of expand my target range outward after that."

Lola poked her spoon into a crème brûlée that crackled easily beneath the light pressure of her spoon, the warmed vanilla wafting upward through the broken crust and promising delight for her taste buds.

That's when it sunk in, as the custard melted in her mouth, delivering on its promise. She'd just negotiated a relationship rule for the first time in her life. Always before, the only two rules that existed had remained unspoken, known by both parties going in: for the fun of it and no commitments.

Now with Tim she was making relationship decisions, ones that she knew he would honor until the day they died. It was the kind of man he was, a good man that you'd only have to tell once.

Until the day they died.

How in the world could she even have a thought like

that? Give it another week or two, and it would all blow up and they'd go their separate ways with no bad feelings. But that wasn't right. This time she'd signed up for it, this time there would be hurt feelings.

And not just Tim's.

She might feel safe around him, rubbing knees once again under the table, but she was also flying fully exposed, no armor left. It scared the crap out of her.

"Ms. LaRue."

She jumped a little in her seat before turning to face the President.

"Heads up! Incoming!" Emily called out and they all ducked and spun to look around. At least everyone at the table except Daniel and the President. Even the Secret Service agents had a hand in their jackets and were scanning rapidly.

"Sorry." Emily turned to the agents on one side. To one in particular she said, "Sorry, Frank. Wasn't thinking."

He grumbled an acknowledgment. Some signal passed to the others in the room, and they settled back into invisibility.

Emily raised her glass of ice tea in a toast to Lola as if wishing her luck. "Here comes his favorite question."

The President grimaced at her like a teenage boy would at a girl who'd just stolen his thunder. All she did in turn was wave her glass for him to continue with his question.

He huffed out a breath and turned to face Lola.

"Why?"

"Why what, Mr. President?" She'd missed the preceding topic.

"Call me Peter."

"Sorry, sir." She swallowed hard, the smooth crème brûlée suddenly sticking in her throat. "I can't do that, Mr. President."

He harrumphed, but Emily was hiding a smile in her ice tea, so Lola would assume she was doing okay so far.

"Let us then for the moment pretend that we're on a first-name basis."

"If you wish, Mr. President."

That got a bit of a laugh as he accepted some decaf coffee from Mark who'd ended up sitting on his far side.

"You know that I never served in the military."

"Don't say I didn't warn you," Emily chimed in, but the President ignored her.

"Why do you?"

"His other favorite question is, 'Who wants to play poker?'" Emily offered up.

"You play poker, sir?" Lola shot for the subject change but could see it wasn't going to stick.

Mark leaned in to offer a loud whisper in the President's ear. "Don't even think about it, sir. She cleaned Connie's and my clocks on the flight over. I'm not even sure I want a rematch, though I am a sucker for punishment, which is why I married Emily."

He winked at Lola as his wife punched him on the other arm.

"Seriously, Ms. LaRue. Why?"

"Why do you, Mr. President? What made you want the all-consuming job that you have? One that pretty much guarantees that you'll never be employable again." Lola could think of few harder jobs on the planet and none that could interest her less.

That actually stopped him. The President leaned back

in his chair and inspected the distance. She'd wager he wasn't watching the ordered chaos in the kitchen that was only now winding down with the tail end of the dinner rush.

"You'd think that question would have an easy answer."

The table had gone silent. Emily rested her elbows on the table. Lola could feel Tim lean forward to be able to see the President clearly.

"Maybe—" Daniel stopped when Peter Matthews raised his hand.

"My deceased wife is the one who made it happen."

No need to ask, the events of her death had been international news. The pilots miraculously survived the helicopter crash and the resulting fireball that had scorched the face of the White House for the first time since the British invasion during the War of 1812, but the First Lady had not survived. Everyone knew Emily Beale had been one of the surviving pilots. Something clicked in a shared glance with her husband, and Lola realized that Mark Henderson had been the other pilot.

Suddenly, what had been a tragic accident mourned round the world took on different shading. SOAR's two best pilots had somehow both been on the helicopter that had killed the First Lady. With the slightest shake of her head, Emily warned her off the topic. Lola shoved it aside for future consideration as the President continued speaking.

"She pushed and shoved and drove. Wanted the power and prestige. That's how it happened, but not why." He toyed with his coffee a bit, shook in a tiny spoonful of brown sugar and stirred it idly.

"I—Hmm, not really inspiring confidence as the

leader of the free world, am I? I can see it, but I'm finding trouble tracking down the words."

"That was a cheat, anyway, Chief Warrant." Major Henderson again aimed that smile at her. "The President asked first."

"Right." Peter sat up straight and turned quickly to face her directly. "I did. You answer. And if I like your answer, I'll unravel this mess I call a coherent thought process and answer yours."

Lola looked over at Tim, who nodded. Not as if she needed help, but as if he had absolute confidence in her answer. She turned back.

"Do you sleep well at night, sir?"

"Reasonably. Except when Daniel calls at the strangest hours with the next crisis, but yes, I sleep pretty well, considering."

"Good. That's why I fly."

He frowned at her.

"My life changed on September 11th, 2001. Vastly for the better. I was headed right down that proverbial highway to hell, one step from falling off the damned edge. Probably that very day." Lola briefly considered that the girl who'd skipped school to hang with a bunch of hookers, trying to get her nerve up before the first john showed up, was now sitting next to the President of the United States. Just more proof of what was possible.

"Except the world changed and I stepped up instead of down. I fly so that you can sleep. So that Americans can sleep. It makes me feel..." She looked around searching for the words. Looked at Tim as he squeezed her hand as if she were speaking for both of them. She returned the gesture, wondering at what moment he'd snagged her hand, and faced the President once more without letting go.

"It makes me feel strong. Powerful. Who knows? I may have already helped stop the next jet plane before it crashed into another building. I'll never know, but it feels amazing that maybe I have that kind of power in my hands. I like that a lot. Guess it strokes my ego, but in a much healthier way than I'd been doing it up until that time." She considered for a moment, but it was the best she'd ever been able to explain it to herself. Part of that was sharing stories with Tim through the morning and afternoon.

"I like flying the world's most kick-ass helicopter and, well, kicking some ass with it. But I like what that results in even better. Tim's got a nice family here. I like being a part of protecting that." She spooned up some more of the custard and savored the sweet taste. Then she grinned at the President a little wickedly.

He raised his eyebrows.

"Your turn, President Peter," she let the first name linger for a tantalizing moment before continuing, "Matthews, Commander-in-Chief, sir."

Chapter 40

THE PRESIDENT SCOWLED AT EMILY ACROSS THE TABLE as she burst out laughing at him.

Lola figured that scowl could stop most other world leaders, but it did no good on Major Emily Beale.

"She got you, Sneaker Boy. One for the home team, Chief Warrant. Now pony up, and make it even half as good or we'll make you stand out on the Ellipse in your underwear and recite the poetry of Theodore Roethke, maybe the one about the biddly bear. And don't think we can't do it."

"I'd have you court-martialed."

"You can try, Peter, but the judge will be too busy laughing himself sick to put us away. Besides, it will be our word against yours as to why you're doing it. We tried to stop you, honest." She fluttered her eyelashes at him in a very un-Emily-like fashion. "Didn't we, Frank?" she called to Agent Frank Adams where he stood behind the President.

The head of the Presidential Protection Detail didn't even try to hide his smile while he spoke as if talking to a room of reporters. "The Secret Service does not comment on the actions of the President."

"Crap."

"It's our job to keep you safe, sir." Adams continued, clearly enjoying the moment. "Our job does not require that we keep you from making a fool of yourself by reciting poetry in your underwear, should you suddenly find it necessary to do so. The choice of underwear is completely up to you. Personally I'd recommend something with color. White doesn't play as well on camera."

The President glanced back at his senior agent, who shrugged.

"Man's gotta have some fun, Mr. President." Adams's grin revealed exactly who would be enjoying himself.

"I get to take pictures," Lola piped up.

Tim started giggling. "Does it have to be in English? Can you read Spanish, Mr. President? Bobbi," he turned to the service line and called out to his sister. "Do you still have that collection of erotic poetry?"

"Under my pillow every night," she chimed back before heading out into the dining room with a tray of desserts.

Daniel's phone rang.

The President swore just loudly enough for Lola to hear while the others at the table still bandied back and forth suggestions of appropriate hats to be worn with underwear while reciting risqué Spanish poetry, and perhaps patriotic socks.

Daniel stood and stepped aside for a quick whispered conversation lost in the various sounds of the kitchen.

She could see the President keeping a weather eye on his Chief of Staff.

"Bad news, Mr. President?"

He faced her with a long-suffering sigh. "It's never good when his phone rings. Damn, I was actually enjoying the evening."

Daniel came over and tapped the President on the

shoulder. He leaned forward to whisper in Peter's ear, but Lola could hear.

"President Javad Madani would like to speak with you. In thirty minutes if that is convenient."

Lola felt the shock ripple through her. The president of the Islamic Republic of Iran was the last person on the planet she'd wager the U.S. President wanted to hear from. Not mere days after SOAR and Delta had just run a clandestine operation deep into his country.

"Of course." The President looked grim, then nodded to Daniel. "Yes, of course, it would be our pleasure to speak with him."

Daniel moved off to finish the call and the President started to stand.

Major Henderson clamped a hand on his shoulder.

The President jolted, probably not used to being touched by anyone, certainly not restrained.

"Sorry, folks. I have to—"

"Answer the lady's question," Henderson finished for him.

Lola could see Frank Adams moving forward and the other agents rising to their toes.

The President held up a hand to wave them off.

"And then if there's anything my team can do to help, we'll go with you."

The President considered for a moment, then nodded. He took a deep breath and turned to Lola.

"I have to be quick. And I wish I could say this better, but I can't. And the reason that I can't? You already said it for me. I am President so that my country can remain a unified country. Not fractured under a thousand vying demands by a hundred times that many special interests.

I try to make small bits of peace where I can. I seek a balance between oil demand and ecologists, foreign trade and domestic production, and so on across more venues than you can imagine. That's what lets me sleep at night, knowing that I tried my best to help. That I made our country run even a little better than it did the day before."

Lola waited until he finished. His words slammed home. That's why she flew. So that someone could try to do just that. Here was immediate proof of the rightness of her choice to fly with SOAR. The President was the ultimate search-and-rescue pilot, definitely in full combat, even if not down in the frontline skirmishes.

She leaned in and hugged him briefly and whispered in his ear, "Thank you. Thank you for doing what you do, Peter."

Chapter 41

LOLA LOOKED AROUND THE SITUATION ROOM AND tried to figure out how in hell she'd ended up here. You'd expect to find the President and his Chief of Staff in the White House Sit Room. General Brett Rogers, the Chairman of the Joint Chiefs of Staff, made sense, even if there was no way Lola would be speaking in the man's presence. Couldn't if she wanted to.

Brett Rogers had started in Special Forces in Vietnam. Been instrumental in dozens of operations that had helped maintain peace through the Cold War years. Led Special Operations Command for almost a decade, right through Iraq and into Afghanistan, and now sat as the Chairman of the Joint Chiefs. He was the senior-most soldier on the planet. It would be like a first-year acting student trying to have a nice sit-down chat with Meryl Streep.

That the Majors had been invited didn't seem completely odd, especially considering the history between them and President Matthews and their knowledge of the operation. When Emily had insisted that her copilot be included, Lola had freaked. All of her protestations had been to no avail, not even the silent but desperate plea she'd aimed at Tim had saved her. Her protests had died when Major Beale rested a hand on her still flat belly. Right. Lola was backup coverage for a "what-if" scenario.

Tim had managed to toss her a light windbreaker which she'd slipped on over her dress before boarding the presidential motorcade. It looked utterly ridiculous, the flirty red skirt popping out below Tim's worn, dark blue windbreaker. But it was better than sitting in a red cocktail dress in the Sit Room. Major Henderson had worn a jacket and had likewise wrapped it around his wife's barely more modest dress.

Lola tried to concentrate on the images being flashed up on the screen. She recognized many of them but hadn't seen the drone's footage of their departure from the Iranian desert. Hadn't known there was a drone overhead watching. Her move with the helicopter to build the dust cloud captured in perfect, night-vision detail.

Major Henderson whistled. "Slick move, honey. Damn slick."

"That was all Lola." Emily nodded in her direction, sounding at perfect ease in a room that was about to cave in and collapse on Lola's head.

"Nicely done, Chief Warrant. A damn fine piece of flying."

In any other circumstance, Lola might have brushed it off or sent back some dismissive riposte. Instead, she found herself inspecting the table's surface and blushing. Not something she ever did.

A figure slipped in the door, unnoticed by those farther away, and sat beside Lola. She glanced up and recognized Colonel Michael Gibson of the D-boys. They shook hands in silence and exchanged simple nods. His handsome face was grim, the scar along his chin deepening as he frowned at the film, perhaps remembering his own narrow escape. This just kept getting uglier by the moment.

They ran the footage of some Iranian fast movers sweeping in low across the desert. She hadn't known the jets were there. By the time stamp on the video, the choppers had cleared the horizon about twenty minutes before the Iranian Air Force showed up and blew the hell out of the site the D-boys had just robbed. The fire plumes were massive, they'd really set out to incinerate the place.

Satellite imagery had traced the Iranian jets back almost two hours to a little known military airbase outside Tabriz, on the opposite side of the country. They hadn't used local forces available at the much nearer Shiraz or Zahedan bases.

That meant the D-boys, including Michael here beside her, had completed their theft between the time of the Iranian flight's takeoff and its destruction of the site. A narrow window after three full days in-country. If either the Iranian jets or the SOAR helicopters had been on just a slightly different schedule, Michael wouldn't be here now. And if either flight had traveled higher than a few hundred feet, they'd probably have seen each other going by with all of the nasty consequences that implied.

Lola could feel a cold sweat at just how close they'd come to dying in the desert.

The other picture, which was even stranger, was a drone image of a cleanup crew.

General Rogers spoke over this piece of film. "This has been identified as an element of the newly formed Quds Unit 400. They were first reported in March 2012 as the top-secret Iranian Special Forces. They were formed to operate strictly overseas to carry out terror on extraterritorial targets. But here we see them operating within Iran against one of their own military plants."

The President glanced at the wall clock.

Six minutes until the phone call.

"So, let's review what was found in the desert."

General Rogers cleared his throat uncertainly, but Michael stepped forward.

"Perhaps I can speak to that, sir."

"Yes. Hello, Colonel, I didn't see you come in. Yes, please do." The general leaned back and rubbed at his temples as the Delta Commander leaned in.

Lola cringed and wished desperately that she was with Tim. Or in Afghanistan. Anywhere but here.

"CIA analysts originally identified this structure just beyond the northwest corner of the city of Ravar. This is part of an ongoing satellite survey of Iranian electrical power infrastructure. Note the large scale of this power station and yet only a single set of electrical lines headed toward the city. Research through prior image mapping revealed the installation of a major power feed to this remote building another mile into the desert. It has since been disguised as an irrigation trench, but analysis shows that while the trench is frequently kept filled with water, it does not in fact flow to the fields beyond."

He called for close-up images of the desert building. Some hidden technician placed them on the screens. A big, squared-off concrete block with no windows and heavily fortified steel doors.

"These photos were taken by cameras on the ground. Hidden machine-gun nests and razor wire fences are clearly visible."

Lola had always felt that CSAR and SOAR were

among the more dangerous occupations in the military. But now that she saw up-close images of where Michael had led his small troop, she felt as safe as if she were flying in the Pauley's Island kitchen. And Michael's team hadn't merely gotten near the building, they'd entered and robbed it.

She looked at him again to see if he'd somehow changed, grown bigger than life, but he was still just Michael-sized.

"Far too large for a pump house," Michael continued, "so we investigated further. The security was immense. No opportunity to infiltrate an agent. The single road is heavily guarded at three points as well as a desert perimeter. I went in with a team of five other operators to investigate. The building goes down for several more stories." He counted on his fingers as he continued.

"Upper floor, guard barracks. The first level underground is, was living quarters, kitchens, etc. The next, offices, small research labs, etc. The bottom floor was a large production laboratory." Then he stated, even more dryly if that was possible, "We managed to borrow a vehicle."

The master of understatement.

Daniel pulled up a photograph of the captured truck. The door had an emblem of two leafed branches and crossed swords behind a central shield showing through the dust. An official vehicle of the Iranian Army.

"What this truck contains is all of the documents and computers we exfiltrated from the site. As our final action, we grabbed what we considered to be their primary computer server and reference files. As expected, the loss was noticed almost immediately, but we had a head start of over three minutes. Thankfully the Black Adder flight was prepared for immediate departure on our arrival. Our thanks." He nodded to Lola and the Majors.

Lola remembered the five guys on weird, hopped-up bicycles, the racing truck, and the line of vehicles chasing them. They'd arrived within thirty seconds of plan, and she now understood that if they'd been even a full minute late, at least the man next to her would no longer be alive and probably none of his squadmates either.

"So far we have unraveled evidence of a fearful biocide—"

Lola hadn't meant to cry out but couldn't help herself. Everyone's worst nightmare, a true weapon of mass destruction. The Majors paled and even the President looked quite ill, though he must have already been told that much.

The Delta operator continued with an impossible calm. "This biocide has a very high dispersion rate, very low dissipation rate, and unstoppable lethality. The vector can be either air or waterborne. It's designed to go everywhere quickly, not run down in potency, and kill everything it touches. Introduced into a small town, it will kill every mammal within three days before it runs its course. Introduced into a sizable city…" He shrugged.

"We saw no evidence of the chemical itself at the plant. This means the research could still be purely theoretical. Or perhaps it's manufactured off-site. But the nearby power station is primarily serving the bottom-story, large underground production lab at the Ravar site. We had very little time to investigate, less than six minutes, but there was simply no chemical there. Though the scientists were, presumably, still in residence when the site was destroyed by the Iranians. They certainly were twenty minutes earlier when we departed."

The silence hammered down on them.

The image of the truck remained on the screen.

No one was meeting anyone's eyes.

Lola finally managed to look up at Major Beale across the Situation Room table.

This is what they'd signed up for. To defend the nation against attacks like this. Just like this. They shared a nod. Come what may, they'd see it through.

They, and Colonel Gibson of Delta Force, were the only ones who didn't jump when the phone rang.

Chapter 42

"Good evening, President Matthews."

Lola listened to the voice on the speakerphone.

Cultured, smooth, careful. She looked at the biography now showing on the main screen of the Situation Room. A slender man with a short, graying beard. A pleasant smile graced his face in several of the photos. Educated at Oxford, and still the Iranians had elected him president. A surprise there. A Western-educated leader.

Or was he chosen by the latest Ayatollah? Lola couldn't remember quite how their government worked.

"Good evening, President Madani. How can we help you this evening?"

"I am hoping that just you and I could discuss a small problem we are having."

President Matthews glanced around, signaling that they should all remain silent before he spoke.

"A small problem, Mr. President, perhaps in the desert outside Ravar requiring the attention of three of your Phantom F-4E jets and a third of your Unit 400 forc—"

"They were the ones I killed there." Madani cut him off harshly.

President Matthews didn't change the tone of his voice in the slightest, calm and steady. Having forced Madani, by his very reaction, to confirm the existence and involvement of the secret-ops unit, Lola hoped he wasn't going to push harder.

"Yes, I am aware that you've had some difficulties. How may we be of help?"

There was a long pause and Lola wondered if the man was going to continue, but the President didn't look worried.

The sound of a sigh over the phone proved him right. It finally sank in where she was sitting and a cold shiver ran up her spine. She'd much rather be sitting in the windblown seat of her Black Hawk than the comfortable armchairs of this room. To lead here, to be the Commander-in-Chief, President Matthews would have to be a truly exceptional judge of character. Far more specialized than herself or the Majors. In this room, there was only one person on the planet of sufficient caliber every four to eight years. Or at least one hoped so, and this president did have a reputation for being the right person in the right place at the right time.

And at least from the seat of her helicopter, a poor decision couldn't affect the fate of millions.

She took a calming breath, and then another. It didn't help in the slightest.

"You are a very wise man, Mr. President."

"Thank you, President Madani. And might I point out that you have also managed to rise to the presidency of one of the few space-faring nations on the planet. But your difficulties are earthbound."

Again the long pause.

"You are very... American."

Lola had to bite her lower lip hard to suppress her laughter. It was true. Peter Matthews had all of the direct, forthright, self-assured American attitude that flustered so many foreigners. Something she and the

President had in common. His easy attitude made the room feel a little less weird, but not much.

President Matthews waited out another silence.

"There is little liking between our countries..." The Iranian leader hesitated. "Do you not think so, Mr. President?"

"Far too little." He looked around the table to see mostly shrugs about what was going on.

Lola wondered if... Something was familiar in the way the Iranian president was dodging around the meat of the matter, but he wasn't going away either. As if he was... afraid?

"Perhaps, President Madani, there is a problem that we may solve together?" Clearly the President was a step ahead of her again.

"Yes. Yes, that would be good." Mandani almost stumbled over himself being pleased. "You and I, we can perhaps solve this thing together."

President Matthews glanced at General Rogers, then at Emily. At a thoughtful look from the former and a nod of encouragement from the latter he continued.

"Mr. Pres... May I call you Javad? You may call me Peter if that would be easier."

"Yes, that would be better."

"So, this problem in the desert, this laboratory, it is—"

"A terrible thing, Peter. A terrible thing. I had it destroyed as soon as I heard about it."

General Rogers turned to glare at the phone in surprise, opened his mouth to speak, then remembered and shut it again. He scribbled furiously on a pad and shoved it to the President even as he was finishing it.

Lola leaned forward.

He's in trouble. The religious right made it, he de-stroyed it. They'll come for him.

The President nodded with surety. He'd clearly come to the same conclusion.

Lola wanted to tell him that this was no time to be playing poker. *Lay down your hand and maybe he'll lay down his.* She could barely suppress her exclamation of surprise when he did exactly that.

"Javad, there weren't any chemical or biologic weapons at the site when you bombed it."

There was a gasp, then silence. Such a long silence that the President leaned forward to inspect the phone to check the connection.

"So it is true." The voice was small, as if coming from much farther away than half a world. "The weapon is in transport. I was too late."

"Do you know where?"

Everyone in the room strained forward in their seats to listen though the sound was clear in the room.

"Only a few clues, nothing concrete yet."

"But we may assume that it is coming to America." President Matthews didn't make it a question.

"With our countries' relations, that is a reasonable assumption, but I can only confirm it is upon a ship. I do not know its type, name, or destination."

"Is there a cure?"

Lola could barely swallow after the worried intensity of President Matthews's question.

"If there is, Peter, I destroyed it along with everything else at the site."

Not everything. Would the President play that card? Major Henderson had said that the President played

poker with more enthusiasm than success. He clearly
made up for that playing in the international arena. Lola
couldn't even guess which way would play better.

"Javad." Matthews's voice had the perfect balance
of calm and surety. "I have your computers and the research references here."

This was clearly the table where President Matthews
played a masterful game. One way over Lola's head.

"How? No, I don't care. Praise be to Allah. Then you
know what it can do. Can you stop it?"

"I don't know, Javad. We are working on the how,
but we need to know where and when."

"I will try, Peter. I swear that I will try."

Help him, Emily mouthed at him. And Lola could
see why she didn't play poker. Childhood friend or not,
Major Beale couldn't see that the President was five or
six moves ahead of her. It was the same way she flew,
straight ahead without any games.

The Iranian president had just reached out in secrecy
to help the most hated foreign power. The personal and
professional risk of doing so was immense. If he were
caught, it wouldn't be execution. It would be torture of
him, his families, his friends, and every member of his
political party. It might unleash an extremist jihad of
unprecedented proportions.

"What can I do to help you, Javad?"

President Matthews was clearly searching for an idea,
any idea. And just as clearly he didn't have one.

She scribbled a note, thought better of it, crossed it
out, wrote another, and shoved it across the table so that
it slid into his range of vision.

The President read it, and read it again, clearly thinking

very hard and fast. Then he nodded sharply without looking up. Decision made.

"Javad."

"Yes, Peter."

"I regret that I don't know who is murdering your top nuclear scientists one after another."

Iran had lost five and nearly lost a half-dozen more as someone used weapons, poisons, and car bombs to kill the country's top physicists. Lola had crossed it out because clearly Israel was doing the assassinations and they had to have at least tacit U.S. approval to proceed. So, stopping that just wasn't going to happen. The United States needed at least one friendly nation in the Middle East too badly to mess with that.

"However, perhaps I can ease the international banking sanctions associated with your space program. Space only. I still cannot condone any nuclear research or related efforts."

Again the silence was long enough for the President to check that the connection remained active.

"Yes, Peter. That would be enough. If I could show them that I had negotiated the release of foreign-held funds that rightly belong to Iran, that might be more important than the destruction of Ravar."

"We'll be in touch, Javad."

President Matthews finished the pleasantries and cut the connection. He looked slowly about the room, offered the general a nod of thanks, then glanced at the two notes in front of him. Comparing them.

"Whose writing is this? Sure isn't yours, Brett. Way too nice. Thanks, Em. It was the perfect carrot. Even the crossed-out teaser of what he'd ask first but I'm certainly not going to do."

Emily pointed across the table at Lola.

President Matthews slowly turned to face her.

"Perfect timing, Chief Warrant. Exactly what I was looking for."

Again she could only nod.

Then he quirked that nationally televised smile that he wore so easily.

"You tell Mr. Maloney to keep you close, Chief Warrant LaRue. If he doesn't, I might be trying to steal you away."

For the second time tonight and perhaps in her life, Lola felt the heat rise to her face as she looked down at the table.

She and Tim had been much less circumspect than they'd thought. And the heat she felt thinking of Tim was echoed by a warmth much closer to her heart.

Chapter 43

LOLA TOLD TIM ALL SHE COULD REMEMBER OF THE phone call and the meetings that followed, going over it again and again until she had every detail clear. She'd done it while curled up in his arms, just letting him hold her close and safe in the apartment's bed. Her head on his shoulder as she spoke, a leg hooked over his hips, and her fingers tracing out her memories on that perfect chest of his.

A Secret Service agent had returned her to the restaurant's back door and there he'd been. Sitting outside the kitchen door, still wide awake though it was two in the morning. Tim sitting in a pool of brightness cast by a single light over the door was the best welcome she'd ever had. He must have been worried because he hadn't even taken the opportunity to razz the agent.

Now the telling was done. Lola hadn't left out a single thing. Not how out of place she'd felt. Not how her flight had looked in the drone's camera. Not about the fears of living in a world where such hatred didn't just exist but created horridly lethal weapons of mass destruction and where people could be so twisted that they'd want to wield them.

She lay in silence now as Tim stroked his hand up and down her bare back. She'd never lain naked with a man when it wasn't about sex; either the sex that had just happened or the sex that was about to. But for this instant, for this precious moment, they simply lay together in companionship. In comfort.

He twisted his head enough to lay his lips on her hair. Tim was the perfect gentle lover, the considerate man, the good son.

"How, Tim? How is it that you ever left your family?"

She could feel the lips against her hair shift into a smile. She'd bet if she could see, it would be a sad one. The sigh that rippled across his chest beneath her spread hand and draped arm confirmed her guess.

"It'll sound stupid."

"Good, that way I won't be the only one."

She could feel him trying to look at her. "You're not stupid."

"You have no idea. Now give. Henderson's dad was a SEAL. Beale's such a goddamn overachiever that she couldn't help herself. Connie was born to it. Kee will fight anything she meets to the death. What is someone like you doing as a lifer in the Army?"

Tim relaxed back against his pillow, probably contemplating the dark ceiling barely lit by the alley's light shining up through a narrow opening in the window curtain.

"I had this great childhood. I was a cutup, the class clown, and I was good at it. Got jazzed up on the attention, I guess. I occasionally feel bad that Mrs. Wilson retired unexpectedly at the end of my fifth-grade year. I think it might have been because I automated her desk. Silent remote-control motors. I could open or close the drawers when her back was turned. Make her chair wander away. Once I got it out the open door and a dozen yards down the hall before she noticed."

Lola giggled against his chest, feeling a bit guilty about laughing at a woman she didn't know.

"Once I got a taste of it, I couldn't stop. I reprogrammed the school's master clock to play AC/DC's 'Back in Black' each time it was supposed to ring the bell for class change. I rebuilt my uncle's transmission linkage, installing a reverser gear in the drive train so that he had three reverse gears and one forward one. That car could go really fast, backwards."

That got her to laugh.

"Then I started getting stupid."

His suddenly serious voice sobered her instantly. She might have tried to raise herself to look at him, but his hand no longer stroked her back. Instead it clamped tight across her shoulders as if holding on.

"Worked my way up into a chop shop for a while. I'm a damn good mechanic, and I learned a lot taking cars apart and putting them back together so that they didn't look stolen. I made good money, too good for a teenager, but thankfully, other than a few drunken escapades, I didn't get too stupid with all that cash. It was the cars I liked. The mechanicking. I did a lot of stupid shit. Even stole and striped a cop car once, as if that wasn't about the dumbest thing you could do."

His body was rigid with memory.

"I'd go home, come here to the kitchen, and Ma would know. Maybe not exactly what, but I could feel her shame of me. Which only pushed me further. To this day I don't know what I was rebelling against. As far as I can recall, I didn't know then, either."

He took a deep breath, raising her head as his chest filled with air that he then released in an exasperated puff.

"I still don't know. I was just stupid. Right until the day I saw that jet airliner fly into the side of the Pentagon carrying a bellyful of helpless passengers. That was the moment I woke up. That's the day I understood that the world was way bigger than what shit I could spread around on it. My parents love me the way they do because they know what I crawled out of."

Tim wasn't just a good man, he was a good man by conscious choice. That in some ways made him an even better man than she'd already thought he was. And made her feel even less that she deserved to be with him.

"They loved you anyway. You just gave them a reason to be proud."

"Maybe. I guess."

Lola could feel the tension remaining in him like hot steel.

"Never told anyone any of that. Not Ma. Not John."

Trust. He treated her with such absolute trust. She didn't deserve such a thing, such a gift.

"So you really are 'Crazy Tim.' Dumb enough to trust a Creole bitch." Her mind latched on to a joke and spit it out before her thoughts could go any deeper. Before they could lead somewhere she didn't want to go.

"Yep." The soft chuckle rippled across his pecs. "I guess I earned that one fair and square. Earned it long before I was tagged with it, if they only knew."

But Lola's thoughts continued despite her best attempt to sidetrack them.

"Your parents love the man you've become."

He shrugged. "I guess. Maybe for the man they think I can be. I haven't been tossed in lockup for a couple years, not since before I made SOAR. But they saw plenty of the bad years. I don't think they trust those are really gone."

"Are they?"

He released his tight grip on her shoulder and started toying with her hair. It seemed to hold endless fascination for him. He was always combing his hand through it, twirling a bit around his finger. A dozen, a hundred little tugs on her scalp like a gentle massage.

"I don't know. The Majors sure put up with enough crap from me. Now I just do the practical jokes on Rangers, which nobody seems to really mind except the Rangers." His tone clearly indicating that their opinion didn't matter in the slightest.

"I usually manage to make it look as if another Ranger did it. Like the guy I sewed into his bunk while he was sleeping. I used the suture line from a half-dozen med kits that I lifted from his squadmates and just happened to leave lying about where he could see them. They had to cut him out of the bed. It was especially funny because he kicked and screamed every time one of them came near him with a knife because he was sure they were the ones who'd sewed him in."

He tugged at another little clump of her hair.

"My parents always wanted me to be a better man, didn't help much. The Majors definitely did. I think it's you that I really want to be the best for. I feel different around you. As if I'm the one that's important, not who I'm supposed to be. Not who my parents think I'm supposed to be. Just me, as I am."

They lay together with Tim's absolute honesty between them. Lola couldn't turn away from that. She wanted to use sex, wash away the moment, but that wasn't honest either.

"That's my dad."

"What is?"

Lola hadn't meant to say anything, but Tim had given her such a gift that she had to return it in kind.

"The way I use sex. Used sex. Or don't use it. I don't seem to do it with you, though I'll be damned if I know why." Or maybe she did, but it was not something she'd ever admit out loud.

"Sex is power. Dad taught me that."

"He didn't?" Tim jerked half upright.

"No." Lola patted his chest to ease him back into place. "He was an abuser, just not a physical one. He absolutely controlled me by proving just how thoroughly he could ignore me. I was never good enough, always a disappointment, didn't meet standards. When he had a woman, he made sure they were loud, usually right in the living room so I couldn't even escape my room. Sex is power."

She pushed herself up on one elbow to look down at him. Just the least hint of light brushing Tim's beautiful face.

"You may be the first man I've ever been with where sex wasn't some weapon to wield, some way to distract myself so that I can fly under the radar and avoid how screwed up my past is. To dodge what a mess I am. How screwed up my family is."

"Is? You have family? I thought your parents were dead."

"No." Her voice was the barest whisper. "No, I just wish he was."

Tim pulled her back down to his chest. He could feel her blinking hard, fighting against the tears he could hear in her voice but she was too stubborn to release.

"He? Your dad? The one you said was run over by the beer truck while lying drunk in a tavern parking lot?"

"Yes. That one." Her voice was a small, distant thing as if she weren't just flying under the radar but was falling off its most distant edge.

He stared up at the ceiling, considering if he should be offended by the lie, but he wasn't. He knew the self-protection of a lie. But he was learning from Lola that it wasn't necessarily the best protection. Telling her the truth, he'd surprised himself. He really was his best self around her. Something about her made him want to be the strong, solid, reliable person that he'd only pretended to be before.

"Tell me about him." He felt the shiver run up her spine, but no tears splashed onto his chest and her head didn't turn into his shoulder to avoid the question. She simply lay in silence and Tim let her.

"Ricky LaRue." Her voice little more than a whisper. "Deputy Sheriff of New Orleans Richard LaRue. Used to say he always wanted to be a cop so that he could lock others up for the shit he did. Never wanted to be sheriff, 'because those idiots get elected, then thrown back out.' He just wanted the power, didn't care about the title. He ran a bunch of brothels, a couple drug rings, had three or four street gangs that reported to him. Who knows. Some corrupt judges, which the Big Easy is known for, he has his hands into several of those as well."

"How did you get away from that?" Lola might project wild, but she was forthright and had apparently become best friends with Emily Beale almost overnight, which was high praise indeed. Lola was a woman of such integrity that it was impossible to reconcile that with such a past.

"Mama Raci." Her voice sounded solid for the first time. "Old crone who ran a brothel not under my father's sway. She'd started in the front of the house as a child prostitute. Ended up working in the place and, sixty years or more later, ran the house from the kitchen with an iron fist. Found me bruised, battered, and bloody in the back alley at twelve. Couple of my dad's criminal buddies went after me and he did nothing to stop them. Said he owed them or some such crap. I beat them off, cut one up pretty good, and got away."

Tim held her tighter, could feel the rage building inside him. No child deserved that kind of past. Lola lay against him totally passive, as if she were talking about the day's news of some far-off place.

"Mama Raci took me in but never let me into the front of the house. I worked in the kitchen with her. Ran errands. I guess I'm the one she decided to save. Got me to go back to school, let me sleep in the kitchen as long as I did my homework. Always made sure I was safe and fed."

She let out a long, slow breath. "Already told you the rest."

Yes, the same thing that had happened to him. She wasn't kidding when she said she'd been born on September 11th, 2001. They both had.

The woman she'd become was a magnificent

statement of her strength of will. Made him feel humble and stupid. He'd struggled against a great family and barely found the fortitude to crawl out of it. Lola strode out of Hell with the power of a goddess of old.

Now she did turn her face into his shoulder, and sniffled.

Tim held her tight and rocked her back and forth. Lola's voice, so carefully flat, clearly hid a tidal wave of pain and anger and old scar tissue.

He knew about old scar tissue. Could feel himself shedding the last of it as they lay there.

He hoped there was some way he could return the favor.

Chapter 44

LOLA CHECKED OVER THE HUEY UH-1M HELICOPTER.

Tim was preflighting the exterior under Anacostia's helipad lights.

Lola was going down the checklist, powering up the different systems, checking fuel, making calibrations, and tuning radios as she went.

They'd been trying to figure out how not to go insane while awaiting orders when Tim remembered that he had to requalify. Each year, everyone in SOAR had to requalify for their seat, and Tim's renewal cycle was coming up. Deployments didn't count, combat gave practice but didn't require standards of excellence.

On only an hour or two of sleep they'd driven up to the Aberdeen Proving Ground range. Lola ran through the target and free range, sharpshooter, and kill-house trials to keep Tim company and keep a bit of edge on. She'd always thought herself good, but Tim was clearly in a whole other league, easily outshooting her scores. Didn't worry her too much, she was a flier first and they each were there to do what they were good at.

It was only on the range debrief that she realized two things. First, shooting beside Tim had made her top any prior score she'd ever achieved. And second, what Tim was doing. He wasn't just trying to requal; he was trying to bust Kee Stevenson's record scores. He was close, damn close.

It would all depend on the night-flight tests.

He didn't match Kee's sniper skills, but on the heavy guns he was a damned artist. He shredded pop-up targets almost before they flipped into position and didn't lose a single point for a "friendly" kill.

The range officer was pretty psyched about the scores. He was so cheerful that Tim didn't think to do anything evil until they'd already gotten back on the road and it was too late.

They'd caught a dinner of blue crab at a dive along the Baltimore waterfront while waiting for sunset. Tim swung by the family restaurant and prepared a huge picnic basket. Clearly he had some other plans for after the night-range flight and she was good with that.

Now they were prepping to fly out of Anacostia.

Tim shoved the picnic basket in the back of the Huey and strapped it down out of the way.

Lola switched over to the right seat for this flight. It only took one pilot to fly a Huey, and it was nice to sit pilot's side again. For the test, General Arnson had arranged for a minigun rig in the center of the cargo bay door and a shooter's seat set up exactly as a Black Hawk's would be.

Now it was up to Tim to show what he could do.

Lola glanced up as he climbed aboard and strapped in. He pulled on his helmet and turned on the intercom.

"Good to go."

In answer Lola fired up the turbine.

And it was up to her to make sure he had a challenging flight.

That was gonna be fun.

—∿∿—

Tim knew he was in the groove. He'd often hit high score records in one of the tests, sometimes two, but never six on the same day. Right now the only place Kee still outranked him was fixed and moving targets at five-hundred-plus yards. And the only one she was out of the ballpark on was the two-thousand-meter bench-rest range. Since she was currently the U.S. Army's number one ranked at that range, he didn't feel too bad. Damn, he could barely see the target. How did the woman bull's-eye it?

He rubbed his hands together as Lola flew them down to the Wallops Island Navy range. Not that his hands were cold; D.C. April nights were rarely cold.

It was that the scores were so close he could feel the magic buzzing in his hands.

"Coming up."

Tim kicked on the power to his night-vision goggles and double-checked his seat harness.

"Do me proud, Chief Warrant." A slack flight would downgrade his score even if he shot dead on.

"Roger that." He heard the excitement in her voice easily matching his. For half a second he wondered if he should be worried, but he'd trust Lola over any pilot other than Major Beale. He dismissed the itch between his shoulder blades.

They crossed over Wallops Island and the Chincoteague National Wildlife Refuge. Yeah, couple of things down there he wanted to show Lola, but he couldn't think about that right now.

Focus, dude. Be loose and focus.

They flew another mile or so out to sea and the off-shore target area.

"Range, this is Marine thirty-four thirty." Their tail number to identify their flight. "Ready for Qual Run." Lola let the range controller know they were ready.

Tim flexed his fingers again, made sure the cartridge belt lay clean from can to feeder, and flicked on the power switch. The minigun's six barrels spun to life with a high whine and the familiarity of an old friend. He set the selector for the low-rate of three thousand rounds per minute. At fifty rounds a second, he had to be careful not to destroy a target past any ability to score it.

"Marine, this is range. Range is clear. You may commence your run."

And the helicopter tumbled toward the ocean.

Tim hung on to the handles of the gun to keep himself stable.

"Lola!" he cried out. She was going to die. They'd both be...

Nothing was making sense.

The engine sounded normal.

But they were falling like—

Tim saw a clear target, marked by bright infrared beacons, bobbing on the waves. Without thought, he jerked the trigger for a half second. The gun burped and threw twenty-five rounds at three times the speed of sound. Every fifth round was an infrared tracer streaking bright green across his night-vision goggles.

He dead-centered it. How?

Lola had flattened the flight at the perfect instant, a wholly unexpected attack from an unusual angle.

She spiraled upward and a half-dozen remote-control drone weather balloons with tiny engines floated across the night sky. Friendlies had star markers, enemies big

X's. Each dangled a target barely five feet square; at a hundred miles per hour, that was pretty damn small. Goal was to dead-center the *X* targets without bursting their balloons. Killing their drones always pissed off the range guys.

Lola was weaving like a mad woman, and it was all he could do to separate and nail targets. One would be a dozen rotors out and the next one so close that the IR markers were blindingly bright.

"Fire below," Lola called out and stood the chopper on its side.

Tim hung in his harness looking straight down at the midnight blackness of the choppy ocean surface. A dazzling sparkler of brilliant green rocket fire came roaring up at him.

RPG!

His breath froze, but his reflexes didn't. Knowing it was impossible and that they were about to die, he zeroed on the nose of the rocket-propelled grenade and shot a long burst.

It went off like… a firecracker. A little fizzle of bright streaks to show it had been disabled; the blue "safe" color just another shade of green in his night vision.

He'd never flown a range like this, at the edge of chaos, and he knew he couldn't think about it.

Trust your pilot.

That's the rule.

Trust your pilot and your training.

Tim shut off his brain and kept his attention on the targets that the pilot presented outside his side of the chopper. In battle, someone else would have his backside, the field of fire behind him, out the other side of the chopper. In range practice, the pilot would always present the threats to his side.

All he had to do was select and shoot.

Short bursts. Range didn't mind having their targets hit, but they hated when they were torn up needlessly.

Tim fired short bursts.

Let the flow take him.

Kept his focus and his wrists loose.

His instincts had a decade of training and led him through the course as a blur; every moment crystalline clear, but all part of a loose, easy flow.

When Lola coaxed the Huey into a full roll, he shot the last target while hanging upside down by the straps of his harness.

He killed it dead.

Chapter 45

"You were goddamn awesome! Did you hear the range officer? He was just shitting bricks!" Lola danced around him on the sand like a warrior princess. Starlight and a thin crescent moon traced her path. The Huey, a dark shadow, loomed beside them.

Tim still floated in that place of perfect, mellow flow. He'd heard buzzing in his ears. Remembered the range officer talking about something.

"Perfect score," Lola shouted up at the vault of the heavens. "I threw all that extra shit at you just to mess with you, and you still nailed it." She sent up a war whoop and started dancing a one-woman conga around him on the sand. Each head toss, flinging her glorious mane of hair like a banner flying high.

He remembered directing them from the range down to the family cabin on Sandy Cove, right across the water from where the Assateague wild horses ran. She'd settled them high on the beach, had to pull him out of the harness where he still sat after she'd powered down the chopper.

He shook himself, feeling like a wet dog just waking up.

The next time Lola circled in front of him he snagged her around the waist and pulled her in hard.

Front to front, she continued to dance and writhe against him in celebration, snapping her fingers to the beat.

He felt like a goddamn god.

Tim took her then. No gentle lovemaking that he'd brought her here for. No slow rise of passion.

Just blistering need burning up his veins and his body.

In moments he'd stripped her naked and shoved her to the sand.

She opened to him and he sated himself on the taste of her, her feel, her shape. He drank deeply, took from her body until she exploded with a cry that shattered the darkness. Her fists pounded his shoulders as a release for the power that surged through her body in great waves.

Still more than half wild, Tim plunged into her welcoming embrace. The pressure built and built.

Trust your pilot.

He let his body take as he'd never taken before. Driving home, nailing the target until he found his own release, a release that tore from his throat with a roar like a lion's. Or like the righteous glory of a minigun pounding down out of the sky and landing in the dead-center of absolute glory.

———

A dead man.

Tim lay atop Lola like a dead man. His weight a warm comfort on a cooling night. She held him tight, arms around his neck, legs still locked around his hips. The crumpled clothes beneath her a thin buffer from the sand.

She held him and looked up at the stars.

No one had ever taken her like that. No one had ever needed her so badly. And no one had ever given her so much back.

Her body held on to Tim as she stared out into the

infinity of space. She was so far gone on him. There had to be something she could do about that, some way to stop it for both their sakes. There was no way she was good enough for him. Not for a man like Tim.

Returning from wherever he'd gone, he didn't move to ease his weight as if still incapable of such an effort. But one hand, a single finger, moved in a slow circle near her ear, slowly winding a bit of her hair about it. So gentle she wouldn't have felt it if he hadn't done it so many times since they'd become lovers.

Experience had taught her that it couldn't last anyway. Military relationships were strictly about sex, passing ships in the night scenario.

That was all it had ever been. Ever should be.

He nestled more comfortably against her, covering her body, toying with her hair.

Why couldn't she ease her hold on the man whose heart still pounded against her chest?

Chapter 46

THEY HURRIED INSIDE THE CABIN IN THE CHILL LIGHT of dawn, running naked up the beach. They'd gone for a long skinny dip. Damn, Lola missed swimming. And she'd felt so strong after the great sex that she'd swum way too far and barely made it back to the beach in absolute exhaustion.

The shower had been fast, especially with someone to scrub her back, and the collapse into bed equally quick. They barely snuggled up and she was out like a light.

When at last she woke, Lola could only blink at the dim light beyond the lace-curtained windows. A bedroom clock built into the face of a coconut informed her that it was six o'clock. A.m. or p.m.? The whole room had been done in tropical island, but with a sense of humor. Rather than the clock being kitschy, it was a joke playing off the soft blues and yellows of the rest of the room's decor. The light green sea-wave bedspread only completed the theme.

She stretched, wincing only a little at a few of her sorer spots, and felt surprisingly good. P.m., she decided. That meant a dozen hours of sleep rather than a mere one or two.

Tim was gone. Only the slightest warmth lingered on the sheets beside her. He'd clearly been up a while.

She wandered back outside into the evening light.

Other than the squat helicopter parked in the middle

of the view, it was a stunning place. The long cove sported only tiny waves along the achingly white sand. Across the cove, a long barrier island drew a line along the horizon. Low sand dunes with only the occasional high point, it did nothing to block the smell of the sea.

Salt and seaweed. A warm breeze that had been heating since it rolled off the Gulf Stream current, fresh from the warm Spanish beaches three thousand miles away.

The sun had indeed set, the sky had darkened even as she stood on the cabin's threshold.

With the fading light, she caught the barest flicker through the Huey's windows. She'd parked it parallel to the water on a broad rock patio that separated lawn from beach. In the cargo bay, a warm light teased behind the clear plastic.

She walked up close enough to see through the closed near-side door that the sea-facing one was slid open to the view, so she circled the nose and stepped barefoot onto the sun-warmed stone. Tim sat on the lip of the deck, so quiet, so at peace.

Lola leaned in to kiss him, but what she saw in the cargo bay was so perfect that it stopped her. Once again, Tim had revealed himself to be truly exceptional in judging her mood. Inside the chopper lay a tiny world of cozy wonder.

He'd unrigged and stowed the gunner's seat and the minigun. The stretch of the cargo bay was now covered in a cheerful red-and-white-checkered cloth. A half-dozen candles lit the shadowed interior of the Huey, revealing the results of Tim's ministrations.

A couple of pillows that had been on the couch when they crawled into the cabin this morning were now set on the hard deck. They were decorated in the same red-and-white checker, with a bit of blue piping around the edges. The pillows would make comfortable seating; not that she and Tim wouldn't both be at perfect ease without them. They'd both spent too many hours aboard to not be comfortable anywhere on the chopper under almost any conditions.

Now she saw why the picnic basket was so big. It was partly basket and partly an ice-filled cooler. A dozen plastic containers were scattered about, and she knew they'd be filled with Pauley's Island-style culinary heaven.

A pair of wide-based mugs, filled with tiny bouquets of flowers, completed the scene.

As Tim pulled her into his arms, Lola decided these were near-perfect flight conditions. Rather than kissing her senseless, he swept her up in those powerful arms of his and set her on one of the pillows inside the chopper.

She folded her bare feet under her, as if they were surrounded by sunlit green grass rather than enough dusk-shadowed firepower to punch a fair-sized hole in an armored battle tank.

He stepped aboard and sat opposite her. Then he reached into the basket and extracted two exquisite china teacups and saucers. She couldn't help herself. She felt all girly as she picked one up to inspect the fine filigree of pink roses, the cup's delicate handle, and the gold along the rim.

Then he pulled out the prize, a matching teapot clearly meant for just two people.

"I cheated." Tim spoke while wearing that soft smile that kept melting her heart.

"Please, cheat some more."

He dug out a tall thermos that billowed steam when opened. On the tail of the steam rose a scent of herbal tea and… "Chocolate?"

Tim emptied the thermos into the teapot and tucked it back into the basket. "Mama's special blend with just a dash of the best dark cocoa powder. I practically grew up on this. Hot, iced, sometimes with a shot of brandy on Christmas Eve or if one of us was sick to help us sleep. I swear it just gets better with the years."

He poured from the pot very formally and very carefully. Lola wondered if Mama Cara knew her prize teapot had gone walkabout on a Huey helicopter.

"Hey! Isn't the general going to be missing his helicopter?"

"I tried gaming him—"

Lola laughed.

Tim smile turned to one of deep chagrin. "Yeah, it worked about that well. General Arnson said something about not messing with someone who'd been all over that since when my mama was still in grade school. So, I told him there was this girl."

"You told a Marine Corps general that you were having an illicit affair with a superior officer?" Lola wondered just how crazy Tim might really be.

"Hell no! I'm not that nuts. Just mentioned a girl and our family's beach cabin and begged on my knees like any other natural-born American boy."

Lola turned to look at the pale pink sky over the settling water out the cargo-bay door.

"Well, you done good."

She tested the tea. The first sip promised wonders and the second delivered. She'd save the third until she'd eaten some of the spread laid out before her. No plates, just a napkin, fork, and spoon. Perfect. She began poking through the containers and peeling back lids at random.

Each required a brief moment held close to her nose. The containers, some cool from the ice, some room temperature, offered up scents pungent, spicy, sweet, and mellow. She reached into one and slipped a stuffed cherry tomato into her mouth.

When she bit down, flavor burst forth in a splash and the top of her head nearly blew off. She liked spicy hot. Tex-Mex or Cajun, she didn't care, bring it on. This was something else again.

Tim laughed as she gulped tea and blinked back tears.

The heat continued to roll, spilling layers of flavor. As the heat mellowed, the tomato's slight acid rolled smoothly on her tongue, the cinnamon wafted up to her nose, and the finish of something nutty was absolutely exquisite.

"We usually eat Pa's stuffed cherry tomatoes in this." He uncovered a container of shining white yogurt. "It makes a better balance."

Lola sipped a little more tea and took a spoonful of yogurt to finish cooling the heat.

"Got any more good surprises?"

Tim nodded happily.

"What's the best one?"

"Later. It's for later."

"Dessert? I want it now. Life is uncertain. Dessert comes first. C'mon, Timmy, I want it now. Now. Now!" She bounced on her cushion. He brought out a silly side that surprised her more than it did him. She pouted like a little girl, crossing her arms and offering her best frown. "I'm not gonna eat no more of your food till I gets my surprise."

"Nope."

"Then no more sex."

"Ouch! Pulling out the big weapons."

"Damn straight!" She gave one emphatic nod. "Gimme!"

He didn't reach into the basket.

Instead he reached into his pocket.

For some reason, her first thought was that was a terribly strange place to keep dessert.

Then, in the candlelight, she saw the glint of gold and silver and ruby he now held between his fingertips. Her second thought was how stunningly beautiful the perfect ring was.

She never had time for a third thought because of the soul-freezing shock.

"Lola, this is my grandmother's ring. I ask—"

The rest of his words turned into a harsh buzzing in her ears. Something about permission and ever after and—

A hard twitch shot through her body with a whip of pain, and she was gone.

Lola dove out of the helicopter, hit the ground in a tight roll that brought her to her feet, and took off running down the beach.

She fell, sprawling face first into the sand.

Heard dishes clattering and banging together where she'd shoved off.

And just as she regained her feet, she heard what could only be the sound of a falling teapot shattering against the hard stone.

Chapter 47

TIM ALMOST MISSED HER IN THE DUSK WHEN HE LOOKED down the beach. Had to walk halfway to her before he was sure.

Lola was huddled a hundred yards down the beach, almost at the water's edge. Her arms wrapped around her knees, pulled so tight against her chest she could rest her chin on them.

For a moment he considered leaving her there.

Hadn't he been clear? There couldn't be anyone but her for him. And he knew it was mutual. There'd never been anyone who made him feel so schoolboy happy. They held hands everywhere except when they went running. They communicated with an ease, with a silence that often didn't need words.

He wanted to shout at her. To rage. About betrayal. About breaking so many silent promises. About his family teapot. He raised his hand to look at the handle still clutched there. His mother's favorite piece of china now just a handle connected to nothing. Tiny trails of pink roses leading to jagged and sharp edges where it had been shattered. All been shattered.

A deep fury boiled up within him. That she had led him so far astray, so wrong. That she'd broken his grandmother's teapot.

Perhaps it was the absurdity of that last thought. Perhaps it was knowing he'd have to explain the loss to his mother. For whatever reason, the anger that was nearly blinding him drained abruptly away and left him ragged and exhausted. Worse, far worse than the adrenal letdown after battle.

To hell with Lola. He thought it, but knew it was wrong. It didn't find its target. He tried to restir the righteous anger he wanted to wrap around himself. It only made him even sadder and lonelier.

On the verge of turning away he noticed she still hadn't moved. He was close enough to see she was shivering despite the warm evening breeze, staring sightlessly toward Assateague Island.

At a loss, Tim moved until he was just a pace away and slowly sank to a squat beside her. She didn't turn to face him. This close, he could see that she fought the shivers coursing in waves up and down her frame.

Without thinking, he reached out to run a soothing hand down her arm, but she flinched away ever so slightly and he withdrew before he touched her. Still she didn't turn to him.

He tried to think of ways to break the silence, but none of them were right.

At length, Lola's frame stopped shaking like some terrified rabbit. She closed her eyes and finally rested her forehead on her knees, the arms not releasing the tension in the slightest.

Her voice barely a whisper, he had to concentrate and turn his ears clear of the gentle breeze to hear her.

"I'm so sorry. I can't. I just can't. You don't know. I just can't."

The hysterical edge to her whispered voice finally broke through his own miasma.

"Shh. Easy. We'll figure this out."

"No!" She popped up her head and shouted at him. Her voice enough of a slap that he lost his balance from his squat and fell back until he too sat in the sand. Her eyes blazed red with pain and her running tears caught the last of the day's light, but her words were sharp, hard-edged.

"No! 'We' won't figure it out! There is no 'we.'" She huffed out a breath, shook her head to clear the hair from her eyes, and looked right at him for the first time. Her voice softer, if not kinder.

"Goddamn it, Tim. I can't be part of a 'we.' Nobody can be enough of an idiot to want me to be part of their 'we.' You're better than that. Go find someone. But not me. Find some sweet, gentle-hearted woman. One who will make you and your family happy. Not some screwed-up, harpy bitch."

"I already did." And he had.

But all she did was laugh bitterly and look away again.

Not knowing what else to do, Tim sat with her. Cross-legged beneath the emerging stars, he stared at the teapot handle still clenched in his hand. He set it carefully on the sand, the handle sticking up into the air as if the teapot were but buried spout down.

He opened his other hand, the one that had been fisted closed since the moment Lola dove from the helicopter. Closed tight until the fingers were numb from lack of blood flow. Forcing the fingers open, he managed to create an opening big enough to see to his palm, the first tingles of pain arcing up his fingers.

His grandmother's ruby wedding ring. The heirloom his mother had offered him with such hope last night.

For one heartbeat, then another, he considered casting it aside. Throwing it into the ocean, or better, into the Potomac. Let the ring join Washington's apocryphal silver dollar beneath the muddy waters. If he could have flexed his numb hand, he might have thrown the ring away and damn the consequences.

He stared down into the shadowed cup of his hand at the shimmering circlet that caught even the starlight with such hope.

Then, without looking up at Lola, he slowly forced his fist closed, a motion twice as painful now that the blood was returning. He would keep it safe, hidden. It would wait, like a Night Stalker waited in the dark, until the time was right. Until that perfect moment of flight.

He stood, steady on legs that moments before couldn't hold him upright.

"Come on. I need to clean up, then we'll return the chopper and I'll get you to a hotel."

She nodded but didn't move.

He left her there and turned to go sweep up the pieces.

Lola watched Tim walk away. Not directly; didn't want to be caught watching if he looked back to check on her. Which he did several times, as if she were a phantom who might disappear into thin air.

Maybe if she just kept running down the beach she'd never have to see him again. Going AWOL wasn't exactly on the list of experiences she wanted to try. Nor did she want to abandon her post, she'd worked harder to make SOAR than anything in her life. And harder still to live up to Emily Beale's standards. "Away without leave" was one of the nastier crimes in the military, right up there with fraternizing with an enlisted.

She rested her forehead back on her knees. How had she crash-landed in such a place? All she'd wanted to do was have a little fun. She didn't want to be someone's dream. Didn't want to own someone else's heart. Not even Tim's.

Out of the corner of her eye she saw the brilliant white arc of beautiful teapot handle still rising from the soil. The small section of pot that remained, awash with tiny pink roses. It was the most romantic gesture anyone had ever made to her.

Living with Mama Raci, a living she'd earned in scrubbed pots and cut vegetables, had left her on the outside looking in. Hers wasn't the world of TV sit-coms with happy families. When she wandered out of Storyville into the French Quarter or Metairie, she'd watched people happily strolling through the neighbor-hood, enjoying their family sit-down dinners, relaxing in front of the television behind brightly lit windows of nice homes.

It wasn't for her. Whatever was going on in Sergeant Tim Maloney's mind, whatever madness had taken root there, it wasn't her problem.

Lola looked up at the starry sky, so different from the sky she'd watched last night from her lover's arms. Different too from the heavens of her youth in New Orleans. The Gulf always cast some high weather system, the heat a palpable shimmer that battered at a person, made the world difficult to see clearly.

Here in D.C., it was a sky of spilled paint. So picture perfect that nothing could go wrong beneath it.

Nothing but Lola LaRue.

She hid her eyes and did her best not to think or feel.

She struggled to her feet and shook the feeling back into her legs. She didn't want Tim to come find her. Didn't want him to touch her. Didn't want what she knew she would feel if he did. A joy like none she'd ever found in being with another. A peace she didn't deserve or understand.

She reached down and grasped the teapot handle. It felt oddly light, her muscles still expected the mass of the full pot.

Lola tucked it out of sight under the edge of her shirt as she climbed the beach back toward the chopper.

Chapter 48

THE WHIRLWIND DESCENDED AS THEY DROVE BACK into the city. For something to do with her hands, for something to do in the silence that descended as dense as any sandstorm between her and Tim, Lola fished her cell phone out of the fanny pack she'd tossed on the car floor while helping to clean and stow the Huey.

A message flashed, now an hour old, calling them to the Treasury Building in less than an hour from now.

Tim laid down on the accelerator and raced through the streets like a madman. She'd managed to make it up the stairs to the apartment to bathe and for them to pack their gear. She transferred the teapot handle to her duffel with Tim none the wiser.

Tim ducked into the kitchen to return the apartment keys. She had to sit and wait for several minutes.

Was Tim telling his mother about the teapot?

Lola felt cowardly leaving him to face the rocket fire when she'd been the one to destroy the family heirloom, but though she reached for the car's door handle several times, she never actually opened it.

Or was he making some excuse why Lola wouldn't come in to say good-bye? Possibly cursing her mere existence?

She'd liked his family—Cara always so willing to give of her love and his father, Jackson, always ready with a smile or a wry joke. Having just refused their son, there was no way on the planet that she could face them.

When Tim returned to the car, he looked grim, and she didn't dare ask. She wasn't just cruel, she was a coward on top of it.

They raced in silence to arrive at the Treasury Building with minutes to spare, not having exchanged a single word since the beach other than her reading their orders off her voice mail. Orderlies swept aside their gear on arrival. They were ushered through metal detectors, each leaving a couple of knives and their sidearms in security's lockbox.

Down a long hall, where their passes were checked twice more, they entered the White House basement, arriving exactly on time in a concrete conference room. It was twice the size of the Situation Room but with none of the niceties. This was a room where serious work was done and nothing wasted on such luxuries as a comfortable chair or even a water pitcher.

The other members of the two DAP Hawk crews were there along with two D-boys, Colonel Gibson and a Captain Thomas. Emily looked at Lola strangely when she neither chose a chair by Tim nor by her. Lola's heart hurt too much to care.

Seeking a quick distraction, Lola dropped into a hard plastic seat next to Kee. Thankful for the distraction, she offered the woman her friendliest smile.

"Where's the kid?"

Kee unwound enough to answer, "Probably in the Oval Office. Her grandmother's in town, so she's staying with Calledbetty, but they're meeting with the President at the moment."

Lola tried to think up something to say, something to expand this momentary bridge between them, but she came up blank. So the little squirt hadn't been making it up. She did know the President and therefore, almost certainly, the head of the Presidential Protection Detail.

Before she could form her thoughts into a coherent response, General Brett Rogers tromped in and Lola was back on her feet even before she heard Viper Henderson shout out, "'Tenshun!" or the general's, "At ease. At ease," that let them settle back slowly into their chairs.

Chief of Staff Daniel Darlington followed him in, shut the door, and began speaking before he even turned to the room.

"The President is unavailable at the moment, but this"— he dropped an envelope on the table bearing the presidential seal—"is National Security Presidential Directive Number 73. General Rogers will explain the contents."

Rogers stood at the head of the table in silence and scanned the room.

Lola did the same. Two D-boys and eight fliers. Seven of them tried-and-true SOAR pilots and crew chiefs, and then Lola. She suppressed a sudden desire to laugh at her inclusion in this circle. Even Sergeant Kee Stevenson belonged here more than she ever could. When their gazes met, she could see Kee making a similar assessment of her. "You don't belong here." No kidding.

Lola was flying with the likes of Mark Henderson and Emily Beale. How was she ever supposed to measure up to that?

The General cleared his throat, drawing everyone's attention back to the head of the table.

"Based on the Insurrection Act of 1807 and Posse Comitatus Act of 1878, you are not allowed to enter into a military operation on U.S. soil except as required by the Constitution and an Act of Congress. Not even to enforce law and order. It does not permit aggressive action against U.S. nationals. This"—the General tapped the envelope—"on the advice of the National Security Council, permits exactly that." He pulled it out of the envelope, even as Mark and Emily groaned aloud.

The General shot them a withering glance, but Emily just reached out to take Mark's hand.

Lola could see that they'd clearly read a similar document once before, but that the General hadn't. He too quickly took in the implication. The Majors had known and performed some secret mission, secret even from Chairman of the Joint Chiefs, that had required broad sweeping powers from the President. Oddly, as she scanned the room, no one else in their crews seemed to know either, except Daniel. The President's Chief of Staff clearly had a few guesses even if he didn't show a look of absolute certainty.

The General harrumphed, then read aloud, "You are hereby authorized to use any force at any place and any time at your commander's discretion that is deemed necessary to protect the safety and sanctity of the United States and her people. Signed, President Peter Matthews."

Emily covered her face as, with obvious reluctance, Major Henderson took the paper presented by the General.

"No word of this mission is ever to reach beyond the people sitting in this room. Is that clear?" The last had a snap of command that had the ten of them jumping to their feet and responding with a shouted, "Sir, yes, sir!"

"Unknown to the Iranian executive branch," the General continued his lecture in the conference room beneath the White House, "and possibly unknown to the clerical branch of their government as well, a secret laboratory was constructed in the deep desert outside Ravar, Iran. A dreadful biocide was produced there. Soman is a Schedule 1 substance deemed to be a weapon of mass destruction per UN Security Council Resolution 687. It is a nerve agent that specifically targets all mammalian life forms and is one of the two or three most lethal such agents on the planet."

Lola saw Emily place her hands over her belly, as if she could further protect the month-old fetus.

"Based on the research data your teams recovered from the desert, it is prepped to be released in an aerosol form, an airborne attack. We know the target is the Southern United States, and that's where you're headed. You're being dispatched immediately to Fort Rucker to prepare for on-call action. You will pick up additional crew there as needed. CIA, FBI, and NSA assets are scrambling to get you a point of interdiction, but if it is airborne, your teams will be the spearhead once we identify the target. Questions?"

"What's our cover, sir?" Lola's voice felt rough from not being used in the last several hours.

"You'll be making the crossing tonight under cover of darkness. After that, if daytime actions are required, you'll be a training-and-testing flight. At Rucker, your birds will be rearmed with Hellfire IIIs. These are brand-new, nano-thermite-equipped missiles. Based upon the

CIA experts' calculations, they should burn hot enough to vaporize the Soman, and being FAEs, fuel-air explosives, hopefully they'll be able to do so across a large enough area." Then the old warrior looked exhausted.

"This assumes that you can arrive at a biocide launch site before it has had a chance to significantly disperse. You are authorized to use this weaponry over citizen populations if the Soman has been released before you arrive. Trust me, it will be an act of kindness to those who might be already exposed."

He dropped into the seat at the head of the table and hung his head.

Lola looked around, wanted someone to give the rallying talk she'd always heard in these types of situations. To know that someone had that absolute conviction of success.

She could see Emily Beale struggling to find the right words, but her face merely looked white and drawn.

"Well…" Lola leaned forward. "I'm sure there is something brilliant that can be said right about now. Regrettably, it needs someone smarter than me to say it." Her irony earned her a soft laugh.

Her brief meeting with Emily's gaze told Lola to keep going, even if she didn't believe it herself.

"All I can think to say is: We're the Night Stalkers."

Emily echoed it softly along with a few of the others, "We're the Night Stalkers."

"NSDQ." Lola made it a flat statement, each letter distinct.

"NSDQ," was mumbled around the table as a benison. Lola repeated it with more strength, more force. It was the Night Stalkers' motto.

"Night Stalkers Don't Quit!" She nearly shouted it.

"Night Stalkers Don't Quit!" Emily hammered down her fist as she replied.

"Night Stalkers Don't Quit!" roared from the throats of both crews, their fists landing once, hard enough to shake the table.

She whispered it one more time to herself, searching for that absolute commitment, as others rose to their feet and began heading for the door.

"Night Stalkers Don't Quit!"

Chapter 49

Lola knew it was a cheat, but she managed to end up in the other SUV from Tim and in the far back-seat after making sure Emily Beale was sitting up front. The Delta Force colonel sat beside her and showed little inclination to speak. Good.

She pressed the heel of her hand against her chest, feeling the pain. A sharp physical bite that she'd diagnose in an older person as a heart attack. She pushed harder, which only worsened the ache.

The irony of the situation was not lost upon her. She needed to feel, even if it was only physical pain. Or perhaps especially if it was pain. After a decade of sliding easy, it suddenly felt hard. An impossible burden to carry. She didn't like what she was facing.

Ever since 9/11, she'd flown down a path that had unfolded in front of her like a yellow brick road. Her life—while not pure hell, certainly hadn't been a lot of fun prior to that moment—had started to make sense. In her last year of high school, all it changed was that she graduated. But in college she'd built up some speed. ROTC, swim team. Afterward, helicopters, Air National Guard. Army, Special Forces. Rangers, Airborne. CSAR, SOAR. She and Dorothy had it easy. Nothing ten tons of military helicopter and a pair of ruby slippers couldn't solve. At least not that she'd admit to.

She'd hit turbulence before. Been bucked down a

grade for kneeing a lieutenant in the crotch when he'd really deserved it. But the harder challenges of military flying had come to her easily. Army discipline had given her a framework to rebel against, but not too much. MFEO—she and the Army had definitely been made for each other.

For all the pain of her childhood, she'd had a fairly easy ride of it since then. Learned early how to emulate the college swim-team girls who'd grown up with mothers who had taken them to swim practice since they were five in the family's silver minivan. She learned how to charm the boys and bought her acceptance there with her body when she cared to.

Knew how to do Army. Had that down cold. Just do it. All that emotion, worry, and fear, there was no more place for it in the Army than in her father's house. Shove it down and out of sight. You don't show any feelings to anybody, then nobody steps on them. Don't show them long enough, and you never have to feel them yourself.

And it worked.

It worked fine.

Lola glared out the SUV's dark-tinted windows at the Lincoln Memorial.

It worked right up until the moment she'd met Sergeant "Crazy Tim" Maloney.

"Never comfortable, is it?" a male voice asked.

"Not even a little!" Lola almost laughed before she realized that the question and her answer had both been spoken aloud, not just her own thoughts.

She turned to face Colonel Gibson.

"What?"

His silence was the only answer as they swung onto

the bridge she and Tim had run across together not five days ago.

"What!" She needed somebody to throttle, and maybe today would be a D-boy's day.

Still silence.

She fired off a short jab at his ribs.

It was as if she was moving in slow motion.

Less than halfway to his rib cage, her wrist was completely immobilized in an impossibly strong grip. Once stopped, he paused just long enough for Lola to realize that he could snap her wrist with as little effort as she tied her boots. That even as he'd stopped her attack, some autonomic part of his training allowed him to judge the most advantageous angle of grip to set up the next move. And probably the three after that. Even she didn't have that kind of speed, nor Tim that kind of strength.

"Sorry," she managed to mumble after he released her wrist still in one piece. What had she been thinking in attacking the Delta Operators' highest-ranked field officer? A colonel in his early thirties, impossible to believe until you were face to face with the man. One look in his eyes and you knew he'd earned it, earned it the hard way.

"Normal." He rested his hands back on his thighs. Not folded together. Not arms crossed. Just resting on his thighs. A position from which he could move to defense or offense most rapidly. She hadn't even seen it and he lived that way. In a world where that was required. "You're faster than most."

"Didn't work though, did it?"

He offered her a soft smile. A smile on a face so

grim seemed out of place, the scar-puckered skin along his jawline pulling his lips off center, but the eyes, the ever-present mask that somehow clouded the crystalline blue eyes, uncovered to reveal an absolute genuineness. Contrasted with his Irish black hair, he was, in this moment, handsome enough that she almost wished she'd met Michael before Tim.

Almost.

And there was the real problem. It was Tim she wanted, she simply couldn't live with that truth.

"You're right," she finally answered in little more than a whisper. "It's not even a little bit comfortable."

Chapter 50

AGAIN THEY WERE WAITING. MADE TIM MORE THAN A little bit crazy, but it was most of what they did in Special Forces.

Train and wait.

At the moment, the Black Adders team wasn't training.

The eight of them were sitting around Fort Rucker, waiting for the mission "go." On a lot of Special Forces missions the "go" never happened. This probably wasn't one of those. It wasn't an "if," more of a "when."

Normally you only returned to Rucker for one of two reasons, either you were gonna "go ACE" or "have a heart-ATTC." Either you were shipped to the U.S. Army Aviation Center of Excellence for more training, or to the U.S. Army Aviation Technical Test Center when helping test new gear. SOAR fliers were often here for both.

But with neither happening, just squatting on hold in southern Alabama, Mother Rucker had way too much moist heat, far too many hurricanes, and not a damn thing to do. Which was okay, usually. Neither the training nor the test staff had any idea what the words "reasonable workload" meant. Mother Rucker busted your behind either way. So spare time wasn't an issue.

Except this trip.

They were there to squat out of sight and await orders. SOAR didn't like their stealth birds just hanging out for anyone to see, so they were tucked away deep in a hangar vacated just for their use.

The first night, they'd long-hauled down from D.C., midair refueling en route.

The second night they'd flown out to the firing range and kicked off a couple of the nano-thermite-rigged Hellfire III missiles at a derelict tank. Tim had thought the fire had been pretty impressive, until they landed to inspect the remains of what they'd shot up. They'd all sobered when they saw the results. The damned missiles had melted whole sections of the tank. As if it had been made out of butter and someone had dribbled boiling water all over it. Anything they hit with a couple of those Hellfires was done for. And they were going to be flying over U.S. soil.

But the two days and nights since, all they'd done was waited.

Still, even here, waiting didn't usually get to him. Hang out, lift some weights, maybe pick up a likely lady or two.

Right now was exactly the right kind of environment for that last activity. He and Kee were shooting some pool. At the next table Lieutenant Trisha O'Malley was working the balls and clearly trying to work him as well. Just his type—smart, sassy, cute as hell, a flier deep in SOAR training, and tough as an Abrams tank.

Not much taller than his shoulder, with flaming red hair and a toothy, come-and-get-me smile, she also shot a fine game of pool. She'd wiped the table with Connie, and now Big John was getting his face smeared into the green felt. She'd kept teasing them about being the toughest bitch left alive in the mud hole, which actually raised a rare laugh from Connie and simply left Big John looking ill. Clearly Connie and John had been part of her SOAR interview week.

And somehow, every time he went to line up a shot, there she was in the space between their tables, lining up some trick shot that it was hard not to be impressed by and watching him with those electric blue eyes.

He could take her. He'd hustled enough pool to know he could. Unless she was even more of a hustler than she was pretending to be.

Kee got him off to the side after he'd screwed up an easy two-bank shot.

"What the hell are you doing, Maloney?"

"What?" Did she mean mooning over Lola? That was a tender point. And he'd rather Kee didn't pound on it with her sharpshooter targeting.

"Why are you flirting with that LT? You know that's not what you want."

Of all damned things. Kee had made it abundantly clear that she despised Lola, and now she was defending her?

It would have helped if she hadn't been right.

Sergeant Crazy Tim enjoyed flirting with the cute Lieutenant O'Malley.

But Tim Maloney only wanted one woman and it wasn't the cute lieutenant.

Kee rested a hand on his arm. A hand of comfort.

"Do you want her badly enough?"

Tim nodded even as his brain tried to shake his head in denial. All the pain of being rejected. All the anger he still felt. All of it was nothing compared to the bald truth. He'd only be happy if he was with Lola LaRue.

Kee nodded solidly. "Archie wanted me that way. I

fought and struggled against him, almost broke his arm in the process. But he knew. And he finally convinced me. So if you want her that badly, get out of here and go be stubborn, right-in-her-face stubborn."

"I…" Tim had thought of a dozen, a hundred different ways, but Lola had said no in no uncertain terms and still hadn't spoken to him since. "I don't know how."

Kee rested a hand on the center of his chest and looked up at him. "Don't think, flyboy. Just go do it."

Tim spotted Trisha O'Malley swinging back around her table, setting up the final shot that would knock Big John out of the game, put another twenty dollars into those tight jeans pockets, and leave him a wide-open opportunity.

He handed his cue stick to Kee as he turned for the door.

Colonel Gibson wandered in through the door and held it for Tim.

He nodded to Michael, then thought of the look that the disappointed lieutenant was probably aiming at his back.

"Colonel, there's a lady over there looking for a worthy opponent."

Michael glanced over Tim's shoulder, then offered him a nod and a thin smile before moseying over to the table Tim had just abandoned.

So that's how Archie had caught Kee, sheer persistence and determination. He'd always wondered. Well, Tim knew how to do that. He was a Night Stalker, and Night Stalkers Don't Quit.

"NSDQ," he said as he stepped out into the heat blast of the day and the blinding sun. He did know who he wanted. Now he just had to find out where in Mother Rucker she was hiding.

He leaned forward into the humid air, like a helicopter tipping down its nose to gain forward speed, and set out to find her.

Tim spent the morning and part of the afternoon trying to track her down. He even wandered into the Army Aviation Museum to catch a break from the heat. He'd never had time to go there before, but without Lola, it wasn't particularly fun. Now he stood outside the door wondering what to do next.

Two days and nights without a single word. Not a single sighting. He didn't even know where to begin.

He'd never considered himself a deep person. Pretty happy just going along living his life. Damn good life, damn fine family, and the best team ever to fly the skies. All a man needed.

But the more Tim thought about it, the more he knew what a complete crock o' crap that had become. He was miserable. If he didn't know it himself, he'd seen it reflected in John's eyes. And Connie's. Even Kee appeared ready to cut him some slack about Lola, and he wasn't ready for that either.

He didn't need slack.

He needed Lola.

Knowing that somehow made it easier. A clear target now in his sights, it was only a matter of getting there.

He considered a strategy.

He considered making a plan.

Instead, he set out to just find her.

Mother Rucker was only eleven square miles, five thousand full-time residents, and another couple thousand transients.

How hard could it be?

—⁓—

Half a stroke before she hit the wall, Lola executed a somersault flip-turn and headed toward the other end of the pool with a mile-eating freestyle stroke. She'd lost count around fifteen laps but had swum a long way since then. At least two miles were gone, maybe most of three.

She was no sprinter, never was built for that kind of hundred-meter speed. Lola was fast but not that kind of fast. What she had was serious staying power. Could outlast any field of competitors on a long swim. She'd already burned out half a dozen grunts who thought they could rule the pool and the woman in it.

Male egos didn't take well to being lapped. Especially not in their first five. After their macho sprint burned out, Lola just ate 'em alive. *Don't be no messing wit' da Creole lady, mon.* One Army grunt became so angry at not being able to outpace her that he'd punched the wall at the end of the lane. By his scream and rapid exit, probably busted his wrist. Be funny to hear him explain that one to his buddies.

After a while the pool emptied and it was just her.

Back and forth.

Just her.

Usually this kind of a long swim charged her up. Made her feel strong, capable, and tired enough to know she'd sleep well.

At the moment all she felt was wound up, cranky,

and exhausted in a way that would just leave her tossing and turning.

She spotted some movement at poolside when she turned her head for air.

No longer just her. Another contender.

The figure loomed at the end of her lane as she swam toward it. Not moving. Not getting into the pool to try and swim her down. Just standing there, arms crossed, silhouetted by the lowering sun. Watching her.

She didn't need the broad shoulders or unconsciously arrogant, shoulder-wide stance to know who stood there. His body knew he was better than most men, even if he didn't act that way.

Lola did another turn and headed back up the pool as if she hadn't seen him to give herself time to think.

Maybe after another lap he wouldn't be there.

Maybe she'd just climb out at the far end of the pool, sending a clear message that she didn't want to be with him.

But that was the problem.

She slapped the far wall, flip-turned, and headed back.

That was the real problem.

She arrived at the end of the lane by his feet and drifted to a stop. Crossed her arms and hooked her elbows on the gutter to hold her in place as she pulled her goggles down around her neck and looked up at him.

The problem was that she did want him.

Chapter 51

"How do we do this?" Lola broke the silence that had lasted since they'd climbed up onto the Aviation Center of Excellence hangar roof to watch the sunset.

Spread out below them were two dozen Chinooks. She'd never seen so many of the giant choppers gathered in one place. Like a Chinook convention all sitting around the bar telling tall tales of mountaintops and drug lords, of massive troop loads and extended over-water flights, and maybe a quiet one, sitting in the corner, never talking about a certain nighttime trip into the Iranian desert.

Next week it would probably be all Black Hawks with their war stories, or OH-6 surveillance Kiowas chattering like magpies about "you'll never guess what I saw." "No, no, first guess what I saw."

Thankfully, it hadn't been all silence with Tim as they'd walked halfway across the base, but they sure hadn't known what to say to each other. They'd talked of the mission. He'd told her about his first trip to Mother Rucker. She talked about SOAR interview week. Harder in some ways than the monthlong hell of quals for Ranger school.

Talking with Tim had been easy, comfortable, and she'd missed it. Terribly. When she toyed with the phrase in her head—"Missed him. Terribly."—it didn't sit so comfortably.

"How, Tim?"

He sat beside her, looking out at the world that was Fort Rucker. Close, but not quite touching. Both facing out at the world, but focused on each other.

"I don't know. I honestly don't. But I can tell you that being apart doesn't work."

It didn't.

"Not for me anyway. I've never wanted a woman in my life the way I want you. The longest I ever had a girlfriend was about six months, no, nine."

"Who was she?" Lola found herself curious. Not jealous. It was far longer than any of her relationships had ever lasted.

"Bess Thompson. Half of senior year of high school and a great summer while I worked the restaurant. Then she 'Dear Tim'ed' me during Basic. I'd told her I was going real Army, not just a two-year tour, and she didn't want that. Can't blame her. Her dad was on Navy subs, gone six months at a time. Hard life for the woman and impossible for the kid."

"Were you that serious?"

Tim inspected the sky awash with orange and gold for a while. "We thought we were. But we were eighteen. What did we know."

"A whole decade older, are we any wiser?"

That got a laugh. A warm, gentle sound that included her.

"I like to think so, but I sure buggered it, didn't I?"

No need to question what "it" was.

"No, Tim. You did perfect." A helicopter, the closest she had to a home. A sunset picnic, so charming and cozy. The flowers and teapot were the perfect touches.

How much time had she spent sitting on her bunk these last three days, just holding the damned broken teapot handle while she tried to figure out the mess going on inside her head.

"Guys always make me feel like a female of the species. They can't help it with the way their bodies react to mine. You're the first who ever made me feel feminine. No one ever gave me such a gift."

"Then why? Can you help me understand why?" He was begging.

Lola had been trying to avoid that question herself for days. But he deserved an answer, even if she didn't have one to give.

"Every time I answer that one in my head, I just sound stupid or petty. All I know is that I can't. My past—"

"Is the past." His voice sounded soldier rough. "My past is a loving family. Your past isn't. My past was most of the way to prison, yours just as close to being a hooker. Does it matter? What really matters is now!"

Again she didn't know how to respond. How could she explain to someone who had so much what it was like to have nothing?

She'd run into the same problem with the swim girls at college. They'd go out on team shopping sprees, waving their parents' credit cards like magic wands. She'd gone along once or twice, but never bought anything. Even with ROTC, the swimming scholarship, and waitressing, she barely made ends meet each quarter.

When cornered about it, she'd tried to explain. Other than her dress uniform and one new swimsuit a year, her clothing budget was spent at Goodwill. The other swimmers had nodded in understanding the one time she tried to explain, but were confused on the next trip when again she'd try things on but buy nothing. She'd stopped going.

"You're right, Tim. Only the here and now should matter. But it doesn't work that way. I wish it did, but it doesn't."

They sat in silence as the oranges faded to reds, the reds to dusky gray. On the verge of true darkness, a dozen crews came running out of the building below them, sixty men and women sprinting toward the dozen machines for some simulated combat alert. Within minutes, she and Tim couldn't have spoken even if they wanted to. Each Chinook spun up a pair of five-thousand-horsepower turbine engines.

Lola realized she was counting seconds in her head from the first alert. One minute… Two… Three minutes beyond when they should have been airborne, the first bird wallowed into the night sky. It was a full thirty seconds before the next was away. Their ascents were spread over the next four minutes instead of the group departing in a single clean flight, the last bird seven full minutes slower than it should have been.

She shared a glance and smile with Tim in the dim light cast up from the lit field below. There were gonna be some very unhappy trainers during post-flight debrief. Even for regular Army, they'd been sloppy. Definitely not SOAR.

"Rooks."

Lola could read the word on Tim's lips as the final Chinook roared close overhead, its turbines definitely past yellow line as its crew abused the machine to try and make up for their own lateness. Definitely rookies.

"Probably visiting Air Force."

They were all going to catch hell at the debrief. The last guy for abusing the equipment and the first one for not waiting to form up. She remembered that lecture with soft nostalgia. First didn't matter. Team mattered.

Together they waited, listening to the choppers fade into the night.

She'd come a long way since those days. Lola remembered the struggles to remember the preflight checklist that was now instinct, hunting for the right switches for startup that she could now hit every time in blackout conditions with incoming live fire while attempting to restart a flamed-out turbine.

She'd come a long way since those days.

Tim's head was still turned to the northern sky though the choppers were long gone.

When she rested a hand on his shoulder, he faced her.

Their faces inches apart, she could read the question in his eyes in the reflected light and shadows.

"No promises."

He waited the length of a long breath and release before answering with a slow nod.

She leaned in the last inches until her lips were on his.

Chapter 52

LOLA KNEW SHE'D NEVER FORGET THIS MOMENT. THE two of them wrapped in the night, sitting above an airfield still well populated by silent helicopters, nothing beneath them but a hard-surfaced roof.

Tim's lips gentle, so soft on hers she could barely feel them. Their lovemaking hadn't always been wild, but there'd always been a strength that bordered on or crossed over into ravenous or a playful battle. They'd each sported their fair share of bruises after their sexual bouts in D.C.

Now he held her as if she were something precious. A strong arm cradled her against him, holding her as no one had ever done. His fingers inspected her cheekbones, brushing her eyes closed, traced her lips as lightly as if they were feathers, not human flesh and blood.

Lola kept her eyes closed, unable to focus on anything but where he touched her. So completely was he focusing her attention that she couldn't tell if it was pleasure or pain. An exquisite agony pulsed through her, like a foot gone to sleep and now tingling awake. As if the blood flowed into her body for the first time.

She too touched him in wonder. Studying the angles of his face until she knew her fingertips could never forget them. The taste of his skin by his collarbone, the heat of his chest, the sound of his heart when she laid her ear upon it. Each sensation to be studied, relished, remembered.

His exploration was as slow, as careful, as thorough. His rough hands, his soldier-strong hands, were weapons able to dispense the most feathering of touches, arousing her skin like never before.

An exquisite eternity later, waves of heat pulsed through her, pounding against her senses, leaving her aware of nothing except how she felt and the man who sent her there.

But the heat didn't pulse upward from between her legs. Instead it originated in her chest and rolled outward in broad concentric rings that heated, burned, scorched. It burned away layers of Lola LaRue, old layers, cracking and flaking aside like the rolling brownout she'd created along an Iranian highway. Shedding old dust until she lay totally exposed and new in his arms.

For the first time in her life, her heart lay wide open to the world. And she felt so perfectly safe in Tim's gentle hands.

Chapter 53

"HOW MUCH LONGER?" PRESIDENT MATTHEWS LOOKED at Daniel and the General. They were the only occupants of the Situation Room. The Director of the CIA was on secure link from his office, his face an image in the corner of the main screen.

"Give the Coast Guard another half hour. We have to be sure. You should get some sleep, Mr. President."

The General was right. But that wasn't going to happen. Not while Emily was flying out there.

The main image across the screen showed the night-vision view from Emily's Black Hawk. Mark's chopper hung just visible in the upper right corner. In front and below rolled the midnight dark sea and four small boats. Apparently boats filled with Cuban refugees a dozen miles from the promised land of the Florida Keys rather than deadly chemicals.

The reason they'd called out the Night Stalkers was the speed with which these boats were moving. Most Cuban flotillas were slow, poorly guided, often dangerously off course, headed for open ocean. This particular group had been moving solidly in a straight beeline for Key Largo, the closest U.S. island to the Cuban mainland, at a very respectable eight knots. The U.S. Coast Guard had been sent out to investigate. With the Night Stalkers for close, unseen support just in case.

"We should have sent our people," CIA Director Bill Smith complained for about the tenth time.

"Bill, until your Special Activities Division can best the Black Adders, shut the hell up."

There'd been an ugly mission in North Korea about six months before. An operation that the CIA's own experts had decided was beyond the SAD's paramilitary group. Emily and Mark's crews had to fly it instead.

Peter exchanged a look with Daniel. The slightest nod confirmed he hadn't gone too far out of line. That Daniel had found his Alice as a by-product of that particular operation added some bias, but the CIA had to learn they weren't the only specialists in the world who could get things done.

The General, as former commander of U.S. Special Forces, was almost smiling at the slap at the CIA. A near smile from Brett Rogers represented the height of hilarity for the Chairman of the Joint Chiefs.

But, political expediency being what it was, Peter gave Bill another excuse to focus on.

"We need to keep this quiet as long as we can."

"But you have choppers out there—"

"That won't show up on the Coast Guard's radar as more than sea clutter at their present altitude."

The rolling waves did indeed appear to be mere inches below the Black Hawk's cameras, causing a slightly seasick feeling if Peter watched the screen feed for too long.

"How long, Mr. President? How long can we do this without changing the alert status? Without expanding the team?"

It was a good question. The problem was, when you

jumped up defense alert levels, people starting asking what to look for. Even the U.S. Coast Guard out there right now in the night were told only to watch for non-Cuban nationals or unanticipated equipment or cases.

A Cuban national could easily be bought with a simple bribe like a free ride on the very craft they were now inspecting. It was a seaworthy boat, stoutly made with plank framing and a heavy plastic tarp pulled over it to make a mostly waterproof hull, and it had a sufficiently large motor. Also, it didn't help that enough poison to destroy a city would fit in a couple cases of two-liter soda bottles and the dispersal mechanism could be a crop-duster aircraft rented anywhere on U.S. soil.

Expanding the team had other risks. The more people in the know, the greater likelihood of a report from "an informed government source." The press would ramp it up, perhaps without exaggerating but by reporting truth about the Soman nerve agent and how it could be spread. There'd be a panic of national proportions. A risk Peter wasn't yet willing to take.

President Madani was feeding them whatever information he could. And Bill's people were working the captured data, but the destination and delivery method were never recorded. Or if they were, it was in some of the heavily coded information they'd yet to crack, though there was very little of that left with the NSA helping out.

A phone buzzed and the General answered it. He listened for a moment, then hung up.

"USCG says they're clean and they're taking them in tow."

"Call off Emily."

The General placed another call. Thirty seconds later, the two Black Hawks veered off and headed back over the dark sea to Rucker. It was the fourth call out in three days. They couldn't sustain this much longer.

None of them could.

But he didn't have a better plan.

Chapter 54

WHEN THEY LANDED, NO ONE WAS MOVING QUICKLY. Lola checked the mission clock. They'd been out there for three hours hovering on station during the Coasties' inspection, plus two hours in flight each way. Even taking turns in flight didn't relieve the stress or the toll it was taking on everyone's patience.

They all sat around the debriefing table too frustrated to speak. Almost too tired to care. They had to do something, if only she could think what.

Sergeant Kee was texting on her phone.

"How's the kid?"

Kee looked at her, startled to be directly addressed. "Uh, she's fine. She's with Archie and his mother. They're trying to work the shipping angle."

"She's a bright kid."

"Smarter than any of us."

Lola heard the motherly bias but didn't doubt it. One year in their culture and the kid's insights were startling. Had learned enough English to jump all the way into *The Secret Garden*.

"How are Mary and Dickon and Colin doing?"

Again Kee studied her carefully before answering, "Colin can run now, but he's in the chair still around the house, pretending he's a cripple. Dilya's having trouble understanding that. After crossing the Hindu Kush on foot, she thinks he should want to stay in the chair and be rolled around."

Lola began a light laugh, picturing the incredibly active kid choosing to live out her days in a wheelchair. "Wait, did you say she walked across the Hindu Kush?"

Kee nodded. "Most of it. Barefoot besides. That's where we found her." She returned to her texting.

Lola remembered how much she'd enjoyed the book. A secret among children. A place of absolute safety. A false presentation to the outside world.

A falsehood. There was something there.

"We're sure they're bringing it in by ship, not by air?"

A couple of the crew raised their heads from where they'd been nodding with exhaustion. They blinked in her direction, like owls woken in midday but ready to go back to sleep.

Kee and Emily nodded.

Tim answered, "That's based on President Madani's intelligence. Yes. The Gulf. But that's all we really know."

"Okay, so let's trust that he's good that far. But what if that's false?"

"False like a cripple in a chair?" Kee asked, jumping straight to where it had taken several minutes for her to reach.

"Yes. So, if it's by sea, what haven't we thought of?"

Kee glared at her for a long moment, ready to fire off a quick comeback.

"Look, for the moment just put aside whatever it is you so despise about me and think about it. Okay?" Lola returned heat for heat. At the moment she had bigger concerns than why one of her crewmates despised her.

Kee took a breath, let it out, then finally nodded her acquiescence.

"Little boats," Tim picked it up before she and Kee could go another round. "We're watching those. Big ships. Cruise boats. Military rigs. How can we check all of the possibilities?"

"Port of New Orleans gets a new boat arrival about every twenty minutes, right around the clock." A fact Lola had learned flying patrol for the Air National Guard.

"Crap!" Kee dropped her chin onto her fists resting on the table.

"What else is in the Gulf?"

"Everything." Kee waved her hand to the south. "Oil rigs, shrimp boats, and a raghead with a load of hate on and a chemical to wipe out a city."

"Not if it spreads." Big John looked over at the map of the Southeastern United States they'd tacked on the wall. "It could wipe out a whole lot more than that."

"Thanks, John. I really needed that image."

He shrugged. "Just saying."

Connie went to a whiteboard and started writing. Lola dragged her head around to watch. Doubtful if she had the energy to stand herself.

Connie started with the list they'd already spoken about, then kept going. Soon people were calling out suggestions.

"Pleasure yachts. Tugs. Sailboats. Racing boats. Fireboats. Cop boats." They moved on four or five more before Tim's curse brought them all to a halt.

Connie didn't speak; she simply stopped writing and turned to face Tim.

—◆◆◆—

Tim groaned. This couldn't be happening. He'd finally managed a partial peace with Lola, though it was wearing thin under the exhaustion and frustration they were all feeling.

He turned from the whiteboard, folded his hands on the table, and faced Lola, ignoring the rest of his crewmates. He took a deep breath and decided he had no choice but to bite off the next piece. He just hoped he could handle it.

"When I called your dad—"

"You called my father?" Lola looked as if he'd just slapped her.

Tim ignored the others remarking that they thought she'd said the man was dead.

"You called my father?" He could read the silent repeat on her lips.

"Yes, before I…" How much was he willing to humiliate himself? A lot apparently. "…before I proposed. I called to ask his permission."

The room went silent. Everyone alert.

Well, he'd been wondering if she'd run from him because he'd called her father. It didn't help that it had been even stupider than he'd thought at the time. But she hadn't heard that part of his proposal. Now that he thought back, she'd already been running as the words of his carefully rehearsed speech had continued to dribble out onto the hard stone. He'd driven her away with the proposal itself. He didn't know if that made him feel any smarter.

Kee was the first to break the silence. Her voice dripped vitriol as she turned to face Lola. "You refused Tim? For what goddamned, idiot-dumb—"

"Can it, Kee!" Tim didn't look at her. Didn't let his attention drift even for an instant from Lola's face.

Kee sputtered at his command, but subsided. For the moment.

"You called my father?" He could hear the ire taking root. He knew once it took hold, she'd be too stubborn to hear him.

"I'm a good Catholic boy. Okay, I'm not. I'm a bad Catholic boy with good Catholic parents. I wanted to do it right."

"By calling my father!" It wasn't quite a shout, but it was getting close.

He considered telling her the other reason he'd called. He'd wanted Lola to see Ricky LaRue. Just once. Not as a rejected and ignored little girl, but rather as the woman of immense beauty and power that she now was. For Lola to understand how far she'd come, how magnificent she really was.

But he'd bet that at the moment, in front of all these people, it would sound even stupider if spoken aloud than if he just kept it to himself.

"Can we just ignore that for the moment?"

He decided to take her indecipherable growl as a brief window of opportunity.

"When I spoke to him, I tried to find some common ground to, you know, get the conversation going okay."

"And you found?" This time he was able to translate the growl, but it had a building ferocity.

"Boats."

"Boats?" That stopped her for a moment.

"You said he was into a dozen different criminal activities. Well, I looked him up on the Internet, and he's now deputy sheriff of the New Orleans harbor police. If anyone knows about criminal activity in the Gulf…"

"He's the man who would know."

"A criminal posing as a cop." Tim closed the circle. "Like a boy hiding in a wheelchair."

"Shit!" Lola swore. "You know what this means?"

Tim knew but played dumb.

"It means I'm going to have to talk to the bastard."

Lola looked at him, and a silence seemed to wrap around them as others burst into conversation. In the background, Beale called someone, probably the White House, about the possible lead.

Her voice was a harsh whisper for his ears alone. "You actually called my father to ask for permission to marry me?"

Tim nodded carefully.

"Knowing I'd kill you if I found out?"

He nodded again, momentarily glad for the table between them.

"You're not just crazy." Her smile cracked forth, turning into the lopsided, dimpled grin that had stolen his heart. "You're also the bravest man I've ever met."

Chapter 55

"Too many hours. You've already flown your birds too many hours today. You are not cleared for flight." The flight-line officer tried to block their path.

Lola considered punching him or busting a kneecap.

Major Henderson moved until he was toe to toe with the lieutenant. "Can you read my lapel, mister?"

"Yes, sir, Major, sir."

"Good, remember that the next time you try to give an order. Now, if you didn't get our birds refueled, you have a C-135 tanker meet us at the shore. We're airborne in five minutes."

Lola had stopped along with all of the others to watch the show.

Viper glared over at them, no question what mode he was in at the moment as his command rang out. "You, too. Move your asses."

"Sir, yes, sir." They shouted in unison and sprinted for the birds to run preflight.

The two D-boys lagged behind to make sure the flight officer didn't offer any other interference.

Tim shot her a cheeky grin as she peeled off toward *Vengeance*.

"Well." She sent a thought to Dilya thankfully safe in Washington, D.C. "Let's see just how bad vengeance can be."

Both birds were airborne in three minutes. All armor

checked, all lights green. Luckily for the flight-line lieutenant's continued well-being, he'd already had both Hawks fully refueled.

Ten minutes later, they blew past the coast and out into the darkness of the Gulf of Mexico at night.

"Keep low and—" Viper's voice cut off with the grunt of a high-gee turn. "Watch out for ships."

Trailing a half-dozen rotors behind, Lola barely had time to correct past the stern of a fishing trawler. She popped up to ten meters above the waves and retuned the radar for ocean clutter. The Gulf was an obstacle course of ships moving about. She'd forgotten how busy the seaway was here. In the Air National Guard, you flew a hundred or more feet up to be clear of the shipping. But who knew what was watching for them at the moment.

"Okay, Chief Warrant." Major Henderson's voice still had that ring of command that no one could ignore. That tone he'd taken the moment she'd identified the transport method.

"Care to explain to me what we're doing redlining across the Gulf at two in the morning? And why we're visiting an oil rig in the middle of the Gulf at this time of night? I show you have twenty-eight minutes until contact to explain this to me."

She checked her own mission clock and agreed. Tipping the nose ever so slightly down and right improved the airflow to the engine intakes, causing the navigation computer to recompute. That would save her another thirty-five seconds.

It was only now that she realized the Majors hadn't questioned her. She'd said where and they'd gone at a run. They trusted her and her instincts.

She glanced over at Beale who simply flew with one hand riding lightly on the cyclic. The Major's other hand didn't hold the collective as Lola's did. Instead it rested on her belly. Perhaps sensing Lola's glance, Beale shifted her hands to the proper position, but there was a hesitation, a reluctance that worried Lola. A pilot couldn't afford to have split attention in combat. And Lola had little question that's where they were headed.

"Chief Warrant?" There was no avoiding Henderson's demand for an answer.

"Prior to Katrina, New Orleans had a history of being the deadliest city per capita anywhere in the U.S. Worse than Detroit. For six months after, it became an amazingly safe city. Why? We'd exported all our criminals along with all of the other refugees." Lola corrected around a container ship, clearing it by a half rotor of distance.

She felt an unexpected resistance on the controls. She slanted a glance over, moving her helmet as little as possible. Major Beale's hand was now clenched tightly around the cyclic control. Lola wiggled the stick slightly, just as Beale had done to her on their first flight, and the Major eased her grasp immediately.

"It took a couple years, but they're back. Having left behind nasty little nightmares in Houston, Nashville, and Little Rock, they came back in force. Scared judges, or ones that are just plain lazy, make it easy to hit the streets, often within hours of an arrest. Some of them were just dug in from the beginning and never left. My father started out as a cop, accepting bribery from and later running whorehouses in Storyville."

Mama Raci's hadn't been one of his, the reason Lola

had chosen it as a refuge at first. Later because Mama Raci was the first person who'd set standards and expected her to live up to them.

"His control grew and so did his greed. Who needs a warlord when you have him for a deputy sheriff?"

"So what did he say on the phone?"

"I quote, 'Heard from a buddy that Pikes has a rig expecting some inbound traffic tonight. Something hot and quiet.' The way he said it, he was pissed that he didn't have a part of it."

She'd not mention that he asked who the hot rod was that had called about marrying her and how much was she getting paid an hour for it? She couldn't imagine what he'd said to Tim.

But Tim's answer had been to propose to her.

And she'd turned him down.

"Well done, LaRue. Glad to have you aboard."

For a moment she'd thought he was saying she'd been smart to turn down Tim. Then she realized that Major Henderson was trying to pay her a nice compliment. A compliment for her dedication to SOAR and its mission.

But it didn't offset the chill that threatened to consume her. The chill that maybe her rejection had been too well done and Tim wouldn't ask her again.

Chapter 56

THEY CAME IN LOW, FIVE FEET OFF THE WAVES. They swung wide and came at the Pikes oil rig from opposite sides.

"Be careful, Major," Lola called over the radio. "This is a GVA 4000 model rig, not a lot of extra space around the helideck."

Just as they swooped up from wave tops at two hundred klicks per hour to a full stop six stories up, Lola once again felt resistance on the cyclic. Knowing exactly what it was, she flicked the control, hard, knowing she'd lose a little momentum on the climb. Out of the corner of her eye, she saw the Major snatch her hands off the controls, an uncharacteristically dangerous action.

But now the controls were free and it was all Lola could worry about at the moment.

Just as her nose cleared the edge of the platform, an RPG streaked by not ten feet in front of her windscreen, thankfully passing between the spinning rotor blades. If she hadn't hesitated to knock the Major's hand clear, she'd have taken that right in the belly.

"Steel!" she yelled into the headset. "We Deal in Steel" was the motto of the Direct Action Penetrator Black Hawks, and almost before she could finish her call, the two crew chiefs were laying in as only a DAP Hawk could.

Twin arcs of green death lashed out of either side

of her helicopter. Kee's hand-steerable minigun was throwing three thousand rounds a minute, pouring death into the control cabin where the RPG had originated. It sounded like a monster buzz saw driven by a Peterbilt truck engine, that sound of pure, lethal power.

Connie's opened up on the other side, having found some appropriate target.

Lola spotted the other Black Hawk.

"*Viper*'s hit. Going down on the deck. Give him cover." Her training let her register the event and react before she'd even focused on it.

They'd clipped his tail and he was trying to auto-rotate onto a platform not much bigger than his bird with a six-story drop to the ocean on two sides and a nightmare of helicopter-eating cables and structure on the other two.

She moved in right above him, using the Hawk's ADAS camera which projected what was going on around her ship across the inside of her helmet visor.

Viper made it down. Hard, skidding to the edge, sheering off his blades against some low steel structure, but he did it without tumbling off the edge and into the ocean below. He came to rest right side up. A quick burst of green fire lancing out of the wreckage showed that at least one of his crew chiefs was still functioning.

Left side. Tim was okay. At least okay enough to keep fighting.

No time for real relief, just acknowledgment that his continued survival was a very good thing.

Lola twisted her fuselage so that she was turned a quarter turn from the Black Hawk on the deck below her. Now between his crew chiefs and her own, they could cover a full circle of fire.

A sharp patter of gunfire across her windscreen drew her attention up.

Bright flashes from the control room dead ahead. They'd clearly dug a nest in there, one that Kee's gun hadn't been enough to eradicate.

Lola sighted and, pressing a safety on the collective, she thumbed the fire button on the cyclic. No way to miss at fifty feet.

Thankfully the Hellfire missile bored deep into the room before it went off. She tipped her nose down to hold her position above *Viper* as the shock wave rolled over them, scattering bits of glass and metal at her like ten thousand angry hornets. Lola could feel the wave of heat despite the windscreen and all of her helmet and flight gear.

Two men, their clothes ablaze, ran from the fire only to fall to their deaths when they slammed into and over the walkway guardrail. Another staggered free of the flames, an RPG launcher still clutched loosely in his hands. Colonel Gibson dropped him where he stood with a shot through the forehead. He must be leaning out the cargo bay door.

Lola's visor showed no more incoming threats, the area appeared clear. Neither she nor anyone on *Viper* moved for a full sixty seconds as the control room continued to burn under the searing heat of the nano-thermite reaction.

"You guys okay down there?"

"Richardson's down. The rest of us are okay. Nice work, dear."

Henderson must be rattled at how close a call he'd just survived if he hadn't noticed it wasn't his wife's voice on the radio.

Lola glanced over. Beale was jammed back in her seat, both hands over her belly, completely immobile. Catatonic.

Lola keyed the mike back to command-and-control, which routed all the way back to the Situation Room on this one.

"Captain Stevenson, you there?"

"Here, Chief Warrant."

"We have a Hawk down on the Pikes rig. Will need an airlift to fetch it. We need a medic and a fire control team before this thing lights off and another rig burns into the Gulf."

"Roger, already en route."

Right. Mission cameras would be running a live feed to the Sit Room.

Henderson called up. "Chief Warrant LaRue, I think you'd better land. We'll offer cover." At least his head was clear now. Clear enough to know his wife wasn't flying this mission. Beale remained unmoving as Lola shifted carefully toward the far edge of the helideck, dangerously close to a crane hoist.

"Roger, sir. Stay on your toes, Chiefs," she called back to Connie and Kee.

She brought the Hawk down, ready to twitch if her chiefs called out any corrections.

Even before her wheels touched the deck, Henderson yanked open Emily's door, had her snapped out of her harness, and had her sitting on the deck. He began twisting and turning her to check for injuries.

"I'm fine. I'm fine. Stop that."

Mark stopped his searching hands, finding no blood on his wife, no telltale stain like the one running down Richardson's chest from where an armor-piercing round had punched through windscreen and visor to remove most of his face. Four years they'd flown together, and in an instant the man was gone.

Yet all Mark had been able to think as he'd watched the *Vengeance* descend from the night sky was that his wife had never flown a Hawk that way.

Chapter 57

LOLA CLIMBED DOWN TO THE OIL RIG'S HELIDECK. THE broad white circle and large *H* in the center shone bright under the remaining floodlights. Most lights flickered or were gone, but a few remained here and there about the rig, outlining it in the middle of the night darkness. Oil rigs, at least when they weren't shot up and on fire, smelled mostly of the ocean. People expected the stench of heavy crude, but rigs were designed to be very clean. The last thing you wanted was oil dripping into the water below.

She watched Major Beale's knees let go, and only her husband's assistance kept her from collapsing completely. Though she did bat at Henderson's hands as he checked her over for wounds one more time.

The Delta operator from the *Viper* sat on the deck beside the downed bird. His leg at a grotesque angle, clearly snapped in the middle of the shin. But his rifle was at the ready as he scanned the oil rig structure towering above them. Colonel Gibson was already disappearing toward the burning control room, light as a cat, his rifle at his shoulder.

The four crew chiefs were standing loose. Perhaps unable to believe that Viperess Beale lay on the deck. Lola couldn't look down at her, because there was something wrong with a universe that could cause the Major to react the way she had. Or maybe something right. That need to protect new life against all comers had overridden a decade of training in a single moment.

Lola swept her hand to get the crew's attention. When she did, she pointed two fingers at her own eyes, slapped the FN SCAR rifle strapped across her own chest, then indicated John and Tim should patrol up through the rig and Connie and Kee downward.

They snapped into action like windup dolls suddenly released. Rifles at the ready, they were in full soldier-mode between one heartbeat and the next. As they faded into the shadows cast by the still blazing fire and the rig's few remaining work lights, Lola unslung her own rifle and started scanning the rigging through the night scope to provide cover for the two officers.

Major Beale was clambering back onto her feet. Lola could hear the Major's voice but didn't stop her scan.

"I don't know what happened. All I could think about was what if I was shot in the gut. It won't happen again."

The Major was still as white as a sheet. At least she'd unslung her rifle from across her chest and held it two-handed, but her eyes were glazed over. In her present condition Beale wouldn't see a terrorist at five meters.

Lola spotted the Delta Force colonel slipping along below the sill of the blown-out control room windows. Every few meters, he'd pop his head briefly up to glance into the inferno blast of heat for a quick scan. Once, he swung his rifle into place and fired a quick double-tap round before ducking back down. A distant scream of agony that Lola hadn't really registered before cut off abruptly.

"Friendly!" Kee shouted as she ran back up from below.

Lola covered her with her rifle as another figure came up behind her making the same call.

John and Tim slid down the wire rigging from higher in the rig announcing "all clear" as they descended.

"There are three dead guys in oil worker clothes," Connie shouted in between gasps for breath after running up six flights of stairs between the water and the helideck. "A small twenty-foot runabout boat with a civilian still bleeding out in the driver's seat."

"And cut ropes on the boat dock. There was another boat. It's gone. We've gotta go," Kee managed to finish for her.

Major Beale started toward the chopper, pulling her arm out of Henderson's hand. He didn't move, perhaps too startled to stop her.

Lola stepped into her path. "Where do you think you're going, Major?"

"You heard her, we have to fly." Beale tried to push past her, but Lola grabbed her by her vest and shoved her backwards into Henderson's arms.

"Emma, you can't—"

Beale cut Henderson off with an elbow to the gut.

Lola pulled back and sucker-punched the Major right on the point of her chin.

She flew backward, almost taking her husband to the deck when she fell into him.

"You can court-martial me when you wake up."

Lola looked up at Major Henderson. He could take her down right now. End her career for striking a superior officer.

He concentrated on the woman limp in his arms for a long moment before looking up to inspect Lola.

He mouthed, "Thank you."

She turned away to face the four crew chiefs and Colonel Gibson staring at her slack-jawed.

"Okay, I'm taking over now. You and you." She jabbed fingers at her two crew chiefs. "Get aboard. You two"—she indicated John and Tim—"which of you would make a better forward gunner?"

Big John slapped Tim on the back hard enough to send him stumbling toward the chopper. "She's talking to you, buddy boy."

Henderson went to step forward, but she held up a hand to stop him.

"Your mind is here, sir. Do the math. Right now I don't want you on my ship. John, you make sure they get out of this alive and in the meantime find a fire hose for that damned mess up there. Colonel, you're the only other mobile shooter whose thinking I trust at the moment. You need to stay here, watch John's back, and make sure this crazy rig is clean of hostiles and nasty chemicals. You know what to look for."

He nodded.

"And the rest of the rig's original crew may be locked up somewhere if they're still alive."

He faded out of sight in that way that only a D-boy could do.

Tim had stopped short of the copilot's door. Though the controls were identical, the copilot usually ran most of the forward weaponry from the left seat and the pilot flew from the right seat. But she didn't want to have to adjust her thinking at the moment and opted to stay in her current left-hand position at the identical controls. And she didn't want to sit in Emily's seat.

She aimed a finger at Tim's chest and jerked it toward Beale's door. He could fight just as well from there.

He went.

Chapter 58

BACK ALOFT, LOLA CIRCLED THE RIG TWICE. SPIRES OF metalwork, drilling derricks, and cranes sprouted like a heli-pilot's worst nightmare. She stayed well clear as she continued her inspection. The infrared imaging was wonky with all of the heat streaming from the control room and the machinery, but she didn't spot any lurkers in the rigging.

On her next circuit she spiraled the DAP Hawk down along one of the submersible rig's pylons to the boat dock. Definitely empty.

She pulled to hover on the north side of the rig.

"Which way?" The whole Gulf Coast spread before them. Alabama to the right, Mississippi and Louisiana close enough to straight ahead.

"I'm guessing that Florida Panhandle and Texas are too far," Tim spoke slowly over the headset.

"Why?" She aimed the question at him.

"The size of the runabout they left behind."

"Good. But what the hell are we looking for?" That earned Lola silence from the crew.

The baddies had clearly planned to use the small boat. Smart. Low and slow to avoid attracting attention. But they'd changed plans. Changed them recently enough that there was a still-warm body at the dock.

"They left in an awful hurry." It was the only thing that would explain everything.

"Why?" This time Tim was hitting her with the question.

"Because… Oh! Damn it! I know what we're looking for. A goddamned police boat." She aimed the chopper's nose down and slammed the cyclic forward. In moments they were rocketing toward the coast.

"I don't get it."

"Simple, Tim. Dad was ticked that there was something important enough going on that his estranged daughter would actually get in touch with him. I caught him on his cell phone, so he must have been out here and decided to swing by and see if he could horn in on the action." She started sweeping arcs side to side, slowing to check any small boats she overflew.

"He must have told them we were inbound, so they hijacked him and cut out so fast that they cut the ropes rather than untie them." Lola was afraid that he was dead already, though for the life of her she couldn't think of why she cared. Maybe because it would deny her the chance of gunning him down herself.

"Would he go straight to land? Or another ship?"

Tim was still thinking. And at the moment she was glad for the second mind sitting next to her. All hers could see or think about was the blinding red of a desire to murder the SOB if he wasn't already dead. If he'd stayed out of the way, they'd have captured the baddies flatfooted at the rig or in a little runabout that couldn't break twenty miles per hour.

"He's an arrogant son-of-a-bitch. Dangerous, but he'll trust his strength. If they give him a choice, he's going for shore."

She traced arcs back and forth across the ocean to make sure she didn't miss any of his most likely routes back. Keeping her attention split between looking for a small police boat with enough biocide to kill millions and not running headlong into a container ship was making her head hurt. Normally the tasks would be divided between pilot and copilot, but Tim wouldn't have the honed skills of a trained copilot. This meant she had to fly even more slowly.

Each mile from the rig, she had to swing wider and wider to make sure she didn't miss his possible paths back to the shoreline. At this rate, he'd be there while she was still carving aerial arcs back and forth over the waves.

A glance over showed Tim checking his weapons, getting his hands used to the unfamiliar position of the forward weapon controls. Clearly, he'd practiced a lot because his hands settled rapidly without applying more than stray pressure to the flight controls.

She returned her attention to the Gulf. This was familiar. This she could do. With the Air National Guard she had flown hundreds of missions over the Gulf traffic. The subtle bob-and-weave of boat tracks as they crossed the rolling waves. The rigs as brightly lit as cities, dotting across the surface of the ocean, promising oil and prosperity to the region.

A bit of relief eased over her as she fell into the practiced regimen of the search part of search and rescue. Lola hadn't been aware of her own shock at Beale's reaction. It was like waking up one morning to discover that the sky was purple and the earth was made of cream cheese, simply too wrong to comprehend.

Yet it made some sense, as Lola made her turn from a northeasterly track to a northwesterly one. It was like a flight crew. Any one of them would rather be shot than see a crewmember shot. Command was crazy, the baddies were crazier, but your crew lay as close as your heartbeat.

Lola had felt it before, but never like this. Could she imagine standing in front of Big John or Captain Stevenson and telling them their wives were dead? Could she face Cara and Jackson to report Tim's demise? She'd rather take the round herself any day. No one to tell. No one to care if she died.

Except maybe this crew. And Tim.

She turned back northeast, continuing her shoreward sweeps. The widening out of each pass would soon have her running farther side to side than forward. Damn it! Nothing.

Beale. It was impossible to imagine that anything could make Beale fold. This crew was her lifeblood.

But it wasn't. Or rather she'd discovered a higher call, the life growing within her. No wonder the woman had gone catatonic. Her world had shifted far more suddenly than Lola's. In one instant she went from one of the top fliers in SOAR to feeling absolute terror for her child's life. Having crossed the threshold, she might have been safe to fly now, but her reactions would still be dulled, hesitant, and they couldn't afford that right now.

Would that happen to her someday? If she were carrying a child? The shock of the thought was only exceeded by a clear image of it being Tim's child. If it was Tim's child, she might well react as Major Beale had.

"Look!" Tim called out. "Two o'clock going north-northwest."

Lola stared ahead, glanced over at Tim, and looked forward again.

Nothing.

"Look through the visor."

Lola's attention had been wholly focused on the camera feed across the inside of her visor. The projected view of the dark night world outside the helicopter as if she flew free of any mechanical structure. The illusion was broken by tactical readouts, targeting information, radar and satellite feeds, and a submenu of the Hawk's mechanical well-being.

She shifted her focus through the visor and saw it clear as day. A long line of phosphorescence striking northwest like an arrow. No need to check her instruments to see that it drew a straight line from the Pikes oil rig to the mouth of the Mississippi River. Algae, a cold light, so no heat signature to show up in her visor.

"Good one, Tim."

Now that she had a path, she climbed to five hundred feet to clear any boat traffic and lay down the hammer. The DAP Hawk leaped forward like an eager dog hot on the scent.

Her father had clearly hot-rodded his boat for him to have gotten this far. But the track continued, growing brighter every minute due to the fresh turbulence exciting the algae.

"Okay, everyone. Game time. Get ready to burn 'em."

"Chief Warrant?"

Her title sounded strange in Tim's voice. "What?"

"We should try to take them alive."

"Why?"

There was an awkward silence.

"Why?" All she could think about was the excuse to bury the bastard in a couple thousand feet of cold ocean.

"We need the information. Maybe to make sure this is the only shipment."

He was right, and she hated that he was right.

She took a deep breath and did her best to let it out slowly.

"Okay."

But it still wasn't. She could feel she was holding on too tight and loosened her hands on the controls. But she couldn't shake out the knot between her shoulders.

"Okay. Kee, get out that rifle of yours and get over to Connie's side. Tie yourself in there. You'll try it the nice way, but Connie, you be ready to bury their asses with your minigun. Tim, keep your finger on that Hellfire. If it gets ugly, we'll need to incinerate this chemical but good. If it goes aerosol, it could still sweep ashore in an invisible wave of death."

Five more long minutes before anything showed. She followed enough phosphorescent tracks over the years to know this was unusual. Even the big cigarette boats should have been in view by this time. When she finally spotted the boat, it took another two minutes to catch up with it.

Then she saw why it had taken so long to catch. Painted the blue and white of the Harbor Patrol, the offshore race boat was skipping wave top to wave top in a mad dash for shore. He was running toward a lost bayou backwater.

"Tim, lay some fire across his bow."

Tim chose a trio of FFAR Hydra rockets that augered into the waves just ahead of the boat and fountained three geysers of water fifty feet into the air. The boat powered right through the spray as Lola swung wide to get clear of the towering columns of sea water.

As she came clear of the water and could see the boat once again, Tim shouted.

"RPG!"

Even before the threat detector went off.

What the hell? No time to think.

She slammed the cyclic forward and down and rammed in the left pedal. In a moment they were tumbling and the black ocean was coming up fast.

Connie and Kee were squawking in protest, trying to compensate.

Lola slammed the cyclic back and right, presenting a minimum profile, most importantly aiming the whirling rotor disc edge on. The RPG flew by so close to the cabin that Lola could almost taste its bad breath.

She managed to recover before they plunged into the waves. Tim's sharp lookout had saved them.

So, they were playing it that way.

They?

Her father might be a maniac, but there was no way he'd shoot at an Army helicopter. So there was definitely someone on the boat with him. If he was still alive, he might well be captive.

Whoever they were, they thought shooting at a U.S. Army helicopter was fair game.

She climbed back into the air until she had a little space to maneuver.

The boat had clearly opened its throttles wider, had pulled ahead once again, and was slaloming side to side.

"Kee, watch for shooters aboard. At least one..." No,

there was the RPG shooter and whoever was either driving the boat or, more likely based on the driver's obvious skill, keeping her father at gunpoint while he drove.

"There are at least two shooters, and Dad's the driver. Baddies have had time to reload. Tim, I'm going to roll in and set you up to take out his propellers. And if you hit a gas tank, I won't complain."

Three massive outboard engines were positioned across the stern of the weaving boat, an almost impossible shot. But Tim was right—they needed information almost as badly as they needed to stop them.

She popped up over a thousand feet and then did a rolling dive just like the final one on the range. The DAP snap rolled with far more willingness than the Huey. Sure enough, another RPG roared upward, but nowhere near the blacked-out helicopter. The roll made them a really lousy target.

At the last moment Lola steadied the chopper into a nose-down-and-diving-hard attitude. Tim lit off with the minigun mounted on the weapons pylon inboard from the Hellfires and poured the flying fusillade into the water barely a foot off the boat's stern. He'd read her move as if they'd flown together for years.

The boat stumbled, then nosed in hard at the abrupt loss of all three screws. Nose down, it kicked the stern into the air. Two propellers were gone and the third was dangling; Tim had sheared all three in a single pass.

The bow dug in so deep that a wave rolled down the length of the boat. Nothing new for an ocean racer, still impressive to see.

A sharp crack sounded over the intercom as Lola recovered from the dive barely feet over the boat.

"I nailed one," Kee reported. "But that's all I saw other than the driver."

Maybe Lola had miscalculated. She circled to face the now wallowing boat head-on, staying well clear of the oily smoke swirling upward from the ruined engines.

Small-caliber fire pinged against her windscreen.

He always was a persistent bastard.

"Tim." He laid into the 30 mm cannon, dropping the inch-and-a-quarter shells at ten rounds a second in a blazing arc that encircled the boat.

Lola flipped on the outside speaker when he stopped.

"Stop being stupid. Put down the gun and come out with your hands up." She could feel the bile rise, the rage swelling from every bone of her past. Every bit of it that she'd thought long since laid to rest.

"Just do it, Dad!"

Chapter 59

A BIG MAN SLOWLY ROSE OUT OF THE BOAT'S COCKPIT, his hands not raised, but both holding the upper edge of the windshield. In plain sight.

She fingered the control. One 30 mm round through the center of his chest. So close. So easy.

"Don't do it." Tim's voice was barely audible over the intercom.

Lola didn't answer. Her finger actually ached from her desire to end it. Screw the information. Screw the chemical. It didn't matter if she hit the payload and was caught in the resulting cloud of Soman. At least he'd be dead. Once and for all.

"Don't." Tim's voice was gentle. As gentle as when they made love. "You're better than that, Lola. We'd cover for you. No question. But he's not worth it. You're better than that."

She knew there was no need for anyone to cover for her. She'd seen the Presidential Order granting her full authority to blow the bastard back to hell.

She held the hover tight, her whole hand now aching with the desire, the need to finish him off. A scream ripped up from her belly, hurt her ears amplified by the intercom. Now she knew how an animal denied her fair kill must feel.

Well, she wouldn't be denied. Maybe if the Major was here aboard *Vengeance*, maybe she could stop this, stop what had become inevitable from the moment in the desert when the D-boys found the chemical lab.

The *Vengeance*.

The moment before she plunged down the trigger, Lola remembered a small voice. The voice of a young girl sitting in a gunner's chair and deciding that vengeance "just make everybodies sad."

She screamed again as she released her hold on the safety. The scream twisted inward and nearly choked her, coming out as a single sob when she eased her finger clear of the trigger.

A sharp double crack sounded over the headset. Kee's rifle.

"What the—"

The windshield next to her father exploded. A bright muzzle flash flared skyward from close beside him.

She'd been right the first time. There had been a second shooter, he'd just been hidden.

Lola slid the Hawk around until they could look down into the racer's cockpit. A man with an AK-47 still clenched in his hand lay sprawled on the deck; one shot had shattered the windshield, and the second had bored a neat hole where his temple should be.

Chapter 60

THE COAST GUARD HAD RUSHED A CUTTER TO THE scene from where it had been patrolling farther west. For twenty long minutes she had waited, hovering fifty feet from the boat and staring at her father in silence.

His smirk had grown.

When he took a hand off the windshield, as if to scratch his head, Lola sent a round whistling past his ear to slam into one of the engines. The force of the 30 mm shell actually ripped it off the mounting and sent it plunging into the ocean depths.

The hand reclamped to the windshield and the smirk went away.

Lola considered dropping the crew chiefs on the deck to secure him. But didn't want to risk her team. She knew how fast his hands could deliver pain, though he'd rarely done more than slap her, how powerful he would remain despite his age. No one would ever be exposed to that again, especially not her crew.

Her crew. They were her crew now. Sure, she'd flown command, but they were her crew.

The Coasties swarmed aboard the racing boat. Once they had it secure, Lola settled the DAP Hawk on the helideck of the Coast Guard boat.

"You done good, team." She wanted to make sure they knew, somehow understood how important they'd all become to her. "You done real good."

"You too, Chief," echoed back to her, from all of them one by one.

The situation remained stable while the Coast Guard secured everything. Her hand still aching from not firing that single 30 mm round through his chest. Even after the moment had passed and she knew she wouldn't actually do it, resisting the urge to let fly had remained a struggle.

As soon as the Hawk was secure on the deck and she had it shut down, she clambered out of her seat. At first she'd thought to go down and confront him, stare down the demon from her past face to face. Had thought how it would feel to spit in his face. He was going to get off scot-free, and she'd lost her chance to just shoot him.

Instead, she sat on the cargo deck of the DAP Hawk and watched the action from her perch high atop the helideck.

She sent Tim and Connie down to make sure the Coasties handled the Soman with the respect a weapon of mass destruction deserved.

At first the Coasties had been solicitous of Deputy Sheriff Ricky LaRue, checking him for injuries from his ordeal. Then there was an abrupt shift of attitude. Tim climbed up from where he'd gone below, carrying a plastic bag of something white.

Suddenly the Coasties had Ricky LaRue slammed against the side of the cockpit and were reading him his rights.

Her father looked up at the helideck as they handcuffed him, and Lola had to resist the urge to flinch away.

Instead, she sat up straighter, holding his gaze until he looked away first. Somehow he shrank in size as they dragged him toward the boarding ladder hanging down from the cutter's tall side.

Kee sat down beside Lola to clean her sniper rifle. The sounds slowly descended to the steady background hum of a military ship going about its duties, a sound so familiar it was akin to silence.

"Thought you were a phony."

Lola looked up at the radar mast etched white against the night sky. Kee was right. Nothing about her was real. The competent soldier Chief Warrant 2 Lola LaRue. A facade. The woman who has her act so together, a complete and utter fraud. Some persona she'd made up out of poor assumptions and insufficient bravado.

Lola turned to watch the Sergeant sight the barrel, then set to running a BoreSnake down it to remove some stray residue.

Finally Kee stopped what she was doing and turned to stare directly at Lola with those narrow, penetrating eyes of hers.

"I thought you were all flash. And no f'ing way you deserved someone as good as Tim. I could see you caught him from the first second. Knew that wasn't right." Then she flashed a smile that lit her up. "Should've known you were okay when Dilya liked you."

Kee snapped her gun back together without looking down to see her motions. She turned to stow the gun in its case, then stood for a moment before Lola.

When Kee glanced down at the deck, Lola followed her gaze.

Her father stood there, drawing himself up tall despite the handcuffs and four-guard escort.

Kee turned back to Lola and snapped a smart salute

to her. Clear for all to see. Making it obvious to the man below exactly who had taken him down.

Lola returned the salute. Didn't even bother to look down as they led him away. He no longer mattered and she didn't need to witness his final demise.

Kee then cracked a smile, more welcoming than any salute. "You done really good, Chief Warrant." And she headed down to the main deck.

Lola stared up at the sky and contemplated the night. A moon, a spread of stars now that the helideck work lights had been shut down. A night lit much like the roof of the Fort Rucker hangar where Tim had made impossibly gentle love to her.

Made love to her.

She closed her eyes, remembering. And she had made love to him. Had felt as if... No, she had belonged in his arms. The safest place in the world. Now maybe she understood Emily a little better. To have a part of a man she loved so much growing inside her, nothing could be more important when that was happening.

She wasn't ready to quit flying. Not by a long shot. And she'd bet that Major Beale would find a way back into the sky after the birth.

Maybe it wasn't the flying that made it worth the effort and hardship and pain. Maybe it was who you flew with.

Lola looked back down from the sky, and there Tim stood in his unconsciously competent pose, not five feet away, swaying ever so lightly as the cutter rode the waves. The race boat now in tow as they turned for port.

"Twenty cases of one-quart steel bottles. Enough to take out a dozen cities. He thought it was moonshine.

Went sheet white when he discovered he'd wanted to sample some of the product. The guys with the guns had yelled at him when he tried."

"So, he gets away with it. Again." She should have shot him when she had the chance.

Tim grinned that easy smile of his. "Not so much. That bag I found wasn't the only one. He must have been out on a run when you called his cell. That's how he got there ahead of us. It just happens that he also has a quarter ton of heroin aboard. Wonder how much cash that cost him?"

Lola nodded. He'd go down hard for that. This wasn't some local judge in the Big Easy. With the Coasties involved, this one would hit Federal court. Maybe she was finally done with her past. Maybe, just maybe, she was who she said she was, Chief Warrant 2 of the Army's SOAR, a Night Stalker of the 160th.

"They've got a nickname for you now."

Lola grimaced. "That doesn't sound good." She'd left behind more than few black eyes when various crews had tried "Stripper LaRue" and a dozen variations on it.

"They're calling you 'Hammer LaRue.' Kinda fits."

She looked at him in silence, knowing full well exactly who had started that nickname—the oh-so-pleased-with-himself man right in front of her.

"Just 'The Hammer,' for short. Personally, I kinda like it."

She rolled the sound back and forth. She liked it, too. The power, the strength, but still herself.

"Hammer LaRue and Crazy Tim. Quite a pair, huh?" It wasn't until after she said it that she realized quite what she'd given voice to.

Tim went all quiet. Hands rammed deep in his pockets. So still that he almost faded from sight like a D-boy.

She knew what was in his pocket. Knew what he hoped for and wanted.

Lola also knew that there would never be anyone who could know her the way Tim did. Who had been able to talk her back from that cliff edge where warfare turns to murder. Had found her in the dark shadows that surrounded her soul.

And no one that she'd ever known so well. No one who made her feel safe and loved and important. No one else had ever made her feel complete, and Tim could do it with the simplest gesture of merely taking her hand.

There wasn't anyone that she ever could love the way she did Crazy Tim Maloney.

He voiced no question. But he was asking.

She'd been sitting in almost exactly this spot on the edge of the Huey's cargo bay that day. It had been spread for a picnic, not dusty with blowback from the miniguns. But he'd asked the question again no less clearly.

And she had given one answer the first time, smashing an heirloom and his heart in the process. The joke had been on her. Who'd have thought that Lola LaRue also had a heart that could be shredded.

Who'd have thought that she had a heart that could be healed by the love of a good man.

This time she knew her answer to his silent question.

She pulled up her legs, shifting back into the shadows of the cargo bay, sitting out of the reach of the sole work-light atop the cutter's helideck.

Then she extended her left hand back into the soft

light to beckon Tim to join her. She held her hand out to him, with the ring finger slightly raised.

A sigh ran the length of her body as the cool gold slid onto her finger and his warm lips marked it in place.

Curling his fingers into hers, she pulled him into the dark shadows of the chopper and the dark shadows of her life, where Tim spread nothing but the brightest light.

Chapter 61

L<small>OLA</small> L<small>A</small>R<small>UE</small> <small>STOOD AT A MOMENT AND A PLACE SHE'D</small> never imagined.

A simple "I do" joining her life to Tim's. The two simple words completed her declaration that matched his.

When he kissed her, tears flowed and she couldn't stop them. Tears and laughter and one of his searing kisses that made her know she could fly.

In moments, her laughter had swept the wedding party and then the rest of the crowded restaurant closed for the occasion. Mark Henderson, who'd escorted her down the aisle, now close beside Emily, her maid-of-honor, still barely showing despite the clingy bridesmaid dress. Big John, looking absolutely amazing in his best man's suit swept his quiet wife into his arms and delivered a smacking kiss that she wholeheartedly returned.

Dilya ran forward, still carrying her near-empty basket of rose petals, to offer her a quick hug before dodging back to her parents barely in time avoid Tim's family descending on her.

Lola let herself relax and lose herself in their unstinting welcome and was quickly buried several people deep until Tim rescued her.

Food flowed from the kitchen, and they gorged on delicacies and delights. None of them were on call, but even the second glass of wine wasn't finished by any of the Night Stalkers; they were giddy enough without the alcohol.

She felt beyond giddy herself and couldn't stop smiling each time she saw the gift table piled high. She knew that in the depths lurked a double present from bride to groom. The first had cost her a month's pay, an antique teapot as exquisite as the one she'd shattered. The second, a plaque. The engraved brass plate noting the date of the first shared kill of Sergeant Tim Maloney and Chief Warrant 2 Lola LaRue and mounted above it, the original teapot handle. A joke on both of them that would make Crazy Tim the butt of a joke that his friends would never let him live down, no matter how many years they were together.

When she retreated to a quiet table for a breather, she found Emily Beale sipping from a glass of sparkling apple cider. It somehow seemed the first minute they'd had together. Lola had been too wound up to be coherent in the upstairs apartment as the three women of her crew had helped her get ready.

Perhaps it was the first time they'd been alone together since… Lola could feel a blush rising to her cheeks.

Emily considered her for a long moment.

Lola inspected her hands.

"Hell of punch you have, Chief Warrant."

"Uh. Thank you, Major. Sorry, Major."

When Lola managed to look up, the Major was watching her closely.

"I'll have to remember to return the favor some day."

"The favor?"

Now it was the Major who looked away, contemplated her cider for a long moment before speaking.

"There will come a time when you have to face choices, Chief LaRue, choices that you don't want to make for what seem many and good reasons. But to which the answer is obvious. I should never have set foot on that chopper. I knew it, but commanding the *Vengeance* had defined me so completely that I didn't know how to be anything else."

Lola nodded. She knew all about fighting the right choice for the wrong reasons. All she had to do was look up and spot her husband laughing with his best friend, a smear of cake on his cheek that still no one had told him about. He looked up to see her, and again Lola felt the smile bloom from deep inside her.

"I'm resigning my commission."

That shocked her attention back to the Major. "No! You can't."

"Already did. And I browbeat Peter into accepting it, though he was pretty grumpy about it. Especially when Mark turned his in, as well."

"No! Emily, that's not right. You can't just throw all of that away. How did the President ever agree to let you go? I need to talk to him."

She'd half risen to her feet to go find him. There. Flirting with Tim's mother. Emily stopped her with a hand on her arm.

"Actually, Peter's sponsoring us in a little endeavor."

"What endeavor?" Lola dropped back into her seat.

It had been strange to fly without Emily beside her, even after the few short weeks they'd been together as crew. But to have her not in the service at all, that absolutely wasn't right.

"Ever flown a Firehawk?"

Lola could only shake her head. Had seen the footage. Sikorsky Black Hawks rigged with spray equipment, fighting forest fires in places that ground crews could never reach.

"One of the odd things about flying a Firehawk, very few people shooting at you. The other oddity, well, countries are always glad for help from a Firehawk team, even countries where there's normally no way to get in, even undercover. You should come fly with us some time. It's going to be fun. Mount Hood Aviation, up in Oregon. Look us up when you're ready."

Lola knew about Mount Hood—part firefighting, part CIA undercover transport, an odd leftover of Air America back in the 1960s. That could be interesting. But not where she wanted, needed to be at this point of her life.

"Maybe we'll fly together again some time."

Emily looked at her. Took her hand and squeezed it hard. "I'd like that, Lola. Truly I would."

She returned the gesture, fighting back the tears. The unquestioned truth of that from Major Emily Beale took her breath away.

Tim came up beside her before she could get her breath back. She rose to her feet and kissed away the icing still on his cheek. He looked goofy happy as he pulled her away from Emily.

He danced her out onto the cleared center of the restaurant's floor. He snapped his fingers and pointed at his cousin Jimmy who punched a button on the screen in front of him.

A tango washed out of the speakers and Lola couldn't think of when she'd been happier. Perhaps dancing with Tim that very first time on the dusty Afghan soil, surrounded by helicopters. Perhaps that had been her glimpse of what was possible.

No. She looked into Tim's eyes as he swept her down and then back up into his arms.

There, in his eyes, there was the glimpse of the possible.

Notes

The curiously straight line and large power station in the Iranian desert outside Ravar may be viewed by pasting 31.30593, 56.76981 into your favorite map viewer. Perhaps just an irrigation ditch, it was still enough to inspire this bit of fiction.

Desert One is located at: 33.083236, 55.799088.

For a great view of real-time ship movement at ports all over the world, including New Orleans, visit www.marinetraffic.com.

Watch for *Pure Heat,*

the first book in Firehawks, an exciting new series by
M.L. Buchman, coming May 2014
from Sourcebooks Casablanca

The daredevil smokejumpers of Mount Hood Aviation
do more than fight wildfires. Led by retired SOAR pilots, they fly elite operatives into places that even the
CIA can't penetrate—and Charlene Thomas and Steve
Mercer are the best in the business.

While battling the summer's toughest fire, the pair un-
cover a terrorist camp in the remote forest of Oregon.
Using specially equipped helicopters and a stealth-
modified drone, they take on the camp. The mission—
and the flames—are combatable. For Steve, it's the heat
from Charlene that might just scorch him to the core.

The Night Is Mine

by M.L. Buchman

NAME: Emily Beale

RANK: Captain

MISSION: Fly undercover to prevent the assassination of the First Lady, posing as her executive pilot

NAME: Mark Henderson, code name Viper

RANK: Major

MISSION: Undercover role of wealthy, ex-mercenary boyfriend to Emily

Their jobs are high risk, high reward:

Protect the lives of the powerful and the elite at all cost. Neither expected that one kiss could distract them from their mission. But as the passion mounts between them, their lives and their hearts will both be risked… and the reward this time may well be worth it.

"An action-packed adventure. With a super-stud hero, a strong heroine, and a backdrop of 1600 Pennsylvania Avenue and the world of the Washington elite, it will grab readers from the first page." —*RT Book Reviews*

For more in The Night Stalkers series, visit:

www.sourcebooks.com

I Own the Dawn

The Night Stalkers

by M. L. Buchman

—◆—

NAME: Archibald Jeffrey Stevenson III

RANK: First Lieutenant, DAP Hawk copilot

MISSION: Strategy and execution of special ops maneuvers

NAME: Kee Smith

RANK: Sergeant, Night Stalker gunner and sharpshooter

MISSION: Whatever it takes to get the job done

You wouldn't think it could get worse, until it does...
When a special mission slowly unravels, it is up to Kee and Archie to get their team out of an impossible situation with international implications. With her weaponry knowledge and his strategic thinking, plus the explosive attraction that puts them into exact synchrony, together they might just have a fighting chance...

—◆—

"The first novel in Buchman's new military suspense series is an action-packed adventure. With a super-stud hero, a strong heroine, and a backdrop of 1600 Pennsylvania Avenue and the world of the Washington elite, it will grab readers from the first page." — *RT Book Reviews*, 4 Stars

For more Night Stalkers, visit:

www.sourcebooks.com

Wait Until Dark

by M.L. Buchman

NAME: Big John Wallace

RANK: Staff Sergeant, chief mechanic and gunner

MISSION: To serve and protect his crew and country

NAME: Connie Davis

RANK: Sergeant, flight engineer, mechanical wizard

MISSION: To be the best… and survive

Two crack mechanics, one impossible mission

Being in the Night Stalkers is Connie Davis's way of facing her demons head-on, but mountain-strong Big John Wallace is a threat on all fronts. Their passion is explosive but their conflicts are insurmountable. When duty calls them to a mission no one else could survive, they'll fly into the night together—ready or not.

"Filled with action, adventure, and danger… Buchman's novels will appeal to readers who like romances as well as fans of military fiction." — *Booklist* Starred Review of *I Own the Dawn*

For more M.L. Buchman, visit:

About the Author

M.L. Buchman began writing novels on July 22, 1993, while on a plane from Korea to ride a bicycle across the Australian Outback. M.L. has been a substitute instructor for the University of Washington's Certificate in Commercial Fiction program and spoken at dozens of conferences, including RWA national and BookExpo. Past lives include: renovating a fifty-foot sailboat, fifteen years in corporate computer-systems design, bicycling solo around the world, developing maps for a national franchise, and designing roof trusses, in roughly that order. M.L. and family live on an island in the Pacific Northwest in a solar-powered home of their own design.

"To Champion the Human Spirit, Celebrate the Power of Joy, and Revel in the Wonder of Love."

M.L.'s website: www.mlbuchman.com